Pitch black had settled in outside. With it, a deep, biting cold swirled into the cave.

She really should put out the fire.

But it was so warm and friendly. And Anya felt so alone.

Put it out. It was time to get going. Although the cave entrance was partially blocked, someone at the perfect angle might see the light. Maybe that one, last, persistent pilot—although she hadn't heard the craft since noon. He must have given up, too. For now.

Unfolding her trowel, Anya chipped up a mound of frozen ice and mud and cast it onto the fire. It flickered, but didn't go out.

"Don't put it out on my account."

The low, rough voice made her gasp, and she whipped out her laser.

Joshua.

He seemed to fill the entrance. The elite, cream military parka made his shoulders seem wider, his body more solid and forbidding.

"You." Hands trembling, she lowered the weapon.

"Of course it's me. I'm your protector, foolish girl. Who did you think would come for you?"

Palpable fury simmered in him, deep and hot, yet tightly leashed, as were every one of his emotions, always. In the past, she had wished that just once she could break through the impenetrable shell he enclosed around himself. Just once, she'd like to see him snap, to glimpse the true man underneath all the medals and the power that fit him like a glove. To especially see beyond the shiny honor of hero worship with which she'd clothed him when they had first met. She had always wanted to please him.

No more.

Also by Jennette Green

Romance Novels

The Commander's Desire
The Pirate's Desire
Her Reluctant Bodyguard
Snowstorm
Ice Baron
Ice Master

(Kaavl Chronicles Quadrilogy)
Kaavl Conspiracy
Kaavl Quest
Kaavl Calamity
Kaavl Conqueror

(Christian Apocalyptic)
Beyond the Rapture

Castaways
(a novelette)

Shorter Works

Toot of Fruit
(a children's story)

Murder by Nightmare
(a novelette)

ICE BARON

Jennette Green

DIAMOND PRESS

This is a work of fiction. Names, characters, places, and incidents either are the product of the author's imagination or are used fictitiously, and any resemblance to actual persons, living or dead, business establishments, events, or locales is entirely coincidental.

ICE BARON

A Diamond Press book / published in arrangement with the author

Scripture quotation taken from the New American Standard Bible®,
Copyright © 1960, 1962, 1963, 1968, 1971, 1972, 1973,
1975, 1977, 1995 by The Lockman Foundation .
Used by permission. (www.Lockman.org)

ISBN: 978-0-9844044-4-5

Library of Congress Control Number: 2011932402
Library of Congress Subject Headings:
Love stories
Romance fiction
Futuristic romance
Science fiction
Man-woman relationships—Fiction

Diamond Press
3400 Pegasus Drive
P.O. Box 80043
Bakersfield CA 93380-0043
www.diamondpresspublishing.com

Published in the United States of America.

"Have I not commanded you?
Be strong and courageous!
Do not tremble or be dismayed,
for the LORD *your God is with you wherever you go."*

JOSHUA 1:9 NASB

PROLOGUE

Former Kazakhstan
Astana, Donetsk Territory, year 3145 A.D.
(Millennial Ice Age, caused by Nuclear holocaust)

ANYA PRESSED HER FOREHEAD to the cool, curved window of the school library and looked down at the earth, a kilometer below. She felt safe here, although she was no longer a child. Unfortunately, the feeling of peace was an illusion. Soon her protector, the current Baron of Donetsk Territory, would find her and she would have to face her future.

If only she could escape. If only she could ride down the slender metal umbilical cord elevator which anchored the sky city of Astana to earth, and flee what was coming.

The glass felt cool against her skin, and the room behind her lay silent, as it was nearly time for supper. Quiet, too, was the vast wasteland of ice and snow which stretched out as far as her eyes could see—land that had been ruled by her family, the Dubrovnyks, until her father had died ten years ago. The frosty view remained the same all year round. Spring and summer were too cold to melt the snow. On a clear day, she could see the great Tien Shan mountain range far to the south. Her uncle lived south of the Tien Shan, and her territory had been engaged in a bloody war with his for her entire life. To the east, Donetsk Territory fought a different, but equally vicious war with Altai Territory. Altai's leader, Onred, was Astana's special guest this weekend.

"Anya." Joshua's deep, quiet voice startled her.

She drew a dismayed breath.

Footfalls noiseless, Joshua Van Heisman appeared by her side. Her nerves prickled up in awareness of him. Nostrils faintly flaring, she surreptitiously inhaled, savoring the clean scent of his pressed uniform, and the warm, faintly spicy scent of his skin. His physical presence, as always, filled Anya's senses. She was always aware of him—too aware of him. She didn't have to look to see how his solid, muscular shoulders filled out his cream baron's uniform. Also etched forever into her mind were his tanned skin, flashing white teeth, and his barely tamed tawny hair, which was the exact color of the extinct lion.

In her mind, he was her lion. He had been her protector since she was thirteen, and he'd been the interim Baron of Donetsk Territory ever since her father had died. She had hero-worshipped him with all of her devastated young heart at thirteen, after losing both of her parents. Now, at twenty-three, his close presence made her feel something entirely different...something completely forbidden. She swallowed the lump in her throat. She had always wanted to make him proud of her, but this...

With a determined turn to her head, she met his gaze. His dark eyes were devoid of their usual warmth, and were instead a commanding brown. Not a good sign. He'd come to give her orders, and she was to obey—for the peace of Donetsk Territory. To save tens of thousands of lives.

"It is decided." His voice sounded impersonal. "Onred has agreed to take you as his bride, for peace. The bride price is set."

Only Joshua's steady gaze kept her knees firm, and prevented her from bolting from the room in sickened horror. Onred made her flesh creep. When she had met him this afternoon, he had been polite, and had bowed over her hand with great chivalry. But she didn't trust the bloodthirsty baron.

Anya wondered briefly if this was a horrible nightmare. It couldn't be happening. And yet she had known it would happen. Her fate had been set. And if she wanted to forge a peace that would save the lives of thousands of her citizens, she would agree to marry Onred.

Joshua's gaze continued to hold hers. The force and strength of his personality shored up her horrified, collapsing dreams. It felt like her very soul was shattering. As if she had been ordered to marry the devil.

"I can't," she breathed. It was unlike her to flounder, but her world was imploding. Joshua was ejecting her from his life. She would have to abandon her brothers and sisters and live in Onred's capitol city of Bogd for the rest of her life. Tears threatened. "I *can't.*"

Joshua's strong, steady hand closed around her upper arm. "You must. For the peace of Donetsk Territory."

Silently, she stared at him. Did she have a choice?

Under the Old Barons' Law, the answer would be *no.* Joshua's order alone, as Baron of Donetsk Territory, would be enough to seal her fate. But Joshua had come to seek her compliance...or maybe this was only a token gesture. Suddenly, she wasn't sure of anything anymore. Had he already accepted the bride payment? Although the bride price was largely a symbolic gesture, if Joshua had accepted the payment, it would mean that both the marriage and peace contracts were already signed. It would mean that she already belonged to Onred in all ways except for one. The marriage ceremony would put the last, pretty flourish on the contracts, finishing the vow before God, and sealing the peace agreement for the rest of her life. And it would grant Onred his final right—conjugal visits. Panic beat in her breast. Surely Joshua hadn't accepted the bride price. Not without talking to her first.

She managed, "Have you...accepted it?"

"No."

Her swift feeling of relief didn't last long. A decision still needed to be made. She wondered what would happen if she refused to accept her duty.

Joshua watched her intently, as if able to read into her soul—an uncomfortable, perceptive quality that she had rued as a teenager. His grip on her arm gentled. "You are a brave woman, Anya. And I know that with you in Altai Territory, I can trust a permanent peace with Onred."

Of course, Anya wanted to protect her people from Onred's bloody hordes, and to save thousands of lives. And she wanted to make Joshua proud. But more than any of that, she wanted her life to have meaning and purpose. She was a Dubrovnyk. Her family had ruled Donetsk Territory for almost two hundred years.

She must give her life to serve the territory. If marrying Onred was her fate, then so be it.

Unfortunately, although her mouth opened and closed, she could not choke out the words to accept her fate.

His grip tightened when the silence uncomfortably lengthened. Voice a gravel rasp, he said, "Do you understand?"

So, it was an order after all. She was to be given no choice.

Mutely, she stared at him, in silence accepting her duty, although her very soul revolted against it.

Something bleak and black flashed in Joshua's eyes, and then vanished. "Good." Another silent moment passed, and she sensed conflict waging within him. But when his fingers released her arm, she felt his emotional withdrawal at the same time he stepped back. "I am proud of you, Anya."

When he strode from the room, leaving her behind, Anya's heart felt like it crumbled to nothing.

CHAPTER ONE

Astana
Lunch, the next afternoon

ANYA DUBROVNYK EYED her future husband across the lavishly appointed banquet table. She hated him. Everything about Onred Stoystiya—from his beard, trimmed into a pointy goatee, to his dark hair, shorn so short that the middle-aged thinning at his crown was obvious. Most especially, though, she despised the territory baron's black eyes, in which festered greed and lust.

"Good one, Joshua!" Laughter boomed from Onred's barrel chest. It appeared he appreciated her protector's dry witticism. It was a lie, as was everything about him. An hour ago Anya had learned, to her horror, that a demon lived in Onred's black soul. He had proven it in a dead-end hallway, where he had cornered her with a chilling leer, and a hard grip on her arm. He had said that he had already bought and paid for her. Now she was his. Those had been the longest, most degrading seconds of her life, until she'd twisted free of his grasp and escaped; thankfully, fairly quickly. All the same, she felt soiled and devastated, and wanted a shower. Nothing, however, could cleanse her mind.

Joshua Van Heisman did not seem to realize what a snake he entertained under his roof. That was because he focused only upon peace. Thousands of men had died last year at the hands of Onred's bloodthirsty forces. Last night, Joshua had publicly accepted the bride price and ruled that

Anya—as the deceased baron's oldest daughter and his only legal heir according to the Old Barons' Law—would marry and form an alliance with the Altai territory lord, Onred.

Peace on their eastern, mountainous border would finally ensue. However, the bloody skirmishes to the south, with her uncle, would continue.

Joshua's gaze sought Anya's; probably wondering why she didn't smile. Keeping her features purposefully expressionless, she stabbed her fork tines into the red berry cobbler and twisted it, shredding the chef's perfect arrangement. Forget Joshua. After all, for all intents and purposes, he had sold her to Onred last night. He had purchased his peace, and had forced her into a betrothal with the very devil himself.

Even worse, he was unwilling to reconsider the matter. Before lunch, when with a trembling voice she had tried to explain to him why she could not marry Onred, he had listened. However, she'd been unable to force past her lips the details of what Onred had done to her. Joshua had dismissed her concerns as nerves, brusquely told her she'd be fine, and strode away. When she'd called after him, he hadn't turned back. Clearly, he didn't care how she felt. It had stunned her that her wishes meant nothing to him.

Had they ever? She bit the inside of her mouth to prevent unwanted tears.

What a fool she had been, and for so long. She had always believed in Joshua and trusted him. He had been honored and respected by her father, to whom bone-deep respect had not come easily—after all, Joshua had been young, at twenty-three, when he'd been promoted to second-in-command. And when her parents were murdered shortly thereafter, when she was thirteen, Joshua had become protector to Anya and her siblings, and soon afterward promoted to baron.

Anya had always believed that Joshua was special, although she'd always known that her aching hero-worship of him could never grow into anything more. Protectors and their charges were forbidden to commit the mortal sin of romantic involvement. Punishment, through the Old Barons' Law, was swift, terrible, and irrevocable—for both parties.

In her secret heart, though, Anya had always adored Joshua. He was brilliant and fair-minded, and wore his role of command easily, as if it were a natural part of him. He knew who he was. But his eyes were what had caught her fancy at that young age. Those changeable eyes. Velvet brown most of the time, or a warm, rich tawny color when he laughed, or when he tried to mask deep emotion. Kind eyes, she had thought then.

And he *had* been kind to her and her siblings. He had also been a little distant, prodding, and challenging...especially to her. As the eldest child, she had taken on the mother role to the younger children. Joshua had approved, and had even expected her efforts. Once, he had told her that she'd done a good job. Anya had held that bit of praise close to her heart for a long time.

Anya cast Joshua another expressionless glance. Yes, she had always thought Joshua was quite perfect. These last twelve hours, of course, had proven something altogether different.

A giggle caught her attention. Marli, her youngest sister, whispered to Onred's daughter. Marli was eleven, Emelie fifteen. Onred's daughter appeared to be a very serious girl. She wore gobs of black eye make-up, which unfortunately brought to mind a raccoon, rather than a beautiful young girl. Her hair was bleached white. Never once had Anya seen her smile. Secretly, she wondered if the girl was lonely. The teenage years were hard without a mother, as Anya well knew.

Marli seemed to like Emelie. Anya's sunny sister had spent the last two days dragging her new friend all over their sky city of Astana, trying to impress her. However, the city's many technological innovations appeared to be the only things which sparked Emelie's interest—especially the new DiaMoRCs (diamonite morphing resculpting compounds). Anya was lucky enough to enjoy a prototype in her compartment. Unfortunately, she had been alarmed to catch Marli demonstrating its abilities to Emelie this morning. It had been too late to stop the demonstration.

The Altai girl had watched in amazement as a graceful, potted red orchid had melted into a shimmering gray ball, and then reformed, sprouting four long legs and a circular table top. Marli had evidently typed "various" colors into the diamonite remote, for the tiny diamonite silicon chips had shockingly transformed the gray table top to look like a rainbow swirled lollipop. With an eye roll, Anya had shooed them out, pretending the incident meant nothing. In truth, she had been deeply concerned, since she was certain that their Altai enemies weren't supposed to know about the new invention.

It was on her way to apprise Joshua of the situation that Onred had waylaid her. His request had been reasonable; to walk with him so they could become better acquainted. Against her better instincts, Anya had agreed. And then he had trapped her in that quiet, dead-end hallway, and muffled her screams with his meaty hand.

Onred now pushed back his chair. It squeaked alarmingly, probably because of the extra stone of weight around his middle. His thick tongue flicked out and ran over his lips, catching the last crumbs of the cobbler. Squashing his linen napkin into the table, he lumbered to his feet. "Thank you for your hospitality, Joshua." He shook her protector's hand and then bowed to Anya, pretending chivalry. "I will see you soon, my dear. Emelie, it's time to go."

Relief lightened the girl's sallow face. Without a word to Marli, she hastened to her father's side and out the door, heading for the shuttle bay.

Marli didn't seem to notice the snub, and eagerly wolfed down the last of her dessert. "Can I be 'scused, Joshua?"

"Of course."

"Me, too." Anya stood before Joshua could speak. When she had gained the empty hall, she discovered she was shaking. She could not marry Onred. She would not.

"Anya." Joshua's voice came as a shock, for she had not heard his following footsteps. "What is wrong?"

"I told you before. I can't marry him." Her voice trembled.

"Don't you want peace?"

"Yes, but not with him. I don't trust him, and I don't like him."

"He gave us his word. We have to trust him. In any case, the deal is done. You will marry him tomorrow."

"I won't!" she gasped.

Something wild must have flashed in her eyes, for Joshua caught her wrist and held it firmly. "You have no choice. I told you. The deal is sealed. He paid the bride price."

"I don't care," her voice rose. "I *won't* marry Onred."

"You will marry him."

"I won't!" Anya struggled to free herself, but in one blindingly swift move, Joshua jerked her up tight against his chest, her arm bent double, so she couldn't move. His show of superior strength infuriated her.

"I am your protector. You will do as I say."

"I won't."

"You will."

"I hate you, you *jerk*!" She had never said such harsh words to him before, and guilt pinched. But it all was too much. Worse than anything, she felt betrayed. That this man, whom she had looked up to all of her life, would relinquish her to the Altai wolf—and all for a price. Because it would bring peace. ...Or was peace the only reason why Joshua refused to reconsider the matter? A completely new, shocking scenario entered her mind, and she wondered why she hadn't thought of it before. Had he instead approved the match because it would protect his power? Was she merely a pawn, to be used to further his political goals? Nausea rolled through her. All of a sudden, she feared this was the truth.

Through clenched teeth, she gritted, "I will do nothing to please you again. Ever."

His grip tightened. "You act like a child. Grow up!"

That he would discard her like this, as if she meant nothing to him—but perhaps this is all she had ever been. A game piece. A responsibility he had willingly taken on, all for the profit of payoff. After all, if she married outside their territory, he would stay baron forever. Had this been his plan all along?

Well, his plot had come to fruition. The good she had believed she had seen in him—their rare moments of laughter and equanimity, and sometimes even a deep, uncanny understanding of each other—must have been a product of her own fantasies.

At the same time, she had known this day must come. According to the Old Barons' Law, it could be no other way. Once she achieved a certain age, Joshua would discharge his duty of her. All the better if he could successfully—from his viewpoint—marry her off to a territory baron who would promise to become Joshua's blood ally. Her blood, of course, being the tenuous thread that would bind the two men and strengthen each of their territories and power.

She stopped struggling. "I *hate* you."

His eyes gleamed a tawny color, which matched his hair. A paradox, for his eyes were in truth a deep, velvety brown. His lips curled back so his white teeth showed in a smile. "You love me."

For a second her heart stopped, and then it slammed harder. She felt cold, and then hot. "You mean nothing to me. Just as I mean nothing to you." She twisted her wrist, and to her surprise, freed herself. "Isn't that right?"

"I expect you to be on the next shuttle."

Anger tightened like a knot in her chest. It felt like a fist squeezed her lungs so hard that she could barely breathe. So Joshua thought it would be simple to get rid of her? That she was still a child, eager to do his bidding, to please him?

No. At last, she had grown up, and now she understood that the heart of a snow leopard lived in him. No warmth. No laughter. Those fictions had been proven a lie. How quickly he was willing to sell her. For power. For peace. Should she feel flattered it was to the highest bidder?

Abruptly, she said, "How many Detsk did he give you?"

He didn't answer.

"I want half. It's my life that's been sold, after all. Don't you think I deserve something?"

Something flickered in those brown eyes. Guilt? Grim triumph flared. So, she'd struck into the heart of this cold, self-serving man, whom she had apparently never known.

"I'll give you five hundred. It's all you'll need for your travels. You will need no money there."

A more than generous sum, if it was just for travel money. But they both understood it was the bride price. Her life price.

Silently, she held out her hand.

Joshua hesitated for a moment, and then dipped into his pocket and withdrew a folded stack of bills. He didn't bother to count it. Neither did Anya. But it was clearly more than five hundred.

Joshua silently watched her push the bills into her pocket. "The shuttle leaves in two hours. I expect you to be on it." Abruptly, he turned on his heel and left her. His cream uniform, edged with gold, stretched crisp and taut across his straight, well-muscled shoulders. His tawny hair was so short now it didn't even touch the collar.

Anya watched him go. With each step, her heart broke a little more, until it felt like millions of pieces of glass punctured her soul.

He had sold her.

He was finished with her.

Maybe this was the end of one part of her life, but Anya absolutely would not marry the powerful Altai baron.

She wanted peace, just as Joshua did. But she would not give her life to Onred to ensure it. Onred's word could not be trusted. History had proven that he was a bloodthirsty monster. His moral character had been further proven in the hallway. He was cruel, perverse, and corrupt to his very soul. Once he took all that Joshua had promised him—goods, exchanges of minor sections of territory, and herself—the peace would end. This, she knew.

All the same, she would get on that shuttle, as Joshua dictated. It would appear to everyone, including Onred's watching men, that the terms of peace were being met. But on the trip to the sky city of Bogd in the Altai Mountains, she would disappear. It was the only way to ensure peace. Forever.

❈✻❈✻❈✻❈✻❈

"I have to go," Anya said again to Marli, and stuffed another dress she would never wear into one of her mammoth suitcases. The other four were already filled. She had known since yesterday evening what her fate would be, and in the back of her mind a plan had emerged. The battle with Joshua in the hall had been a last attempt to delay the inevitable.

Anya told herself that she hated the cold, unfeeling man. She did.

"But *why?*" As the only child with blue eyes and blond ringlets in the family, Marli was adept at wrapping all of her older siblings around her little finger. Joshua, too, if the truth were told. But the tears in her voice now were real. "You don't want to go! I heard your fight in the hall. Why is Joshua so mean? Why do you have to leave?"

Anya stopped packing and pulled her little sister into her arms. Marli's tears soaked into Anya's simple black shirt. Underneath, Anya wore an even thinner polymer shirt, suitable for regulating body temperature when subjected to extreme weather. She would need it later.

"I'm sorry, honey." Anya's own unhappiness gathered into an aching lump in her throat. "I'll miss you. But I'll come back." If she could. She fiercely loved her brothers and sisters, and Astana was her home. She couldn't imagine living anywhere else, and she couldn't bear the thought of parting with her family. Marli needed her. She was the only mother figure the young girl had ever known. Anya blinked back tears.

Marli looked up. "You promise?"

Anya pressed a kiss into the soft hair at her sister's temple. Marli's baby fine skin was damp from the exhausting ordeal of crying. "Sometimes life turns in directions we don't want," she murmured. "But I'll get it back on track." She bit her lip. She shouldn't have said that to her unusually perceptive sister.

"How?"

"I don't know. I'm making it up as I go along." That was true enough. "Now." She squeezed her sister tighter, and then released her. "Will you get the others? I'll need help to the terminal." She had to try to be strong. If she could project confidence to her siblings, they would believe everything would be fine. It would give them a measure of peace.

How sorely Anya wanted to believe it, too. But her plan was far from failsafe.

Her sister paused near the door. "Joshua, too?"

Anya averted her face. "No. Not Joshua."

"I'm mad at him, too," Marli said. "I won't talk to him for a month."

"Listen to him. He wants what's best for you."

"But not for you. If he wasn't so stupid..."

"Marli!"

"I'm going," the girl sullenly muttered, and the gun metal gray door slid shut behind her.

The dull gray walls of the room matched the bleak feeling in Anya's spirit. She had programmed the depressing color into the paint's tiny, diamonite silicon paint chips last night. Normally, she preferred a warm, toasted almond hue, with a mirage of surging and crashing ocean breakers on the wall across from her bed, but she couldn't bring herself to enjoy the scene any longer. She had even turned off the sound system. It was utterly silent and barren in the room. It matched the desolation in her soul.

Anya lugged the suitcase to the floor to join the other four. Her fingers curled around her black overnight bag. She would carry this one herself. In fact, she wouldn't let it out of her sight.

Don't cry, she told herself again. But that was impossible moments later, when her siblings entered the room. The four were her only family in the world, except for her uncle Richert (Rik' ert), a baron to the south, who had started a blood feud with her father shortly after Anya's mother had married him, instead of her uncle.

Her twin brothers, Damon and David, approached first. They were fourteen now, and taller than she. Elise held Marli's hand. Elise was sixteen, and with her long dark hair and blue eyes, looked very much like Anya. Elise's features were perfect, whereas Anya knew her own nose was too sharp, and her mouth too wide. Like all of the inhabitants of Donetsk Territory, the five siblings were a mix of Eastern European and Russian descent. Once the nuclear holocaust had decimated the earth, the survivors had scrambled to claim new land. Eurasia, even now, was barely habitable, and covered with a thick ice sheet, which covered the deep scars in the earth.

Tears blurred Anya's vision, and a sob closed her throat. "Let's say goodbye now. I don't want to make a scene in the terminal."

Her brothers hugged her first, their arms all gangly bones and lean muscle. "We'll come rescue you, if you need it," Damon said. "The guy's a jerk." His face looked pale and sick in its earnestness.

"Don't," she told him firmly, with a rush of protectiveness. "Remember, I want peace. I want you to be safe. I'll be fine. Don't worry."

Yes, she would pursue peace, but by her own means. In fact, in the days to come, others would label her actions as selfish and immature. The truth was far different, of course, and far more dangerous. Even better, if her plan succeeded, she would win peace with *all* of their enemies—not just Onred.

"Take care of them," she whispered to Elise, and then hugged Marli last of all. Her little sister sobbed without restraint, and clung to her tightly.

"You can't go. You just *can't!*"

Anya held her for a long time, and tears ran down her own cheeks. Then, gently, she untangled Marli's arms. "It's time to go." Her heart felt sick, empty, and fearful. She may never see any of them again. Her plan had so many holes. So many uncertainties. "I love you."

Words seemed inadequate to express the deep emotions overwhelming her. It was a good thing Joshua hadn't come. She just might fly into him for forcing her to leave her family.

For peace, of course. But for once in his charmed life, Joshua was wrong. The sweetest revenge would be to prove it.

✖∗✖∗✖∗✖∗✖

Anya sat with her arms tightly crossed, struggling to barricade her emotions inside. She sat on a plush, cushioned seat in the baron's official government shuttle. Beside her, the window radiated in the mercilessly cold, late afternoon sun. Tears slipped down her cheeks.

Inside the terminal, her younger siblings mingled with other well wishers, and waved whenever she managed to look. Each glance at her family stabbed a fresh knife of pain through her heart. Anya disengaged a hand and waved again. A hot lump closed off her throat, and she stared down at the black bag at her feet, willing the tears to stop. The bag contained everything she would need to survive in the snow for several weeks.

Of course, her five monstrous travel cases, stuffed with her superfluous belongings, had been checked into cargo. To all appearances, she had packed for a permanent farewell. No one had noticed her best winter boots on her feet, or the ultra thin, but heavy duty parka she wore. Underneath her black pants and shirt, she wore fiber thin snow wear. She had set the thermostat to cool, so she wasn't too warm inside the winter layers. A solar panel was built into her parka hood, and would provide all the electricity she would need.

Onred's men occupied seats nearby. Anya had placed an electronic notebook on the seat beside hers, discouraging others from sitting there. Her gaze strayed again to the terminal and she found herself searching the dwindling crowd for tawny hair. When she realized what she was doing, she berated herself.

The shuttle jerked, and then slid forward, propelling her in a direction she did not want to go; taking her from her beloved city of Astana, possibly forever. Childhood images tangled with a flood of memories: Astana's warm, sparkling walls when crisp, summer sunshine streamed through the windows; the laughter in Marli's eyes at Christmas time; coming home after a two day military survival trip with her father and Elise... How beautiful Astana had looked then, growing larger and larger as they'd flown home; a silvery, saucer-shaped city perched on a steel stalk, far above the earth.

And now she was leaving her home and family—perhaps forever. Anya blew a flurry of emotional kisses to her siblings. A flash of cream on the upper concourse caught her eye.

Joshua. Her hand froze, lips puckered, still in the motion of blowing her last kiss. He watched as the shuttle slid forward, faster, until he was out of sight.

Anya jerked her chin forward. Her heart thumped in uncomfortable, erratic beats. So he had seen her off? It meant nothing, of course. He had probably watched to make sure she had obeyed him. Well, now his duty was fully discharged, and he could retreat to his office and toast his success at having won the most important peace negotiation in Donetsk Territory's history. And he had ensured his title of Baron for life.

Anya closed her eyes. She didn't care.

She *didn't*.

Time to orchestrate her disappearance.

CHAPTER TWO

JOSHUA SLAMMED BACK another shot of raw alcohol. He rarely drank liquor, and this particular brand tasted bitter and foul. The truth was, he wanted to punish himself. And he wouldn't mind deadening the pain roaring through his heart and mind, too. Nothing would ever be the same again. But he would live with it. It was for the best.

With a curse, he hurled the glass into the hearth. Flames exploded up into a hot, roiling inferno. Joshua seethed another curse, this time at himself. "It's for the best."

Why couldn't he believe it? Why did fear clench his gut? Why did he feel like he had just made the biggest mistake of his life?

"It's for the *best*." His jaw hurt from clenching it so hard.

Was that why he had agreed so quickly to let Onred have Anya? To get her out of his life and his city, so he wouldn't be tortured by his own dishonorable weakness anymore?

But this didn't feel better. It felt like death.

Ten years ago, it had all started so differently, and with such promise. When Joshua had learned that Jason Dubrovnyk's will had designated him to become protector to Jason's young brood of five, along with the help, of course, of their nannies, he had felt honored. It was nothing short of a miracle, for a man from his background. His new duties wouldn't be strenuous; be a strong male influence on the boys. Keep the girls in line.

But then proof surfaced that the baron's first-in-command had poisoned the baron and his wife. The murderer had wanted power, but wasn't willing to trust fate for it.

Fate. Joshua smiled without humor. Fate and superstition tangled through the odd laws of the Old Barons in middle Asia, frozen in a perpetual ice age ever since nuclear war had destroyed most of the earth a millennia ago.

Although the Old Barons had wanted to keep power in their families, they had superstitiously chosen to surrender the ultimate, trump card to fate. They believed power should flow to its intended recipient—whomever that might be. As a result, the Old Barons' Law stipulated that only the oldest child could inherit. If the oldest child died, or if the girl child married out of the territory, power would go to the late baron's first-in-command. Unless, of course, the baron bequeathed power before his death. A rare occurrence. Jason Dubrovnyk certainly had not done so.

Shocking to all, after Baron Dubrovnyk's first-in-command was executed, Joshua, as second-in-command, was next in line for power. He had become interim baron; a position which would last until Anya grew up and married, when her husband would become the next baron. Joshua had taken the job in stride, and with single-minded tenacity had learned all the intricacies of the baron's duties in six short months. Plenty of advisors helped him, but he had found his own way, all the while negotiating the far more tricky duties of protector.

The oldest of Baron Dubrovnyk's children was Anya, and she had been thirteen when he had been thrust into the role of protector. His own life had turned upside down at a similar age, so he empathized with what she was going through.

At first, Joshua had believed himself blessed. To become both baron and protector at such a young age was an unbelievable honor for a young man who had come from absolutely nothing. He had been twelve when he had joined the army. By sixteen, he had earned more medals for valor than most men twice his age. Afterward, he had transferred to the air fleet. He was fearless in battle, and praised by all of his commanders. And shrewd. A man they wanted in their corner.

When Joshua turned nineteen, Jason Dubrovnyk heard about Joshua and enlisted him into the elite service. The rest was history.

Overall, Joshua thought he had done well. The job of baron was difficult, but a perfect fit for his aggressive, take-no-prisoners personality. He had even grown to like the children, which was a good thing, as protector. The world was his...except for one thing. Protector was a sacred trust. On oath, the baron's family had become his own. He could not become romantically involved with one of his charges.

Of course, the Old Barons' Law was meant to keep protectors from gaining power by unscrupulous means, such as by marrying the oldest female heir. If Joshua did break this sacred trust at any small point, all power and position would be stripped from him. He would become as an enlisted soldier again, and the baron's daughter would lose her inheritance to power. But even worse, if a larger offense was proven, both culprits would be stripped of all possessions, and cast from the territory forever. Joshua's honor would be forever lost, for he would have taken advantage of one of his charges. A heinous crime, especially to the Order of the Barons, who highly prized their children.

And now Joshua had finally discharged his duty. Anya was about to safely marry another. He had kept his honor and pledge to her father. And, by an undeserving twist of fate, he would remain baron.

With a mocking twist to his lips, Joshua raised his glass to heaven. "Your daughter is safe from me, Baron. Of course, Onred..." A hoarse bark erupted. It should have been laughter, but it burned, as if the very flames of hell licked down into his soul. Just the thought of that grubby bastard touching Anya... All rational thought abruptly left his head.

He snarled out a string of curses, wishing he could send Onred to the blackest pit of hell forever.

✳✳✳✳✳✳✳✳✳

Anya surreptitiously checked her watch. Ninety minutes of the journey had elapsed. Time to put her plan into motion. Finally.

She pulled her carry-on bag onto her lap. With a fake frown, she rummaged through it, aware that Onred's men watched her every movement. At length, and with an audible sigh of success, she pulled out a compact. Of course, she had known its location the entire time. Although the compact appeared to be a frivolous item, it also doubled as a compass.

Anya peered into the small mirror, pretending to study her face from all angles. She squinted, as though it were hard to see. Finally, with a sigh of disgust, she shoved the compact back into the bag and stood. Handles slipped over her fore-arm, she headed for the women's restroom.

Onred's men, and one of Joshua's, hidden in the last seat, continued to watch her, but did not interfere. Where could she go? Already they were speeding over frozen waste-land, several kilometers above the earth's surface. She glanced outside, at the massive Tien Shan mountain range rapidly approaching from the south. In half an hour, the shuttle would pass over the northeastern ridge and head southeast to Bogd, Onred's main city.

After locking the restroom door, Anya quickly set to work. She pulled off her jacket and slipped on an ultra-light, specialty vest, and then she slipped knives, a laser gun, and back up solar charges into the loops in her belt. Next tucked in were matches, a solar light, rations, and a cup-sized water purifier, complete with instant heater, to melt snow into a hot drink. The minimum needed, should she lose her bag. She pulled her parka back on, and adjusted the top pouch of the underlying vest. Last of all, she tied the bag to her arm with thin black rope, which matched the color of her parka.

Done. Although her heart beat rapidly and nerves twisted through the pit of her stomach, Anya left the rest-room with a bored expression on her face. She wandered to the window and looked down at the barren wasteland far below, which was bordered by the craggy Tien Shan moun-tains. She searched for the dip, indicating the pass through the towering mountain peaks. There it was, to the south—the Dzungarian Gate. Her second destination.

Her first destination, however, was this white, barren, no-man's land; but at a point as close as possible to the Dzungarian Gate. She glanced at her watch. Previous calculations told her that only two minutes remained. Heart beating harder, she swallowed and stared outside. From this vantage point, it was impossible to tell that lakes lay beneath the unending sheet of snow. Snow drifts had claimed frozen Lake Zaysan to the east, and to the west, Lake Balkhash. This wasteland, with temperatures which reached as low as -42° C in February, was far too desolate for human habitation, but she would survive well enough. Her hard, militaristic father had trained both of his oldest daughters in the basic elements of survival. He had wanted them to be prepared for everything.

Anya was glad for that now. But she hoped she would meet no snow leopards. The animals, which used to prowl the higher mountains, now hunted the warmer, lower elevations in search of food. Her laser would protect her, of course—provided she saw the animal before it sprang upon her.

Beneath her lashes, Anya glanced sideways at the cabin. One of Onred's men watched her, but the others had closed their eyes, intent on a nap between here and Onred's home city of Bogd, more than an hour distant.

She wandered toward the pilot area. No one followed her. This was going to be easy. Anya actually felt disappointed. She found she was itching for a fight. Was it because she was sick of feeling impotent, with her entire life dictated by others...duty, the Old Barons' Law.... Ultimately, of course, by Joshua. The gray door to the cockpit was at hand. She pulled the laser from her belt, yanked open the door and barged into the small space.

"Hey!"

"Get out," barked the pilot.

"You don't belong..." The sight of Anya's laser shut up all three crew members.

Slowly and distinctly, she said, "Open the emergency door." As trained by her father, she knew that the cabin, at these low altitudes, was not pressurized. Opening the door would harm none of the cockpit crew, who were seatbelted, in any event.

One man's hand crept across the dashboard. Anya whipped her laser toward the emergency door handle and fired. Green lights flickered in the cockpit, and something sizzled. An acrid smell drifted to her nose. Everyone froze, staring at the madwoman who had invaded their cockpit. Anya shoved the laser into her belt, ran for the door, and rammed a shoulder into the emergency release bar. The door jerked right, and air blasted into the cockpit. A hard lunge, and she was through, falling into empty, cold air, hurtling toward the earth.

Soft snowflakes brushed her skin as she yanked and jerked at the vest under her jacket collar, searching for the ripcord. Where was it?

Below, the flat snow pack and a few huge drifts rushed closer. Her fingers finally brushed the knotted cord and yanked. With force, the parachute popped the back of her head as it shot from beneath her jacket collar. The next second, the billowing chute jerked her body, stopping its death fall.

All was silent. She didn't hear the shuttle. It was probably long gone. Cold snowflakes kissed her cheeks. The earth continued to drift closer—faster than she had expected. She bent her knees, bracing for impact. One of the drifts looked huge and bulky, as if it hid a gigantic boulder, but before she could adjust course, she hit the ground with teeth rattling impact. Clearly, an ice sheet lay beneath the surface of the deceptively soft looking snow. She tumbled hard and spun sideways into the craggy rock. Pain slammed into her shoulder and head, and then she lay blessedly still.

She was safe. And, for the first time in her life, completely free. No one—not duty, not the Old Barons' Law, and not Joshua—would ever rule her life again. It was a surprisingly freeing thought. With a faint, grimacing smile, Anya slipped into blackness.

CHAPTER THREE

Astana

"SHE *WHAT*?"

"Anya skyjumped from the shuttle, sir. Onred is furious. He thinks this has all been a trick."

Joshua's curled fist went to his head, as if that could put a lid on this insane turn of events. "She didn't. She wouldn't."

"She did, sir. What are your orders?"

For a moment, Joshua couldn't think. Anya could be.... No. He would not allow the thought to form. She couldn't be dead. He would feel it. Somehow, he would know.

His natural command swiftly returned. "Send out aircraft. Search the area where she went down."

"She jumped in the middle of the wasteland, sir. A storm is coming."

Joshua swore. "Get my flight gear."

"But sir..."

"*Do it.*"

Flying through storms had been his specialty in the elite air fleet. He would find Anya. Never would he leave her out there, alone, in the middle of a storm.

He *would* find her. But when he did, he would kill her.

❈✳❈✳❈✳❈✳❈

Anya's eyelids fluttered open. Frigid, furry snowflakes clung to them. It was so quiet and still.

Cautiously, she moved her head. It ached. A glove touch to her chin came away bloody. Her shoulders and back felt sore, but nothing to write home about. A grim smile curled her lips at that absurd thought.

Carefully, Anya sat up. So far, her body seemed to be in working order, although her head ached more sharply now. Gripping the fingertips of one glove in her teeth, she pulled it off and felt the back of her head. No blood. Just a small bump. Good. She slipped the glove back on again. It wasn't too cold this afternoon—maybe -23° C, but extremities cooled rapidly. She didn't want to risk frostbitten fingers.

She opened her snow covered pack, still tied to her arm. Quick use of her compact and the first aid kit dealt with the gash on her chin. Then she pulled on a warm face mask and pulled up her parka hood. Last of all, she pulled out her heat insulating camouflage tarp, re-zipped her bag, and slid her arms through the loops, using it as a pack.

The tarp was white on one side, and black on the other. After casting a look to the north and noting the dark, heavy gray clouds advancing across the steppe, she smiled. Good. A storm was approaching. She pulled the white side of the tarp over her head and around her shoulders like a cape and tied it securely in place with the rope. Blizzards were common, and she didn't want to lose her prized tarp in the storm.

Micro-sensors were built into each side of the camouflage tarp, which enabled it to change colors like the rare chameleon. It would allow Anya to blend into her surroundings, so the search fleet Joshua was certain to send wouldn't find her. Even better, the tarp would act as a shield, preventing her body heat from being detected from overhead. She would be virtually invisible to all searching aircraft. Even so, she intended to travel at night as much as possible, until she passed through the Dzungarian Gate. Travel might be slow going, and she estimated it would take three or four days of steady trekking south to reach the Gate.

Snow continued to gently fall as she walked across the wasteland, heading for the shelter of the Tien Shan foothills. The snowfall would mask her footsteps, and the coming blizzard, although it promised misery, would obliterate her path. Good.

Satellite images had helped Anya plan this trip, and she knew where a few snow caves were located. She would spend the days in those—as long as wild animals, such as bears, hadn't already claimed them. She shivered, and tried not to think about that right now.

She trudged for the foothills. It would take until nightfall to reach them. If all went well, she'd continue walking until dawn.

❋**❋**❋**❋**❋

Astana

Gray, thick clouds roiled outside Astana by the time Joshua's small, single pilot airbird flew from the hangar. A kilometer below, snow dusted the clear, pod base encircling Astana's stem, which secured the city to the earth. From the sky, the stem looked like a long umbilical cord, interlaced with steel supports. The pod base was a domed greenhouse, warmed by the heat generated from Astana's life support systems.

Joshua pushed the throttle to half of Mach 1 and allowed the familiar weight of gravity to push his body against the chair. It still felt strange to him to live so far above the earth's surface. He and his brother and sisters had been born and raised in caves, deep inside the earth. Astana was as different from his childhood home as night from day.

Sky cities like Astana had become popular two hundred years ago when lighter, cheaper, and stronger construction materials became available. It was an advantage to live in cities high and free of the ever-encroaching ice pack and snow drifts. But mostly, the Old Barons had liked looking down on their domains. Maybe a lingering desire to escape the damaged earth had played a part in their construction, too.

The cities looked like the flying saucers of old.

Joshua chuckled grimly to himself. How naïve people had been before the nuclear wars. Mankind had more to fear from his own destructive nature than from scout ships from another world. Just now, the space academy was starting to open its doors to all recruits; even the disadvantaged poor, as he had been. If Joshua had still been in his twenties, he might have joined. If he wasn't a baron. If he wasn't a protector to five Dubrovnyks; the eldest of which had just pulled the stupidest stunt imaginable.

His fist tightened on the throttle. When he found her...

He wanted to thunder at her, and shake her for scaring him like this. But he would not. Losing control of himself was never an option. Ever. He would not be like his father.

Joshua slowed to 100 kilometers per hour when he reached the spot where the shuttle pilot reported that Anya had parachuted to the earth. She couldn't have gone far. She had been wearing all black. It would be easy to spot her.

But it wasn't.

The wasteland was a sea of white. No black anywhere. Where was she?

The small flurries thickened. What if Anya was injured, and now covered by a layer of snow? Joshua's pulse felt thick and sluggish with anxiety. He programmed the computer to scan the landscape for signs of body heat.

The scan came up clean—no readings of heat anywhere in the wasteland at all, except for a few small, faint readings of warmth—probably voles burrowed beneath the snow, in the earth.

Joshua circled a ten kilometer area once, twice, and then three times before a frown locked his brows together. Visibility in the growing blizzard had become nonexistent, but his instruments did not lie. Anya had vanished.

Violent gusts shook his craft now. He couldn't find her. Fear and powerlessness were old, unwelcome emotions, and Joshua battled to suppress them. He had never failed a mission. Never. And yet he was failing Anya now. If he didn't find her, she could die in this storm. Where *was* she?

✹∗✹∗✹∗✹∗✹

The blizzard whipped the tarp and buffeted Anya's body. At times, the wind felt like a giant, invisible hand, repeatedly shoving her and trying to push her down. Every few steps, it succeeded.

She fell to her knees again in the deepening snow. Walking in the storm was miserable, but at least the snow wear kept her warm, and her compass kept her on track. And the rope she'd cinched around her waist prevented the tarp from ripping free. She would be in big trouble if that happened. If necessary, she could wrap up inside the tarp and use it as a shelter. She could survive the blizzard within its cocoon, as long as she wasn't smothered by a mountain of snow.

But wrapping up in the tarp was a luxury she could not afford right now. The angry, spitting blizzard was doing her a favor by erasing her tracks from the pristine white wasteland. Once she reached the mountains, the clumpy vegetation would help to hide her trail. But for now, cruel and wretched as it might be, the blizzard was actually a blessing. Neither Joshua nor Onred would be able to follow her tracks, and that meant her plan to forge a lasting peace with all of their enemies—not just Onred—had a fighting chance to succeed.

So Anya kept walking.

Storms came from the north, and so she pocketed the compass and allowed the wind to drive her south, toward the mountains. Sooner or later, she would run up against the foothills, and if the storm was still raging at nightfall, she would take refuge in one of the small snow caves until its fury subsided.

First the Dzungarian Gate, and afterward, Tarim Territory. Her uncle's land.

CHAPTER FOUR

JOSHUA FLEW HIS AIRBIRD like a possessed man during the bright, sunny days following the blizzard, only stopping long enough to snatch the required hours of sleep. His elite pilots traded off in shifts, keeping a total of seven birds patrolling the steppe. But so far, no trace of Anya had been found.

Birn, his first-in-command, suggested calling off the search after two days.

Joshua had succinctly told him where he could go.

In the meantime, Onred had delivered several broadcasts—actually, temper tantrums disguised as newscasts—threatening an offensive strike if Anya wasn't delivered to him within 72 hours.

Onred could take a trip to the fiery furnace, too.

Joshua's respect for the Altai leader had disintegrated, and a knot of self-condemnation and fury lodged in his throat when he realized that he had almost delivered Anya into that jackal's hands. Within the last few days, Onred had revealed his true colors. He was hot-tempered and undisciplined, and Joshua now doubted if Onred's desire for peace was genuine. He had rejected Joshua's attempt to return the bride payment, and instead had called Joshua every foul name under the sun. Each day seemed to prove more clearly that Onred took after his father, a devil named Jacan, who had passed baronship to his oldest son before he had a chance to die. Now *there* was a living baron unwilling to surrender his territory to fate. If Onred failed him, Jacan's other son, Cadmus, would take over.

Anya had to be somewhere in this frozen wasteland. Joshua's eyes hurt from scanning the glittering white snow pack.

Was she still alive? Sometimes, his brain felt too bleary to think logically.

She had to be alive. He was her protector. That job always came first in his heart. The title of Baron meant little by comparison.

He would find her, even if it killed him.

❋∗❋∗❋∗❋∗❋

Three and a half days had passed, and Anya estimated she would reach the Dzungarian Gate sometime tomorrow night. She stirred the fire in her latest cave—a larger one than most—ignoring the fact it was finally dark outside. It was time to leave her warm sanctuary.

Anya was sick of hiking through the black, bitterly cold nights. So far, she had encountered no animals, except for a few rodents. What did it say when she found their quiet rustlings in the back of the caves a comfort as she slept?

Anya had never felt so utterly alone in her entire life. She thought about her family all the time. She missed them so much. And Joshua... It was hard, but she struggled not to think about him. Always a painful, losing battle. It didn't help to remind herself that he cared nothing for her wishes, and that he had basically sold her. Even though the bride price was largely symbolic, she didn't feel any less like a sold piece of meat after Onred had manhandled her.

The leaping flames warmed her face. She needed to start walking again. With any luck, her ambitious plans for peace would make all of this misery worthwhile. And hopefully when she arrived in Tarim Territory her uncle wouldn't shoot first, and ask questions later.

Maybe a few more minutes by the warm fire wouldn't hurt.

❋∗❋∗❋∗❋∗❋

Joshua had flown in the dark for over an hour now, sweeping over the Tien Shan foothills. Tonight, something in his gut wouldn't let him give up and go home. But how much searching was enough?

It didn't matter.

He would not give up. All the same, he felt so worried that he'd found no trace of Anya that it made him feel sick. In his deepest heart—a place he didn't look often, for as a child he'd found things hurt a lot less if he shoved his emotions deep into a black place inside himself—he was afraid he would never find her. Clearly, if she was alive, she was working hard to avoid being found. Fear and anger knotted harder, and for a second, felt like a sharp ache in his chest. She had to be out here. Somewhere.

More on impulse than by design, he set the bird down on a level plateau. The engine whispered into silence, and Joshua ran a palm over his rough, whiskered face. Should he give up? Even Ray, his analytical second-in-command, was now quietly recommending that he do so.

But Anya was alive. Joshua felt it, deep in his gut. In fact, he had the insane feeling he could reach out and touch her right now...as if she were that close.

This illogical perception did not leave him, even though his logical side said to dismiss it. After all, he was woolly-headed from exhaustion. But the soldier in him had been trained and honed to act on both logic and instinct.

"Why not?" he muttered, and unstrapped his safety belt. He was sick of being trapped in this bird, using only his eyes and computer instruments to search for Anya. The primitive urge to stride into the wilderness and use brute, physical strength to fight the obstacles keeping him from Anya overwhelmed him.

It was illogical. Joshua knew it. All the same, he pulled on his protective gear and stepped into the dark night. A wisp of a moon and millions of stars leant feeble light to the stark landscape. Cold bit into his exposed face, and he closed the door behind him. It was so quiet out here. Lonely, too.

It felt good to stand up and stretch. A hill rose before him, and so he climbed it. The exertion felt good, too. At the top, Joshua gained a better view of the landscape than he'd had before. He scanned the horizon, then the foothills, and finally a small, flat valley before him, edged by rocky foothills on the other side.

"Anya, where are you?" Frustration roughened his voice. His gaze flickered to the starry heavens. The cloudy gauze of the Milky Way, sparkling with millions of tiny stars, was breathtakingly beautiful. God had made it. God knew where Anya was right now.

Joshua wasn't in the habit of talking to God, although he did completely believe He existed. "Help me find her," he muttered. "Please. I need h...I need to find her."

Desperation and growing fear twisted his gut. His gaze searched the horizon again. Nothing but blackness. Moonlight glinted white off a few snow-spangled bushes, and yellow rocks glowed...

His gaze swung back. A fire. Someone burned a fire out here, in the middle of nowhere. A jagged bolt of hope shot through him. Anya.

So. She was here. She had come a lot further than he had expected.

The sound of the aircraft might spook her, so Joshua left it, and walked swiftly by the light of the moon across the frozen terrain. The light dimmed to almost nothing as he reached the lower elevation, as if hidden behind a rocky outcropping. The fire had to be in a cave.

She was there. He felt it.

And yet a few minutes later, when Joshua truly saw Anya's dark head bent over the fire, something settled inside him. Relief. And more.

Shortly following, a whole lot of anger welled up to replace it.

CHAPTER FIVE

ANYA STILL DIDN'T WANT to put out the warm, comforting fire. What did another few minutes matter? So far, she had eluded Joshua's air fleet. Now freedom was as close as her next frosty breath. Only one aircraft whispered through the skies now. The others had given up. Soon that one, lonely one would, too. Perhaps then she could walk during the daytime.

After she traversed the Dzungarian Gate tomorrow, it would be another week, perhaps, before she reached her uncle's nearest outpost. Hopefully, Richert would welcome her. Every bit of her outrageous plan hinged upon this tiny hope.

Pitch black had settled in outside. With it, a deep, biting cold swirled into the cave.

She really should put out the fire and get going. Although the cave entrance was partially blocked, someone at the perfect angle might see the light. Maybe that one, last, persistent pilot—although she hadn't heard the craft since noon. He must have given up, too. For now.

She wondered if Onred's men would join the search. Thankfully, her sisters were too young to be considered as an exchange for a bride. If it had been different, she would never have left. But she did trust Joshua to protect them. He'd never think to relinquish one of them to the wolf. He had always expected more of her. Demanded more, really.

Home. It hurt unbearably to think that she might never see her family or Astana again. If her plan failed, she would not. Even if it succeeded, would Joshua allow her back into the city? Surely he would not be cruel enough to forbid her. But he was not a man who suffered insubordination well. She had disobeyed the baron's direct orders. Banishment would be acceptable punishment in the eyes of the Donetski people.

Tears filled her eyes, thinking about Marli, Elise, and her brothers, but she blinked them back.

She really should put out the fire.

But it was so warm and friendly. And she felt so alone.

Put it out, Anya. After all, when she reached her destination, she could light as many fires as she wished. And after she fought for peace, she would be her own woman. No one would ever rule her life again. No one would ever sell her again. Like Joshua had, for peace. And to keep his title of Baron, she reminded herself.

Unfolding her trowel, Anya chipped up a mound of frozen ice and mud and cast it onto the fire. It flickered, but didn't go out.

"Don't put it out on my account."

The low, rough voice made her gasp, and she whipped out her laser.

Joshua.

He seemed to fill the entrance. The elite, cream military parka made his shoulders seem wider, his body more solid and forbidding.

"You." Hands trembling, she lowered the weapon.

"Of course it's me. I'm your protector, foolish girl. Who did you think would come for you?"

Palpable fury simmered in him, deep and hot, yet tightly leashed, as were every one of his emotions, always. In the past, she had wished that just once she could break through the impenetrable shell he enclosed around himself. Just once, she'd like to see him snap, to glimpse the true man underneath all the medals and the power that fit him like a glove. To especially see beyond the shiny honor of hero worship with which she'd clothed him when they had first met. She had always wanted to please him.

No more.

Anya realized now that Joshua was the lone pilot. Part of her had known it all along, and it was why she had worked so hard to stay hidden. Joshua was clever and the bank of medals on his uniform proved the Donetsk legend that he was difficult to outwit. Apparently, she hadn't done a good enough job.

"I didn't want to be found," she said shortly, reholstering the laser.

"Then you should have put out your fire."

Yes, she should have. So, was this to be the end result of all her efforts, of walking at night, freezing the exposed bits of her skin to a brittle crust? All for what? To be found in three days?

Joshua entered her cave. Invaded it, it felt like. His personality and presence felt as strong as a magnet to her soul...to her foolish heart. She looked away. "I didn't want to be found," she repeated. "Go home."

"What was your goal? To go south? Meet your uncle?"

He was too smart by half. But he didn't need to know her true plan. He'd only forbid it. Then she would need to mutiny against him again. Simpler to stay silent and plot her escape.

He said, "Onred thinks the marriage offer was a trick. He's threatening to attack."

Anya had hoped that wouldn't happen. Now she'd need to get to her uncle's stronghold even faster.

"Onred can take a trip to hell," she bit out, ignoring the inbred guilt for uttering the crude words. After a moment, she baldly finished, "And so can you." That should make it clear that she would not return home with him.

"I've never allowed you to swear at me before." His voice held a soft bite. "I won't begin now."

Heat flashed. She didn't want to feel guilty. However, ingrained respect made it difficult to ignore the quiet chastisement. As well, his soft tone was misleading. She knew the inflexible steel that lived inside him. And the unswerving determination to have his own way, no matter the price.

But the real truth was far worse. She wanted to please him. Still.

"I'm sorry," she allowed. "But you're no longer my protector. You discharged me, remember? Your authority over me has ended."

To her complete, consternated surprise, he swiftly closed the distance between them. She leaped to her feet, reaching for her knife.

His hand was on her jaw before she could draw a breath, and he tilted up her chin. His fingers felt cool, yet firm, and her heart pounded much harder than she liked.

"What happened to you?"

Disconcerted, Anya jerked her chin back. "It's from the fall. I mean, the landing."

"It's a bad gash." Ignoring her retreat, he cupped her chin again, angling it up so he could see better. His fingers unexpectedly gentled, and for a second felt unbearably tender. "You are all right?"

Flustered, she swallowed. "Yes."

A heartbeat elapsed, and then he released her. He loomed very close now, a few inches taller than she. His broad shoulders blocked part of the firelight, and his tawny hair was rumpled. He looked disarmingly approachable. But she knew better. He hadn't accomplished his mission yet.

She took a step back. "Go." Distinctly, she added, "Just so we're clear, I won't go home with you. I will not marry that disgusting Onred."

The dark eyes held hers. "Is there someone else?"

"No."

No one but you. Anya swallowed. She would never admit that wretched truth to her unattainable protector. How could her heart so quickly forget that he had sold her and refused to reconsider his decision, even after she had begged him to do so?

Again surprising her, he went down on his knee and took up a cross-legged position near the fire. "Perhaps we can negotiate."

Another disarming pose. She had sensed the heat and force of his anger when he had first arrived. Once again, he was strictly under control. Wasn't he always?

Anya sat, but not too close. The fire felt warm, and that heat doubled when Joshua fed a branch into the licking flames. A blast of warmth hit her face as the flames leaped higher. She shivered.

"Cold?" he murmured, not looking at her, and fed in another branch.

"I can take care of myself."

"I can see that."

"I don't need you anymore."

Quietly, Joshua said, "I need you. Your territory needs you. We can make things right."

"No!" Agitated, she sprang to her knees, but his swift, light pressure on her wrist stayed her.

"Thousands more will die."

"Thousands will die anyway. Onred is dishonorable. He won't keep his word."

Joshua's gaze cut sharper. "You don't trust him."

"Of course not! Not after..." She cut the words short.

He prodded, "After what?"

Anya refused to reveal her humiliation to him. Joshua had a way of making her feel far more vulnerable than she wanted to feel. She wouldn't slice that part of herself open to him, too. He already wielded far too much power over her heart.

"Nothing. It doesn't matter."

His thumb rubbed her wrist, as though absently, but his brown eyes gleamed tawny and warm in the leaping firelight. They held hers. "Tell me." That gaze softened something inside of her, and beckoned her to give him everything he wanted.

She closed her eyes to break the spell. How weak she was to him. Did he know? Did he suspect? She should hate him. He had sold her!

He waited.

Why not tell him, she thought recklessly. It would shock him, as he deserved. Yes. Why not?

So, looking into the fire, so she wouldn't have to see his expression of disgust when he learned of the soiled creature she had become, she told him everything that Onred had done. Bitterly, she finished, "Onred said that he'd paid for me. That he had the right to do anything he wanted." Then she shot a glance at him.

Joshua stared into the fire, too. His shoulders moved up, and then down, matching the movement of a barely audible breath. His shoulders heaved again, and his skin unexpectedly flushed dark. He bolted to his feet and strode to the back of the cave.

She had shocked him; and a bit more violently than she had expected. Meanly, that felt good, after all that he had put her through.

Joshua silently paced for long minutes. After a while, it unnerved her.

"Well?" Anya said. "Aren't you going to speak?"

He ground out, "You don't want to hear it."

"Are you really so shocked?"

"Yes!" The one word hissed through his teeth. "It's my fault. I failed to protect you."

Now her revenge felt petty. "It wasn't your fault, Joshua."

"It was. He knew." His voice sounded rough.

Anya frowned. "Knew what?"

"That I..." His fists clenched, but he did not complete the sentence.

Joshua said no more, but his pacing stopped. He stared out of the cave, as if picturing a scene in his head. No expression flickered across his face. It disturbed her. Once again, he had bottled up his emotions.

"I won't marry him," Anya repeated, just to try to break through to him.

He nodded, shoved his hands in his pockets, but said nothing.

"Joshua, what are you thinking? You're scaring me."

❋*❋*❋*❋*❋

Joshua could barely think for the white fury searing his brain. He burned to kill Onred, the fiend. The depraved demon. He'd finally come to realize he was a jackal, but this...

His fingers itched to squeeze the life from that bastard's throat even now. He had touched Anya. He had hurt her. Joshua's mind would let him go no further. The broken, wild hellion of a boy he had once been wanted to break free and scream his rage to the heavens, then annihilate the man, his troops, his territory...everything Onred held dear.

A fine tremor seized Joshua as he struggled to keep himself under control. A violent loss of self control would accomplish none of his goals. The perverted bastard would die. This was a certainty. Now he just had to plot how.

"Joshua, you're scaring me." Anya touched his arm and with a desperate twist to his head, he looked deep into her beautiful blue eyes. They were like clear waters that lapped at his soul and calmed him. They always had. They always would.

"You won't marry him," he said gruffly. "Come home with me."

❈*❈**❈**❈**❈

Relief was so swift and strong that Anya swayed a bit, feeling light-headed. Could it be so simple? She could go home. Everything would go on as it had before. She looked down at her fingers, still on Joshua's arm.

Then, slowly, she removed them. No. It could not. For the first time, she saw this truth clearly. She would die. She would waste away from wanting a man who would never want her...who *could never* want her. "What about peace?"

"Peace will wait for another day. Pack your things. We're going home."

She stepped back. "I won't go with you."

Joshua's gaze narrowed.

"I've made a clean break. I want to start a new life."

"No."

"I've said my goodbyes."

"Your family needs you."

It was the one card he could play that would break her heart, and he knew it. After all, she had never wanted to leave home—at least, not forever. "Marriage to Onred would have done the same thing."

"You have no need to leave. I will protect you from Onred. You can marry whomever you wish."

"No. I can't." Anya turned away before he saw the truth in her eyes. He was a perceptive man. It wouldn't take a space scientist to see through the flimsy, self-protective layers to her heart.

Silence elapsed. "I won't leave you here."

Anya gathered up her things and pushed them into the black bag. "I'll go with you under one condition."

"What?" He sounded grim.

"Fly me to my uncle's territory and leave me there."

Joshua's gaze flickered.

"No tricks," she cautioned. "Or I'll escape again. You can't keep me a prisoner."

Softly, he said, "Now I am your captor? Your guard?" Temper heated his eyes to tawny fire.

She stiffened, and lifted her chin. "Of course not. But I need freedom. I want to find out who I am, apart from you...and my family."

"Apart from me."

"You are no longer my protector, Joshua. Let me go."

His fingers curled around her wrist, and he drew her close to him. "I will always be your protector," he said through his teeth. "Accept that. Finally."

"Let me go." Her voice lowered to a whisper. "Please."

His gaze remained locked with hers, but he did not release her.

A piercing shriek broke the silence. Then came a distant, guttural boom and a hissing whoosh, like the explosion of an air cannon. The ground shuddered.

"What was *that*?"

Both bolted into the night. Far to the north, low on the horizon, a bright yellow ball mushroomed, rimmed with crimson. Whatever it was, it had happened a great distance away.

Anya stared in shock. "What..."

"No. God almighty." Joshua's words sounded like a strangled prayer.

"What *is* it?" she cried out.

Surely it was too far away to be...

"Astana."

The yellow mushroom roiled higher, billowing into an angry, orange-red cloud, rimmed with black, devouring its prey like a greedy, voracious monster.

CHAPTER SIX

"*No.*" It could not be Astana.

Anya staggered backward. It wasn't. It *couldn't* be.

But Joshua's very silence terrified her. He stood completely still, staring north, his features rigid.

"It *can't* be!" Anya cried out.

"It is." The horrible deadness in his voice made her gasp. Suddenly, she couldn't catch her breath. It felt like all of the air had been sucked from her lungs.

"No," she whispered, her voice tight and choking. "*No!*" Not Astana. It couldn't be. And yet a descending, horrible certainty told her otherwise. No other city lay in that direction. What else could it be?

Joshua said nothing, his features as still as stone. But the bleak acknowledgement in his eyes struck to her very soul.

Something crumpled inside of her.

"*No.*" A high, keening wail left her throat, and Anya fell to her knees. It couldn't be true! Her family. Marli, Damon, Elise, David... "No. *No,*" she screamed again. "Marli..."

Joshua's arm clamped around her shoulders and held her tight. He was on his knees too, staring at the far horizon; at the inferno that had been their home. She wasn't sure who held the other up.

Her home was gone, destroyed forever in one thermonuclear fireball. A hysterical sound rose in her throat, and she cried out gasping, incoherent belts of misery.

New thermonuclear bombs were clean and precise, and the modern weapon of choice for mass destruction. They left behind no radiation, unlike the nuclear bombs which had destroyed the planet one thousand years ago, and left it in a permanent ice age.

Astana was gone. *Gone.* She could not comprehend it. It could not be true.

"*No.*" She wept in gulping, uncontrollable sobs. Time became meaningless. Her throat felt raw and her jaw ached.

Slowly, after many long minutes, logical thoughts formed. She choked out, "Who could do such a thing?"

"Onred."

"Why?" And then it hit her. "Because of me. It's because of *me* they're all dead!"

"Anya, no."

"Yes. It's because of *me.* Oh God, what have I done?" Weeping, she fell face first on the ground and screamed her inconsolable torment into the snow.

"Anya. Anya!" Joshua pulled her up.

Her wet face felt frozen. She didn't care. She wanted to die right now. She wanted to be with them. "I should be there. Why them, and not me?" She could barely think.

Joshua's arms went under her knees and he lifted her. She fought him. "Put me down. Put me *down.* That should be me." She wept without ceasing. "Put me *down!* I need to go to them."

"They're dead." Through her own torment, she heard his voice break. "Stop fighting. We've got to go inside. I have to think."

Think? What good would thinking do? They were dead. All of her family was dead. Bitter, piercing wails tore through her as Joshua carried her inside the cave. He gently set her down against the wall, near the fire. Anya wrapped her arms around her knees and rocked back and forth, wretchedly weeping.

Joshua paced, his strides jerky. Anya pressed streaming eyes into her jacket sleeve. The world had ended. What else was there to live for, to fight for?

Onred had taken it all. Every vile word she had ever heard in her life spit from her mouth, relegating Onred forever to hell. She didn't feel better afterward, just more filthy. Guilty. It was all her fault. If she had just sacrificed herself, maybe peace would have come. It had been arrogant of her to try to achieve peace on her own. Who *was* she, anyway?

"I'm sorry," she whimpered. "I'm so sorry."

"It's not your fault, Anya."

"It *is*."

"A man who wants peace wouldn't take the first opportunity to attack. You were right. We couldn't trust him. He probably planned this all along. After he got you..." Joshua's harsh words broke off, sounding strangled.

Anya wiped her face and took several deep breaths. "He's won. Just like that, he's won. The whole territory is his."

"No, it is *not*," he said with low intensity. "I am still alive, and so are you."

"The other cities will be next."

"No. He needs our greenhouses. Destroying Astana was symbolic. He destroyed our power base to send a message to the other cities."

"They'll surrender."

"Not...." A crackle came from the gold, triangular patch on his collar.

"Alpha Victor; Tango Bravo. Copy?"

Joshua pressed the microscopic send button. "Go ahead, Tango Bravo."

"Thank God!" Relief mingled with the panic in the young male voice. "I'm flying the northern border. Astana's gone. Did you see?"

"Affirmative. Report."

"Onred arrived at twenty hundred hours. I don't know how he got through our defenses. I got a distress call from Control fifteen minutes ago. Onred's shuttle left ten minutes later. Then Astana blew up."

Joshua bit out an expletive. "Replay the distress call."

Static crackled, and then a precise, clipped woman's voice said, "They're shooting in the halls. Onred's men are armed. They're sweeping the baron's level. They're..." hissing crackles popped. "They're breaking in here." For the first time, a small note of panic entered the woman's voice. "What's that?" She seemed to be listening to something else. "Report. They've kidnapped the Dubrovnyk children. I don't know..." An explosion sounded, and the sound of running footsteps. A grunt. "No!" Then silence.

"Copy, Alpha Victor?" The young man's voice shook.

"Retreat to Zebra Charlie Alpha," Joshua barked. "All units report."

"They're tracking me!" Fear elevated Tango Bravo's voice. "I'm taking evasive action. Get rid of your transponders, Alpha! Once you're dead..."

Complete silence.

Joshua swore and stripped off his jacket and shirt. He wore thin snow wear beneath. He thrust one garment at Anya. "Cut out the transponder. We need to go. Now."

With shaking hands, Anya flipped out her utility knife and hacked out the rectangular transponder from the back collar of Joshua's shirt. For security reasons, the small device tracked his movements. She had already cut them out of her own clothing. As she did so, she wondered how Onred had breached Astana's entire defense network. How else could the warhead have punched through their defense shield? And how could he track the pilots? To do it all, he must have gained access to Central Command and the military's highly protected computer transponder codes. But *how?*

While Joshua yanked back on his shirt and jacket, Anya swiftly finished packing. She pulled out her heat reflecting tarp.

"Let's go." Joshua strode fast for the cave entrance.

"What about the fire? Should we put it out?"

"Leave it. They'll think I'm hiding here."

Anya followed him into the freezing night. Moonlight glinted off the white snow. Dark rocks looked like unfathomable black shadows.

Joshua said, "Onred's men will be here soon."

"What about your aircraft?"

"No time."

Silently, Anya handed him one end of the tarp. Casting her a quick, approving glance, he took the end and pulled it over them both. Although the heat insulating tarp was large, they had to walk shoulder to shoulder. Joshua pulled her black bag from her hand.

She protested, "I can carry it."

"Don't argue."

They walked fast over the frozen snow, heading uphill, deeper into the mountains.

Anya couldn't seem to feel anything. Maybe she was in shock. She peered around the edge of the tarp at the glowing orange slice on the horizon. "Do you think they're alive? Do you think Onred kidnapped my family?"

How could she feel any hope when all the other inhabitants of Astana were dead?

"Maybe. They could be insurance, in case they can't kill me. Or you."

"Hostages, you mean."

Joshua didn't answer. He didn't have to. Now a whole new set of worries tortured her. If her brothers and sisters were still alive, what would Onred do to them? Horrible images flooded her mind, making her feel sick.

"Maybe it would be better if they were dead," she whispered. No. She couldn't think like that. Anya didn't dare cry, for it was so cold now that the liquid might freeze her eyelids together.

Joshua still didn't answer. That scared her, for if he could reassure her, he would. That was his nature.

They both heard the whisper of approaching aircraft at the same time.

"Over there. Behind the rock," Joshua said, and they swiftly knelt behind a huge rock topped with a deep cap of snow. Anya peered through a crack formed between the tarp and the rock.

Yellow lasers shot from the incoming aircraft. One flamed east, and a muffled explosion broke the quiet night. Joshua's ship, no doubt.

Another aircraft shot at the mountain cave where they had been minutes before, and where Joshua's transponders still lay on the floor.

Anya watched in silence. It seemed surreal. Onred *had* gained access to the military's transponder codes. He had tracked Joshua to that cave. Onred had breached Astana's high security military defense systems. But how had he done it? And when?

Another aircraft, close enough that Anya could see the black underbelly of Onred's distinctive, v-shaped airbird, joined the first. Their mingled laser beams focused on the cave, and it collapsed in a thunder of rubble.

The two aircraft dipped to hover inches above the ground, while the remaining bird swooped over the terrain, undoubtedly seeking glimpses of heat or movement. Joshua slowly pulled the tarp down to the ground, forming a tent about them. They could not see the enemy, and hopefully the enemy could not detect them, either.

Boots scrunched in the snow. Anya's heart beat faster when the heavy footsteps crunched closer. Beside her, Joshua crouched as solid and motionless as a stone. He gave no inclination of his intent until he whipped up the tarp and shot blue flame into the night. His laser was on stun. Less likely to be seen in the dark.

He darted out and the tarp fell in crisp, cool folds around her. Moments later, Joshua returned, pulling an inert man under the tarp. "I'm going to disable one of the aircraft. Cover me." Before Anya could blink, he was gone.

Onred's unconscious soldier breathed in muted whistles. It creeped her out, having him behind her, not knowing when he'd wake up. And Joshua. She pulled out her laser and crept around the corner of the rock, tracking his movements. Where was the other pilot? Each airbird carried one pilot, although the standard issue craft could carry up to four in a pinch.

She finally glimpsed Joshua's cream jacket melding with the shadowed lumps of snow near the cave base.

What was he *thinking?* She had assumed they would hide until Onred's men left. But passivity wasn't in Joshua's nature. Conquering was. Over the last ten years, seeing him only in civilized, diplomatic environments, she had forgotten the stories of his legendary—and often risky—heroics on the field of battle.

Both enemy airbirds continued to hover, engines softly whispering, above the snow. Red lights chased in circles around the lower edges. Orange lights from the console gleamed through the dark windows.

Joshua moved forward in a low crouch, laser at the ready.

Where was the enemy airman? Anya swiftly searched the landscape for movement, but saw nothing. Then she searched the sky for the remaining airbird, but it had faded into silence.

All at once, Anya guessed Joshua's plan. He would disable one of Onred's ships and steal the other. Once they'd ripped out the transponders, they could fly on blackout to her uncle's territory. A terrific plan, of course. Only one man stood between death and freedom.

Anya edged out a little further, searching for Joshua's target. Yellow light flashed toward Joshua. Anya pinpointed the source and fired. Blue light fizzed. Wrong setting. She kicked it up a notch, but before she could fire, Joshua shot and a dark shape fell.

Both of Onred's men were down. They were free! When Joshua darted for the far ship, Anya grabbed her bag and tarp and ran for the nearest one. She could search for the transponders and rip them out.

"Anya, no!"

In surprise, she glanced at Joshua. His face was shadowed in the darkness, but his arm cut downward at a violent angle. Without thinking, she dove to the ground. Yellow flame seared her arm.

CHAPTER SEVEN

ANYA INSTINCTIVELY ROLLED into the snow, cooling the burning pain. Fiery lasers hissed above her, then stopped, leaving darkness.

Pain and fear seemed to freeze her thoughts. Who had won?

Joshua's face appeared above her.

"Should have known," she murmured. "You never fail."

He swiftly carried her to the nearest aircraft.

The pain in her arm burned like crazy, but Anya managed to climb into the dimly lit aircraft on her own. "Don't forget my bag...and the tarp."

She took the seat behind the pilot's chair and eyed the orange instrument panel. Finding and removing the transponders had been such a clean and simple goal a minute ago. Now her brain felt fuzzy. Where was Joshua?

A glance outside spotted her bag and tarp, still lying on the ground. Beyond them, a fallen man. His body was long and lean. He wasn't the beefy man Joshua had first stunned and dragged behind the rock. The lean man who had shot her must have come from the third airbird.

Yellow light flickered from the direction of the boulder. And then Anya understood. Joshua had returned to kill the first man. But why? He was no threat to them now.

Queasiness twisted in her stomach. She felt sick.

Joshua dashed across the frozen snow pack, scooped up the fallen bag and tarp and deposited both in the ship. Cold air and the metallic scent of snow billowed in with him. He slammed the door. With bare fingers, he ripped off the black instrument panel cover and jerked out wires. Metal pieces clattered to the floor. He grunted in satisfaction.

The engine whirred louder, and they shot up, dizzyingly fast, into the air. Anya's stomach dropped with a sickening lurch.

Joshua pushed overhead buttons, and the next moment the airbird swirled right. Yellow fire spit. A sharp turn left, and more yellow fire lit the black landscape.

"You...blew up the birds?" Anya managed to keep her voice level. The truth was, the pain searing her arm choked her mind.

"No one will follow us. For a while."

"Good." Anya sat quietly, breathing shallowly, not wanting to draw attention to herself. They needed to escape this airspace, and fast. The craft's antiradar field would help hide them from enemy radar, but nothing could disguise their movement. Satellites would pick it up within minutes.

An Altai voice spoke from the console, startling her. "Report, AirOpsOne."

Tersely, Joshua muttered, "In pursuit."

"We're not tracking you. Blue and Nine are not responding. Report."

"Damage. ...Fading." Joshua clicked off the microphone and pushed the throttle. The ship shot forward, and gravity pressed hard against Anya's body, pushing her deep into the seat.

Silence ensued for long minutes.

"How long...do we have?" she got out.

"They're busy, fighting resistance. We could have thirty minutes to an hour before they become suspicious. Don't worry. We're flying open aces. They won't catch us."

Anya didn't need to ask what "open aces" meant. Obviously, it meant flying as fast as a demon escaping hell.

For the first time, she mustered the courage to look at her upper arm. The dim light filtering back from the instrument panel revealed that several inches were charred black. The wound didn't appear deep, though. Was the black color her charred skin, or her snow wear, melted into her skin? Anya swallowed back bile and searched for the medical kit.

A white box was snapped under the pilot's seat, and she battled the gravitational force to lean forward and pull it out. It contained bandages, healing cream, and an antiseptic healing wand, too.

"How's your arm?" Joshua glanced back, concentration etching shadowed lines into his face.

"I don't think it's deep."

Joshua pressed buttons on the console and swiveled to face her.

It startled her. "Don't you need to steer? I'm fine. I can handle it."

"I'll be the judge."

If she had felt better, she might have rolled her eyes. "Dictator should be your title. Not baron."

"When one knows best..."

This time she did roll her eyes.

His teeth flashed. "Let me see."

It hurt to move her arm, but he solved that by lifting it for her. Gentle fingers tested the edges of the wound.

"I don't think it hit muscle," he murmured. "You're lucky." With two quick movements, he ripped the fabric of her clothing in order to better expose the wound.

"Hold still." He popped an antiseptic healing cartridge into the wand, set the mode on "wide," and pressed the button.

His head was bent very close to her own. Never had Joshua been this close to her before, or gently tended her wound himself. Never. The sweet intimacy of it made her heart both soar and pound—and made her fiercely long for what could never be. *Would* never be. For Joshua did not want her. And yet the way he gently touched her now, with such care, could not prevent her heart from foolishly imagining all sorts of impossible things.

Cool white light stroked over her skin. A fine mist, mixed with healing alpha waves, sprayed from the medical appliance.

She sighed with relief. "That feels good."

He looked up. A devilish grin lifted one corner of his mouth. "You've never said that to me before."

Was he *flirting* with her? Anya flushed in confusion.

His smile faded, and he looked down to concentrate on her wound.

A moment later, his expression remote, he turned off the wand and leaned back. "That's enough. You'll need to apply more in an hour." His warm fingers accidentally brushed hers when he pushed the wand into her hand.

He swiveled back to the console to check the instruments.

Anya didn't know what to think of his out-of-character comment. If he had flirted, he certainly seemed to regret it now.

Of course he did. Or, more likely, she had misconstrued the whole incident. Her brain was overloaded. Too much had happened in too short a time.

"Thank you," she offered.

One shoulder jerked. "It's my job."

Protector, he meant. How Anya had grown to hate that title.

"Rest," he advised. "It'll be another half hour before we reach Aksu."

Her uncle's capitol city.

Anya didn't think she could possibly sleep, but she was tired. So much had happened in the last hour, and her arm still burned from being shot.

Astana had been blown to bits. The image of that horrific mushroom cloud boiling orange death into the night seemed burned into her brain. Darkness lodged in her heart, rimmed by the fire of unquenchable pain. Her home was gone. All of her friends were dead. And it was all her fault, no matter what Joshua said.

Was her family dead? Or Onred's hostages? Grief gathered into an aching knot in her throat, and she wept. Anya rarely prayed, but she did so now. *Let my family be alive, and if they are, please protect them from Onred.*

Anya silently swore that she would rescue them, no matter what it took. As soon as she convinced her uncle to ally with them against Onred's forces, she would hunt down Onred and find her family. She would not rest until her family was free and Astana avenged.

✱✱✱✱✱✱✱✱✱

Anya's eyes opened. Although the interior of the aircraft was dark, orange instrument lights haloed Joshua's dark head. She must have napped, but for how long? "Are we almost there?"

"We'll cross the last of the Tien Shan in a few minutes."

And enter her uncle's territory. "What then?"

"You tell me. What was your original plan?" No mistaking the soft bite to his voice. He wasn't happy that she'd led him on a merry chase over the past three days. Why? Because he cared for her, and had been worried about her? How she wanted to believe that. But she feared it was only because she had put a wrench into his peace plans and disobeyed him.

Anya yawned in an effort to clear her head. "I planned to convince my uncle to ally with us. Onred would fear our alliance. That way, he'd think twice before attacking us. If my plan worked, we'd have peace with Richert, and Onred, too, by default."

"Why would Richert agree to ally with us? Twenty years of blood lies between our territories."

"His attacks have slowed down over the last few years."

"So you believe he wants peace?"

"I had hoped to convince him." Anya didn't want to say more.

"How?"

She should have known he wouldn't let it go. A moment elapsed before she said, "I look like my mother. I hoped he might still have a soft place in his heart for her. ...For me."

Joshua clicked a button on the console and swiftly faced her. His eyes glittered a hard, topaz color. "Are you insane? Your mother started the war."

Anya frowned. "No. My uncle started the war, because he's a jealous tyrant."

"Your uncle hated your mother *and* your father. Why else would he fight a twenty-three year war? I fought his men. They're cutthroat. If Richert had seen your mother again, he would've slit her throat himself."

Surprising anger swelled. "He wouldn't. He loved her."

Joshua stared at her, his eyes hard. Then, softly, he said, "I thought you'd outgrown those teenage love novels. I'm sorry to disillusion you, but real life is not a fairy tale."

"I know that," she snapped. "But I don't think *you* understand the first thing about love. All you know is giving orders. Nothing matters to you except logic, facts, and...and *power*."

He swung back to the console. "Count yourself lucky I'm with you. If you'd followed your plan alone, you'd be dead now."

Anya softly gasped with rage. "You're an arrogant son-of-a...jerk. *That* I know for certain."

His whole body stilled. Slowly, he faced her. "Watch it."

"You're so arrogant you can't see that *you* insulted *me*. I am not an idiot. I wasn't going to sashay into Richert's palace and ask him pretty please to make nice. I was going to offer him...something."

"What?"

She hesitated, unsure how he would receive the linchpin idea of her plan to produce peace. "He wants the Tien Shan mountains. They're beautiful, but barren and uninhabitable. We don't use that land. I planned to offer it to him in exchange for a permanent peace."

Joshua actually threw back his head and laughed.

"What?" she frowned.

"I grew up in those barren, useless mountains," he said pleasantly.

"No one lives there, except..."

"Wastrels? Vagabonds? They live quite nicely, deep under the rocks. Until they decide to throw someone into the cold to die."

Anya gasped. "Not you, Joshua. I thought you came from Japa."

"You thought wrong." He twisted back to check the instrument panel. His skin looked faintly flushed.

"You've never said anything before..."

"And why have I now? I don't know. But I've lived in those mountains, and I've fought for those mountains. My friends have died in the Tien Shan, defending them from your uncle's troops. I'd rather die than give your uncle that piece of land. That mountain range is the only physical barrier keeping him out of our land. Did you think about that?"

"We'd have peace."

"And you'd trust his word?"

Anya didn't know how to answer.

"What's more," Joshua ground on, "he knows you have no authority to give away land."

"I would if I married someone...from our territory." This solution had been her last resort. "My husband would replace you as baron."

Joshua went very still and just watched her. Did he feel betrayed? And yet what had he done to her, by giving her to Onred? He had used her for his own purposes. For peace, supposedly. But really, it had to have been for power. Once again, the hurt of that swamped her—so much so it felt like a burning, physical ache in her chest. And if she was honest, it wasn't just because he had sold her—for whatever the reason; it was also because he'd ejected her from his life for good. Clearly, she had never meant anything to him. Equally clear, nothing mattered to him except for peace and power.

Anya had to know something. "Tell me. Is that the real reason why you sold me to Onred? To marry me, my father's only legal heir, out of the territory, so you could stay baron forever?"

"Anya. *No,*" he said harshly. "I've always put the territory's best interests first. And your father's wishes first, too. I did not agree to the marriage so I could stay in power."

"You sold me, though, regardless." She was surprised by the fury gathering hotter in her belly. He had betrayed her trust, and had refused to listen to her pleas to rethink the marriage and return Onred's money. It still hurt, horribly. Until these last few minutes, however, she hadn't allowed herself to fully feel how much.

A crackle from the console drew Joshua's attention. Words blipped across the computer screen. He said, "This conversation isn't finished."

Anya didn't answer. She was furiously close to tears. Too much had happened. Too much. Astana was gone, all of her friends were dead, her family might be captured by a monster, and now she was arguing with Joshua? And he, in just a few words, had torn apart her plan to make peace with her uncle. Unwanted tears slid down her cheeks.

"Things are about to get worse," Joshua stated grimly. "We're going down."

"Why?" Anya wiped her cheeks with the heels of her hands.

"Your uncle won't let us cross the last mountain range. Either we land, or they shoot us down."

For the first time, Anya noticed the starburst of tiny blips on the radar screen.

Was this finally the end? Instead of dying in Astana as she should have done, would they both die now, at the hands of her uncle's bloodthirsty men?

CHAPTER EIGHT

JOSHUA LOWERED the craft to the snow pack at the base of the mountain. Cold moonlight illumined the flat clearing. Spindly trees poked through the frozen ice.

Richert's red aircraft settled like bats in a circle, enclosing them in a tight web. The lights under-circling their bellies flashed yellow. Anya wondered what color encircled Donetsk's craft. She had never noticed before. It seemed a ridiculous thing to wonder right now, one trigger shot shy of death.

"Distress signal noted," came a voice from the control panel. "Identify yourselves."

"Joshua Van Heisman. Anya Dubrovnyk. We're fleeing Onred's forces. We seek asylum in Richert's city, Aksu."

A computer voice scan would verify Joshua's identity. Anya's heart beat faster with fear. How could Joshua sound so level-headed and calm? Now her uncle's men knew their identities. One laser shot from her uncle's ships would end both Joshua and the Dubrovnyk's reign in Donetsk Territory. An easy win for her uncle's bloody, twenty-three year war.

Wasn't Joshua afraid? Didn't he feel anything?

Silence ensued.

Joshua waited patiently, occasionally drumming his fingers on the console.

Anya's arm hurt. Time to apply more healing mist, but she was afraid to turn on the wand. It's white light might be misconstrued as a laser charge up.

She had to use the bathroom, too.

Why was she thinking these things?

"Exit the bird, hands up."

"Roger." Joshua turned to Anya. "Leave everything here."

"But..."

"Everything."

Some of her fear must have communicated to him, for Joshua reached forward, as if to touch her, but stopped. His gaze, however, held hers. Its steadiness reassured her. "It will be all right," he said softly.

She nodded.

Joshua slid open the door and freezing air rushed in, instantly sticking Anya's fine nose hairs together. Hands raised, Joshua jumped out first. A waiting man grabbed his arm and shoved him hard against a nearby aircraft. Swift, gloved hands patted him down and hurled his laser and knives into the snow.

A man pointed a laser at Anya. "Out."

Her legs didn't want to move. She stumbled toward the opening.

"Hands up!"

Anya tried, but her left arm hurt horribly. Awkwardly, she jumped to the ground.

"I *said*, hands up!" The man wrenched her left arm high, and she cried out.

"She's injured, idiot," Joshua snarled. He shook off a restraining hand. "Be careful with her."

The man didn't listen. He hurled her against another aircraft and slid hands over her body, looking for weapons. He whistled. "You're packing, pretty one." With swift efficiency, he stripped her laser and four knives from her belt.

"Get in the bird." He shoved Anya toward one craft's doorway, while Joshua was hustled to another. They would be separated. Anya couldn't hide the fear in the glance she shot Joshua.

"It's all right," he told her again. Face set like stone, he climbed into the enemy aircraft.

Anya obeyed the prodding of the airman behind her and climbed into the warm bird. The man bound her wrists, slammed the door, and they rose at dizzying speed, then shot forward. Anya closed her eyes. At least they weren't dead. Not yet.

✼✼✼✼✼✼✼✼✼

Anya spent the short flight time thinking up strategies for meeting her uncle. It seemed obvious they would be taken to see him. Otherwise, they would be dead.

Although Joshua hadn't thought much of her original plan, Anya was more determined than ever to sway her uncle to their side. It was the first step she could take to free her family from Onred's prison, if they were still alive, and protect the rest of Donetsk Territory. She would do whatever it took to coerce Richert to listen to them.

But by the time they touched down in Aksu's hangar, Anya had formed no new, solid plan to influence Richert. Truly, why would her uncle want to ally with them? What could they possibly offer that he would want? Besides the Tien Shan, of course. Anya supposed she could try to charm him—although with the history of the twenty year war between their families, it seemed unlikely to be an effective strategy.

Rough hands pulled her from the aircraft, and within moments she walked beside Joshua toward the massive glass doors leading to the heart of the city. People thronged in the inner, circular area. Footpaths criss-crossed it, and these were bordered by flower beds and benches. The outer perimeter of the main circle showcased shop fronts. Wide hallways leading to unknown destinations intersected the large circle like the spokes of a wheel.

He murmured, "Are you all right?"

"Yes."

The doors silently slid apart.

"Let me do the talking."

Anya didn't answer.

Following grunted instructions, they climbed into an open-air vehicle. The white electric train scooted parallel to Aksu's wide outer walkway. After a pause at the master exchange, they rose five floors, and then sped on. This floor was quieter. Potted plants dotted narrower hallways. Crisply dressed men and women walked quickly, some carrying paper-thin computers, others disappearing down unknown hallways.

The train coasted to a halt at the arched entrance of a gigantic room. Three story, floor-to-ceiling glass curved up and arched overhead, allowing the glorious pink dawn to stream inside. Plum colored couches, cream tables, lush carpets on the floor, potted plants, televisions, and a gold bar counter covered with platters of food all leant the feeling of comfortable opulence.

An airman directed them to adjacent chairs and ordered them to wait. A younger military officer guarded them. At least it was comfortable. And warm.

Anya evaluated the plush appointments, trying to get a feel for the man who owned them. Although Richert was her father's brother, Anya knew nothing personal about him. Over the years she had seen clips of him on the news, of course, but those had only left the impression of a big, stooped, frowning man with receding hair and thick, bristling black eyebrows. And a low growl of a voice. Clearly, he was growing into a bitter, angry old man. He also appeared to be much older than her father had been. Perhaps by as much as ten years. That would put him at about sixty now.

A silent *whirr* drew her attention. She drew a quick breath of surprise when she saw her relative.

When Joshua rose to his feet, so did she.

Her uncle rode in a wheelchair. He wore a brown and black flannel shirt, which drooped over his sagging shoulders. His gnarled hands, clasped in his lap, looked like those of a much older man, for the knuckles were round and bony, and the skin papery. Richert held his head erect, though, as if with great pride, and beneath silvered black brows, ebony eyes snapped.

"So. Joshua. You seek asylum with your old enemy." His gaze slid to Anya. "And you." Although the words were sharp and cutting, his eyes lingered; swiftly—perhaps even greedily—scanning her face.

"I'm Anya..."

"Dubrovnyk, I know," he interrupted. "It's my name, too." His gaze returned to Joshua. "Why is she with you?"

Anya didn't appreciate being discussed in the third person. "Joshua accepted a peace agreement with Onred. My bride price was part of the deal. Onred paid it. I ran. Onred blew up Astana."

Reluctantly, it seemed, her uncle's gaze returned to her. "So this mess is your fault." He snorted. "Not surprised."

His words stung. Before she could speak, Joshua said, "Onred never intended to keep the peace. If Anya hadn't sky-jumped from that plane..."

"Skyjumped!" Her uncle's black eyes bored into her.

Enough of the games.

"We're here to ask for asylum. And for your help."

Richert's eyes went to Joshua. "Do you allow her to speak for you? You're Baron. Allow a woman enough rope, and she'll hang you with it."

Anya clenched her fists, sick of her uncle's petty digs, but again Joshua spoke before she could, his voice low and level. "I'm her protector first. Her baron, second."

"Protector, eh?" Richert's gaze traveled from Joshua to Anya, and then back again. Imperceptibly, and without apparent cause, his posture relaxed. "Is she as cold as her mother?" Again, that opaque black gaze flicked to Anya. "You look just like her."

It didn't sound like a compliment, but she said, "Thank you."

Richert snorted again, and turned his full attention to Joshua. "We'll eat breakfast. Then I'll decide if you have terms worth considering."

"My family may still be alive," Anya said. She wished she could erase the tremble of emotion from her voice. "Sources say Onred kidnapped them."

"You think that's incentive for me? To save my brother's family? You're a fool." Richert rolled for a long table adjacent to the bar, which was piled high with food. "Grab a plate."

Anya's arm still hurt, but she decided to wait until after the talks to discuss medical care. An alliance came first; her comfort and well-being, a distant second.

A young woman in a black uniform, whom Richert called "Lisa," appeared and deftly piled food on a plate for the baron. She brought him a steaming hot drink as well. "Leave us," he ordered. As soon she settled the napkin on his lap, she quickly obeyed.

The eggs, bacon, and crisp, buttered toast made Anya's mouth water. After three days of dried rations, the food smelled like heaven. When Richert stabbed into an egg, Anya crunched off a salty corner of bacon and gave a soft sigh of ecstasy. Across the table, Joshua offered a faint smile.

Richert seemed disinclined to speak. He ate like a starving man at his last meal. Again, Anya wondered about his wasted body. Although he had clearly lost a lot of weight, he ate like the proverbial horse. She didn't think he would respond positively to inquiries about his health, however, so she remained silent.

The food rapidly disappeared. Joshua went back for seconds, and brought Anya a cheese pastry; her favorite. The thoughtful gesture reminded her of the Joshua she had known for so long, her stalwart—if unyielding—friend and protector.

"Thank you," she murmured.

Richert dashed the napkin across his mouth and slammed it onto the table. "Let's have it. What do you want?"

"I want our territories to ally against Onred," Joshua evenly replied. "Together, we can defeat him. Afterward, we'll split his land and live in peace."

Richert coughed out a hoarse cackle. "Not good enough, son. Without me, you've got nothing. Give me something I want."

"You can take two-thirds of Onred's territory."

"Not enough."

Anya's half-baked plan to try to charm this ornery man had disappeared the moment she had met him. Curtly, she demanded, "What is enough? All of Donetsk Territory? Our lives? The lives of my whole family? Would that be enough to satisfy you?"

"Anya."

Temper flushed Richert's weathered cheeks. "Let her speak. She's a fool, just like her mother."

"My mother is dead," Anya returned. "So is my father. You can't punish them any longer. And look at you. You've turned into a bitter old man. How long will you wage war against us? How much death is enough to salve your injured pride?"

Richert's fist hit the table. His face glowed a bilious purple. "This is not about *pride*, stupid girl!"

"Then what is it about? Greed? Hatred? Is that what's eaten up your whole heart? And your body?"

Puffs of air pulsed his papery cheeks. "No, you insolent girl. It's about justice."

"Justice? Thousands of men dying is justice? Justice for what? My mother marrying the man she loved?"

"She loved *me!* Jason *stole* her from me!"

Was the man insane? Delusional? Maybe, after all of these years, he had managed to rewrite history in his mind. More quietly, she said, "No. My mother loved my father. It's the only reason she'd leave Aksu—her home."

"No." A hoarse sound huffed from his throat. "She left because she was weak. She couldn't face the scandal."

The young woman appeared again, this time with an oxygen mask. Over the top of it, Richert glared at Anya.

Anya stared back. "What scandal?"

"Forget it." Her uncle closed his eyes and breathed deeply. Moments later, he ripped off the mask and ordered Lisa to leave. She frowned at Anya before exiting.

Richert turned to Joshua, ignoring Anya now. "You're forgetting Cadmus. He's got ties to western Mongolia. If Altai is split up, Mongolia would be on our backs faster than black flies in a plague."

Joshua spoke, his voice calm. "What terms do you want, Baron? You'll have to fight Onred sooner or later. If he defeats our territory, he'll come after yours next. Onred wants our greenhouses now, but he'll want your petroleum next. With our military power, he could defeat you. Choose. Fight with us now, or alone later."

The Baron of Tarim remained silent for a long time, staring into space. At last, he said harshly, "We'll unite. But under my terms."

Joshua glanced at Anya. The subtle stiffness in his straight shoulders indicated tension. "I'm listening."

"I get all of Onred's territory. No negotiations on that point."

Joshua's eyes narrowed. "Agreed. In addition, you agree to a permanent peace with us. Your military never enters our territory again."

"Done." The old man's lips curved up in a satisfied smile. "But you're wrong about one thing, Van Heisman. Onred doesn't want your greenhouses."

Something flickered in Joshua's gaze. He knew what Richert was talking about.

Anya frowned. "What else could he want? We have nothing but open land."

"He probably wants that, too." Richert chuckled, and Anya wondered what the wily old man was thinking. Her uncle, however, did not elaborate, and instead told Joshua, "Your forces are scattered. Unite them. Contact me when it's done, and we'll plan an attack strategy."

"We'll plan the attack now," Joshua countered. "It'll be a two pronged assault. The first phase will be tonight, and Donetski air corps from Omsk, Zyra, Irgiz will strike fast and hard."

"A focused attack, eh? A warhead?"

"No. Assassination."

Richert raised a thick eyebrow. "How many levels?"

"Top three, to keep then scrambling. Onred, for obvious reasons. And both Yegor and Belar are dangerous, sadistic strategists. We've got a better chance to win this war if they're dead."

Richert nodded. "I like it. What about the extraction?"

"The same team will extract. Tomorrow night, our combined forces will attack."

It surprised Anya that Richert had brought up the matter of her family's extraction. At the same time, Joshua's cold-blooded discussion of assassination disturbed her.

Richert said, "I'll give you twenty-four hours. Then my forces attack, even if your team is still at risk."

"Agreed."

"Starting now," the baron added.

"Starting at dusk."

The old man's gaze bored into Joshua's. A silent battle of wills ensued. The old man's fire, drive, and even a bit of contempt battled Joshua's unwavering stare.

With an abrupt nod, Richert pushed back from the table. "Tomorrow at dusk."

"Thank you, Baron." Joshua offered his hand. "We will defeat Onred."

Richert shook it, briefly. His black eyes glittered, and glanced from Joshua to Anya. "I have no doubt." The wheelchair swirled left.

"Before you go," Joshua said, "Anya requires medical care."

The old territory baron rolled away. "I'll send Lisa."

When he had gone, Anya laid down her fork. "That went surprisingly well."

One brow flicked up. "So far. I still need to meet with him to hammer out the details of tomorrow night's attack."

"Do you trust him?"

"No." Bluntly. "But we both want Onred dead. In the meantime, we'll be alert to a surprise attack from Richert."

"When would Richert strike us?"

"When it's clear Onred is defeated."

"Will you really order Onred's assassination?"

"Yes." Joshua must have seen something in her expression that concerned him, for he said more gently, "Why?"

"I hate Onred, of course. But planning his death...it seems like murder."

"He deserves to die."

"I know. It's just so...cold-blooded. Like when you went behind that rock and killed that pilot. You didn't have to kill him, Joshua." Her voice lowered to a whisper. "Why did you?" This newly realized, merciless side of him scared her. It made her wonder again, as when he'd sold her to Onred, how well she knew him.

Joshua's warm hand curled around her fist. It made her feel secure, although her heart beat faster at his touch. "He was moving. In a minute he'd have reached for his weapon or contacted Onred. With Onred alerted, we'd never have escaped to Tarim. I had no choice." He paused. Then, with apparent reluctance, he continued, "Even if he hadn't been coming around, I couldn't let him live. As a soldier, I learned one important lesson. The only safe enemy is a dead one."

"But ..."

His hand tightened. "Listen to me," he said quietly. "The first day I joined the military I was twelve. I lied about my age so they'd accept me. My community had thrown me out—" he grimaced, "—because of a crime...never mind. I knew I'd die soon. I figured it would be better to die as a soldier with warm clothes on my back and food in my stomach."

He drew a breath, and his thoughts seemed to turn inward. "The soldiers didn't ask many questions. They gave me a knife, clothes off a dead soldier, and ordered me to carry supplies. That first day was terrible. I'd never seen so much blood and death. I couldn't imagine any day being worse than that one." He paused again.

"At dusk, we battled Richert's men over the ridge. They retreated, leaving a few bloody comrades behind. Soldiers in my unit cheered. I remember one taking out a flask and gulping from it. His face was so exultant. He was so pumped with victory that he didn't see the dead man move at his feet.

"I shouted, but a laser flashed first. The soldier's mouth opened in surprise. His flask fell, splashing out alcohol.

"Our commander shot the enemy. Afterward, he shoved a laser into my hand and ordered me to shoot every dead soldier I saw, right in the brain." His eyes closed. "For the next two months, I followed behind the battles. I shot every enemy soldier, dead or alive." His eyes opened, and they appeared black. "I don't like to kill, Anya. But in war, men kill, or they die. Onred must die, or he will continue to murder innocents. Do you understand?"

"Yes," she whispered. His rationale was brutal and merciless...but necessary. She didn't like it, but could accept it.

"Good." To her shock, he tugged her fist to his firm lips and kissed the back of her fingers. Her breath caught with surprised pleasure. She didn't move, or speak, for fear of losing the sensation of his warm breath on her skin.

"Come." Lisa's sharp voice interrupted. "I'll bring you to your rooms."

Joshua released her. He rose to his feet and in wordless silence they followed the short, rigid woman to the electric train.

For a second, Anya thought she spied Richert's wheelchair parked in a dark corner, near a potted tree, but the electric train whisked them forward before she could double-check.

CHAPTER NINE

ANYA GAZED with longing at the wide bed in the spacious, opulent room. A pale rose, silky comforter covered the mammoth bed, and the pillows looked deliciously soft. If only she could lie down for a few minutes. During the past three days, she had barely slept.

All the same, Anya held no illusions that she would ever sleep in that bed. She didn't want to. In fact, she would rather forego all sleep in order to rescue her family and defeat Altai Territory as swiftly as possible.

They would have to move fast, before Onred's forces coalesced again.

Joshua had left a moment ago, with the quiet order that she care for her wound and refresh herself. He'd return after he had spoken to Richert and her uncle's commander about the attack. Anya would rather have gone with him, for she was anxious to get moving on the strikes, but that particular argument seemed a ridiculous one to fight. She did need to take care of her wound. At the same time, it felt wrong to partake of the room's luxurious amenities. How could she pamper herself while her family suffered?

Astana was gone, and all its inhabitants dead, all because of her foolish choice to run from Onred. She had been cowardly and selfish. Why hadn't she faced her future with courage?

Tears welled. Anya couldn't wait to leave Richert's city. Her life and her death belonged in the northern territory. She was ready to die in order to avenge Astana, and to free her people from Onred's encroaching, murderous grip. Not for one minute did she think Onred's strike on Astana was the end. For years, he had wanted to conquer their whole territory. Unless they managed to defeat him now, he would succeed.

But for this one moment, Joshua was right. She did need to take care of herself. Then she could fight longer and harder.

A medical wand and five cartridges lay on the bed. She kicked off her boots. As she crossed the room, her toes sank deep into the lush, creamy soft carpet. The bedroom featured all of the newest amenities, including a micro-washer/dryer and computerized closet. After tending her wound, which hurt a little less after applying the second healing alpha mist, Anya stripped off her clothes, threw them in the washer/drier and took a long, hot shower.

Long minutes later, dark hair combed out and a thick towel wrapped around her, she pulled her clean, dried clothes from the micro washer/dryer, and searched the room for a sewing kit. She'd need to mend her parka sleeve so she could safely go out in the cold again. And fast. Joshua wouldn't waste much time. They'd need to contact Donetsk's military soon and plan the attacks. Anya fully intended to be a part of the strategy sessions.

No sewing kit anywhere.

With a touch to a button, the closet door slid open. Beautifully flowing gowns hung from the racks. Anya rapidly slid open drawers and sighed with satisfaction when she found a case containing a small, hand-held fabric simulating machine. She should have known the baron's rooms would carry no items so mundane as a needle and thread.

Carrying it to the bed, she pressed the sensor against the parka material. Cool blue light and invisible sound waves permeated the coat's specialty fabric. The digital readout said "Re1D." She plucked the appropriate fabric cartridges from the case and inserted them into the wand. Meshed fibers, looking like a fine net, extruded from the simulator. A few passes over her parka and the fabric wound was healed. A few minutes to dry, and it would be as good as new. Anya healed the fabric on her shirt and snow wear, too.

A knock came at the door.

"Just a minute." She swiftly pulled on her clothes and opened the door.

Joshua wore a frown. A moment elapsed while he eyed her wet hair. The cool air from the hall swirled in, mingling with the rose scent from her shower, still lingering in the moisture laden air. When she gestured him in, he hesitated before entering.

He crossed to the window, which offered a clear view of the snow-capped Tien Shan to the north. His shoulders looked stiff.

"What's wrong?"

"Onred bombed Irgiz."

Anya gasped. "No."

"He knows we're in Aksu. If I don't surrender, Omsk is next. He's given me twelve hours."

"What about Irgiz's missile defense system?"

"Failed, just like Astana's." He shoved a violent hand through his hair. "I wish I knew *why!*"

Anya rapidly assimilated this information. Onred would not be satisfied with only Joshua's surrender. If he knew she was alive—as it appeared he did, from the "we" in Joshua's words—he would demand her surrender, too. "How does he know we're here?"

Tersely, he said, "I don't know. Maybe Richert let it slip. Maybe they scanned our voices in their airbird. Good news is, Onred confirmed he has your family."

Anya felt relieved—and fearful. "Tell the truth, Joshua. Onred wants me, too, doesn't he?"

His tawny eyes met hers, and they burned like fire. "You will stay here. I'll pretend to surrender to Onred. Meanwhile, the extraction team will rescue your family. I'll kill Onred, if I can."

Completely aghast, Anya stared at him. "No. I'm going with you."

"You won't. That is an order."

Anya's temper flamed. "Forget you and your orders! My family's in danger. It's *my* fault people are dying. I will not sit on my hands and do nothing!"

He turned back to the window, dismissing her protestations without bothering to reply. "I spoke to Richert and his commanders. The extraction is set for zero hundred hours tonight. It's our game. They'll help, if needed. I'll surrender when Onred calls the time."

Anya deliberately relaxed her fists, telling herself to bide her time and get more information. "What's the plan?"

"After I leave here, I'll go to a Donetski outpost and communicate with my men. Then I'll take the enemy airbird and fly to the surrender location. Onred refuses to tell us the location yet."

"When do you leave here?"

"In two hours. After lunch. Richert insists I sleep for an hour."

"I'm going with you. My brothers and sisters..."

"No."

That flat, inflexible command infuriated her. "You can't win this war alone."

"You will stay here, where you'll be safe."

"I failed my people. You *have* to let me make this right."

His brown eyes appeared to be swallowed up by darkness. "Obey me."

"You're not infallible. You don't know what's right."

"I want what's best for you."

"Do you?" Her voice rose sharply. "Is that why you sold me to Onred? Because you wanted what was best for *me?*"

His solid shoulders flinched.

"I wish I had obeyed now." Her voice trembled. "Maybe thousands of our people would still be alive."

"A..."

"I was so angry and hurt. That you could do that to me, when I..."

"Anya."

"You sold me. I asked you to stop the deal, but you *wouldn't.*" Unwanted, angry tears slipped down her cheeks. She hadn't meant to bring this up now, but couldn't seem to stop the storm of words.

He opened his mouth again.

"You *sold* me. Against my will. Two cities are gone because I couldn't take it. I wasn't strong or brave enough to sacrifice my life for you...or for our territory. And now they're all dead!"

"*I'm sorry!*" The words erupted with startling force.

She stared at him.

"I was wrong. I convinced myself that you marrying Onred was for the best."

"Then..." she faltered, "...then you didn't think it was?"

"No. I needed..."

"Peace?" she supplied when he didn't finish.

"I was a gutless bastard, and I'm sorry."

She wasn't quite sure what to make of that statement.

"I was wrong. Please forgive me, Anya." The entreaty in those velvet brown eyes almost melted her heart into a puddle of forgiveness. Almost.

"Would you ever again force me, or my sisters..."

"No!" More gently, he said, "Never again. Never."

"Good." Finally, one terrible weight rolled off of her shoulders. Relief overwhelmed her. Heart feeling a little lighter, she impulsively hugged him. Although he stiffened, his arms closed around her, too.

Awash in a moment of peace, Anya held him tighter, and murmured into his neck, "I forgive you." She closed her eyes, drinking in the comfort of his strong, solid body. He smelled nice. Warm, spicy, and male. The urge to kiss him overwhelmed her, and so Anya turned her lips into the warm skin of his neck. He wouldn't know it was a kiss. Not really. But the texture of his skin against her mouth shot warm, shaky emotions through her. Longing for more swamped her. It took every ounce of her will to step back.

Joshua's eyes appeared a bit glazed. Abruptly, he turned. "I have to go."

Bewildered, she watched him stride from the room. Had he realized she had kissed him?

He must have. It must have shocked and offended him, too, the way he'd shot out of the room. Embarrassment heated her skin. All the same, she knew that when Joshua returned, all would go on as normal—as if the incident had never happened.

But she *had* kissed him. What did he think of it? Was he truly disgusted? Contemptuous? Horrified?

Anya pressed her hand to her lips, deeply regretting her impulsive action.

CHAPTER TEN

BY ACCIDENT, JOSHUA came upon the solarium. It was deserted. Thank God, for he needed to be alone. He crossed the sunny room to gaze out at the desolate snow pack stretching south. Sunlight glinted off the snow and the sky gleamed a brilliant, winter blue. Beautiful, but not as beautiful as the color of Anya's eyes.

For the first time since leaving Anya, Joshua allowed his stiff control to relax. A shudder slipped through him. When her lips had pressed into his skin, his heart had about stopped. It had felt like a caress. It had felt like heaven.

He'd wanted to take her and...

Joshua drew a harsh breath, and then another, willing the images and emotions to leave him. His fists clenched. "You can't *have her*. Stop."

"Why not?"

The raspy voice of the baron made him turn on his heel. Richert had caught him unawares. A bad sign. His preoccupation with Anya had dulled his instincts.

"Why not?" The old man repeated, lifting a heavy, silvered black brow. "If you want her, take her."

Joshua disliked anyone suspecting his deepest, most dishonorable weakness. Especially his lifelong enemy. "Never. I'm her protector."

"Most idiotic law in creation."

Joshua's fists tightened. "She trusts me. I won't betray her." He turned to the window. "Not again."

"You mean like when you sold her to that felon, Onred?"

Joshua's fists briefly clenched again.

"You *are* a fool."

"Thanks," Joshua said tersely.

"Settle up with her." The old man cackled. "You'll feel a whole lot better. And it'll clear your mind for the mission. Think of it this way: if you fail the mission, you lose everything, including her."

"And if I win…"

"You gain power as a true baron. You won't feel like a mistake anymore. No one will see you as a stand-in for the real thing. That's how you feel, isn't it?"

Joshua didn't answer. He would not bare his soul to Richert. But the baron was right. He had always felt that he'd come into power by accident. Anya's father had never chosen him to be baron. As a result, Joshua felt he needed to exceed by double what others expected of him. It was the only way he felt deserving of the role of baron.

Richert said, "If you defeat Onred, you'll gain the power to make your own laws. You can begin your own dynasty. Anya's father's rule will finally die. As it should!" This ended with a snap. "It's part of the reason I'm willing to help you, boy."

Joshua glanced at him, one brow barely raised.

The old baron chucked. "Yes. I thought you'd see the advantage for both of us. If you defeat Onred, you earn the right to the territory. You'll pull it back together from nothing. An impossible task, maybe. Probably. But it will be a new territory. A new start. A new dynasty. You could abolish the Old Barons' Law if you want."

Joshua had never considered this possibility. However, he wouldn't allow himself to hope. Not yet.

"But," the baron finished, "if you fail, you're dead."

"Protect Anya for me, if I don't return."

The old man did not answer.

❆✳❆✳❆✳❆✳❆

Anya set the alarm to ring in an hour and curled up on the soft, pink bed. One hour should leave her enough time, shouldn't it? With a sigh of exhausted bliss, she closed her eyes.

It seemed only a moment before irritating *beeps* awoke her. She swung out of bed, brushed her hair and left the room, still yawning. Hopefully, Joshua was still sleeping. She wanted to speak to Richert alone, before lunch.

A servant in the hall directed her to the dining room, where Richert sat brooding near the window.

"Hello," she said brightly.

The old man sent her a startled glance. A flash of something indecipherable gleamed in his eyes, then disappeared. "What do you want, girl?"

"Thank you for your hospitality."

He grunted. "Get on with it. No one speaks to me without a reason."

"I need your help."

For the first time, she noticed the cane in his hand. Noticing the direction of her gaze, he prodded it into the floor. "I can walk, you know."

"Why don't you?"

A coarse chuckle erupted. "I'm afraid I'll fall."

She hadn't expected honesty, nor the vulnerability he had allowed her to see. After a moment elapsed, she dared to ask a personal question. "What happened to you? You're not that old."

"Doctors don't know. Maybe I have a parasite." Richert levered himself to his feet. Slowly, he shuffled forward, a few centimeters at a time. It was painful to watch. Anya tensed, ready to run to his aid, should he need it. He now rested his weight on the dining chair back. A feeble plucking, and he dragged it back enough so he could plop down on the cushioned seat. Harsh breaths rattled in his chest.

Richert propped his cane against the table, and with a wheeze took up the conversation again. "A viral one, they're guessing. Or maybe someone's poisoning me."

Anya was surprised he'd speak so matter-of-factly of possible assassination. "Who's next in line for power?"

"My son. He's sixteen. Two years until he reaches his majority. Or it could be my first-in-command. But I think it's Lisa. She hates me."

"Probably."

He chuckled loudly.

"Maybe you should get a new cook."

The black eyes glittered. "What do you want, Anya?"

It was the first time he had ever referred to her by her Christian name. "I want to go with Joshua. I need to fight Onred and protect my people."

"He asked if I'd watch over you when he dies."

Alarm rushed. "He *won't* die."

"He probably will. He's a brave buck, but he's going against impossible odds."

"I want to go with him."

"You'll die, too."

"So be it. If Joshua dies, I die. It's the way it has to be. It's the way I want it to be. Let me choose my death."

"You love him that much?"

Anya swallowed, and then said, "Yes." It was the first time she had ever admitted that to anyone.

His eyes glittered. "Against my better judgment, I'll help you. Listen carefully."

Anya wasn't fooled by her uncle's sudden generosity. Richert didn't suddenly like her. For one thing, she still physically reminded him of her dead mother, whom he despised. For another, if she and Joshua died, it would give Richert the perfect opportunity to conquer her territory. With two of Donetsk's cities gone, he would likely succeed with ease.

Richert had just finished outlining his plan when Joshua entered the room. "We were just talking about you," her uncle said.

Anya cast Richert an uneasy glance. Would the unpredictable baron let a clue slip about their plans?

But Richert only told Joshua to pull up a chair, and then rang for lunch to be served. "Eat up," he advised. Ghoulishly, he added, "It may be your last meal."

Lunch consisted of hot rolls, slabs of ham, and cheesy potatoes. Joshua ate silently. He also looked tired.

"You're boring guests," Richert growled.

"How did you come to power?" Anya asked. She didn't really want to talk. Worry about her family, Onred's threats, and, in a short while, mutinying against Joshua's orders again, all coalesced into an uncomfortable lump in the pit of her stomach. Getting Richert to ramble on about himself seemed the best plan. Most people loved to talk about themselves, and she felt certain Richert was no different.

His heavy brows lifted. "You want a story? Fine. My father was Baron. He passed the title on to me when I turned thirty-six. It was about the time your mother married my brother." His lips twisted, as if tasting something sour.

"Your father didn't die before you took power?"

"No. He tested me first. I was a protector for eight years. I started at twenty-five. Most protectors are older. But my father ordered it, because he thought it would mature me for the job of baron. He wanted to test my mettle—for me to prove I could control myself." His lips twisted into a faint smile. "I was quite the lady's man in my day. But I did a fair job as protector. I watched over two teenaged girls and their brother. Their father died in the old wars. The mother needed help." Richert lapsed into silence.

"What happened?" Anya asked, assuming he had a point to his story.

"The oldest girl was your mother."

Anya stared at him in complete silence.

Richert's fiery, obsidian gaze bored into Joshua. "So you see. We have much in common."

Joshua's gaze flicked to Anya, and then back to the baron. Quietly, he said, "What happened between you and Anya's mother?"

"I loved her. Rachel loved me, but refused to admit it, because of the scandal." Richert huffed a laugh. "My father saw, of course. He warned me to stay away from her. If I broke the protector's sacred trust, he'd disown me. The title of baron would go to my brother."

Anya squelched a disbelieving snort. Her mother had never loved Richert. But better to let Richert talk. Then she could better understand what made him tick now.

"Then my uncle died in an attack, and the northern territory—your territory—" this to Joshua, "—needed a baron. My brother was nominated. Jason asked Rachel to go with him. Not because he loved her. But because *I* did. He'd always been jealous of me, and all I would become. He wanted to be Baron of Tarim Territory, but he didn't have the guts to kill me for it. So he took my Rachel."

Anya bit her tongue. Rachel had hardly been Richert's.

"The night before she was to leave, Rachel came to me in tears. She said her mother and Jason had come to an agreement. She had to marry Jason, but it wasn't by her choice." Richert's face gentled. "She said she loved me, and didn't want to leave me. But she also didn't want me to lose my future, either, as I would if I married her. All the same, I asked her to marry me, and she said, 'Yes.'"

Richert's voice grew quieter, and he looked into the distance, as if into the past. The true past? Or one he had reengineered for his own comfort? "I was ecstatic. I figured I could get my father to overlook my transgression, eventually. After all, he didn't have any more sons to become baron. It seemed like all of my dreams were about to come true. I should have known."

"Known what?" Anya said, beginning to feel impatient with the story that Richert clearly wove from figments of his imagination. She had to bite her tongue to keep from asserting that her mother had loved her *father*, not Richert.

"I should have known when she gave herself to me that night, that something wasn't right. Waiting until marriage was ingrained into Rachel's character. But I was a fool, and took her for my own. When I woke up, she was gone. So was my brother."

Richert sat silently for a long time. "She married him. I waited like a fool, hoping she'd be miserable and leave him. Finally, I wrote to her, begging her to return to me. My brother wrote back. He said he'd kill me if I wrote another letter like that to his wife. Rachel was his, forever. Rachel wrote a note, too, saying that she'd never loved me. Later, I believed it. But not then. And then you were born." Richert spared a brief glance for Anya.

The full implication hit, and she gasped.

"Don't worry," Richert snapped. "DNA proved you were his. Plus, you were born too late, in May."

Anya had been born in March. Joshua met her gaze and held it, but Anya said nothing to put the delusional old man straight. As Richert had said, DNA had proven that she was her father's child. And her mother had loved her father. Anya had seen it in the way she had kissed him goodbye in the morning, or smoothed his collar. The way she'd given him five children. Bitterness had bent this old man's mind and warped his body. Anya would provide no more fuel for his twisted fantasies. It was time for peace. Time to put the past to rest.

"So you started a bloody war, all in the name of love," she summed up.

Color rushed to Richert's face. "I started the bloody war because Jason stole her. Then he held her prisoner. The first skirmishes were to try to steal her back." He waved a bony hand. "Matters escalated from there."

Anya gasped. "Thousands of people died! Your jealousy has caused heartbreak for..."

"Anya," Joshua said.

Joshua was right, of course. What did she hope to accomplish? Richert would never see the truth. He had given his entire life to pursuing "justice." What were the chances that he'd admit to being wrong all this time? That he'd wasted his entire life, as well as the lives of thousands of young men, on a war spawned by his crushed pride and jealousy?

The old baron glowered at her, his black brows beetling over burning black eyes. Did she want to start another war right now, when Joshua had just negotiated peace? When Richert had just "magnanimously" agreed to help her?

"I'm sorry if I spoke out of turn," she managed.

"You're *not* sorry," Richert snapped. "Don't lie to me, like your mother did."

In a flash of understanding, Anya guessed that this was what had hurt Richert most of all. Rightly or wrongly, he had given his heart to her mother. She had betrayed his trust, and so had her father.

Drawing a deep breath, Anya touched his cool, papery hand. To her surprise, he didn't snatch it free. "I'm sorry," she repeated in a low voice. "I'm sorry for the way my mother hurt you. And I'm sorry that both of my parents betrayed you."

Richert looked away. A deeper scowl knit his brows. He fumbled in his shirt pocket. As if summoned by an invisible command, his wheelchair noiselessly rolled up to his chair.

"I'm glad for a chance at a new beginning," she pressed on. "For you, me, Joshua, and my family."

The black eyes glittered. "I don't trust you, you know. I don't trust anyone."

"I know. But we've taken the first step toward peace, haven't we?"

Now he jerked his hand free. "We'll see." With shaking arms, he levered himself up and plopped into his wheelchair. With an impatient poke at a button, he whirred away.

"Good job." Amusement lurked in Joshua's eyes. "Ready to sweet-talk Onred next?"

"You'd let me come?"

"Not a chance."

Lowering her gaze, Anya spooned up soup and blew on it. Joshua could read her too well. She was afraid her eyes would give away her true intentions. He would be livid when he found out what they were.

CHAPTER ELEVEN

JOSHUA SLOWED to a stop before Anya's door.

It was almost time for the mission to begin. He looked forward to seeing Onred face-to-face—his visceral desire was to kill the monster with his bare hands. First, though, he had to say goodbye to Anya. She had left the lunch table shortly after Richert, and it was why Joshua stood outside her door now.

He didn't want to leave her again. What a waste, to never be able to show her or tell her how much she meant to him. His overwhelming longing to hold her in his arms threatened his rational mind; even worse, it threatened to undermine his fierce vow to honor, loyalty, and duty. He had to control himself one more time. And he had to be prepared, too, for he knew she'd beg to come with him. Part of him selfishly wanted to grant her wish. He wanted her with him, so he could see her as long as safely possible before he left for his ultimate mission. But Anya was too unpredictable, and might find a way to follow him. So he absolutely could not allow it. It was far too dangerous. Protecting her was his number one job. And he'd continue to do so until his dying breath.

So now he had to tell her goodbye.

What if this was the last time he would ever see her? Would it matter if he broke his sacred protector's trust? She would forgive him. Joshua knew it.

If he died, his sins would die with him. If he lived, perhaps there was a chance...

No, there wasn't.

Joshua had lived so long tamping down his hopes and his desires that it had become almost a reflex action, the word "no." Was it easier to say "no" than to experience the capricious uncertainties of a risky, joyful "yes"?

In battle, he had never accepted less than complete conquest. It was easy, because it was the right thing to do. He could follow through on his basic, primitive instinct to conquer. But with Anya, he could not do the same. Always, he had to put the brakes on his feelings and deny the deep desire to make her his.

It was hard. But one more time, he would do what was right.

Joshua knocked.

❃✲❃✲❃✲❃✲❃

Anya drew a breath and schooled her features into petulant lines. She had to make this look real. Joshua couldn't suspect her true plan until it was too late. Her boots and parka lay in the closet, ready for hasty donning. She already wore snow wear under her black clothes.

At Joshua's second knock, she opened the door.

Those velvet brown eyes looked serious, and a faint frown drew his straight brows together. He wore his cream parka and boots, and he looked bigger than normal. He was ready to go.

She shut the door after him.

"I'm leaving," he said, his mouth a straight line.

"I could help you," she told him, keeping in character. If she had truly been about to be left behind, she'd argue with him, even at this late hour.

Tersely, he said, "Stop it." Afterward, he stood before her in silence, as if not sure what else to say. His fists tightened and relaxed.

Anya drew a shaky breath. "I may never see you again."

"Probably not."

Anya clenched her teeth. The stubborn man. If he let her come, his chances of survival would improve. A welling, sick feeling in her gut told her he'd die if she didn't. It was one of the reasons she was dead set on going with him. She couldn't lose him. It was absolutely unthinkable. And so she would deceive him now, and it had to be a good performance. He could suspect nothing, or else he might lock her in the room until all chances to follow him had vanished.

"I want to go with you." The emotion in her whisper was real.

"Goodbye, Anya." He gazed at her for an eternal second, and then unexpectedly, roughly, pulled her into his arms and hard against his chest.

With a small, contented sigh, she slid her arms around him.

Joshua stood stiff and still. She pulled back a little, so she could look up at him. To her surprise, he watched her. His face was very near her own.

His breath touched her lips, and she closed her eyes.

She stood motionless. The heat of his body, his scent, and his nearness drugged her senses. She longed for his kiss. Of course, he never would kiss her. And she didn't want to be the one to kiss him. His quiet rebuke—gently put, of course—would crush her heart. And so she stood very still, enjoying the sweet torture of his breath caressing her skin.

Soft moments passed.

His lips brushed hers.

Her breath caught, and her hands fisted into his parka in complete shock. She was afraid to move, for fear he would stop.

He did not. His mouth lingered on hers for long, sweet moments. Unable to stop herself, her hands slid up to his shoulders.

His muscles tensed, and he pulled back slowly, but his breaths still caressed her lips in quiet, silky whispers.

"Anya." The murmur sounded tortured.

She slid her fingers into the thick hair at his nape. "Joshua."

"Red One. Copy?" The voice from his parka came as a shock. A new rectangular, silver transmitter was clipped to his lapel.

Joshua touched the "send" button. "On my way." He released her and stepped back. "Goodbye," His voice sounded rough. With a duck to his head, he headed for the door. He did not look back.

Anya's fingers went to her lips. She didn't know whether to feel elated or to cry. Joshua believed he would never see her again. For him, that had been a goodbye kiss. Would he want to kiss her again when he saw her in thirty minutes? Probably not. More likely, he'd want to kill her.

Unease slid through her. Anya didn't want to think about it.

CHAPTER TWELVE

ANYA BOARDED Richert's small, private airbird five minutes after a military aircraft flew Joshua out of the gigantic hangar. Her pilot, a burly man, merely grunted, "Put on your seat belt."

Within minutes, they shot after Joshua's transport. According to Richert's cunning plot, after the military transport dropped off Joshua, her pilot was to land a good distance from the Altai airbird they had stolen. The pilot would stop just long enough for her to jump out, and then he'd speed away.

From there, Anya would be on her own.

She laced and unlaced her fingers. Nerves knotted her stomach, but she tried not to think about Joshua's reaction to being marooned alone with her and the enemy airbird.

Her stomach swirled up in a sickening leap as they dropped to the earth. And then, blessedly and all too soon, they were still. "Get out."

"Thanks," she said, and stepped into bitterly artic air. It was a bright day, and the sky a cold, polarized blue.

Cold snow swirled up, stinging her cheeks, as the pilot rose, then shot south.

Onred's black airbird rested across the clearing, but she didn't see Joshua. Was he inside? She'd better hurry before he took off. Anya ran as best she could. Her boots crunched deep into the snow with every step.

The airbird's door was shut, the engine silent. She pounded on the door and waited.

Nothing. The silence of the landscape seeped into her bones. The aircraft appeared empty. Where was Joshua? She triggered the door's release button. No one was inside. Her black bag and tarp still lay on the floor, where she had left them.

Worry crept in. Where was he? She grabbed up the bag, stuffed the bulky tarp inside, and then spent a minute rooting in the snow for the laser and four knives Richert's men had stripped from her belt. She found the laser and two knives. Someone else had dug through the snow, too. It had to be Joshua. Footprints headed west.

Anya gave up on her two missing knives. She had wasted enough time. Where was Joshua headed? Anya ran in his tracks. By her calculations, he must be fifteen minutes ahead. She couldn't lose him. Not now.

❈✻❈✻❈✻❈✻❈

Joshua strode fast for the secret command base. Richert's satellites might be tracking him, but that didn't matter. The baron would think Joshua planned to meet the few troops permanently stationed inside the caves of these isolated, southern mountains; Joshua's home. Maybe Richert knew that. Maybe not. Either way, it meant nothing.

The old man didn't know the real truth. No one but his most elite pilots knew the location of Zebra Charlie Alpha, for it was written nowhere. Once inducted into the elite force, his most trusted men memorized its latitude and longitude. It was never mentioned again.

Joshua trusted no one except for his select force.

Somehow, Onred had discovered Donetsk's transponder codes. Onred's men had been able to track down Joshua's pilots and destroy their craft. Worse, Onred had been able to disarm Astana and Irgiz's missile defense systems. Joshua meant to speak to his brother about it.

He strode down the last, steep hill.

The huge cavern leading to the heart of the mountain loomed ahead. The two men guarding it raised their lasers when they spotted him. Joshua cut his hand through the air in a short, three motion signal. Immediately, the men lowered their weapons. A moment later, however, they raised them again. They aimed at a spot behind Joshua.

Joshua spun, whipping out his weapon.

A slight figure, all in black, ran down through the snow. Dark hair floated in the breeze and a black bag slapped against his—no, *her*—thigh.

Anya.

Disbelief...frustration...and finally fury consumed him. What was she doing out here? She was supposed to be safe!

But she wasn't safe anymore. Despair hit him.

Joshua chewed out a string of curses bluer than the cobalt sky.

❊✲❊✲❊✲❊✲❊

Anya halted in her tracks. Joshua's words didn't frighten her, but his expression did. His reaction was worse than she had imagined.

The two soldiers guarding the cave entrance leveled lasers on her, stances wide and threatening, their weapons no doubt set to kill.

"Baron?"

"Stand down." Joshua's eyes did not leave Anya. With purposeful steps, he advanced toward her.

She swallowed. Hadn't she known this would happen? *Time for courage, Anya.* Slowly, her feet moved toward him. Unfortunately, her heart beat faster as his expression grew sharper, in full, livid detail. Had she ever seen him this angry before?

Nope. Didn't think so.

"I'm here." She stopped a meter shy and lifted her chin. "You can't make me leave."

He didn't answer, but his topaz gaze burned like unholy fire.

She dared add, "What assignment will you give me?"

"To start, how about you bend over my knee?" he suggested in a very soft voice.

Anya flushed. "You don't frighten me. I'm a grown woman..."

"Who behaves like a child!"

She didn't like the look in his eyes. The guards, watching now with interest, increased her feeling of discomfort. "You're not a barbarian..." She gasped when he grabbed her arm and dragged her close to him.

"I *am* a barbarian," he said through clenched teeth. "And I'll prove it, right now."

"No!" Suddenly panicked, she tried to free herself, but his wide grip was too strong. It burned her skin as she struggled. Tears blurred her eyes. "You're hurting me," she whispered.

At once, he let go. He stared at her, his chest heaving. Frosty white blasts expelled from his lips. "Go back to the bird that brought you here. Go back to Richert."

"I can't." She licked her lips. "It's gone."

He cursed.

Anya rubbed her smarting wrist. Her own anger rose to match his. "*Back at* you," she told him. "I have every right to be here. My people are in danger. Have you forgotten it's my fault this war started in the first place?"

"What do you plan to do? You can't fly. You're not trained for combat."

"I can do *something!*" she cried out. "I won't be shut up like a child in a nursery. I'm an adult. Don't deny me the right to help my family. To help *you.*"

He ground something under his breath.

"Let me help you. Onred wants both of us. We'll go together to free my family."

"No!" That violent bellow startled her. "I will not let that bastard touch you. Not again."

"Joshua. Onred has to think he's getting both of us. I have some ideas. Together, we can beat him. I know we can."

He briefly closed his eyes. "For now, you'll stay with me. But when it's time to meet Onred, you'll stay here. Or I'll chain you down myself."

Not a full victory, but a start. "Thank you."

He frowned, and then took her arm and bared her skin at the wrist. Three finger marks reddened her skin. "I'm sorry." He stared at it, as if unable to accept what he had done. "I'm sorry," he said again, his tone even quieter.

"It's all right."

"No, it's not." His lips whitened.

"Kiss it and make it better," she dared to say, and added a small smile.

He stared at her in clear disbelief.

"That's how my mother made hurts go away." Anya could barely believe that she'd just asked him to kiss her. She continued to smile, letting him know that she had already forgiven him. After all, she wasn't without fault. She had disobeyed a direct order from her baron. She had gone into this situation knowing full well that he would be livid. And rightfully so.

To her full surprise, Joshua lifted her wrist. When his lips touched her skin, his lids lowered. "I'm sorry," he murmured. His kisses felt as soft as butterfly wings on each of the marks. Shocked joy streamed into her heart.

"See?" she said, voice shaky, when he let her go. "All better."

Bemused, he looked down at her.

"Now," Anya glanced at the huge cavern, "what are you doing here?"

"This is Tash. Home. I need to speak to my brother."

CHAPTER THIRTEEN

THIS WAS JOSHUA'S HOME? Anya had read about the primitive conditions of Tash in her school texts. She wondered now if Joshua had landed the Altai airbird near Tash's entrance on purpose, while at the same time appearing to comply with the Tarim demand to stay out of Tarim airspace.

Anya hurried to keep up as he strode for the wide entrance into the mountain. Now that he had accepted her presence, Joshua seemed to be in a hurry to reach his destination.

With a brief word of greeting to the two guards, he entered the dark, empty cave.

She said, "I thought people lived in this cave."

"No." He didn't seem inclined to talk.

During the last twelve hours Anya had come to realize how little she knew about him. She wouldn't keep quiet now. "Tell me about your family." He'd briefly mentioned a brother once, long ago, but that was all she knew.

Joshua didn't answer. They had come to a metal door. He punched a button beside it. A creaking groan sounded from inside the mountain.

"Surely you have a family," she pressed.

The door slid open, and Joshua stepped inside. A pale, vertical strip lit the elevator. It leant a greenish gray hue to the utilitarian chamber. Joshua punched the "down" button.

"My father is dead." He stated it as a fact, without emotion.

"I'm sorry."

"I'm not."

He stared straight ahead, his face resembling a stone mask.

"What about sisters, or brothers?"

"I have one brother. Three sisters. Probably more I don't know about."

The door slid open to reveal a humungous cavern, lit in the center by a leaping bonfire. An invisible draught of air sucked the smoke skyward, toward a black opening.

The cavern was jammed full of all sorts of people. Flat, plastic television screens dominated the southern wall. Images flickered on them. One repeated the Astana and Irgiz explosions. The orange, billowing cloud that was Astana, stamped in violent color across the black night, hit Anya like a fist punch to her gut. She gasped, and her steps faltered. Her home...her friends...all dead. Joshua's shoulders stiffened, but he kept moving toward his intended destination. Few Tash residents paid attention to the silent screens.

Drawing a steadying breath, she hurried after Joshua. Wasn't that why they were here? To avenge Astana and Irgiz, and defeat Onred.

Most inhabitants gathered around tables, haggling for vegetables and meat. In the far corner, children played with scuttling rodents.

Anya stilled a shudder, and followed Joshua into the noisy chaos. "What about your mother?"

"Dead." He strode for the northern side of the chamber.

As they passed a table of snow boots, an old man's face lit up in a toothless smile. "Joshua!"

Others quickly turned and cried cheerful greetings to him.

Joshua replied curtly, still heading for his unknown destination, which appeared to be a passageway coming up on the right.

"Joshua, I love you," cried out a blond girl, and then swooned into the arms of an irritated looking man.

Anya caught up when he entered the dimly lit passage. Overhead, thin light strips dimly lit the hall. "Did these people really throw you out?"

"It's convenient for them to forget now." He stopped and pounded on a scarred wooden door. "Michael. It's Joshua."

The door opened. A man whose features bore a marked resemblance to Joshua's regarded them for a second, and then ushered them inside. The cave dweller was taller and bigger than Joshua, with dark blond hair and sable brows and dark green eyes. A scar marked his face, from left ear to jaw.

"You're alive." Michael's gravelly voice bottomed out in a bass register.

"Surprised? Or disappointed?"

"Relieved."

The two men eyed each other. No familial warmth lurked.

She held out her hand. "I'm Anya."

Michael enveloped hers in a warm shake. "Michael. Joshua's younger brother."

Anya returned the firm pressure. "Pleased to meet you."

Michael's attention returned to Joshua. "We intercepted Onred's transmission to Richert."

"So you know I'm supposed to offer myself as a sacrifice for peace."

His brother's gaze traveled to Anya. "Her, too."

"No. Nonnegotiable."

"Do you trust her?"

When Joshua's gaze rested on Anya, a hint of amusement warmed it. "In every way—except obeying me."

Michael's lips twitched. "Tough for a baron. Zebra Charlie Alpha?"

Anya recalled Joshua ordering airships to retreat to a location named Zebra Charlie Alpha. She had never heard of it before, and now wondered why Michael mentioned it.

"Yes."

Following Joshua's tersely spoken affirmative, Michael headed into an inner room. It must be Michael's living area. It contained a sagging, puke green couch, an ornately carved rocking chair, a table, and furry skins on the floor. A fire blazed in the hearth, and a paper thin television, made of the usual flexible plastic, hung by nails from the rock wall.

It was warm inside, and for the first time Anya realized she hadn't spotted any vents pumping central heating through Tash. In fact, the short impressions she had formed of this underground community were a strange mix of savage and civilized.

"Leave your bag here," Joshua said, so Anya left it near the door.

Michael shoved aside a floor-to-ceiling wall tapestry. It hid an elevator. After they stepped inside, its sudden jerk sideways made Anya stumble into Joshua. His strong arms closed around her, holding her upright. Unfortunately, he released her the moment she regained her balance.

With interest, Anya examined the square "elevator" box in which they rode. "Is this an electric train?" she asked in surprise.

"And an elevator," Michael rumbled with a faint smile.

It was hard to guess how fast they were speeding, but from the initial jerk, it couldn't be slow. "Are we going to Zebra Charlie Alpha?"

Joshua met his brother's gaze over Anya's head. "Not exactly. It's the ZCA command center."

She suspected he had filtered the information. That was fine. She would discover more facts later, when she needed them. "What will we do there?"

"You'll send messages to Donetsk's cities," Joshua told her. The elevator jerked and slowed. "Orders are to evacuate, except for mandatory personnel."

Anya was pleased to be given a task. All the same, she said, "Where will the people go? It's too cold outside for the babies and children."

"Tell them to take solar tents and provisions for a month. They'll need to scatter into the hills so Onred's ships can't use them for target practice."

Anya wondered what would be worse for her people— fleeing for their lives across the icy wasteland and hiding in the hills, or sitting in warm, comfortable cities, which were apparently defenseless from Onred's attacks. Maybe it was an easy choice, after all.

The door slid open to reveal a huge, rocky black cavern. Encircling the room was a seamless, floor-to-ceiling television screen. Below the multitudes of flickering images, men operated glassy computer work pads. The room's center area housed a medium-sized conference table and more computers, but those screens were smaller.

This cavern rivaled Astana's Command Central.

Relief hit Anya by surprise. "I thought when Astana was destroyed, that that was it. I didn't know..." She gazed around in awe. "How long has this been here?"

Joshua smiled. "It's been operational for five years. I ordered it built two years after becoming baron."

"It's ingenious! And no one knows about it?"

"If Onred did, it would be dust." He strode for an empty computer pad.

"I still don't understand how Onred got past Astana and Irgiz's missile defense systems."

Michael spoke. "I've been wondering the same thing. It's clear he disabled the defense system before he kidnapped the Dubrovnyks. Otherwise, he would never have been able to land in Astana in the first place. Once the defense system was breached, and the Dubrovnyks kidnapped, sending a warhead into Astana would have been like shooting a bomb into a baby's crib. But here's the real question. How did he get the key codes to the system in the first place?"

"A spy. Or a traitor," Joshua said shortly.

Shocked, Anya said, "You think one of our people is working for Onred?"

"What other explanation is there?" Joshua leaned over the work pad. Fingers flying, he typed in a series of letters and numbers. "Our first job is to change all of the codes, and jam the transponder frequencies."

"What if he's accessed our entire satellite computer system?" Anya said. "He might see the new codes, or delete them."

Joshua looked at Michael, who said, "Del is working on that right now. He's found a remote virus hacking the satellite system, feeding data to Onred. We can't tell where it originated, or when it was planted. We do know, however, when it started corrupting the system."

"When?"

"Minutes before Onred scrambled Astana's air space circuits and kidnapped the Dubrovnyks. Del has cut out the virus's main heads, but now the end code is manufacturing new data processing hubs. It's like cancer."

"The whole satellite is infected?"

"Everything but the housekeeping network."

Joshua opened his mouth, but Michael raised his hand. "We're on it. Del's set up firewalls on the housekeeping network. For now, they're holding. His men are rewriting code so Onred's computers are directed back to the main system. Onred hasn't tried to breach ZCA's firewall, because he doesn't know we exist."

"Yet," Joshua said grimly. "Cut information packets to short bursts."

Michael nodded.

"Tell Zyra and the other cities to take their systems offline and go to internal backup systems. Change all codes. No communication through the satellite except through housekeeping."

"Done."

"Anya, write the messages to the cities, and Del's men will send it. Michael, do we have contact with our pilots and the army?"

Anya moved to the work pad, and swiftly typed in the evacuation order.

Michael answered Joshua's question. "Yes, but sporadic. Estimates are, half the airbirds are down. The army is pretty much intact. Onred's men bombed two military fields an hour ago. The men were gone, though."

"Good."

"I'll talk to Slovic about jamming the pilot transponder codes. Most men have destroyed theirs, but a few are flying solo—we haven't heard from them in hours. I've ordered a blackout on communications. I hope that's okay."

"You read my mind." Joshua gripped his brother's shoulder. "Tell me when we've got a secure line to the commanders. We won't use ZCA's channel until we're sure Onred can't access it."

"Right." Michael headed across the room.

"I'm finished, Joshua," Anya said, after rereading her brief message. "But how will people know it's really from you?"

"We'll attach a short video link." Joshua's fingers flew across the keypad again, and then his arm unexpectedly went around her shoulders. He drew her close against his side. "Smile for the camera," he murmured.

A red feed line indicated recording had begun. "Anya and I are alive," Joshua said in a cool, level voice. "Our territory lives, as well. We will defeat Onred. Follow my instructions for your own safety." Another touch, and the feed glowed green.

Joshua's warm arm left her shoulders, and he touched a few more keys. "I sent it to Slovic. He'll send it on the secure network."

Anya had managed to keep up fairly well with the military half-speak and technical jargon Joshua and Michael had exchanged a few minutes ago, although much more would make her head ache. One question had come to mind, however. "Why hasn't the virus infiltrated the housekeeping network?"

"I don't know. Hopefully Michael and Del will find the answer."

Anya had studied Donetsk's general satellite computer infrastructure in school. It had been a core requirement that she had disliked, because it had required unusually boring amounts of memorization. She had forgotten most of it promptly after graduation. However, Anya did remember one interesting detail. "Both the housekeeping network and the children's education network are on the same satellite server. Why would the children's network be infected? Why would Onred infest a network made up of education and games?"

"Good question. I'll put it to Del. Then I'm going for a walk."

"I'll come with you," she said at once.

"Yes, you will." The grim note in his voice made her frown.

After a brief talk with a dark-haired man, Joshua opened a recessed door in the wall. Cold air billowed into the computer room. Anya hurried after him into an enormous black cavern. She stopped dead in her tracks, for its sheer size and contents made her jaw drop.

"So *this* is Zebra Charlie Alpha," she whispered.

CHAPTER FOURTEEN

THE CAVERN'S DOME arched at least a hundred meters over-head, and harsh light strips lit the vast area. Hundreds of airbirds were parked in bays stacked high against the far wall. Mechanics worked on others. A few larger warships, capable of carrying thermonuclear bombs, hovered like sleek black beasts at either end of the long cave. Men bustled about, fueling aircraft, cleaning them, loading supplies... The activity looked like a well-oiled machine.

"I had no *idea*," Anya murmured, zipping up her coat against the arctic air. It took only a moment to realize the airbay lacked one important feature. "Where's the exit?"

"A tunnel. There." Joshua pointed.

The black mouth loomed at the far end of the airbay. Anya saw no tracks. It looked large enough for an airbird to comfortably fly through, but the larger warships must be captained by Joshua's elite force. No one else could safely navigate such a narrow space. She wondered how long the tunnel was, and where it exited.

"Anya!"

She turned at the familiar voice and smiled when she saw flame-haired Pete O'Shea striding toward her. The lanky young pilot had asked her out a few months ago, but they had decided to remain just friends. Recently, he had been reprimanded for hot-dogging in his airbird.

"Pete!" She hugged him while he kissed her cheek. With a laugh, she pulled back. "I'm glad to see you're alive."

Pete flashed a bright blue, devil-may-care glance at Joshua. "Baron's had me doing penance, flying border patrol. Never knew it would save my life." Tone turning more serious, he said, "I'm glad to see you're alive, too. Joshua's been killing himself, searching for you. Riding rough on a bunch of other pilots, too."

Anya glanced at Joshua and was surprised to see faint color wash his cheekbones.

Pete grinned, also seeing his discomfort. "That's right. Ray about sidelined him for short-sheeting on rest. Looks like you finally found her, Baron."

"O'Shea," Joshua said curtly. "You've got orders. Meet me in Command Center in ten."

Pete saluted. "Yessir!" With a grin, he left them.

Anya touched Joshua's sleeve. "I didn't realize you were searching for me night and day."

He didn't look at her. "I was worried," he said gruffly. "I was afraid you were dead." A muscle flickered in his jaw.

He *had* been afraid. Suddenly, she realized just how selfish she had been. She had been worried only about herself—and hiding from him—while Joshua had been searching for her around the clock, probably growing more afraid with each passing hour that she might be dead. And Astana—her home's destruction continued to weigh heavily upon her, even though Joshua believed Onred had planned to destroy it all along. How could they ever know the truth?

"I'm sorry," she said quietly. "I regret what I did more than I can ever tell you."

He finally looked at her. "Don't be," he said. "If you hadn't run, you would be dead. So would I. And Donetsk Territory would be Onred's."

She looked into his eyes for a long moment, finding steadiness and reassurance there. And forgiveness. Feeling a small sliver of peace, she smiled softly. "Thank you."

Joshua's lips curved up. "Come on. I have something to show you."

He strode across the bay, calling a greeting to a grayhaired man in a yellow parka. Silver tape on its back marked Donetsk's circle and cross symbol.

Following close on Joshua's heels, Anya gazed about the monstrous room, trying to drink it all in. Why hadn't she known about this place? Why didn't Onred? Of course, Zebra Charlie Alpha was located underground, so satellites couldn't spot it. As well, the room was freezing, so maybe it didn't show up on heat sensors—or maybe the rocky mountains blocked the signal.

Joshua spoke to the gray-haired man. "Darryl. How's my ship?"

Darryl grinned, revealing crooked teeth. "You're a sight for sore eyes, Baron. I've kept it all polished up and running smooth as a kitten. Right over here." He moved to the wall of floor-to-ceiling bays and patted a black airbird's nose. Yellow painted flames licked down the sides.

Joshua grinned. "Thanks." He stroked the shiny bird like a master his favorite horse. As Anya watched his tanned hand caress the inanimate beast, a ridiculous stab of jealousy hit. Clearly, his heart belonged to this ship.

When Darryl left them, she said, "Did you fly this bird when you were in the elite force?"

"Yes. I still do, sometimes."

"It looks nice," she offered. The shiny craft's nose was a bit blunter than others in the airbay—maybe an older model—and the fierce, iridescent yellow flames made it distinctive looking. A niggling of an idea occurred to her. "You were in the army before the air corps, weren't you?"

Joshua nodded and released the door latch. With a faint hiss, it slid left. After a quick climb inside, he relaxed into the pilot's chair. His fingers gently fondled the bird's control panel.

Anya crawled inside, too, so she could get a better view. Her tiny idea faltered when she examined in detail the multiple control panels and indecipherable markings on some of the keypads. "Was it hard, learning to be a pilot?"

"Not really. It was a crash course. When I joined the air force, they'd just lost a pilot. They needed an immediate replacement. I learned the basics overnight."

"Wow." Anya touched one of the buttons. "What does this do?"

At her request, Joshua explained the function of a number of the controls. He didn't appear suspicious of her sudden interest, for he still wore that fatuous look as he caressed each button, explaining its purpose. Anya refrained from rolling her eyes.

Insight struck. "Will you fly this bird to meet Onred?"

With apparent reluctance, his hand dropped from the instrument panel. "I could. But I won't. Onred won't get both me and my airbird."

"You won't really surrender to him, will you?"

"He'll need to think I will. If I'm guessing right, he'll blow up my airbird as soon as I get off the ship."

"You can't get *off*," she said in horror. "He'll kill you. And that will be the end of our territory."

"There's still you." Joshua gave her a level look, and Anya frowned. Donetsk Territory needed Joshua's strong leadership. "I'll be fine. Don't worry."

"Don't worry?" Anya's brow lifted. "Are you insane? Of *course* I'm worried. What's your plan?"

"You don't need to know."

Anya softly gasped in outrage. "Tell me. I'm not stupid. I can understand."

A smile touched his lips. "I know you're not stupid." Tawny eyes burned into hers. "That's why I won't tell you."

If she had been younger, Anya might have stamped her foot. As it was, she clenched her teeth. "I'll find out sooner or later." She managed a reasonable tone. "You might as well tell me now."

"No. Back up. I'm getting out."

As Anya retreated from the small craft, she changed tactics. "If you won't tell me your plan, then tell me what I can do to help the mission."

Joshua shut the door. "I told you before." His tone was grim again, and unyielding. "Listen to me. You'll stay here, where you'll be safe."

"That song and dance is getting old. By now, you should know one thing—if you don't give me an assignment, I'll make one up."

"Michael will give you a job in the control room."

"No. The control room is well-staffed. I might as well tell you, Joshua, I plan to be in the thick of the battle. Now, you can either keep me in the loop, or I'll find a way to get myself there. I *am* the Baron's daughter, you know. I'm next in line for power if I marry. These people know that. They won't dare shine me on like you are."

Satisfied with her speech, she crossed her arms and gave him a hard glare.

❋∗❋∗❋∗❋∗❋

Anya would not back down. Joshua could see that in her flashing blue eyes and the set line to her jaw. But he hadn't been her protector for ten years without learning a few things about her. On the positive side, she was smart, courageous, and loved her family to distraction. On the negative, she was reckless. Skyjumping from the shuttle had shocked him. So had following him here, to Tash. Richert must have helped her with that one.

So Joshua knew Anya would formulate a risky plot and carry it out if she felt desperate enough. She wanted to help. He understood that. The key was to give her an assignment vital enough that she'd feel content to stay here, at ZCA.

He thought fast. "When Del secures the computer network, we'll need a communications coordinator..."

"No. I am not stupid, Joshua! I know Michael's got a communications expert. Probably three."

That was true. Frustrated, Joshua expelled a breath. "I'll talk to Michael. I'm sure he needs help somewhere."

"I want to come with you." Her blue eyes pleaded with him.

"No!"

The stubborn line of her jaw stiffened. "I know you'll send an extraction team to Bogd. That's where Onred lives. My family is probably there, too. I'll find out who's going. If you won't let me ride with you, I'll fly with another pilot."

Just the thought of Anya with the extraction team, vulnerable to Onred and his filthy men in Bogd, made Joshua's gut burn. "I'll lock you up first."

Hurt flashed in her eyes, and then anger. "Why do you have to be such a stiff-necked, *arrogant* dictator?"

"I lo..." He bit off the unintended words. "I want to protect you. Don't you understand that?"

"I'm not a child anymore. You can't protect me from the world!"

Joshua wished he could order her to her room until this whole disaster was over. But she was an adult, which made everything so much more complicated. In a quieter tone, he replied, "I know you don't want me to be your protector anymore. But I am still your baron. You will listen to me and obey me."

"I *can't*." Her voice caught. "Onred wants both of us. I have to go with you, or he'll launch more warheads. It's only you and me now, Joshua. We need each other. I need to fight with you. We need to fight together."

"I don't want to see you killed."

"I don't want you to die, either. But I have to be with you. I have to help my family. Don't you see that?"

He said nothing for a long moment. "I understand." And he did. But Anya coming on the mission was out of the question. He said, "Let me think about it," and then felt like a wretch when her eyes lit up. He had just lied to her. A first, and he hated it. But for Anya's safety he would do anything. Of course, he'd willingly lay down his life for her, but if a small half-truth would keep her safely here, then all the better. "Give me some time," he managed to finish. "I'll let you know what you can do."

"Thank you, Joshua!" Anya threw her arms around his neck and hugged him tight.

Weak as he was, he couldn't stop his own greedy desire to wrap his arms around her and pull her soft body against his. He rested his cheek against her silky hair and swore to himself that he would die before he allowed her to put herself in danger. His first order of business would be to talk to his men and warn them not to give in to her forthcoming pleads and demands. Prior to that, he would need to convince her to leave ZCA, at least for a while, so he could formulate his plans in peace.

❊*❊**❊**❊**❊

Anya followed Joshua back inside Command Central. It felt blessedly warm, after the artic temperatures in the air-bay. She was encouraged by Joshua's promise to think about allowing her on the mission. Of course, he'd likely assign her to the back of the fleet, but she wouldn't have to stay there.

If only she possessed useful military skills. Skyjumping from shuttles, surviving in the wild, and a fair knowledge of computers were all she could offer. Surely, she could make those count.

Learning to pilot an airbird appealed, too. Anya wasn't foolish enough to think that she could learn to fly before Onred announced the surrender location. And she certainly didn't think Joshua's elite force would let her fly a bird, either. However, if she knew piloting basics, wouldn't that be helpful if an aircraft went down, or if a pilot died? If necessary, she could salvage the craft and perhaps fly injured people to safety. After all, Joshua had learned the basics overnight. She could do the same.

The idea appealed to Anya more by the minute. How could she find a piloting manual?

Joshua's voice interrupted her thoughts. "It'll probably be a few hours before Onred contacts us," he told her. "How would you like to explore Tash while we wait?"

The offer took her by surprise. "Would you come, too?"

"I need to speak to Michael about a couple of matters. I could call one of my sisters to come meet you."

Anya eyed him. For the first time, suspicion entered her mind. Was he trying to get rid of her? If so, what would he try to accomplish while she was gone? What if he flew out of ZCA? He had never actually *promised* to put her on the mission, she realized now. He had just promised to think about it. Probably that thought had lasted one second. Hurt and anger arose. It wasn't like Joshua to be deceitful, but his decision to skate the thin line of truth gave a clue to his deep determination to keep her out of the mission.

What would be the best way to play this? Pretend she still blindly trusted him? Or confront him outright? She wanted to confront him. Outspoken directness was in her nature. However, if she did so, his guard would go back up. He just might lock her up before the mission, like he had threatened.

So Anya managed a fair semblance of a smile. "Ordinarily, I would love to meet your sister and learn more about where you grew up. But I was thinking more about the communications assignment you mentioned. Maybe I could be helpful if I learned ZCA's communications systems. Do you think one of Del's men would be willing to show me how they work?"

Now it was his turn to eye her. Unknown thoughts flickered behind the brown gaze. She kept her expression expectant and open.

A faint frown drew his brows together. He wasn't pleased. Likely, he didn't trust her, either. But if Joshua attempted to throw her out of ZCA again, she would blandly smile and hang on by her fingernails.

"These computers are taken," he said abruptly. "I'll set you up in another room."

"Where?" she asked warily.

"It's a back up command center. It's cold," he warned, "because it's right off the airbay."

Anya smiled. "Sounds perfect." She pulled on fiber thin black gloves and followed him back into the airbay. They walked to the far end of the hangar, where an open door led to a small, brightly lit room. A burly man with a shaved head and his back to them typed with lightning speed at the glass console. Five computers took up the room, and a mini version of the wrap around screen in the Command Center took up two vertical meters of wall space.

"Slovic," Joshua said. "Meet Anya."

The burly man turned, revealing ordinary features but intelligent, pale green eyes. "Nice to meet you." His hand engulfed hers. "You here to learn the system?"

She smiled. "I'd appreciate whatever you're willing to teach me."

"We've got a tutorial. I'll start you on that. Take the computer down there. I need lots of elbow room," he explained with a grin.

This suited Anya just fine. Hopefully, it meant he wouldn't be looking over her shoulder every minute. While she did want to learn the communications system, and she wanted to hear Onred when he came on the air, she also planned to find the pilot manual and open it up in the lower left quarter of her screen. That way she could learn two things at once.

After Anya was set up, Joshua hovered in the doorway for a long moment, probably wondering if he could trust her to behave after he left. She didn't bother to give him a reassuring smile. That would only encourage his suspicions. Instead, she settled down to speed through Slovic's tutorial. On the subscreen keypad, however, she sent a search for the pilot's manual.

❊⁑❊⁑❊⁑❊⁑❊

Anya had memorized the main airbird controls by nineteen hundred hours, and she had also learned that the aircraft possessed a sophisticated autopilot program. That was great news, since she didn't have much confidence in her ability to fly an airbird by herself tonight. She spent a good deal of time learning the requirements necessary to run the autopilot program. She had also applied more medication to her wound with the medical kit Richert had given her, and had eaten military rations for dinner.

By her calculations, Onred could call anytime in the next two hours. ...If he hadn't called yet. She couldn't access any communication channels, which frustrated her. The interface was fairly straightforward, but she had discovered that every level required security access codes.

Heavy footsteps approached, so she minimized the pilot manual and resumed her investigation of the communications system.

"How's it going?" Slovic asked.

"I think I understand it. But it's hard to tell, since I can't access the communication channels. They're locked."

"I know." Slovic straddled a chair beside her. His thick fingers moved with surprising speed over the pad. "We're only working three lines, plus the ZCA channel. ZCA's a security level you don't have."

"Why not?" Anya watched him enter passwords into the three channels. "If I'm going to help, I'll need access to all the channels."

"I'll talk to Joshua about it later. Look here. We've got one open channel. We call it Alpha. Anyone can speak on it. It's blocked, though, so we can't send a return message. If we do, Onred could trace it and find us."

"Onred will send his message on this one?" she guessed. "Or has he already?"

"Not yet." Anya relaxed. "The other channels feed through the housekeeping network. One is a text channel. One is voice. We've just hooked the military commanders into it. We won't say much on those channels, because they could be compromised at any time."

"Is the virus still replicating?"

Jaw tightening, he said, "It's a mess. It's like a blow torch melted the satellite's circuits. Whoever made that virus is a genius. I've never seen anything like it."

Anya wondered how he could sound so awed by malignant software.

Slovic said, "Use these buttons to send and receive. These codes are yours." He shoved a slip of paper across the console. "Use it when you access the computer. It gives you access to the system and tells the recipients who's sending the message."

"Thank you. Can I practice sending messages to you?"

"The internal server should be open." When Slovic clicked a button, her pilot manual screen blew up, filling the entire screen. "What's this?" He turned a wide, surprised smile upon her.

"Nothing." She hastily minimized it again. "I was just curious. Joshua showed me his airbird, and I wondered what all the different buttons were for."

"Uh huh." Slovic's gaze appeared entirely too intelligent. "In any case, here's the internal system. "I'm Sl1. Practice sending me text and video messages."

Anya waited until he had returned to his seat before she opened a new window in the bottom corner of her screen and accessed the Alpha channel. Now she would see Onred the instant he sent his message. She also memorized the access codes Slovic had given her. For the next half hour, she practiced sending messages to Slovic. He shot back speed tests, measuring her response time to questions he put to her.

"Good," he said, from across the room. "You're improving. I'm sending you an old report. Read the information, then send me a message stating the main points. Speed counts. If the system cuts down to one channel, life and death could depend on how fast you relay messages."

Anya worked so hard at accurately speeding through Slovic's assignments that the flicker of static, and then the empty white image on Alpha channel didn't register for a second.

"Good evening." Onred's nasally voice stilled her fingers. His headshot filled the screen. She pushed "send" to Slovic, then maximized the Alpha channel, her gaze glued to the computer screen. Onred looked meaner than she remembered. His black beard appeared more menacing, and his dark eyes were as black as a demon's.

His lips thinned into a false smile. "Citizens of Donetsk, I propose peace. I am not an unreasonable man. I would be pleased to spare your lives and your homes. I need workers. If you serve me, you will live long and prosperous lives. Under one condition, of course. Joshua Van Heisman and Anya Dubrovnyk must surrender. If they sacrifice their lives, you will keep yours."

All pretence of a smile fled. "Surrender, Joshua and Anya. Meet me at the wreckage of Astana in sixty minutes. Both of you must come, or in sixty-one minutes I will annihilate Omsk. Next, I'll order my pilots to hunt the hills and exterminate your people like rodents. Count starts now." The screen turned black

One *hour?* Anya choked on a breath. It would take at least fifty minutes to fly to Astana—unless the fighters chose to break the sound barrier. Possible, but unlikely, when dealing with an enemy that could crop up anywhere, at any time. She had to speak to Joshua, and now. Punching a countdown timer into her watch, she bolted for the Command Center.

CHAPTER FIFTEEN

WHEN ANYA BURST through the door into the Command Center, Joshua gripped her arm and hauled her none too gently into the elevator.

"What are you *doing?*" she gasped aloud, taken too unawares to do more than give a token struggle.

He punched numbers into the elevator keypad. "We're taking a trip."

"Where?" She didn't appreciate being manhandled, and wrenched her arm free. All the same, at least he was with her, so he couldn't meet Onred...yet.

She eyed him while her heart rate settled. It disturbed her that Joshua had appeared to be waiting for her. As if he'd known she'd come running in, full of fire and brimstone and demands to take her on the mission.

He had succeeded in removing her from Zebra Charlie Alpha.

Anya crossed her arms. "Tell me your plan."

Topaz fire burned in that dark gaze, but he did not answer.

"Tell me!"

He still did not answer. The elevator slowed, and stopped with a jerk. Joshua took her arm again, firmly, and pulled her into Michael's shabby living room. Anya struggled. "What are you *doing?*"

"Keeping my promise to you. And your father."

Finally, she understood his plan. She felt foolish it had taken this long.

Joshua shoved her down the hall and into a narrow bedroom. Inside, she jerked free and faced him across the small space. A snarl thinned her lips.

"He'll kill everyone, Joshua. He'll kill them *all* if I don't surrender, too."

"He'll kill them anyway."

"What? He said..."

"Do *you* trust him now?" Joshua's lips curled back in a humorless smile. "Surrender will never satisfy Onred. He can't gain full power over Donetsk unless he's killed both of us, and your family, too."

Anya gasped. "He wouldn't! If he'd wanted my family dead, he'd have killed them already."

"They're bait. If he captures you, then you'll be bait for me. I can't allow that."

"So you'll surrender to him?"

"No. I'll meet him. I'll tell him that you'll surrender in a second location. He'll fly there to get you. My men will ambush him, and we'll fly for Bogd to help the extraction team."

"That's crazy! Why would Onred go to your location? He'll suspect a trap."

"I'll fly with him. If he doesn't follow instructions, my men have orders to shoot down his bird." His face was grim.

"With *you* inside? No!" she cried out.

"Don't worry."

"Don't *worry?*" she gasped aloud. "You're insane. It's a suicide mission. I won't let you do it!" She launched herself across the room, intent on getting out first and locking *him* in, instead. His solid body blocked her. She fought him with every ounce of strength she possessed, pummeling him, tears streaming down her cheeks.

"Stop it." He gripped her wrists hard. She twisted, burning her skin in the process, and struggled, kicking him, fighting like a mad woman.

"I won't let you," she gasped. "I won't let you *die* like that. ...No!" He forced her backward, and she didn't realize his intent until the bed hit her knees and she toppled backward onto it. His full weight fell on top of her. Now his sheer size subdued her every movement.

"Get *off*. Get off!" Their hands were caught between them, and it hurt horribly. "Ow," she panted, grimacing.

Joshua forced her arms overhead, onto the bed, relieving the pain. Anya struggled again, futilely, against the unyielding bands on her wrists. Her breaths heaved, and she glared up at him. He was so close now that the hard planes of his body intimately imprinted into every soft place of hers. She had dreamed of being this close to him, but never like this. "You stiff-necked dictator," she spat. "Get off me."

"I am your baron, Anya. And your protector. I will protect you until the day I die."

"No!" She arched her back, trying to roll him off. "*No. No!*"

He remained as steady as a rock. She couldn't budge him. "You're a beast! An animal," she told him. "Only savages treat women like this."

A smile ghosted his lips. "I told you I was a barbarian. It's how I was raised. Sometimes my base instincts rule."

"Get off."

"No." His eyes gleamed.

"You like this," she accused. She struggled again, but with less fervor.

His lids lowered. "Stop."

And then she understood why. Her whole body flushed, and she went still. "Joshua." Her heart thundered into a gallop. Long seconds ticked by.

Infinitesimally, and completely involuntarily, she pressed closer to him.

"Anya," he murmured. His gaze smoldered fire, and slowly it drifted, as soft as a caress, from her lips to her throat.

She arched her neck. "Yes," she whispered. It was a plea and a prayer.

He muttered a soft word, and leashed emotion pulled his features taut. With agonizing slowness, his head lowered and his warm lips buried gently in the hollow of her throat.

She gasped with the pure, wondrous pleasure of it. "Yes, Joshua," she whispered again. "Please."

He drew a shuddering breath, and his soft, lingering kisses burned a molten trail up her neck. His breaths felt like heavy, sultry fire against her skin. Just when she thought he would kiss her lips, he kissed the tender place at the base of her jaw and then traced warm, feather kisses back down her throat. He nudged aside her parka and snow wear and buried his lips in the sensitive place between her collarbone and shoulder. Breaths coming faster, she again involuntarily arched against him, seeking more of his body against hers. Blindly wanting all of him, now and forever.

His warm mouth abandoned her shoulder, but his breaths still seared her skin.

"Anya." The word sounded anguished. "You're so beautiful." He lifted his head, and his eyes were black with torment, need...and self-condemnation.

"*No*. Don't look at me like that." With no difficulty now, she pulled her wrists free and cupped his face in her palms. She stroked his bristly beard and rose to kiss him, full on the mouth. At first he devoured her kiss hungrily, like it was a balm to his soul, and then his tongue slid past her defenses and possessed her mouth. His slow, savagely gentle strokes pooled heat low in her body. He kissed her until she was mindless, drugged with love and feverish with longing. When he pulled away, she wasn't sure what he meant to do. Her mind still felt fuzzy from the bliss of finally holding the man she loved in her arms.

He was halfway to the door when she realized his intent. "Joshua!"

"Stay here," he said hoarsely. "For me." And then he was gone. The lock tumbled into place.

Anya put her hands to her face and cried out in torment.

❈*❈*❈*❈*❈

Shaking, Joshua stood very still outside the locked door. His hand clenched the doorknob.

Abruptly, he strode down the hall, heading for the elevator. Once inside, he punched in the code to ZCA and leaned against the wall. He closed his eyes, battling to control his emotions. Anya's soft, urgent pleas for him to kiss her had undone him. For long, disorienting minutes, he had lost all grip on space and time. Overwhelmed by his relentlessly suppressed, fierce need to make her his own, he had nearly forgotten his mission.

Summoning the strength of will to leave her had taken superhuman effort, because for the first time in his life he had glimpsed, in Anya's arms, what love could be. He wanted her with a need that bordered on desperation. Only protecting her, and freeing his territory, meant more to him than satisfying that desire.

The doors slid open.

"Been waiting for you." Michael thrust a vest into his arms and walked fast for the door to the airbay. "The ship is ready." He cast Joshua a penetrating look. "Are you?"

Joshua zipped the vest, then pulled his parka over it. "Yes. ZCA channel?"

"Open. Use housekeeping, though, until it's compromised."

Joshua nodded, striding fast across the airbay to the hive of hovering black airbirds, all awaiting his arrival. He hit the door release button of the lead craft, then looked at his brother. "Take care of her, Michael." If he didn't return. It didn't need to be said. They both knew he would probably be dead within the hour.

"Take this for back up." Michael shoved a small plastic capsule in his hand. "In case you're in a bind." He smiled, but it didn't reach his eyes. "Don't bite too soon."

Joshua's fist curled around the object, and then shoved it into his pocket. A smile ghosted his lips. "You and your technological wonders." For a second, he eyed his brother, and then reached out and gripped his shoulder. "I'm proud of you, and everything you've become. You're a good man."

In response, Michael gripped Joshua's shoulder, too. "You'll make it. Our father couldn't kill you. Neither will Onred. You'll come back and take care of Anya yourself."

Joshua allowed himself to smile, although in his gut, he didn't believe it. He released his brother and swung into the aircraft. A touch to a button, and the door slid shut. Another few strokes across the control panel, and his bird shot for the black mouth of the tunnel.

❋*❋**❋**❋*❋

Anya lay on the bed for a full minute after Joshua left, weeping with fury. He had tricked her. How much of his lovemaking had been real? How much had been manipulation?

She had *begged* him to touch and kiss her. Anya closed her eyes in utter mortification. How pathetically weak and eager she had been for his caresses. And how swiftly Joshua had taken full advantage.

She hated him. Yes, she did. And she despised herself.

Fed up with self-pity, propelled by anger, she rolled off the bed and attacked the door, shaking the knob viciously. Locked, of course.

He had left her. He had locked her in Michael's bedroom! Anya let out an animal sound of fury and searched the room for a weapon she could wield against the door. A key would work best. Otherwise, she'd have to break it down.

One part of her mind realized that Joshua must be back in ZCA by now. She didn't have much time if she wanted to catch up with him.

Anya rummaged through the drawers in the dresser beside the bed. They were empty. So, this wasn't Michael's bedroom. It must be the guest room. She shoved open the closet, but found nothing but hangars. The thick wire wouldn't fit in the old fashioned keyhole.

She surveyed the room. It was bare, except for the bed, dresser, and a picture on the wall. In two strides, she plucked it off. A thin wire on the back balanced it on the nail. She smiled. Here was the advantage of being locked in a half-primitive society. Pictures in Astana were hung with plastic suction tags.

Impatiently, she twisted and pulled at the metal filament. The wire poked into her fingers, pricking up a bubble of blood, but she freed the wire from the picture and inserted it into the pinhole lock. The keen awareness of time slipping by inspired quick, urgent jabs into the keyhole.

She checked her stopwatch. Fifty minutes left until Onred bombed Omsk. Right now, Joshua must be preparing to fly.

She jabbed the lock again and again. Dead, metallic clicks resulted.

Joshua couldn't leave without her. He just couldn't. He needed her. So did Donetsk Territory, and her brothers and sisters.

Anya took a breath and slowed down. Delicately, she probed the lock. She had to escape right now. She *had* to. Joshua couldn't go without her. Much as she was furious with him at the moment, the persistent, deep certainty that he was flying to his death lodged like an unmanageable boulder in the pit of her stomach. Tears of frustration hovered. "Please God," she whispered. "Help me. Protect him."

Anya picked again and again at the lock, but it refused to release. She glanced at her watch.

Forty minutes left.

Joshua was long gone. She had failed.

A helpless moan escaped, and she squeezed her arms around her middle. She felt sick. He was gone. Forever.

"*No.*" With a gasp, Anya lunged across the room. She yanked out a drawer and then spun and swung it with all her strength at the door handle. "No," she panted, and struck it again and again. "No, no, *no!*"

❈**❈**❈**❈**❈

Joshua broke Mach 1 all the way to the remains of Astana. Twelve of his fighter birds peeled off seconds after swarming up from the western end of the Tien Shan, heading for the decoy destination. It had taken two minutes to fly out of ZCA's fifteen kilometer tunnel, which was designed to protect ZCA's location. Satellites had probably picked up the exiting aircraft, but hidden, well-armed sentries guarded the secret exit.

For now, it didn't matter. Joshua shot a glance at his black wristwatch. Five minutes until Omsk blew. His radar screen picked up twenty of Onred's airbirds hovering on the southern edge of Astana. A few others slyly slipped in lazy patterns to the north. A few scooted east and west. He spoke into his transmitter, which was programmed into the house-keeping network. "Red team, time to play."

Six birds broke free from the pack to play chicken with Onred's fey forces.

On the ground, far ahead, all of Onred's birds looked the same size. No warships were in sight. A few men stood on the moonlit snow pack, waiting. Joshua's fingertips slid digital pictures of Onred and his favorite bird into the craft's recognition system. He muttered, "Find Onred." His computer screen zoomed in on the enemy, enlarging the pinpoints to full figures.

Three minutes now. One until he touched down.

Joshua's bird screamed in at Mach 1, cutting the frosty air so fast that muted thunder signaled his arrival. Unease registered on several enemy faces.

"Onred not found," the polite female computer voice stated. "His ship cannot be located."

Joshua's quick scan had net the same conclusion. He had, however, spotted Onred's second-in-command, Belar, on the ground. "The nest is empty," he reported into his microphone. "But the crow is hungry." Time for plan B.

He braked a hundred meters distant from the hovering enemy airbirds. With slow deliberation, Joshua pulled on his gloves and stuck the capsule into the secure pocket between gum and cheek. He shot a glance skyward. "If ever I needed help, it's now, God."

Hood down, he slid open the door and jumped lightly onto the moonlit snow pack. Arctic wind ruffled his hair. He tapped his transmitter to open broadcast.

His fighters kept to the air, but the comforting lights of two birds flanked Joshua as he left the safety of his aircraft. He faced the hovering pack of enemy craft. The black and silver, twisted steel of Astana rose behind them, a silent graveyard of death.

Joshua set his jaw, dismissing his emotions, and advanced at a controlled pace toward the five waiting men.

CHAPTER SIXTEEN

IT TOOK FIVE precious minutes for Anya to beat the doorknob crooked. It took another five to figure out how to release the bolt.

Thirty minutes remained. She would never catch up with Joshua now. But she could still be useful. If only she could figure out where he meant to lure Onred, perhaps she could reach that location before Onred's bird arrived—with Joshua probably inside it. If he would ever need her, it would be then.

Anya sprinted into Michael's living area and searched for a communication device. Surely it would be logged into ZCA's communications system. She swiftly scanned all surfaces. Finding nothing, she pawed through drawers, leaving behind a scrambled, disordered mess. She forced herself to slow down. *Think, Anya.*

Surely Michael had a back up phone somewhere. If he was sleeping, he'd want double warning in case of an emergency.

His bedroom! Anya sprinted back down the hall. The first door she opened made her pause. It was filled with technological equipment, most dismantled—or was it in the process of being created? In any case, she didn't have time to do more than give it a cursory glance. No phone. She darted to the next room and skidded to a halt before Michael's dresser. A small black phone rested in a cradle.

Yes. She scooped it up and swiftly scanned the networks. The phone was logged into Alpha channel. She tapped open a small window for this blank channel. Michael's phone wasn't programmed for the housekeeping network, but she had paid careful attention when Slovic had first redirected her computer's system in the airbay, and with only a few missteps, replicated his procedure. Two channels materialized, and below them, the closed ZCA channel.

With swift finger taps, she entered her personal codes and opened the housekeeping channels on separate, tiny windows. A quick dig in Michael's drawer unearthed the wireless earplug, and she took off for the front door. Her bag lay near the door, where she'd left it, and she scooped it up on her way out.

ZCA's channel code was the only vital piece of information she lacked. While Michael might have hidden the code somewhere in his cave, she didn't have time to look for it. Time was slipping by much too fast. The pilots would probably use the housekeeping channels for now, anyway, and keep the ZCA for back up. She hoped.

She dashed down the long hall, brushing by strangers she barely noticed. Out in the crowded main cavern, she skirted the wall, and made for the elevator.

"Fruit?" cackled an old woman as she passed.

"No. Thank you." Anya ran for the elevator and pushed the button.

It seemed to take an eternity to arrive. Finally, with a clunk, the doors crept apart. Anya squeezed inside and punched the "up" button. With another faint groan, it lurched upward. She pulled on gloves and zipped her coat to her chin.

When the elevator finally stopped, Anya bolted through the cracked doors and sprinted for freedom. Moonlight on snow glazed the cave's entrance. She had forgotten it was nighttime.

"Hey! Stop." A guard blocked her path.

Bright light blinded her eyes, and she lifted a hand in protest. "Excuse me. I need to get out."

"You're Anya Dubrovnyk." A smile lightened the heavy voice.

"Yes." She favored him with a strained smile. "Let me pass. I have an assignment to complete."

"Funny thing. The Baron left orders to keep you *inside* Tash."

✻∗✻∗✻∗✻∗✻

"Baron," Belar rumbled. He was a big man with shorn black hair and a goatee. In fact, all four Altai men with him sported shorn heads and goatees. Except for variations in body type and facial structure, each could pass as a clone of Onred. "Where's Anya?"

Joshua assessed Belar and the other men, measuring their threat level. "At another location. I'll take you to her."

"No, you won't." Belar lifted a finger. Fire spit from an Altai aircraft and the ground behind Joshua shuddered. His bird had exploded.

Joshua didn't bother to look. "If you want Anya, you'll follow my instructions."

"Report." A voice crackled from Belar's transmitter.

"Van Heisman is here. Dubrovnyk is supposedly in a different location."

The voice swore. "Kill him."

Four lasers leveled at Joshua.

Belar raised a hand. "What about Dubrovnyk? He says he'll bring us to her."

Another oath. "It's a trap." Silence elapsed. Belar waited patiently. "Go. But send in your fighters first. If it is a trap, send Van Heisman here. I'll torture the truth out of him myself."

"Roger." Belar smiled at Joshua, revealing a broken front tooth. "You're going for a ride, Baron. You are a foolish man."

Four men sprang forward and shoved Joshua face first into the snow. Quick hands divested him of all weapons. Tight bands confined his wrists behind his back. They dragged him upright and forced him toward the nearest airbird. An enemy airman climbed in first, then Joshua, and then Belar, who settled into the pilot's seat. Joshua sat behind him while the airman behind Joshua held a laser to his head.

Belar cast him another pleasant smile. "Give me the coordinates."

"I'll give you the first set."

The laser poked harder into his head. "The destination, Van Heisman!"

Belar laughed as the airbird shot skyward. "It's a game, Skylar. Cat and mouse. But we've bagged the prize. We'll play his game for a little while."

Joshua relayed the first set of coordinates. They were also the final coordinates, but Belar did not know that. He also did not know that a dozen of Joshua's birds had stealthily arrived twenty minutes earlier and now waited, armed and hidden in the forested foothills.

The radar screen showed the enemy birds darting at Joshua's nearby aircraft, trying to force them back.

Belar chuckled again. "You are a fool, Joshua. And I always thought you were a worthy opponent. No wonder Onred didn't come himself."

"Where is he?"

Belar snorted. "Readying the warhead for Omsk."

"Why blow up our cities? You need our greenhouses."

"We're not interested in your greenhouses. They're easily replicated, once we win your flatland."

"What do you want, then?" Joshua could venture a guess, but wanted confirmation of his suspicions.

Belar did not answer.

The instrument panel read one minute out from the decoy location. Enemy aircraft shot forward to scope out the rough, hilly landscape, darkened in folds of night.

"I see an aircraft," crackled a voice.

"Blow it up."

"No!" Joshua said forcefully.

The exposed craft had been left for bait.

"Blow it up," Belar repeated with a chuckle. "Then we're heading home." He touched the controls and the aircraft spun. "Our mission is complete, Onred. You can blow up Omsk."

"You don't want peace," Joshua said through his teeth.

Belar grinned again. In the half light, his eyes looked like sunken black shadows, and his mouth a gaping black hole, like a ghoulish specter. "We want Donetskis to come crawling to us, begging for peace. When you and all of the Dubrovnyks are dead, we might take them as slaves."

"Enjoy hell," Joshua said in a pleasant voice. He lurched sideways, punching his elbow into the door release button. Laser fire blazed, licking across his cheek as the door jerked open.

He hurtled out into deep, impenetrable blackness.

Strange. The moon was up. It shouldn't be so dark.

Joshua bit into the capsule.

CHAPTER SEVENTEEN

ANYA TENSED. Her eyes had grown accustomed to the dim light in the huge cave, and now she spotted the other guard strolling closer. Together, the two burly men could easily force her back inside Tash.

She had to get to Joshua. This feeling grew stronger by the minute. Anya slipped her hands into her pockets and felt through the slit opening for her utility belt. She kicked the laser to its lowest possible setting, and then double-checked it. Although using a laser would be her last resort, she'd do anything to get out of this cave and find Joshua. Even if he'd manipulated her and his kisses meant nothing, she loved him. She would save him, or die trying.

"I'm Jason Dubrovnyk's daughter," she stated coolly. "I'm first in line for power. My orders supersede Joshua's. Step aside."

"Sorry." The guard nearest to her did sound apologetic, but he advanced one step closer. Another, and he would be able to grab her. "But our first loyalty is to Joshua."

"I'm sorry, too," she murmured. Whipping out her laser, Anya shot him in the knee. Before the second guard could reach for his weapon, blue light spit into his knee, too. She was lucky they'd both been near enough to hit on the first try. She wasn't an expert markswoman, much to her father's chagrin.

Both men crumpled to the ground, moaning and clutching their legs. Long ago, her father had drilled into her that shooting the knee was the best way to incapacitate a man without killing him. It hurt like a son-of-a-gun, but the victim would fully recover within fifteen minutes.

Anya sprinted outside. Moonlight glittered on the snow. To her left, dark Tien Shan spruce soared skyward. To the south rose the sheer bulk of the Tien Shan mountain range. She pulled on her face mask and slogged uphill, following the deep, snowy path she and Joshua had broken earlier. The hill seemed steeper than when she'd run down it. Her heart hammered. Sharp, cold air prickled her laboring lungs as she churned through the heavy, knee deep snow. Ignoring the painful burn in her muscles and the arctic air searing her lungs, she pressed on.

Long minutes later, panting heavily, she crested the rise. Ahead lay the quiet, moonlit clearing where the stolen Altai airbird awaited.

She had to hurry. Joshua was in danger. She felt it. Heart thundering so loud and so hard she feared it might explode, she plowed through the last two hundred meters. Snow flakes drifted from the dark, overcast sky. Gasping, she punched the door release and tumbled inside the cold aircraft.

Anya settled into the pilot's seat. The Altai control panel was a little different than the manual's example, but it took only a moment to find the two buttons to start the aircraft. The bird hummed to life, and warm air whispered from the vents.

Encouraged, she ripped off her facemask and murmured, "Please God, let there be an autopilot program."

But the series of keystrokes that should have pulled up the autopilot program did not work. She tried again, with no better luck. For the first time, panic gathered in the pit of her stomach.

Until this moment, she hadn't realized how heavily she had counted upon the autopilot program. What had she been she thinking? Could she really fly an airbird by herself? What if she couldn't get it into the air? What if she crashed into a tree and killed herself? Who was she, to think she could fly a sophisticated military craft the first time out?

"Oh, God, help me," she mumbled. Anya closed her eyes, picturing the pilot's manual in her mind. A photographic memory would be helpful about now, but the best she could remember were fuzzy pictures. She had, however, taken care to memorize the start sequence.

First, she located the navigation bar and punched in the coordinates for Astana. When she got closer to Astana, she'd adjust her course for Joshua's alternate location. Hopefully he'd broadcast it.

Next, the altitude. When Anya punched in "two hundred meters," the bird shot skyward, spinning so fast she tumbled out of her seat. Her heart pounded. She was airborne! A glance out the window proved she hovered, spinning like a top, far above the black forest. It was disorienting.

"Whoa," she murmured, and with difficulty clambered back into the seat and clipped on her safety belt. Cautiously, she engaged the navigation button. The spin jerked to a stop and the bird's nose quivered northward.

"Thank goodness," she whispered, and punched "10" into the speed throttle indicator. The ship crept forward. Encouraged, she increased the throttle to one hundred. A bit of gravitational push signaled success. A sea of treetops rippled by below.

A glance at her watch proved fifteen minutes remained until Joshua met Onred. No time to piddle around at one hundred kilometers per hour.

"Let's see how fast you can go," she murmured, and pushed the lever forward. Several Gs of force pressed her back against the seat. Not fast enough. She opened the throttle to Mach 1. The instant acceleration slammed hard gravitational force, like a heavy hand, against her body. A faint scream whistled outside, and fine vibrations shook the bird's hull.

Exhilaration and fear charged Anya's pulse. At least she'd arrive at her destination in a hurry. And then what? Should she land?

Land.

Anya slapped a hand to her forehead and groaned. "I am such an idiot! I am going to *die*."

"I hope not," said a hoarse voice.

Anya gasped, and cast a quick glance about the tiny cabin, seeking the source of the voice. It hadn't come from the tiny earbud in her ear. Joshua's forces were flying on silent. "Hello?"

"Hit the video screen, foolish girl," the voice snapped. "Left button above the throttle."

When she pushed the tiny black button, Richert's testy face stared back at her. How had Tarim's baron accessed Onred's communications system?

An inspired touch to an adjacent button opened up a wide, black radar screen. Orange blobs bobbed on the horizon. They must be Onred's forces, waiting for Joshua at Astana. She didn't see Joshua's birds, but they were probably flying with radar jamming on. Obviously, Onred, in his arrogance, didn't feel the need to jam radar. Or perhaps some of his birds flew invisibly. Likely.

"Well?" Richert snapped. "Why are you ignoring me? Aren't you curious why I'm on Onred's video feed?"

"Because you're in cahoots with him?"

Richert scowled. "You'd be dead if I were."

"So why are you spying on me?"

"Where's Joshua?"

Anya eyed Richert with suspicion. What were his motives? Clearly, he'd compromised the bird's security system. He had probably thought she and Joshua would fly this bird to meet with Joshua's secret forces. Probably the whole cabin was bugged with microphones and tiny video cameras. Richert couldn't, however, hear her tiny earpiece linked into Michael's phone. So, how much should she tell him?

Anya didn't trust Richert any further than she could proverbially throw him. At the same time, he had pledged to help them fight Onred. In the interest of their temporary truce, how much should she say?

It wouldn't hurt to tell him what he probably already knew.

"He's about to meet Onred." She checked her watch. "In ten minutes."

"Why isn't he flying your airbird?"

Anya bit her lip. "He locked me up so I couldn't meet Onred. As soon as he left, I took this bird. I'm following him."

"Where'd he get the new craft?"

Richert didn't know about Zebra Charlie Alpha. So she'd better think up a plausible story, and fast. "He met some old friends. They're helping him out."

"Didn't see him leave Tash."

"Probably jamming radar signals. Do you see me?"

"Only on the monitor." Richert sounded surly. "I'm trying to help you, girl. Stop treating me like the enemy. Tell me the full truth."

"The truth is, Joshua's going to meet Onred. He's got a crazy, hair-brained scheme that's going to get him killed."

"Find that hard to believe."

"What do you *want*, Richert?" Anya's patience frazzled to nothing. "I've got to figure out how to fly so I don't kill myself. I don't have time to talk to you."

"You don't know how to fly?" Richert's cackle blasted, reverberating through the tiny cabin. "You *are* a fool. Or brave. Haven't decided which."

"What do you *want?*" Anya repeated through her teeth.

"I want to help."

"How?" she asked with thinly disguised impatience.

"Are you tied into Joshua's communications network?"

"Yes." She hoped.

"I'm on blackout here. Can't hear anything unless Onred blasts the Alpha. They've gone and switched up all their networks. Tell me what Joshua says, word for word."

Anya supposed it wouldn't hurt to pass along general facts. Although she'd certainly censor any ZCA sensitive information. "Okay. Now, if you'll be quiet..."

"I'll teach you to fly."

"What?"

"It's been awhile, but I'm the best pilot ever flown the skies."

"And the most modest, too."

Richert unexpectedly smiled. "You've got a mouth on you that's nothing like your mother's."

Anya rolled her eyes, refusing to accept that as a compliment. "Fine. Tell me how to land. I'm afraid I'll kill myself."

Richert gave terse instructions on landing and then more complicated lessons on interpreting radar. Thanks to his insights, she speedily read the satellite atmospheric images and learned that the thickening flurries outside heralded the arrival of a severe snowstorm. Great. Another difficulty to navigate. He had instructed her to pull up a third screen to monitor sound wave disturbances—and thereby track radar cloaked ships—when Joshua's first, terse words spit through the tiny ear piece. Anya's heart jerked with quick relief. He was alive. And she was following the right network.

"Richert, I just heard from Joshua."

"Repeat everything he says. Leave nothing out."

Anya would not repeat Joshua's code words to their old enemy. But as soon as he said something intelligible, she would. "Wait," she told Richert.

Soon, it was obvious Joshua had set his transmitter on permanent broadcast. And moments later she gasped when the bloodcurdling order came to kill Joshua.

"Repeat, girl!" Richert snapped.

Anya repeated the ensuing conversation as best she could, and felt supreme relief when Joshua was dragged—obviously still alive—into the enemy aircraft. When Joshua gave the new coordinates, she punched them into her navigation system, and was relieved to see she was only seven minutes distant from the location. Should she tell Richert the coordinates? But what if he took the opportunity to shoot down Joshua's forces? On the other hand, what if he joined them in fighting against Onred?

She didn't know what to do. Clouds of snowflakes drove into the windshield, and a faint shudder indicated that the storm winds had arrived.

A few moments later, Belar's words wiped all thoughts of the storm and Joshua's coordinates out of her head. "Our mission is complete, Onred. You can blow up Omsk."

Anya swiftly repeated the message to Richert. "They're going to blow up Omsk!"

But Richert's screen had gone blank. He was gone.

"Enjoy hell," Joshua said, and then sharp static hissed into her ear.

Joshua! What had happened?

Anya zoomed in the radar to magnify the birds swarming upon each other ahead. A faint orange dot separated from the pack and plummeted toward earth. What was that? Or *who* was it?

A sick feeling in Anya's gut made her fingers fly to disengage the navigational autopilot. Gripping the hand controls with trembling fingers, she flew toward the spot where the figure had plummeted. It couldn't be Joshua. It just couldn't be. She couldn't be too late.

He couldn't be dead.

CHAPTER EIGHTEEN

PAIN AND BLACKNESS engulfed Joshua, and a light, filmy weight covered his face. Michael's capsule had worked. The parachute had triggered. It was the only coherent thought that registered through his fog of pain.

Sizzling sounds rent the air. What were they?

Airbirds fighting? Lasers searching the ground—for him?

Joshua opened his eyes. Or had they been open before? He saw only pitch black. Unless he had fallen in a pit, it shouldn't be so dark. These facts gradually seeped into his sluggish mind. His left cheekbone hurt like crazy. So did his right shoulder and knee.

Mind still moving with frustrating slowness, Joshua took inventory of his injuries. His hands were free. The impact must have snapped open his shackles. He flexed each of his limbs. Everything worked.

Something spit and sizzled nearby. It smelled like a burning tree. Onred's lasers had set it on fire. Birds were looking for him. Smothered by this large parachute, it would take only moments to find him.

Joshua clawed the filmy fabric from his face. His shoulder felt like a ball of fire. He ignored it. Fresh, cold air bit into his skin; it was the only indication he was free. The gossamer parachute had not blocked out the light.

He was blind.

Joshua sat up, shoving the chute off the rest of his body. Turning on his good knee, he awkwardly climbed to his feet. His head swam and his brain pulsed in agony. Softly, he swore. He lurched forward. A tree scraped the right side of his face and slammed into his hurt shoulder. Joshua swore again and hung onto the tree, trying to orient himself. Trying to clear his foggy mind and figure out what was going on around him.

He appeared to have landed in a forest. The solar wind of a multitude of flying aircraft ruffled his hair. Snowflakes brushed his cheeks, too. When he concentrated, he also heard the faint whoosh of the swooping aircraft's engines. Laser fire spit and sizzled off a target overhead.

He had to put distance between himself and the parachute. It would give Belar's men a bull's eye to start searching for him. Joshua left the safety of the pine tree and shuffled forward, arms outstretched. His toe stubbed a rock, but he managed to regain his balance before falling.

Air sheeted off an oncoming aircraft. Faint orange entered his right field of vision, and something sizzled. His chute?

For safety's sake, he needed to hide in the forest, but he couldn't see the trees. Frustration mounted, but Joshua ignored the temptation to sink into self-pity. He was alive. He would survive.

Joshua increased his pace, falling more than once, and taking comfort when rough tree bark rammed into his searching hands.

Orange flares grew brighter in his right eye. Those brief flashes also illuminated large, black shadows. Trees. He sought the dark, formless shapes, knowing they were his only, fleeting protection. Belar's men probably tracked his body heat. It was only a matter of time before they found him. He wished he had Anya's heat reflecting tarp.

Anya. The warm thoughts of being in her arms beat away the cold and despair. He imagined a warm fire, and going to her. "Anya," he murmured. He needed to sit and rest. His brain felt fuzzier, and the cold threatened to take over his mind. Combined with shock and unknown injuries, it tempted him to slow down. To rest and take comfort in warm dreams. "Anya," he whispered again.

Behind him, a tree branch splintered. Joshua ordered his sluggish legs to run, and managed a half-jog before he rammed into another tree. He hung onto it, telling himself to wait for another flash so he could see where to go next. The truth was, his energy was ebbing, and fast. He must have an open wound. He must be losing blood.

Joshua ran his hands down his arms and legs, and then stopped below his right thigh. It hurt like the devil beneath his frost stiffened pants and snow wear. Fingers clumsy, he pulled off his belt and cinched it hard above the wound. That should stop the worst of it.

Overhead, brighter orange lit the sky. Joshua pushed on, heading deeper into the forest. The whoosh and spit of laser fire hit the tree behind him. A pine ignited into a towering inferno, pushing Joshua's dim field of vision out a few more meters. The ground appeared fairly level. Dark forest loomed ahead. He ran.

He needed a snow bank to burrow inside, to hide his telltale body heat.

Men's shouts reached his ears. Joshua increased his pace and ordered his lethargic mind to assess the situation. It wasn't hard to reach a conclusion. With airbirds overhead, tracking his heat source and relaying his coordinates to the men on the ground, he didn't stand a chance. He would be lucky to survive another five minutes.

✖ ✱ ✖ ✱✱ ✖ ✱✱ ✖ ✱✱ ✖

Anya's ship flew into the middle of a brilliant, violently explosive air battle before she realized what had happened.

Slow down, Anya.

She cut the throttle to 100 kph, and the abrupt loss of speed felt like hitting a wall. Laser fire spit across her craft's nose. Was it Donetski fire? She *was* flying Onred's airbird. Stormy wind gusts buffeted the bird.

She needed to land. Joshua was down there, just ahead somewhere, according to the radar sighting of the parachuting figure. It had to be him. She felt it in her gut. An airbird shot by her starboard side, and laser fire spattered at her. Panic hit, and she nosed downward at a steep angle. The fire passed over her, but the tree tops rushed closer at an alarming rate. She pulled the nose up, leveling the craft. Her heart felt like it might beat right out of her chest.

"Oh, God help me," she murmured. Anya had never prayed so much in her life as she had in the last twelve hours. Was God listening to her?

Joshua should be just ahead. She'd touched a trace on his falling figure—if it had been him—shortly after she'd spotted it. Thank goodness, Richert had taught her how.

Now she flew under most of the pecking, spitting airbirds. A few, however, flew just above the treetops, shooting fire to the earth—toward the location where Joshua must have fallen.

An airbird bearing Altai's distinctive red lights suddenly cruised alongside her, as if trying to look in her windows. It gave her the creeps. She had no idea what the pilot might be trying to communicate to her. Richert's men must have disconnected it from Altai's main communication channels when they'd tampered with the bird.

She needed to land.

Onred's airbird veered left and joined a pack of others hovering above the forest floor, and creeping forward bits at a time.

They were tracking Joshua.

She had to get in front of them and land. The best place would be somewhere just ahead of where Joshua might be running. The only trouble was, a jagged cliff loomed directly ahead, bordered by tall, thick spruce.

Anya remembered the tunnel in ZCA's hangar. Surely these pines were no closer together than that tunnel. Or maybe they were, but she didn't want to think about it. She had to land now. She had to rescue Joshua before Onred's men killed him.

Reducing her speed to 50 kph, she cut down, speeding through the forest. She swerved between trees, cutting left and right in jerky swoops around half fallen trees. Radar helped. Her eyes frantically searched for a moving shape on the screen. Joshua should be somewhere to her left. There! A hundred meters north, a man-shaped blob moved. Another hundred meters south, three figures converged on the first man. She dodged another tree.

"Now to land this thing." She glanced at the control pad to slow the speed to 10 kph. When she looked back up, a tree branch hit her windshield. The craft spun sideways, hit another tree, flipped over and over and then rammed backward into something hard. Anya flew forward in her seat. Only the harness kept her from tumbling out. She hung upside down.

A tremendous cracking sound rent the air. Anya only had time to cover her head before a pine crashed across her windshield. The ship shuddered, and then was still.

Anya opened her eyes. She was alive. The ship's hull appeared to be intact. But the instrument panel was black.

Joshua.

Anya hit her harness release button and fell onto her hands and knees. She punched the door emergency release handle, and by some miracle, with her help, the buckled door actually slid halfway open. She crawled outside. Near as she could tell, the rear end of the airbird had butted into the cliff, and a tree lay on top of it. It was a wonder the bird hadn't exploded. It was a miracle she wasn't injured or the bird crushed. Or maybe she was critically injured and didn't feel it yet, and was operating on adrenaline.

But at least she could move and think. Anya pulled out her laser, set it to kill, and burrowed under the fallen tree's branches for the open forest.

❈✳❈✳❈✳❈✳❈

The men were closer. Joshua forced himself to run, although he did more falling and crawling than actual running. He swore in fury. He did not want to die like a blind animal, running like a coward from his enemies. Unable to fight.

He ran into another tree. He saw stars...in both eyes now. His head swam. Grogginess threatened to steal his mind.

"*No.*" He lurched on, forcing his legs to move. "Move it, Van Heisman."

"Joshua!"

He shook his head. Knife-like pain stabbed into his skull.

"Joshua, it's Anya." The voice was very near.

Had it come to this? His hand went to his head. "You're not real."

"I am. Come with me. I'll bring you to safety." A gentle hand took his.

His brain felt fuzzy, but the voice sounded like Anya's. Joshua was unable to resist. He followed the apparition called Anya. If he was about to enter heaven, he didn't mind. If he could be with Anya, maybe death wouldn't be so bad. Perhaps he could go in peace.

❋✻❋✻❋✻❋✻❋

Anya could not believe that she had found Joshua so fast. God must be smiling down upon them both. She breathed an incredulous prayer of thanks and tugged Joshua through the forest, half-blinded by the thick, driving snow flurries. He stumbled behind her, tripping more than once. Something must be terribly wrong with him, but she didn't have time to figure out what, for the distant snap of branches indicated the enemy soldiers were closing in. They needed to hide, and the only safe place was in the aircraft. Once inside, her thermal tarp could hide their body heat from the airbirds swarming overhead.

Of course, right now they were leaving a broken path that a child could follow. Their only helps were that it was nighttime, and snowing hard. Hopefully, tracking in the dark was not the sharpest skill of the enemy airmen. All the same, she'd need to cover their tracks as best she could.

"Down," she said urgently. "Crawl. Grab my foot and follow me."

Severely injured as he no doubt was, Joshua gamely gripped her foot and slithered with her under the tree branches to the door of the airbird. She helped him inside, and then, after a whisper for him to wait, she grabbed a broken branch and wiggled back under the tree. She swept snow onto their tracks and smoothed them as best she could. Gusts of wind battered snowflakes against her cheeks, and added another tender layer of protection to their path. Five meters of tracks were thinly covered. It would have to do. A muffled expletive drifted to her ears. The airmen were almost upon her. Anya quickly returned to Joshua inside the airbird.

At least with the aircraft upside down and the seats hanging from the ceiling, there was plenty of room for Joshua to lie down. Anya pulled the door just short of clicking closed, careful to make as little sound as possible. The enemy airmen were fewer than twenty meters distant now. She scooted next to Joshua and pulled her tarp over them both.

Joshua smelled of dirt and pine...and blood. But he was alive. His warm breaths touched her cheek, and she felt like weeping from gratitude. Now, if only Onred's men wouldn't find them.

Joshua's rough, gloved hand touched her face. "Are you real?" His voice sounded wondering.

Her fingers closed around his, and unbearable tenderness ached through her. "I am," she whispered. "Now hush, so they don't find us."

Men's voices came.

"He was here. Now he's gone."

Someone cursed.

"Can't disappear into thin air."

"Maybe one of his birds picked him up."

More expletives drifted through the howling wind.

Anya barely dared to breathe. Joshua lay very still, too. His breaths were deep, even, and regular. He had fallen *asleep*. Fear crawled into Anya's gut. Something must be terribly wrong with him. Joshua would never fall asleep on duty.

She pulled off her gloves. Gently, she touched his face, which was angled slightly toward her. His right side seemed fine. She remembered the sharp blast of static, and then the silence when his transmitter had gone dead. His transmitter was clipped to the left side of his collar. The left side of his face was angled downward, toward the floor. She pulled on her glove again, not wanting to wake him. Not with the enemy so close.

But what was wrong with him? Had a laser shot hit his head?

More fear pooled in the pit of Anya's stomach. Men's boots audibly crunched through the snow, very close, now. The tree covered the airbird, for which she was grateful. Had she hidden their path well enough?

God help us.

"Report!"

Boots continued to scrunch through the snow.

"Someone met him. We see two sets of tracks, then they just disappear."

"Roger. Matches our sensors. We tracked two systems of body heat. Both are gone." Another curse. "A bird must have picked them up. Join the air fight. Let's put the fear of God into them."

"I don't know..." A man's rough voice spoke. "I *feel* like they're here. Somewhere close."

Fear slammed into Anya's heart.

"Give us five more minutes."

"Roger."

Anya bit the inside of her lip, straining her ears to filter out the rising wind to hear the sounds the men made.

"This tree...just came down. Fresh break. See?"

"What's on the other side?"

Anya closed her eyes and prayed harder than she had ever done in her life.

"These branches poke like a son-of-a..." A muffled expletive.

"Can't see..."

A tinny voice said, "Report to your ship. We need you in the air. *Now.*"

"Roger, Rivner."

The footsteps and voices receded. Anya drew a deep, shaky sigh of relief.

It was a miracle. *Thank you, God.*

All the same, Anya lay very still for a long time, just to make sure that no one had lingered behind to try to trap them. But except for the whistling wind, the forest was silent. Overhead, airbirds streaked, splitting the air with muted shrieks, and spitting weaponry. Eventually, she crawled over to securely shut the door. The bird was insulated, and with the thermal tarp and their insulated snow wear, they shouldn't freeze to death. She wondered who was winning the air battle. No one had spoken in her earpiece since Joshua's transmitter had gone silent.

Awkwardly, she pulled the phone from her pocket and switched to the text channel. A few messages, written in orange light, glowed on the screen.

Where's Joshua?

His transmitter is blocking the voice channel.

Belar is dead. His ship is dust.

Fight to the death.

Anya realized that Joshua's transmitter must still be on, and broadcasting on the voice channel. She needed to turn it off. The fighting men could communicate much easier by voice. Going up on one elbow, her fingers slid up the lapel of Joshua's jacket, searching for the collar. The rectangular metal piece was still clipped in place, and although it felt intact, it must be internally damaged. She lifted the edge. Pulling off her glove with her teeth, her fingernail searched for the permabattery. The round nodule slid into her palm, and her hand quickly fisted to catch the precious piece. If it still worked, it could be a valuable commodity later. After tucking it in her pocket, she pulled on her glove and typed a message into the phone for Joshua's men.

"Joshua alive. Transmitter off. Send help when can." After signing her digital signature code, she sent the message. Somehow, the tarp had slipped down to her shoulders. She pulled it back up.

"Why are the seats on the ceiling?" Joshua's voice startled her.

He was awake again. She drew a small breath of relief. "Crash landing. I flew here. Flying was okay, but the landing wasn't so great. I'd have done better without a whole forest in the way."

Joshua huffed out a quiet chuckle. "You never...fail to surprise me." Silence ticked by. "The men are gone. What happened?"

"They think an airbird picked you up."

Another moment elapsed. "I must have passed out."

Urgently, Anya whispered, "Where are you injured? How badly are you hurt?"

"I'd rather not think about it." The tiniest grunt escaped his lips.

He was severely injured. She had to find the medical kit, and a flashlight. She went up on her knees and crawled the length of the craft, searching for her bag or the kit. She found one near the nose, the other near the tail section. After dragging both to Joshua's feet, she sat up, tarp tented over her head, and clicked on a flashlight.

"What hurts worst?"

"My leg," Joshua muttered.

Anya spotted the belt around his thigh, and the blood darkening the fabric. Swiftly, she pulled the medical wand from the kit, along with assorted other supplies. Then she carefully cut the pant leg and snow wear above the tightly cinched belt, then carefully released the buckle. The snow wear stuck to his leg. Swallowing back a sick pull of nausea, she murmured, "This will hurt. I'm sorry."

"Do it. Don't worry." Just like him; always encouraging. Always trying to reassure her, even though pulling the fabric from the wound would likely feel like she peeled the skin right off his leg.

"I'm sorry," she whispered, and swiftly did what she had to do.

His only reaction was a swiftly indrawn breath and the click of clenched teeth.

"It's a big gash, and a deep puncture wound." She didn't mention it was bleeding like the proverbial stuck pig now, either. The quick flow of deep red scared her. It was too much, too quick. He must have already lost a lot of blood. She set the wand to "cauterize," and set it on high. After one long, distressing minute, the blood flow ceased, and the blood thickened to a thin skin over the wound. It would need to be treated every fifteen minutes for the next hour for best healing. She found a bit of thermal cloth in the kit and wrapped it around his leg to keep out the biting cold.

"Now what?" she said.

"My shoulder hurts, but I don't think it's bad." His voice was fainter than she liked. It might be from the pain, but more likely from blood loss. She pulled a flat, rectangular vital meter from the kit and pressed it into the skin beneath his jaw. Joshua's eyes were shut, his skin tinged gray.

The vital meter said what she'd thought. His blood pressure was low, and he'd lost over two liters of blood. Thankfully, the medical kit carried a blood generator. The instructions were written on the front. Touching the test strip to a bit of blood at Joshua's thigh, the machine read the blood composite and a green light indicated it was ready. Anya punched in the volume needed, and swiftly stripped Joshua's coat, shirt and snow wear from one arm, and then attached the flat, rectangular generator with the hard back and soft bag closest to his arm.

The bottom half was black plastic, and was supposed to be positioned in the crook of his elbow. Sensors would find the vein and insert a fine needle. She attached it securely, then hit the start button. Relief hit her when the green light indicated a vein had been found. A hum indicated that the blood Joshua needed was beginning to be manufactured.

She draped his clothes back over his chest and zipped them all shut to keep his body heat inside.

She caught Joshua's faint grin. "What?"

"You're a good nurse," he mumbled.

While attaching the blood generator, she had taken a quick look at his shoulder. It appeared bruised, but that seemed to be the worst of it, unless he'd torn ligaments. If that was the case, she could do nothing about that here.

"Thanks. Now let me see your face." She trained the flashlight on his jaw. Although the bright light shone into his dark eyes, they didn't blink. Obediently, he turned his jaw, and she drew in a sharp breath. A black burn mark scorched his left cheek, fanning to the corner of his eye, and stopped a centimeter short of his mouth.

"That bad?"

"Oh, Joshua." She bit her lip. Bracingly, she told him, "You'll be fine. It's not too deep. It won't leave a scar." She pulled out the medical wand again and set it high, to "third degree burn," just to err on the side of caution. Cool white light wafted over the charred skin.

"Feels...good," he murmured.

"You've never said that to me before," she teased.

A lopsided smile edged up. "How's...your arm?"

"Fine. Two more applications should do it."

"Treat it next." A hint of the old Joshua came through in that faint command, and it made her smile.

"Yes, sir." After she treated his cheek for as long as she dared, she swiftly treated her own wound. As she'd thought, it was much better. In fact, the dead, black skin flaked off in the first second, leaving behind new, pink skin. She brushed off the burned flakes and set the wand to "finish healing." "It's done," she announced, zipping up again.

A faint twitch of his lips was his only response. His eyes were closed, and his skin had taken on a greenish cast.

"The new blood is making you feel sick," she guessed.

He didn't answer, but just tightened his lips.

"Lie still. You'll feel better soon." She didn't know if this was true, but she'd done all she could for now. She closed the kit and stretched out next to him, wanting to comfort him, but also needing the solid feel of his body next to hers to assure her that he was still alive and, if not well, at least on the road to recovery. He would mend, as long as they weren't interrupted.

It occurred to her that if Onred's men couldn't find them, Joshua's couldn't, either. She could relay their coordinates, if she knew them. Maybe Michael's phone had GPS built in and Donetski forces could lock into that signal and find them. Maybe she could send an SOS. But the air fight still went on overhead. Surely they would contact her via text or voice when they were ready to find them. Anya was suddenly tired, and tucked her head up against Joshua's shoulder.

Maybe a few minutes of rest would do them both some good.

Joshua's hand unexpectedly touched her cheek, and stroked into her hair. Contented, she closed her eyes. This was where she wanted to be, always. By his side. She had forgiven his manipulative kisses back in Tash. She understood why he had done it, and while she didn't agree with his methods, or his decision to lock her in the room, she understood his heart. He had wanted to protect her. When he got better, however, a serious discussion would be in order.

Surely now he would agree that she must be a part of the mission. She would stay on the frontline of the war until both Donetsk Territory and her family were free.

After a few minutes, his fingers stilled and slid down to rest on her jaw. Anya let him rest, but she could not sleep. The spitting, exploding air fight continued overhead. Worry about the fate of Omsk and her family overwhelmed her. Before now, she'd been so busy with the mission that she'd had little time to worry. Now, it consumed her thoughts. Over and over again, her mind turned from Omsk to her siblings...especially Marli's tear stained face when Anya had left Astana. What was Onred doing to her, and to the others? Had the extraction team managed to rescue them yet? Her circling worries always ended with Joshua.

When fifteen minutes had passed, she clicked on the flashlight and treated his leg wound again, and then directed the light to his face. His eyes were open, but he didn't blink when the light accidentally shone into them. In fact, the dark gaze appeared strangely blank.

"Joshua?" She passed a hand across his eyes. He didn't follow the movement. Fear struck her heart. "*Joshua,*" she whispered. "What's wrong?"

CHAPTER NINETEEN

"I'M BLIND," he said quietly.

"You're *blind?*" With horror, Anya noted the way the burn marks fanned toward his left eye.

"Shine the light in my face again."

Anya did so.

"I can see light and shadows in my right eye, but my left..." he paused. "It's black, except for white sparks."

Anya recalled her duty and ran the healing wand over the burn marks. Impotent frustration welled within her. She wished she could heal his eyes, and the damage below the skin; perhaps even in his brain. "Your eye doesn't look damaged." Her voice came out level, for which she was grateful.

Joshua gave another lopsided smile; probably because the nerves on the left side of his face were damaged, she realized now. "Laser fried my brain. I'm lucky I can think."

"Was it set to kill?"

"Blue. Maybe green. He must have powered it down in the aircraft."

Yellow could short out the bird, if it hit the wrong circuit. Blue equaled stun. Green an exponent more. Anya thought about the guards she had shot. Her father had taught her that blue laser injuries could recover in fifteen minutes. But he hadn't mentioned brain shots. Or green laser fire. And she estimated Joshua had parachuted from the airbird at least fifty minutes ago.

"Maybe your nerves are stunned," she suggested. "It was a shock. Maybe they're inflamed."

"That would be the best case scenario."

Joshua couldn't be permanently blind. He just couldn't. "You'll be fine," she told him, swallowing the quiver in her voice. "But you need to rest. Try to sleep, if you can." At least he was alive. He still possessed his right mind. He could still command, as Baron of Donetsk.

He fell silent again, and long minutes passed. A tiny vibration from Michael's phone made her haul it from her pocket.

Text scrolled. "We're retreating. Will return. Ten casualties. J Okay?"

Anya typed back. "Yes. Have Michael's phone. Track his GPS."

"Roger."

"Omsk?" Anya wondered.

"Richert's missile intercepted. O consolidating forces. Out."

Feeling relieved, Anya pushed the phone back in her pocket. "Thank goodness."

"What?" Joshua murmured.

Anya relayed the new information. "Richert saved Omsk."

Joshua lay silently for a few moments. "So. He's taken sides."

"Do you trust him now?"

"Richert does nothing without a purpose."

"You mean he did it to strengthen his strategic position."

"Onred is a threat. Richert wants him cut out. Once he's defeated, Richert will show his true hand."

"I wonder how the extraction team is doing."

"It might be hours before we hear."

Anya checked her watch. "Time to treat your wounds again." Switching on the flashlight, she tended his leg. A firm scab covered the wound now. She set the wand to "deep" and stimulated the cells at deeper levels so they would replicate even faster. An artery needed to heal. So did muscle and skin, before Joshua could move far. To be on the safe side, he needed continuous treatment for the next few hours.

She trained the light on Joshua's cheek again. It was too soon to see healing. Unfortunately, she'd have to wait at least an hour before applying another treatment. Fewer cells needed to be regenerated, and they were all near the surface. They required periods of rest before being re-stimulated. Her glance went to his dark eyes. They seemed to be looking at her.

"Can you see me?"

Joshua gave a lopsided smile. "My right eye can see the shape of your head. And your hair." He raised his hand, and his fingers touched a wavy strand at her cheek.

Anya smiled, holding very still. "And your left eye?"

"You're a black shadow."

"That's an improvement."

When his fingers left her skin, Anya felt overwhelmed by the need to fuss over him. "Are you warm enough? Can I do something to make you feel more comfortable?"

"Lie down, Anya. Rest. When we're found, we'll need to get right back into the thick of battle."

"We?" She smiled. "You mean you'll let me join the battle?"

"I can't seem to keep you out."

It wasn't a promise, nor a complete answer. She said, "I belong with you, Joshua. I want to fight to free our people. And, like you, if that means death, then so be it."

"Rest, Anya." His voice was husky. "Lie by my side until we have to fight the real world again."

It was enough for now.

Anya stretched out next to him and lay her head against his shoulder. Joshua's hand reached for her own, and his fingers intertwined with hers. It was an uncharacteristic move. With a sigh, she closed her eyes. Although everything in her life was so desperately wrong, she felt a sliver of contentment right now. Joshua had deliberately taken her hand. Did that mean his feelings for her went deeper than he could ever admit? What had he truly felt when he had kissed her in Michael's guest room? Had any of it been real? She drifted into a soft slumber.

❋⁑❋⁑❋⁑❋⁑❋

Anya treated Joshua's wounds countless times during the night. At one point, she removed the generator from his arm, for his blood levels had been replenished, and the gray tinge had left his skin. Joshua slept through most of it. In the dark, early morning hours, she felt satisfied that the wound on his leg was beginning to heal, too. No more text messages arrived on Michael's phone. In exhaustion, she lay her head down again next to her baron and fell asleep.

Dawn filtering through the airbird's windows teased Anya awake. Somehow, the tarp had bunched down around their shoulders, leaving their faces exposed. She wasn't cold, but glanced at Joshua to assess his condition.

The perfectly cut planes of his face were relaxed in sleep. The charred line of his cheek looked awful, but new, pink skin should emerge later today. His tawny hair was rumpled, and his changeable eyes, which always drew her like a magnet, were shut. Had his vision improved? Worry for his eyesight, her siblings, and for her people, vulnerable to Onred's attacks, had eaten away at her all night. Belar was dead. Joshua had escaped. If the extraction team had failed, would Onred take out his fury on her family?

It seemed entirely too peaceful and quiet in the aircraft, compared to what her loved ones must be going through, if the extraction team had failed. But she couldn't think like that. At least Richert had saved Omsk from Onred's thermonuclear bomb. A big victory against Onred, for which she was grateful. Was Richert truly an ally they could trust now?

She went up on one elbow and gazed intently at Joshua. What was his big plan to save Donetsk Territory? For she felt certain he had one, although he hadn't confided it in her. He had told Richert that he'd planned three levels of assassination. Belar was gone. Onred and his first-in-command, Yegor, remained, unless the extraction team had managed to kill them both. Anya could only hope for this scenario. If not, her next goal would be to convince Joshua to share the details of his bigger plan, so she could help him achieve it.

Her gaze slipped to Joshua's mouth. His lower lip was cut just a little fuller than his upper. She remembered his kisses in Michael's spare room. Again, she wondered if they had been real on his part. Or merely manipulative? Irrationally, she longed to kiss him again. What would happen if—just for a second—she brushed her lips against his?

If he awoke, would he be shocked? Condemning? Or would he welcome it?

She really should stop staring at him like this.

With a sigh Anya edged back, but unexpectedly, Joshua's hand curved around the back of her neck, preventing her retreat.

"What are you doing?" His eyes gleamed tawny in the dim light.

She swallowed. "Can you see me?"

A long moment passed, and the brown gaze flickered from her eyes to her mouth. "Yes."

"*Joshua.*" Tears of relief sprang to her eyes, but she quickly blinked them back. "With both eyes?"

"Colors are gray in my left. The right is normal."

"Thank goodness." She made another move to retreat, but he still wouldn't let her.

A faint smile touched his mouth—still a bit lopsided. "You haven't explained why you were staring at me."

"I need to monitor your medical condition."

His smile edged up. "What's your assessment?"

Her eyes helplessly lingered on his mouth, and then swept up to his amused, intent gaze.

A bit tartly, she said, "The patient is demanding, and may need to be restrained." When he still wouldn't release her, she said, "Joshua." Instead of sounding reproving, as she had intended, it sounded breathless, and she colored. "Let go."

His fingers fanned out to cup the base of her skull. Soft trepidation built inside her. Joshua fully controlled the moment, as he obviously intended. Anya closed her eyes but, just to set him back a pace, dipped down to kiss him.

She expected surprise. Instead, when his warm lips met hers, Joshua firmly but aggressively commandeered the kiss. A moment later, he teased the seam of her mouth, urging her to open to him. With a shaking breath, Anya surrendered. It wasn't a hard decision. She wanted him so badly that this felt like heaven to her. Slowly, he accepted her invitation, kissing her with exquisite, savagely gentle heat, so that she trembled violently. What was he *doing?* He couldn't possibly...he couldn't possibly *mean* this. Could he?

Anya's senses swam, overloaded, heated and melting into him. This passionate, yet desperately tender kiss was nothing like the controlled Joshua she knew—always restrained, always walking the straight and narrow, always doing the right thing ...and yet it *was* him, fully him, and she helplessly responded to his searing, possessive caresses.

Long, dizzying moments passed, and Anya's heart beat in fast, heavy thumps. She felt like she was drowning in Joshua. In the space of seconds, she wanted more of him—impossibly more. All of her fantasies were coming true, right now.

Did he feel something for her, like she had always hoped? It certainly appeared so...unless this was all a dream. If so, she didn't want to wake up.

Yet how could this possibly be real? In the real world they could not be together. Joshua would lose his baronship. She, her inheritance. They would both be thrown out of the territory forever. What was more, Joshua's first-in-command would become baron if anyone were to see them...fooling around like this. And yet, why would he kiss her now, if he didn't feel *something* for her?

When she made a feeble effort to pull back, Joshua kissed her for another thorough, lingering second. Only then did he release her. His chest rose and fell rapidly, and his eyes burned a hot, tawny color. In a low, uneven tone, he said, "Promise me you will marry no one unworthy of you."

"What?" She blinked to follow his train of thought. "I won't marry. That way you'll stay baron."

"No."

"Yes."

His dark gaze held hers. "I should be dead already. I will probably die today. Promise me you'll marry a worthy man. But not Pete, if you don't mind. He's a hothead."

"I'm not interested in *Pete*." How could he be so obtuse? "I l..."

"Promise me. Consider Birn or Ray." His first and second-in-command. "Or even my brother Michael."

Anya jerked back. "Are you insane? I don't want any of those men. I don't want anyone but..."

"Stop," he said swiftly, and with unequivocal finality. "Promise me you will choose a worthy husband. You will have children and pursue a long and healthy life."

It finally occurred to her what he was doing. He was saying goodbye.

"I'm coming with you, Joshua," she gritted. "You won't lock me out again!"

"When my men come, I'm sending you back to Michael. He'll keep you safe."

"I won't go!" she snapped.

"You will!" His jaw was hard and uncompromising. "Don't fight me again."

She was so angry she wanted to spit. How could they go from lovemaking to fighting in the space of one minute? The hardheaded man—Protector. Baron. *Dictator* was more like it. "I *will* fight you. And you're weak enough now that I would win. In fact, maybe I'll tie *you* up so you'll stay safe."

Anya was flat on her back on the floor before she realized what was happening. Joshua loomed over her, his face frighteningly dark. Her mistaken belief in his weakness died a swift, alarming death. Softly, he said, "Don't argue with me, sweet Anya, or I'll show you the true brute who lives in me."

"You'd never hurt me."

"No. But I could make you hate me. You don't want that."

"I could never hate you."

His gaze, hot now, and dark, grazed down her body. "Yes, you could," he said softly. "How easy it would be for me to ruin your innocent fantasies of me."

Anya wanted to cover her ears. "Stop it." She struggled to get the conversation back on track. "I won't let you die. Donetsk needs you—more than it does me."

"No."

"Yes. And I think Michael would agree with me," she asserted. "You're pig-headed and blind, but maybe together, your brother and I could make you see reason. In fact, I think *you* are the one who needs to be locked up."

He laughed softly, with genuine amusement.

"The territory needs you!" She wanted to slap him. "How can you be so thick-headed? You can threaten and intimidate me, and breathe orders like a dragon, but you can't keep me out of this fight."

"Oh no?" he murmured.

Her heart beat faster. "Get off. You're not a savage, and I am not scared of you."

"You should be," he said softly.

She involuntarily swallowed, finally taking note of the unfamiliar, darkly feral cast of his features. She had never seen Joshua look like this before. "You won't hurt me," she told him again. "You would never hurt me."

But Anya did wonder why he was acting like this. It was as if he wanted to frighten her. But why? Did he want to discourage her feelings for him? Or was something else going on? Was he angry because she refused to stay in the safe, protected box where he wanted to put her? Or was this his means to push her away, because he already regretted their kisses? Hurt flashed, but she stated evenly, "You can't make me hate you."

"You're wrong. Shall I prove it right now?" His head dipped to the side of her neck.

"No." Her heart beat more wildly, confused by the dark, bottomless emotions she sensed in him. Where had they come from? Who was he, truly, this man that she loved?

"Promise me, then." His breath felt warm and thick on her skin, and she shivered.

"No!" Enraged, she spit it at him. "You won't scare me into making promises. Get off me, you big brute!"

With disturbing ease, he stilled her flailing hands with one hand and pinned them to the aircraft floor. "Promise me." His tone was maddeningly conversational, and his breath trickled warm, electrical charges across her skin.

She swallowed, and breathlessly said, "No. I said, get off."

His weight pinned her to the floor now.

"You're not intimidating me," she informed him. "I'm not scared. Now, for the last time, get off."

His lips nuzzled her neck, followed by the barest graze of teeth. Anya went very still and her breaths came even faster. "Joshua, no." He wouldn't hurt her. Would he?

"You see me through rose colored glasses. I am not the man you think I am."

"You are," she insisted. "You're honorable, trustworthy, brave, and..."

"I am *not*. I am not worthy of you. Or the baronship." His head unexpectedly sagged, and his temple pressed into her neck.

Her heart leaped. Was she finally getting through to him? "You are." With no difficulty now, she pulled her hands free and touched his shoulder. The muscles beneath his baron's uniform felt bunched and hard, a testament to the suppressed conflict roiling within him. "Every Donetski respects you. *I* respect you. You're the best baron Donetsk Territory has ever had. You're..."

"A killer. A thief." His soft laugh sounded bitter and grim. He went up on his elbows again. Those dark, unreadable eyes entreated her attention.

Previously, he had told her that he'd been ordered to murder enemy soldiers. But a thief? "No."

"Yes. Don't you know that's why they threw me out of Tash?"

She rallied, "If you stole something, it was for a good reason."

"I stole money to pay for a prostitute."

Anya gasped, then recovered. "You didn't."

"I did. And I've done worse."

She still couldn't believe it. "You didn't steal the money for yourself."

He said nothing.

She was right. He would never do such a lowly thing, and at twelve years old! It was inconceivable. After all, Joshua had said he'd been twelve when he had joined the military. So stealing the money must have happened prior to that. "Who was the money for?"

Joshua heaved a harsh breath. His head unexpectedly dipped closer to hers, so his hair pressed into her cheek. She felt the power of his chest muscles, lightly grazing her breasts, and yet the press of his head into hers felt like a little boy. "Tell me," she said again, but more gently. "Who was it for?"

Joshua said nothing for long minutes, and then heaved himself off to sit beside her. He looked away, out the window. "My father," he said in a barely audible voice.

It was the first time he'd ever spoken to her about his family. And Anya felt horrified. "Your father asked you to steal? Why?"

"So he wouldn't lose his position, if it was found out that he was stealing money."

"What position?"

"He was an elder, and in line for Chief of Tash. He wouldn't dirty his hands, but his children were expendable."

Anya began to see the whole picture, and it chilled her. "You mean he ordered you to steal so he could have prostitutes. What happened if you refused?"

Still staring straight ahead, Joshua raised one brow. "Do you need to ask?"

"Yes. Tell me everything." Softly, she slid a hand across his broad, muscular back, wanting to comfort him, wanting to understand everything about him, but most especially this dark part of his past that she'd never known existed. And yet knowing about it now, certain things began to make sense. Especially the way he held himself back from others—always honorable to a fault—but never willing to get close to anyone. He had set impossibly high standards for himself; this she began to see. Was it his way to try to atone for his past?

Joshua said in a low voice, "He'd beat us, or force us to work in the furnace room all night; sometimes for weeks on end. I tried..." he gave a mirthless smile, "but I couldn't live without sleep. And if I failed at school, the beatings were...bad." Anya suspected that word was an understatement. "Michael was the youngest. I was the oldest. I didn't want Michael or my sisters to grow up like me. I was growing into a soulless wretch. I hated myself, and I hated the world. Every time I stole or lied, a piece of me died."

"Of course it did," she murmured, unable to believe what she was hearing. "You're an honorable man. Stealing and lying and whatever else he made you do must have killed you inside." Anya wanted to wrap her arms around him, but refrained. His posture remained stiff, withdrawn. He was ashamed of his past...and perhaps even unable to see the man he had become.

Joshua swiped a hand across his eyes, and held it there for a brief second. "When I was ten, I told him *I'd* do all the stealing. I told him to leave my sisters and brother out of it. He agreed." A bitter laugh escaped. Joshua's eyes shut and his fist clenched. "I helped him cheat on my mother. I was the reason she died inside, a little more each day."

"Joshua, no!"

"Yes. Yes, I was. When the elders finally caught me and threw me out in the snow, I was relieved. Finally, my miserable, worthless life would end. I only regretted that my sisters and brother would have to take my place." A long pause elapsed. "It turned out I was the lucky one. The military saved me. It disciplined me, and eventually gave me back my self respect."

"Thank goodness." Anya's voice broke with feeling. "Your father was a horrible man." No wonder Joshua had shown no regret that his father was dead. "How lucky you're nothing like him."

Quietly, he said, "I was never meant to become baron, Anya. Your husband will be baron, and that is as it should be. My life is expendable. Yours is not." Intense dark eyes bored into hers. "That is why I will protect you to my dying breath. It is one pledge to your father I will not break."

Implying he had broken others. His kisses, to her? Possibly. In Joshua's honorable mind, those would be a crime. No doubt punishable by death. His own death.

How could she get through to him?

"You are *not* expendable," she told him. "I told you once, and I'll tell you again: You're the best baron Donetsk has ever had. Even better than my father. He was a hard man, and a brutal one, too, sometimes. You have a natural gift for command. All the men respect you. To survive, Donetsk needs *you*."

Whether Joshua realized it or not, he was the glue that had held their whole territory together during the last few years. How could he not see that? Onred knew it. It was why he wanted so desperately to kill him. Once Joshua was dead, and she was gone, the backbone of the territory would disintegrate. She'd heard mutters and rumors of discouragement lately, of a desire for peace at any cost. It was a shortsighted view, of course, and could possibly end in the death of half of her people. Anya would never let that happen. Not if she had any say in the matter.

"It needs you more," he told her.

"I don't think so. But maybe we can agree it needs both of us."

He shook his head.

"Understand one thing, Joshua. No matter what happens, know this now: I will never take the baronship from you. You're the best man for the job. You've earned it, and you deserve it." It was true. It was also true that in order for him to remain baron, she could never marry.

A tortured expression crossed his features. "You deserve children and a husband who loves you."

Anya did not answer. If he could be stubborn, she could be more so. And the truth was, she wanted no man but Joshua. If she couldn't have him, then she wanted no one. She was quite prepared to live the rest of her life alone. "You don't get to choose for me."

"When I'm gone, you will marry." He said it grimly.

"I won't let you die. You know how determined you are to protect me? Well, I'm equally determined to protect you. If it wasn't for me, you would be dead right now."

"I know."

"Then stop fighting me!" she said in exasperation. "Treat me as an equal. I'm going to fight Onred and free my family. Now, I can either do it with you, or I can do it alone. Which do you prefer?"

He pulled free. His gaze flashed a warning. "Don't give me ultimatums."

His hard tone did not deter her. More softly, though, she said, "We both want to defeat Onred, right?"

He did not answer.

Time for a new tactic. "If we don't defeat him, my husband will have no territory to rule." At the word "husband,"

Joshua flinched. Encouraged, she continued. "In which case my birth means nothing. My life means nothing."

Joshua scowled. "An..."

"Let me finish," she said calmly. "Donetskis are my people, too. And my family is at stake. I mean it, Joshua. I would do anything to save them." She crossed her arms and pulled back a little. "Just like I'd do anything to save you."

✖︎✳︎✖︎✳︎✖︎✳︎✖︎✳︎✖︎

Joshua didn't know how to win this argument. In his gut, he knew he'd never keep Anya out of the fight against Onred. She was too spirited, too determined...too smart for her own good.

He didn't like it, and muttered a soft curse under his breath. He wanted to protect her. If he'd had his way, she'd be back at Richert's headquarters now. The man might be a snake, but he wouldn't harm Anya; of this, Joshua felt certain. The cunning old man had plans for her—what, Joshua didn't know yet—but then again, he hadn't intended for her to stay in Tarim long enough to find out.

"What do you say?" Anya regarded him with one dark brow arched. "Will you swear to put me on your team?"

"You have no training."

"I can skyjump. I can shoot a laser. I understand how communication systems work. I can survive in the artic for weeks." She paused, and then finished with a smug note of triumph, "And I'm the bait Onred will take. He wants me. He'll invite me into his palace, into his home, into his..."

Joshua saw red. "*No!*" He raked his fingers through his hair in an effort to obliterate the images that had leaped in living color into his mind.

"I can kill him, Joshua." That feline, confident smile couldn't come from his sweet, innocent Anya.

"*No.*"

A faint frown drew her delicate brows together "Tell me a better plan, then."

"My plans do not include you behaving like a whore."

She scowled. "I won't sleep with him. I'll kill him."

"You will *not* go into Onred's bedroom," he bellowed.

The tiniest smile twitched her lips. "Funny. A few days ago, you ordered me to marry him. Where did you think I would end up?"

He growled, and jerked away from her. "I wish you'd stayed in Aksu." And yet he deserved that barb. He wanted to go outside and pace off his frustration.

"You are so unreasonable," she snapped. "You act like a cave man. This is the fourth millennium, in case you've forgotten. Women can read, write and make decisions about their own lives. We don't need a man's protection. I don't need *your* protection."

"You've forgotten your history. Remember the last millennium? In a barbaric world, only the strong survive. Women were almost wiped out."

"Thanks to terrorist scientists," she agreed. "But they're dead. Things are different now. Protectors and male chauvinism are dead. Join the thirty-second century!"

He shook his head. "I grew up in Tash, and it still lives in the last millennium. So do Donetsk and Tarim Territories. We all live under the Old Barons' Law for a reason. Women must be protected, or they will die. And if you die, our whole race will die."

With a glare, she crossed her arms. "This particular woman's line will die, if a certain man won't give her what she wants."

Heat caught Joshua by surprise. She couldn't possibly mean what his depraved mind instantly imagined. "You don't know what you're saying," he said softly.

"I *do*."

The faint blush on her cheeks disturbed Joshua more deeply than he liked. Time to take command of the situation. Anya would not be deterred, so he'd minimize the collateral damage...meaning no one would ever lay a finger on her. Wherever she went, he would go. Grimly, he reflected that although she didn't want a protector, she had one...for as long as a heart beat in his body.

"You can go on the mission," he gritted. "But you'll do what I say. You'll be my communications officer."

A beatific smile lit her face. "Really?"

"You will obey me," he said through his teeth. "Swear on your honor you'll obey every one of my orders."

The sunny smile did not dim. "Oh Joshua, I will. I promise!" She flung her arms around him and held him tight. "You won't regret it. I promise."

Joshua's arms closed around her slim, fragile body. Regret already pulled at his gut. His arms tightened around her, wanting to protect her. His jaw slid through her clean, sweet smelling hair. "We'll beat Onred," he muttered. "I swear it."

He could not die now. Joshua trusted no one but himself to protect Anya.

CHAPTER TWENTY

AFTER JOSHUA AGREED that Anya could accompany him on the mission to defeat Onred, he seemed to withdraw into himself. When he discovered his transmitter didn't work, Anya handed him Michael's phone, and he texted a message to ZCA. Shortly afterward, he shouldered out of the aircraft and into the crisp white morning.

Fresh snow coated pine branches and softened last night's foot imprints. When Anya followed Joshua outside, her nose hairs stuck together in the frosty dawn. It was cold. Maybe -40° C. The sky was blue, but puffy, dark gray clouds bunched on the eastern horizon. Probably it was the storm that had just left them.

Daylight showed just how lucky her crash landing had been. Joshua examined the crushed rear of the airbird, which was crumpled up against the granite cliff face. A large pine tree pinned the nose to the ground. The bird should be demolished, and yet it wasn't. It was as if the protective, divine hand of providence had curled around the ship, preventing its destruction. In the light of day, Anya marveled at the sheer, crazy stubbornness that had made her pilot the sophisticated craft in the first place. She should be dead, and breathed a prayer of thanks that she wasn't.

The small clearing encircling the airbird's door was completely enclosed by the fallen pine and the cliff; a small, cozy space, and apparently, from Joshua's stiff movements, confining. When he checked the phone again, she said, "When are they coming?"

"An hour."

"I have food. Do you want breakfast?"

Without a word, he followed her inside the aircraft. She divided the rations in equal silence, and they ate. When they finished, she said, "I should check your leg."

"I can do it." He took the healing kit and administered the treatment himself.

It was a rebuff, but she recognized his tactic. She should, for it was a familiar one. He had shut her out. He had done it in Astana, before she'd left for Bogd. And he'd attempted to do it just minutes ago, when he'd tried to put a wall between them and intimidate her into obeying him. Always in the past, when things became too emotional between them—whether she was arguing about a longer curfew, or dating a boy of whom he did not approve—afterwards, Joshua always retreated behind an impenetrable barrier. On the surface, he would return to work. However, usually he'd barely speak to her for a day or more afterward. For the first time, Anya began to understand why.

His childhood had been rough. Certainly, he had received no love from his father. He had taken the role of protector over his younger siblings at a very early age. It appeared his mother had made no effort to protect her children from their father. Had Joshua felt alone as a little boy? Was that why he allowed no one to get too close to him? Was it why he felt he needed to face his enemies alone now? Without a doubt, he felt he needed to prove himself. Perhaps he also felt the need to pay, over and over again, for his past sins—choices that had been forced upon him by a weak, cruel father.

Anya wanted to touch Joshua and reassure him that she would never hurt him. And yet she suspected part of the distance he'd put between them now was a result of anger, and perhaps fear. During the upcoming mission, he would be unable to wholly protect her. She understood his feelings, for the thought of Joshua being hurt—perhaps more severely than last night—scared her to death.

Sharp blasts of static burst from Michael's phone.

"Report," Joshua said tersely.

"Five minutes out. Enemy birds are in the area. Be ready to run."

"Roger."

Swiftly, Anya packed up her bag, tarp, and medical kit and followed Joshua outside, and then shoved the bag under the fallen pine. Joshua took it and helped her through the shallow tunnel through the snow to the other side.

Anya glanced up at the clear blue sky, listening for the slicing *whoosh* of an oncoming airbird. Where were Onred's aircraft? The silence of the still forest around them seemed eerie. As if someone might be watching from beyond the trees.

A high-pitched shriek indicated a bird's fast approach. Anya spotted the dark speck in the southern sky a split second before two black airbirds shot up from the trees. Faint thunder rumbled as they jetted for the incoming aircraft.

"Onred's men," she gasped.

Joshua's expression remained impassive. His gaze swept the northern horizon. Anya followed his line of sight. A sleek, silent airbird approached, flying meters above the tree tops. Blue and cream identified it as one of their own. Within seconds, it dropped into their tiny clearing and hovered above the lumpy snow pack. When the door slid open, Anya sprinted for it. Joshua tumbled inside after her. Even before the door closed, they ascended at stomach emptying velocity and shot north.

"Good to see you alive." Michael rumbled from the pilot's chair.

Joshua slapped his brother's shoulder. "Didn't think anything could get you out of ZCA."

"Only saving your sorry backside." Michael's lips thinned. "Buckle up. We've got company." The aircraft swerved left, and Anya tumbled sideways, slamming her shoulder into the wall.

Joshua's strong hands helped her overcome the G forces of the accelerating aircraft. He saw her settled into the seat behind Michael's before strapping into his own. He directed his words to his brother. "Status on the decoy?"

Michael gave a brief chuckle. "Victor Echo and Yankee Delta are goosing Onred's birds." Faint explosions reached Anya's ears. Grimly, he finished, "The black ones are gone."

"What's the report on the extraction team?"

Michael's fingers swiftly moved over the control board. "Answer my question first. Where are we going?"

"Zyra."

"Zyra?" Anya repeated. "Why?"

"It's closest to Onred's territory." Tersely, Joshua said, "The report, Michael."

"We intercepted garbled messages. Onred must have expected our men. Five birds were shot down crossing the Altai mountains. Three pilots skyjumped onto the city. Two made it inside." Michael spared a backward glance for Anya. "Your family wasn't there. Neither was Onred."

"They weren't?" This news came as an unpleasant shock. "Were the men sure?"

"Positive. Pete broke into Onred's quarters and set up explosives. They got cornered, and the last we heard was static. Satellite shows a big hole in Bogd."

Anya swallowed back a horrified gasp. She fisted her hands, trying to control her emotions. Pete was dead. Just yesterday, he had been happy, teasing, and full of life. Now he was gone.

"They're heroes," Michael stated. "The bomb destroyed Bogd's heating units. The city is freezing. That'll slow them down."

"Earlier, Onred ordered Belar to nuke Omsk," Joshua said. "Any way to trace his transmission?"

"Nope. Tried. He's smart, and routed it through Bogd."

Joshua fell silent.

"My family might still be alive." Anya brushed away welling tears for Pete, and clung to this small hope. "They might still be with Onred."

"Maybe," Michael offered, but Joshua remained silent.

Anya prayed again for her siblings, as she'd repeatedly done over the last twenty-four hours. Where could Onred be? And she offered a prayer for Pete, too. And for the rest of her people, living in the freezing wasteland. What foul plan did

Onred plan to implement next? But the ones in immediate danger were her family, if they were with Onred. They would bear the immediate brunt of his rage over losing Bogd.

Extracting her family from Onred's clutches had seemed like a monumental task from the start. Now it seemed impossible. Where could Onred be hiding?

"How will we ever find them?" she whispered.

The aircraft spun without warning, and Michael's white lasers drilled the sky. Black airbirds peeled east and west. Blue birds followed one, and with a terse word, Michael pursued the other. Within minutes, the black one fell in flames from the sky.

Michael spit, "Onred knows we picked you up."

"Wish we still had that hijacked bird," Anya said. "Maybe we could figure out how to listen in on their transmissions."

"They change frequencies every ten minutes."

"It probably wouldn't have helped, anyway," she said. "I think Richert sabotaged the system."

"What?" Joshua said sharply.

Anya described Richert broadcast while she'd flown the enemy ship. "His techs must have hacked into Altai's communications system."

"Gives us hope," Michael said grimly. "Maybe *he's* following their transmissions."

"We need to contact him," Joshua said.

"How?" Anya wanted to know. "Do we trust him enough to transmit to him over our secure channels?"

Michael barked out a laugh. "Not a chance."

"Onred will intercept if we use the Alpha channel," she pointed out.

"We can't take that chance," Joshua agreed. "We'll use our voice network. I'll warn the commanders it's no longer secure. I'll use your phone, Michael. Anya lifted it from your apartment."

She winced. "Sorry about your door," she said meekly.

"I won't ask." Humor laced Michael's rumble.

"I've got the code to one of Richert's frequencies. Hope it still works," Joshua muttered.

"Put it on speaker when you get through," his brother advised.

Long moments passed, and then Joshua said tersely, "Joshua Van Heisman." Then, "Give me a line to Richert." Frustration deepened his next words. "Yesterday, man. *Now.*"

More silence, then Joshua said, "Richert. Van Heisman."

Static crackled. "You're alive," came Richert's brusque response.

"Thanks for Omsk."

"Now do you trust me?"

When Joshua hesitated, the old man coughed up a chuckle. "Lay your cards on the table, Van Heisman. Our plan still a go?"

"Yes. Like we agreed after breakfast."

"Good. What else?"

"Extraction failed. Onred was probably tipped off. He's in hiding. Anya said your techs compromised the bird's communications system. Any intel to pass along?"

"Word is, Onred's transmitting on Alpha at nine hundred hours." In two hours. "They're scrambling frequencies almost faster than we can keep up. Almost." He gave a dry chuckle.

"We need to find Onred."

"Position yourself as bait. Anya, too. If he wants you bad enough, he'll come get you."

"Our deaths would serve you well." Humor edged Joshua's dry tone.

"Who's in command if I can't talk to you?"

"Birn, Ray, or Michael. Give us one of Tarim's secure channels, and I'll pass those codes to them."

Richert rattled off frequencies and codes so fast Anya wondered how Joshua caught them all. However, his calm, "Got it," reassured her.

"Is this a secure phone?" Richert demanded abruptly.

"Yes."

"We'll analyze Onred's video and pass on our findings to you." He cleared his throat. "How's your military holding up?"

A crafty prodding for delicate information.

Anya glanced over her shoulder and met Joshua's calm, amused gaze. Evenly, he replied, "We're ready to fight."

"Richert out." The line went to static.

Anya smiled. "Can't blame him for trying."

"Convinces me we can't trust him." Joshua switched channels and texted a message—to his commanders, she guessed.

Anya faced forward again. She wasn't sure what to think about her cunning uncle. Joshua was probably right. However, a small part of her actually liked the crotchety old rogue. The discovery surprised her. That same, illogical piece wanted to trust him. After all, he was family. But after pursuing over twenty years of bloody war against her territory, Richert had proven time and again his one true desire; he wanted Donetsk. All of it. Logically, his agenda would never change.

❊⁑❊⁑❊⁑❊⁑❊

Birn, Joshua's first-in-command, met them in the eastern city of Zyra's deserted shuttle bay. The military commander was a tall, bulky man with grizzled black hair and a barrel chest. He wore Donetsk's blue and cream with pride. Two fingers of his left hand were missing, and these were noticeable when he clapped Joshua on the shoulder.

"Glad to see you in one piece."

Joshua's gaze slid to Anya. "Thanks to Anya."

Silver eyes sent her a piercing glance, and then returned to Joshua. Birn's failure to greet her was an insult. Did he think her a coward for fleeing her marriage to Onred? Did he blame her for Astana's destruction? How many others felt the same way?

Guilt settled more heavily upon her shoulders. Although she wanted to cling to Joshua's comforting belief that Onred would have bombed Astana regardless of her marriage plans, in her heart, she agreed with Birn. She was to blame for the thermonuclear strike on Astana. And she didn't see how it could ever be proven differently. Somehow, she had to make things right, at least as much as she could. Less than a week ago, she'd been unwilling to give her life for peace; that was no longer the case. Now she would do anything to secure Donetsk Territory. And if she had to die to gain her people's freedom—it was a sacrifice she was ready and willing to make.

Birn led the way down the hall, still speaking to Joshua. Anya followed beside Michael.

"Richert has pledged to help us," Joshua said. "We'll attack at dusk."

"Good. We'll need it. Last night, Onred bombed three military hangars. At last report, half of our air corps are out of commission."

The two men swerved into a conference room. A handful of decorated military men waited at the oval table.

Ray, Joshua's second-in-command, rose to greet them. He was a tall, bespectacled, fair-haired man, with a gentle demeanor. His intelligence and analytical skill, however, were quietly formidable assets. Few dared argue with him in matters of facts, logic, or science. No one ever beat him in chess.

His long, cool fingers curled around Anya's, and squeezed. She saw no condemnation in his eyes, which comforted her; just sharp, analytical curiosity. "You saved Joshua's life."

"Yes," she admitted. It was a small accolade, compared to the trouble she had caused.

"You'd never piloted a ship before."

"Sometimes I can be impulsive. And headstrong."

His thin lips curved. "An element of chaos can prove quite useful. Please join us."

Great. Now she was the element of chaos. Although Ray had made it sound like a positive quality, she was certain Birn and the others would disagree, if their glacial expressions were any indication. And she didn't blame them. Anya pulled out a chair and sat between Joshua and Michael.

Joshua reported the major events of the last twenty-four hours, and detailed his and Richert's plan to attack Onred's forces at dusk. "I've got frequencies and codes so we can coordinate with Richert's men. I've texted them to your phones."

Ray punched a button on a small, flat computer and a map glowed to life on the conference wall. Upon closer inspection, Anya discovered it was a gigantic, three meter by three meter built-in television monitor. Astana's cities and territory were delineated in blue, Richert's in red, and Onred's in orange.

"Do we focus our attack on their capitol, Bogd?" asked Falcon, one of the older commanders.

"They're licking their wounds. We should finish them off," Birn agreed.

"No." This was from Joshua. "They're vulnerable. They'll be like a mother bear with her cubs. We'll need help."

"Agreed," Ray said. "By my calculations, they'll increase defensive measures by fifty percent."

It was agreed to send three heavy warships to attack Bogd, and enlist more help from Richert. The meeting continued on, and the finer details of airbird and army squadrons assigned to strike each of Onred's cities were decided. Joshua would contact Richert to finalize details of the plan, and to integrate Tarim Territory's massive air defense network with Donetsk's diminished air corps to attack Altai Territory. To Anya's mind, this was all well and good. However, by the time the meeting wound down, no one had spoken of finding her family.

A few men rose, muttering about meeting with troops and giving final instructions. Falcon headed for the door.

"Wait!" Anya exclaimed in frustration. Ten pairs of eyes swiveled in her direction. Birn looked irritated; many of the others, impatient. Joshua's warmer gaze gave her the encouragement to speak. "What about Onred? This war won't end until that snake is dead." Anya could barely believe that now *she* was the one talking about murder.

Calmly, Ray asked, "Do you want to join the assassination team?"

"Yes!"

"No," cut in Joshua.

Turning to him, she said in a low voice, "If my brothers and sisters are alive, they're probably with Onred. I want to be on the rescue team, at the very least. Don't you?"

Curtly, Ray interrupted. "Onred's transmitting. On screen."

The map on the wall dissolved into Onred's grotesquely distorted, gigantic face. He smiled. Each of his glinting teeth looked as large as a skull.

"Citizens of Donetsk, again I come, offering peace. I have called for the surrender of your leaders, but they have refused. Their selfish disregard for your lives does not surprise me. When I win the battle for your territory, you will be grateful to gain a wise ruler. One who puts the needs of his people ahead of his own self interests."

Anya rolled her eyes. For the first time, she wondered if Onred might be a touch insane.

Onred attempted a smile. It looked like a grimace. "In the gentlest way possible, again I urge Joshua and Anya to concede defeat. If not for the benefit of the Donetski people, then perhaps for the lives of the Dubrovnyk children."

Onred's face dissolved into a scene so awful that Anya cried out and fell to her knees in horror. Elise, David, and Marli were in chairs, faces battered, gags filling their widely stretched mouths, wrists bound behind them, and ankles strapped to the chairs. Tears ran down Marli's terrified face. Anya's horrified gaze traveled right, to the worst image of all. Damon cowered on his knees on the floor. Yegor, Onred's first-in-command, gripped him by the hair. As she watched, he jerked Damon forward and sliced an old fashioned machete toward his tender neck.

"*No!*" Anya screamed out.

Onred's chuckle sounded demonic. "Surrender. Or the boy dies. Right now."

Anya gasped. In that moment, her only course of action became clear. She thrust her hand into Joshua's jacket pocket and snatched out Michael's phone. Two finger taps, and she accessed Alpha channel.

"I surrender!" she choked out. "I'll meet you anywhere you want. But if you hurt *any* of them, the deal is off."

CHAPTER TWENTY-ONE

UTTER SILENCE FELL in the conference chamber after Anya's pronouncement.

"You little *fool*," Birn snarled, and lunged for the phone.

Anya scrambled to her feet and backed away, seeking refuge—a safe place to be. Her family! She could think of nothing else.

She bumped into Michael's solid chest and spun away, backing away from the cluster of staring men. Disbelief immobilized Joshua's features, but she didn't care. With shaking hands, she lifted the phone to her lips. "Did you hear me, Onred? I surrender. Let him go. *Now*."

She gazed at the screen. Fear mixed with hope. Yet when Yegor released Damon's hair and her brother hunched forward, unharmed, a tiny cry of relief left her lips.

Onred's enormous face occupied the screen again. "We'll free that one in the wilderness as a sign of good faith." The screen split to reveal Yegor dragging Damon from the room.

"He'll die," Anya gasped. "Give him snow wear."

"*You* bring snow wear," Onred smiled. "We'll release him at these coordinates." Numbers flashed across the bottom of the screen, and in her peripheral vision Joshua and Ray swiftly took note. "You have thirty minutes. If you try to welsh on our deal, Marli will lose her head." The screen turned black.

Anya trembled so hard her teeth chattered. She crossed her arms, unbearably cold. She wanted to cry, but would not.

Could not. Now she had a roomful of angry men she must convince to approve of her plan.

Michael eyed her. "You lost it, little one."

Joshua's silence spoke volumes. A muscle flickered in his jaw.

"I'm going," she said into the silence. "Who'll help me?"

"I will." Birn's caustic statement surprised her.

"Why?"

"You started this mess. You'll end it. My bird will take you to the coordinates."

"Birn," Joshua said in a low, controlled voice. "It's my call. Not yours."

"How about we vote?" Birn retorted.

Joshua's tawny gaze narrowed.

Birn skated insubordination. The big man looked away from Donetsk's baron, his cheeks coloring a little.

"Anya's surrender will end nothing," Ray interposed calmly. "Onred has given us an opportunity, gentlemen. The Dubrovnyk children are within thirty minutes of those coordinates. I've already plotted them in. It narrows their captivity to two cities. Satellite One is watching both. Within minutes, we'll know where they are."

"Onred may be hiding somewhere else. He may not go to the meeting place."

"I'll wear a transponder," Anya said, grasping at Ray's thin straw of support. "You can track me to Onred after I surrender."

"I don't like this." Joshua said through clenched teeth. "It's a trap."

"Of course it's a trap." Anya choked on a laugh. "He's going to capture me. That's what he wants."

"No. He wants your entire family dead. What will stop him from killing both you and Damon, the minute you arrive?"

"But..."

Ruthlessly, Joshua finished, "Then he'll kill Marli, Elise, and David."

"But he...can't," she whispered. And yet, of course Joshua spoke the truth. She put hands to her burning eyes. "What can we do? I can't let them die! I can't!"

"I know." Joshua said gently, and to her surprise, he moved to stand before her. "We'll come up with a plan. Trust me."

"I do trust you. But..."

When she burst into tears, Joshua pulled her into his arms and tucked her up securely against his strong, solid body. His warm lips pressed into her hair. "We'll save them. I promise you, Anya."

She clung to him and struggled to stop crying. She needed a level head. Her siblings needed her to think rationally. She pressed her cheek into Joshua shoulder and, just for a moment, let him be strong for her. Gradually, his strength and confidence of purpose seeped into her. When she looked up, his level, tawny gaze held hers, and hope upheld her spirits. Her rock. Her lion she could always count upon. "I trust you, Joshua," she whispered again. "Tell me what to do to save my family, and I'll do it."

The faintest smile touched his lips, and for an insane moment, Anya thought he just might kiss her. "Good," he murmured.

Michael cleared his throat.

With a guilty start, Anya remembered the others in the room.

Birn scowled at them both. Even Ray's brows had climbed halfway up his high forehead. Hastily, Anya stepped away from her protector. This was the last thing they needed; for Birn and Ray to wrest power from Joshua because of suspected indiscretions with her.

"I'm sorry." Quickly, she wiped her cheeks. "I usually don't fall apart like that. I'm ready to listen to ideas that any of you..." she appealed to all of them, "would like to suggest."

Birn's heavy frown remained, but he said nothing. The men resettled at the table.

"I've got a plan," Michael said. "Now, listen."

CHAPTER TWENTY-TWO

ANYA SAT HUNCHED forward in Falcon's swift warship, hands between her knees. Nerves tightened her muscles. "God help us," she muttered.

Michael's risky plan involved a technological prototype never tested outside of ZCA. He had installed the shield in his airbird two weeks ago, hoping for a chance to test it in the real world.

Now's his big chance, Anya thought grimly. She plucked at her seatbelt's shoulder harness. It felt confining. If only she could pace off her nervous energy. If only Birn had come up with a better plan to finish the coming confrontation.

If only Joshua were here. He had a way of calming her that no one else possessed. Currently, he followed the warship in a standard issue airbird. Both Birn and Ray had vehemently opposed Joshua accompanying the mission. But Joshua had made up his mind; and, as Anya well knew, nothing would sway him from his course. Onred couldn't learn of Joshua's presence, however. If the territory baron managed to kill them both, this war would end now.

"We're here." Falcon tapped buttons above his head and sent her a glance. "Ready?"

Two artillery men flanked Falcon at the helm. Two more covered the rear of the aircraft. They were the best sharp shooters available at short notice.

Anya closed her eyes, trying to calm the knot of fear gnawing in her chest. This mission would be a disaster. She felt it in her gut. Michael's original idea had been good, but the rest of it…no. The horrific endgame plan was Birn's idea. But Joshua had agreed to it. Their alarming orders were to blow up Onred's men and ships once Damon was free. If Yegor was there, as Joshua believed he would be, the second level of assassination would be complete.

And, as a result of their treacherous, double-crossing plan, Onred would murder her siblings. Anya had no doubt about that.

However, her passionate arguments against the plan had been ignored. According to Birn and the other commanders, the Dubrovnyk children were already as good as dead. Onred fully intended to kill them, so Donetsk might as well take out as many Altai men as possible, while they had the chance. Joshua agreed with the last two points, but not the first. He had given orders for an extraction team to fly to Gorno to-night, under cover of the raids, to rescue her siblings.

But they'll be dead by then, Anya thought. Once Falcon killed Onred's men, Onred would murder her siblings right away—and probably on the Alpha channel, for all the world to see. Why would he wait until dusk? Unless he wanted to torture her family still further.

No, Birn's plan would end in certain death for her brothers and sisters—unless she made a move sure to upset every balance of power. This, she planned to do. Joshua would be furious with her yet again.

Tough. He had signed off on the ruthless plan. His decision angered her, even though she knew he believed he was doing the right thing. Well, she disagreed. Someone had to stand up for her family. And maybe her "element of chaos" would prove useful, as Ray had suggested.

Her first goal, however, was to see Damon safely to Michael's airbird. After that, her life would be the only one at stake.

"I'm ready," she told Falcon, and released the confining seatbelt.

"Remember to cut right. Stick close to Michael's bird."

She nodded, and glanced out the window to the scene awaiting her. The cluster of military birds hovered in a small valley. The Altai Mountains—Onred's territory—soared up all around them. Three aircraft faced them, backed by a black warship. Three men stood before them, and one slight figure knelt on the ground. Damon. He wore a T-shirt and shorts, but that was it.

Onred was a monster. Anya spit an angry word between her teeth.

"Be quick," Falcon advised. "Or the boy will lose his feet."

Frostbite. Hypothermia. How long had Damon knelt in the snow? Anger chased off the last of her nerves.

Anya pushed the door release button and jumped down a meter to the soft snow pack. She'd brought snow wear for Damon, including socks, and had packed them in Michael's bird. But she hadn't thought to bring boots. That's because she hadn't known Onred was such a fiend that he'd make a child freeze to death in his bare feet.

Michael's bird hovered twenty meters distant. Even if his technological wonder worked, the next five seconds would prove her most dangerous. Anya darted toward its protective shadow.

Three...two...one.

No laser fire. She had made it.

Onred's men watched her. Although each man wore his hair in a buzz cut and sported a goatee like his foul leader, Onred was not present. That wasn't a surprise. The center man was Yegor—Onred's first-in-command—the one who had held a machete to Damon's neck. So, Joshua had been right. Yegor was here. That would please the men fingering their weapons behind her.

Slowly, she walked forward. Michael's bird kept pace, but Falcon's warship remained stationary.

Yegor raised a hand. "Far enough," he said in a thick accent.

"Release him," Anya ordered.

"Leave the bird. Come closer."

"Not until you release him."

One of the henchmen shoved Damon hard, so he fell face forward into the snow. His wrists were bound, so he could not save himself. Fury knotted in Anya's belly. Slowly, painfully, Damon managed to roll to his knees, and then staggered to his feet. His knees remained partially bent, as if frozen in place. Purple marks underscored his eyes, and blood had frozen in a river from his lip to his throat.

Anya struggled to control her grief and her anger. "Come on, Damon," she called in a firm, encouraging voice. "Come closer, as fast as you can."

Her brother stumbled forward. His feet jarred into the snow, as if walking on deadened stubs. When he had made it halfway to Anya, Yegor shouted, "Stop!"

Damon swayed. His body, except for his battered face, looked the color of a pale, blue ghost.

He was about twelve meters distant from Anya—not close enough to be protected by Michael's ingenious shield. Its range was five meters.

Anya strode fast for Damon. Michael's bird kept pace beside her.

"Stop!" Yegor trained a laser on her.

She dared another small step. Now, seven meters separated Damon from Michael's shield. "Let me help him," she snapped. "He's freezing."

"The bird *stays*." Yegor shouted. All three men trained lasers upon Anya. "You, come forward alone."

She raised a hand to Michael and walked forward four meters. Now three meters separated her from her brother. "Now *he* comes forward," she stated.

The men conferred in low rumbles. Disagreement was clear. In the end, Yegor waved his hand. "Boy. A few more steps."

When Damon was close enough, Anya dared another half step and pulled him into her arms. His cheek against hers felt like ice. Snow wear wouldn't help him now. He needed immediate medical attention. Good thing a doctor flew in Michael's bird.

"Go to the airbird," she murmured in his ear. "No matter what they say, don't stop. Understand?"

"Yeah." It was barely a breath, but it encouraged her.

She directed him behind her. Now, for the tricky part. Falcon wouldn't shoot Yegor until she was safely inside Michael's bird, for no one knew whether Michael's wonder shield would work correctly or not. And yet Anya did not want Yegor dead. His death would mean the deaths of her siblings. Of this, she had no doubt. So she had to save the Altai commander. She needed to get between Yegor and the Donetski air ships' lasers. She had to become a human shield for one of Onred's most despicable men, and she had to surrender now. It was the only way to keep her other siblings alive.

"Stop, boy!" Yegor ordered.

Damon continued to painfully shuffle toward the bird, and Anya remained stationary, waiting for him to get closer. To be fully safe.

"*Stop*. Or we shoot!" Yegor shouted.

Static hissed from the transmitter at Anya's collar. Joshua said, "Get in the bird, Anya."

She didn't answer.

Yegor's enraged gaze latched upon her. "*Dubrovnyk!* Come here. Now. Or we shoot."

"Get into the *bird*, Anya."

It was now or never. Anya drew a fortifying breath, but just as she stepped forward, fire blazed from Falcon's ship. The enemy warship exploded into a giant fireball.

Yegor shouted. Men scrambled and lasers shot from the black beasts. One yellow tongue of flame shot straight for her.

CHAPTER TWENTY-THREE

ANYA DOVE for the ground. Centimeters before her nose, a blue wall of pure energy sizzled skyward, arching into a bubble around Michael's ship. The protective shield darkened and thickened to the consistency of sky blue. She couldn't see through it. Then, slowly, the blue, pulsing field shimmered to nothing. The enemy's laser fire had ceased.

Altai lasers blasted again. Once more, the blue field sparkled into a silent dome over Michael's craft. On her knees now in the cold snow, Anya's mouth opened in silent wonder. Michael's shield seemed to *feed* off of the energy from the enemy laser. Instead of weakening the shield, it appeared to make it stronger. She had never seen such a thing in her life. Of course, shields weren't a new concept, but few could survive repeated laser blasts. And none became stronger.

It was a miracle technology. Michael had installed it in his bird, but who had invented it?

The field faded again.

Joshua ground out, "Get in the bird, Anya." His voice sounded remarkably clear, as if he was right behind her, instead of speaking from the device in her collar. Had the energy field amplified its power?

Anya's gaze remained on the enemy, trying to assess the damage. Onred's men had scattered. One lay dead. Two birds had exploded. But in the sky, black birds advanced, like bees in a swarm. She scrambled to her feet.

Too late to surrender to Yegor. The damage had been done.

"I *said*," Joshua gritted, gripping her arm hard, "get in the bird."

Anya gasped in shock and whirled. Joshua's face looked murderous. Never had she seen him more angry.

He dragged her to Michael's airbird before she could speak. His bird hovered meters behind Michael's. Clearly, Joshua had put himself in danger in order to haul her to safety.

At his forcible shove, she quickly climbed inside the warm bird. Michael greeted her with a frown. The seats had been stripped from the back of his bird, and the floor had been converted into a makeshift bed. The doctor knelt beside Damon, who was already enclosed in a temperature controlled body bag.

Joshua stuck his head inside and addressed his brother. "Does the shield work in the air?"

"Yep."

"Then I'm coming with you. My bird will be toast." Joshua swung inside, and the bird rose at dizzying speed and shot west. Falcon's warship followed.

"Who's dead?" Anya wanted to know.

"Does it matter?" Joshua's opaque, quelling gaze bored right through her.

"Of course it matters! If it's Yegor, Onred will—" her gaze slid to Damon's still form, and her voice lowered, "—*kill* my brother and sisters!"

Joshua moved so fast that he loomed over her within a heartbeat. Face dark with emotion, he gripped her shoulder, hard enough that it hurt. She gasped, frightened by the violence twitching his fingers. Through his teeth, he said, *"Don't you understand?* He'll kill them anyway."

"No, he wouldn't. Not if I went with them."

"Was that your plan?" Fury darkened his eyes to onyx. Like a black hole, no light escaped. "I thought so."

"They didn't shoot me," she cried out. "Don't you see? If they had wanted me dead, they'd have shot both Damon and me. But they didn't. That proves Onred wants me alive."

"And once he has you," he snarled, "he'll kill your family. Then you would be his slave. Forever. Do you understand what that means?"

The bird swerved right, nearly knocking her sideways. "I..."

Abruptly, he released her. His hands were shaking. "You're a *fool*. You can't follow a simple order..."

"You don't care about my family!" she cried out, overcome by rage. "They're expendable to you. They're chess pieces, aren't they? You used Damon to assassinate Yegor. Isn't that right? Tell me. Is Yegor dead?"

"Yes."

Anya put her hands to her face. She was so angry that she wanted to burst into tears, but she did not. Instead, her jaw tightened, and she glared at Joshua. "*You're* the ruler. *You* got your way. Don't attack *me* for wanting to save my family!"

The bird swerved left.

"Uh, kids?" Michael said. "We're in trouble. I need help up here."

Joshua swiftly joined his brother in the cockpit.

Shaking with grief, Anya crawled back to her brother. His eyes were shut, and his skin blue. "How is he?" she whispered to the small, balding doctor.

"Too soon to tell. We need to get him to a medical bay, and now."

"No chance of that," Joshua clipped out. "Falcon went down."

"What happened?"

His jaw clenched.

Michael answered. "Warship shot him down."

Anya glanced outside and gasped. Blue and black airbirds tangled, swooping up and down the mountain faces. Lasers spat like snake's tongues. Donetsk's backup birds, waiting behind the mountain range, must have jetted to meet Onred's forces. Now a hot, savage battle waged.

Joshua muttered to Michael, "Head for Gorno. Can you shake them?"

Anya swiveled her head to listen, spirits rising in hope. Onred held Marli and the others hostage in Gorno.

"We'll give it a go," The big man's fingers sped across the navigation pad. The craft cut downward at a steep angle and only Anya's boots, wedged against the pilot's chair, prevented her from sliding forward. A second later, the craft leveled out and shot forward at dizzying speed. G forces hit like a physical weight against Anya's chest and she fell backward, onto her spine. Swiftly, she pushed up onto her elbows again. They shot for a dark, narrow canyon. Bristly pines bordered the narrow space, and far below, a ribbon of water shimmered.

"We've got a tail." Sliding to his knees, Joshua took over the weapons panel. Video feed revealed two airbirds on their tail, growing larger every minute. The back window afforded Anya the same view—only the black birds looked scarier at full size.

Yellow lasers licked from the lead Altai craft, and Michael's blue shield shimmered into place. "Found a problem," that man muttered. "I can't see when they shoot at max power. The shield gets too thick. I'm flying by instruments, bro. Get them off my tail."

"Mark when you turn off the shield, and I'll fire."

The blue shield shimmered and faded, looking like dancing, sparkling sunrays.

"Three, two, one...Now!" Michael said.

White lasers shot from the rear of Michael's airbird. A black bird exploded in midair.

"Gotcha," Joshua muttered.

One strike! Anya could not believe that one blast had destroyed the enemy bird. All aircraft, from her father's old lectures, could withstand at least two laser hits before shields failed.

"Shield up," Michael said.

Fire spit from the remaining bird. Tense moments later, that enemy craft combusted into a black, smoking ball of scrap, too, and hurtled down toward the water, far below.

"Bogey above us." Joshua switched controls to fire overhead lasers. He swore. "They're all *over* the place."

Suddenly, an enemy swooped ahead of them and jetted straight for Michael's ship, firing all lasers. The blue shield darkened to midnight blue. Michael shot skyward. The shield faded, then darkened again.

Michael swore.

Concentration hardened Joshua's features. "On my mark, lower the shield. Three, two...one." White lasers spit at the same time they took a hit. The whole ship shuddered.

"Another one down."

"The shield's damaged," Michael reported. "Here comes another one."

Anya clung to a safety handle as the craft jerked and swerved. Her stomach lurched with each violent movement. Their shield held, but appeared to be a lighter blue than before. Three black birds pursued them.

"We've got to lose... *What the...*"

Another bird appeared.

Now Joshua swore. "The canyon's skin tight ahead. They want to box us in."

"Why? And how?" Anya dared to ask. She felt sick to her stomach from the violent motions.

"They'll fire everything they've got. Michael, will the shield hold?"

"It'll short."

"On my mark, go vertical at Mach one. Then lower the shield."

"Okaaay, big brother. You're the boss."

Did Joshua want Michael to lower the shields while all four birds fired on them? "Joshua, that's crazy," Anya gasped.

Tight lipped, he said, "You haven't cornered the market on chaos."

Was that a compliment? If so, it frightened her. On second thought, the birds swooping into position—one behind, one ahead, one below and one above them—scared her much more. The black beasts jetted in with blinding swiftness. Lasers spit, and all went blue.

The ship hummed and crackled. Random numbers and shorting images flickered across the console.

"Now!"

The ship shot skyward. A jolt hit, and the ship spun like a drunken man. Joshua hunched over the weapons console.

Simultaneous explosions sounded both above and below them.

A grim smile twitched Joshua's lips. "Got them all."

Michael's tight lips told another story. "We're going down. Brace for impact."

CHAPTER TWENTY-FOUR

MICHAEL'S AIRBIRD STUTTERED and fell.

Anya closed her eyes and incoherently prayed.

Long seconds later the craft jerked up, as if punched by a giant fist, lurched forward, and then dropped more dizzying meters. Anya longed for a seatbelt—although what good that would do when they shattered into a thousand pieces, she wasn't certain. She hung on tight to the safety handle, trying to stay in one place.

"Take the helm," Michael told Joshua. "I'm going into the engine."

Joshua's brother ducked down and ripped off the front control panel. He muttered, "Reroute...energy from shield reservoir to main steering..."

Anya hoped Michael knew what he was doing. He was a fine pilot, and obviously an equally fine commander of ZCA...but was he an aircraft mechanic, too? Then she remembered that he had installed the new shield in the airbird. And what about the electronics scraps she had seen in his spare room in Tash?

It was difficult, however, to think long about the mysteries of Joshua's brother when they'd soon be smashed to smithereens.

The ship's lurches deteriorated into long, sickening plunges. Joshua's firm, steady hand on the controls kept them clear of the cliff faces, but gravity was a master no control could deny.

"Sweet mother of God," muttered Dr. Spalding. Sweat shone on his bald crown.

Damon mercifully appeared unconscious.

"We've got ten seconds, Michael," Joshua warned.

The swiftly rushing river grew larger and larger. White capped rivulets foamed, devouring boulders like rabid dogs. It couldn't be a nice, soft pond upon which they were about to land. Oh, no. Instead, white river rapids with boulders the size of warships.

"Five, four..."

Anya's life flashed before her eyes. Her family, her parents...and Joshua. Always Joshua. Even when he made her mad enough to spit, she loved him. She would always love him. Now, as he wrestled with the ship, his hair glowed tawny in the sunlight streaming through the windshield, his face drawn into grim lines of pure determination. If she had to die, it would be looking at the man she loved.

God, please forgive me for my sins. Take us to be with you...

"Got it!" Michael said in triumph. Power surged through the bird and Joshua pulled up the bird's nose as it shot forward. Its belly skated the swift flowing skin of the river. Boulders, like an obstacle course, hurtled toward them.

The ship rose, but not nearly fast enough. How could they ever...

With swift dexterity, Joshua steered the ship through the maze of boulders. All the while, the bird climbed, bit by bit, until suddenly, just as they faced the largest boulder of all, they skimmed clear and soared skyward.

"Thank God," said the doctor.

"Amen," Joshua agreed.

Michael went back on his heels. "We're good for another ten kilometers. I need to give this ship an overhaul before we head back."

"We're not heading back," Joshua said. "We'll milk this flight to a hundred kilometers, if we can. Then you'll fix the bird while I go to Gorno."

Michael's sable brows rose. "Whatever you say."

Anya cleared her throat, still amazed and grateful that they were alive. "Just so it's clear," she said. "I'm going with you, Joshua."

Dark eyes met hers. "Yes, you are. Because I can't trust you to stay where you belong."

His words evaporated her relief at being alive as effectively as cold water slapped in her face. "We need to have a discussion," she returned coolly. "Before we go to Gorno."

Michael made an "Uh oh" sound under his breath.

Joshua's gaze lingered on her for another moment, and then returned to the controls. "Ten minutes to Gorno."

Anya spent those ten minutes rehearsing exactly what she would say to her dictatorial protector.

✖✱✖✱✖✱✖✱✖

When they were twenty-five kilometers shy of Gorno, Joshua drove the airbird down below the tree line in order to try to camouflage their position from the satellites. As he whipped between pine trees, Anya remembered how difficult it had been for her to navigate through a forest. Of course, she had utterly failed. Success required fierce concentration and flawless reflexes. Michael seemed content to let Joshua steer his ship, and she now understood why Joshua had been given top honors as a pilot. He possessed nerves of steel and faultless technical skill. He also appeared to possess the fearless edge of a daredevil.

The ship glided to rest in a dark glen overshadowed by thick trees. Meters distant, the mountain steeply sloped downhill. Gorno was five kilometers distant, and just before they landed, she had glimpsed its silver, flat dome beyond the trees.

"It's just after twelve," Joshua said. "We attack at dusk. If we're not back by twenty one hundred hours, fly back to Zyra."

"Nope," Michael said. "Won't think like that. When you're ready to escape, hit your transponder's emergency button. It'll transmit your location. I can be there in minutes."

The doctor spoke. "Damon could die if we wait too long."

Both Joshua and Michael turned to Anya.

It was up to her. If she said the word, Michael would return to the safety of Zyra. But that course of action would jeopardize the lives of her other siblings. She touched her brother's cool skin. "Damon would want us to rescue the others. He'd never abandon a fight."

Joshua's smile almost softened her heart toward him. Almost. "I agree," he said. "Michael, if you haven't heard from us by dawn, head home."

Michael grinned, but did not answer.

Joshua's eyes rolled skyward. "Insubordination everywhere I look."

"If we're in danger, we'll move. Otherwise, I'll stick close for as long as I can. I won't leave you alone in that devil's city."

Joshua gripped his brother's shoulder. "You turned out all right."

"Maybe I had a good example."

Joshua glanced at Anya. "Ready?"

At her nod, he slung a pack on his back and the door slid open. He jumped down into the deep, powdery snow, and his gloved hand steadied her as she jumped out, too. The door slid shut.

They were alone in the silent forest.

"Come on." Joshua headed at a fast clip down the slope. Pine trees dotted the pristine white landscape.

"We need a sled," Anya said. "It would be a lot quicker."

He glanced at his handheld computer. Sunlight revealed the raw, black burn mark slicing down the left side of his face. It still looked awful, although she knew it had been treated in Zyra. Hopefully, it would be better soon. "Satellite shows a cliff a kilometer east. Sledding is not a good idea." After checking more images, he shoved it into his coat pocket.

Although Joshua had done a remarkable job piloting the bird, she couldn't help but ask, "How is your eye?"

"Pretty clear. But colors are faded in the left one."

"That's good." Improving. She was glad.

They walked in silence. It didn't feel like a friendly silence, however. Unresolved issues festered between them.

Better to discuss them now, Anya reasoned, so they could focus on their mission later. Hopefully, their "discussion" wouldn't deteriorate matters still further.

She followed behind him, walking in his deep footprints. They hugged the tree line of the pines as much as possible. Although it would be difficult to carry on an argument with the back of Joshua's parka, she said, "Tell me what you're thinking."

Their feet swished and clumped through deep snow.

Shortly, Joshua said, "You don't want to know."

"You're mad I planned to surrender to Yegor."

"I'm angry you won't follow orders."

"Onred released Damon in good faith. We killed Yegor. We ended negotiations before they could begin."

"*Negotiations* would not have saved your family."

"So you say. I think differently."

"As a soldier, you follow orders. You don't *think*."

Anya gasped. "I am not a soldier."

"That's clear."

She snapped, "I'm not brain dead, either. Birn's plan seemed stupid. To him, my family was expendable. He was wrong. You're both wrong."

Joshua abruptly stopped and faced her. She staggered to a stop, just shy of plowing into him.

His hand on her elbow steadied her. "You'd be dead now if you had surrendered to Yegor." Fire gleamed in the topaz gaze.

"So you say," she scoffed.

"So I *know*." His grip tightened. "I know those men. Yegor loved to torture prisoners." At her small gasp, he smiled thinly. "Didn't know that? Yes, Anya. I might, as a *soldier* and baron, know a few things you don't."

"I want to protect my family. I would do anything..."

"And Onred knows that. He's playing you. He dangles hope like a carrot, knowing you'll bite. You let your heart rule you."

Anya wrenched her arm free. "Well, that's better than being cold and analytical, like you."

"I am not..."

"You are! You're supposed to be our protector. But you think my brother and sisters are expendable, don't you?"

"No."

"*Yes.*"

"No!" Through his teeth, he said, "I hate this just as much as you do."

"And yet you ordered the attack on Yegor!" Her voice rose. "You knew full well that would enrage Onred. He's already threatened to..." She drew a gasping breath, unable to say aloud what Onred had threatened to do to Marli. In a thin, furious voice, she pressed on, "But that didn't stop you! Not for one second. Because you've got a heart of *ice*. You're rigid and inflexible and have a conniption fit whenever I disobey you. You know why? Because you're a control freak. *Joshua Van Heisman,*" she mocked. "The mighty baron of Donetsk. Heaven help *anyone* who steps on your..."

"Shut up," he ground out. His fingers bit into her shoulder. It hurt. Even through the snow gear.

Tears smarted her eyes. "You're bigger than me. You're stronger than me. Is this how you'll subdue me, Joshua? By brute strength? Since you don't want to hear the truth, you'll strong arm me into being quiet?"

"No. Would you just..."

"I hate you!" Overcome by the violence of her emotions, she shoved him, hard. Eyes flaring wide in surprise, Joshua toppled backward. Unfortunately, since he still had a grip on her shoulder, she went with him. Anya ate a mouthful of snow, and ice plowed inside her nostrils. She elbowed up, snorting free of the cold, suffocating powder. She'd landed half on and half off of Joshua. He was buried so deep he looked like a sunken snow angel. Shock still registered on his face.

Hot emotion shook through her. Tears burned, but Anya wouldn't cry. She hated arguing with Joshua. But he refused to see her as an adult. He still wanted her to blindly obey him, like a child. Or a soldier. Whether he liked it or not, she was neither. She had a mind of her own. And he wasn't always right. Her planned marriage to Onred was a case in point.

Anya levered herself completely on top of him, deciding to take advantage of her brief moment of control over him. She gazed down into his dark, stormy brown eyes.

"Joshua." She drew a breath. "I hate this. I hate arguing with you. But I will never be a soldier. Not ever. I want to do what's right. I want to help you. But my family is in danger. They come first. Before my life. Before your orders. Don't you see? I love them."

"I love them, too." To her complete surprise, his snowy hand lifted, and then gently cupped her cheek. "But *you*..." He heaved a deep breath.

Her breath caught. "Joshua..."

"Listen," he said gruffly. "When I knew you meant to surrender to them, I lost my head. I can't lose you. I would do anything to save *you*. Do you understand that?"

"Yes." Could he possibly...? "Joshua..."

"Shh." His snow encrusted glove brushed across her lips. "I'm sorry about your family. I truly am. But Onred will never release them. That's a fact. They may still be alive—but not for much longer. That's why we're here now. I'm going to rescue them, if I can."

Her heart melted a little more. Joshua loved her family. That's why he was here. Maybe he wasn't as hard and cold as she had declared.

"Listen, Anya. If we hadn't fired on Yegor first, the Altai would have destroyed us. I'm certain Onred ordered them to annihilate us. It's how he operates. We were lucky to escape with Damon."

Anya finally began to understand Joshua's point of view. "I see," she said faintly. Onred did plan to kill her family, whether she surrendered or not. "I should have listened to you. But I was desperate to find a way—any way—to save my family. I didn't want to believe... I'm sorry."

"Will you trust me?"

She had been foolish not to trust him. If she had truly listened to him from the beginning, her harebrained surrender plan would never have formed.

"Yes. I will."

"Good," he murmured. His hand slid behind her neck, and he drew her down to him. She surrendered utterly when his warm, firm lips parted beneath her own. His kiss threatened to steal her soul.

By the time Joshua released her, Anya felt quite warm, lying in the snow with him. Color washed his good cheekbone. His lips lifted in a faint smile, "We'd better go, or I might keep you here until dusk."

She blushed. "That is not appropriate talk, Baron."

He pushed a wisp of hair behind her ear. "Then get off me. We've got a mission to accomplish."

She gave a tiny gasp. "Like I'm the one holding us up!" Well, maybe she had been. Anya rolled off and offered him a helping hand out of the snow bed. Then she swiped snow off his back and broad shoulders until he tramped forward, leaving her behind.

"Another two hours to Gorno," he reported. "Maybe more, depending on the climb down the cliff."

"How will we get inside?"

"I have a few ideas."

CHAPTER TWENTY-FIVE

JOSHUA, IN TRUTH, had very few ideas about how to get inside Gorno. As a pilot, he had often screamed into battle at Mach 1, with all guns blazing. Sometimes as baron he flew by the seat of his pants, too. Amazingly, it usually worked out. However, he preferred to have backup plans. Not much chance of those now. Formulating a plan B, let alone a plan C, when plan A seemed near impossible, was out of the question.

He slogged through the deep snow, breaking an easier path for Anya, and trying to forget the kisses they had shared. Those had been a mistake. Correction. The kisses in Tash had been his first mistake. What had he been thinking? Their intimacy was a taste of what he'd always longed for—the desire to love her. Now he would have to pay the price for that joy, for it was getting harder and harder to keep his hands off of her. Somehow, he had to find the strength to resist what his whole body and soul had desperately craved for so long.

He forced his mind back to the battle ahead.

It was amazing how easy it had been to slip back into the role of military pilot. Fighting Onred's birds had felt good, as if he'd only taken a moment's hiatus from battle, rather than twelve years. Would it be so bad to lose his baronship, and be expelled from Donetsk to become a pilot—a civilian pilot—in another territory, in order to gain Anya as his own?

His hungry mind again slipped back, reliving their shared passion. Even his soul, which he had long ago thought dead, had come alive, deeply longing for the love he felt in her arms. He wanted a lifetime to love her. He wanted it with a fierce, almost frightening intensity.

But that selfish course of action would destroy her. She'd lose her home and her inheritance. The Dubrovnyks, after two centuries of power, would lose all rights to rule in Donetsk Territory. He would not allow that to happen.

It may be a moot point, anyway. By this time tomorrow, he could be dead. His mission, above all, was to protect Anya and rescue her family. And defeat Onred. He burned for the opportunity to kill that depraved devil with his bare hands. Then he could die a happy man.

Joshua glanced back at Anya. His gut tightened. Maybe not. He was a selfish man. He suspected she loved him. She'd almost told him twice, but he wouldn't allow her to say it. He couldn't allow himself to believe it. And if he didn't know for a fact that she'd follow him on her own, he wouldn't have allowed her to be here now. Better to keep an eye on her, and keep her safe. He'd lay down his life to do so.

Richert's ideas had given him hope. But if he couldn't make things legal and right between himself and Anya, so his passion for her would not destroy her...

Joshua gritted his jaw, and struggled to ignore the pain ripping like claws through his soul. If he couldn't...

To protect her, he'd have to find the strength to walk away.

✳❋✳❋✳❋✳❋✳

Anya and Joshua managed to skirt the cliff face, but the topmost, rocky path down to the canyon floor, where Gorno's base was located, was slick in places, and treacherous. The flat, silver dome of Gorno loomed around the next jut of the mountain.

The canyon toward which they descended now was narrow—perhaps half a kilometer wide, if that—and deeply shadowed. Higher mountains reared on the opposite side. In school, Anya had learned that all of Onred's territory was mountainous. No wonder he lusted for their open land. Even worse, this valley appeared ill-suited for greenhouses. The sun would be lucky to penetrate to the canyon floor for an hour each day. Where *did* Onred keep his greenhouses? Or did he import goods from the east? That would be expensive.

The sun slid behind thick gray clouds as they left behind the steep, rocky cliff face and cut into the fragrant pine forest, trying to avoid Onred's surveillance systems. So far, Joshua's computer had picked up the infrared detectors, and they had skirted them successfully.

"I've been meaning to ask you something," Anya said. Her legs ached from plowing through the deep snow, but she ignored the discomfort. "The lasers on Michael's bird shot white fire. Onred's birds exploded on the first hit. Why?"

"Michael's lasers are prototypes. They're ten times more lethal than ordinary lasers."

Anya gasped. "*Ten* times?"

Joshua grunted an affirmation and ducked under a pine branch. Keeping close to the trees helped hide their footprints from scout airbirds. A few flew at intervals overhead, but no one appeared to be looking for them. Yet.

"Why are prototype lasers on Michael's ship?"

"He tests all the prototypes."

She thought about the DiaMoRCs, and Astana's other technological wonders. Slowly, she said, "ZCA is more than your backup command center. Isn't it?"

"Much more. And it's classified. Only my elite pilots know about ZCA. Birn and Ray know it exists, but not its location. It has to stay that way, for security reasons."

"I understand."

Joshua stopped, so she drew level with him. "Do you? Our enemies would kill for the information you know about ZCA."

"But they don't know it exists. Right?"

"Right." He trudged forward again.

"Why don't Ray or Birn know its location? If something happens to you, who will tell them?"

"Michael. Or one of his officers, depending on the situation. ZCA is on a need-to-know basis only."

"How did you build it, then, without anyone learning about it?"

"I selected military engineers and soldiers who have become permanent residents of Tash. The caverns were already there. Michael oversaw the construction. Piece by piece, we put it together."

"So Richert doesn't know it exists, and neither does Onred."

Joshua tossed a brief smile over his shoulder. "*You* didn't, did you?"

"No." What other details about Donetsk did Joshua know? During the last few days she had come to learn so many things about her territory—and about Joshua—that she had never known before. No doubt many more mysteries remained. She wanted to learn them all, by Joshua's side. If only they could survive the hours ahead. If only they could save her family.

"Are we the only extraction team?" she asked after a while.

"No. The others will parachute down after dusk. My job is to deactivate security."

"Then my job will be to find my family."

"We'll look together."

Anya did not reply. Splitting up made more sense to her. Surely they'd find her family faster that way. But she told herself to trust Joshua this time. He was the experienced soldier. If her family could be rescued, Joshua would know best how to accomplish it.

Trees grew sparser and appeared more spindly as they neared the canyon floor, as if the pine needles had been eaten up by a wasting disease. Shadows lengthened and appeared to darken. Maybe it was Anya's imagination, but the closer they came to Gorno, the gloomier it felt. The mountain was silent.

"It's eerie," she whispered to Joshua. "Why is it so quiet?"

"I don't know."

They edged around the last outcropping of mountain and froze.

Gorno's foundation lay before them on a snowy, frozen lake. Its few maintenance shacks appeared closed. No vehicles or humans moved. Steel columns curved skyward, supporting the sky city. The straight column in the center must be the security elevator. Dark red lights under-circled the belly of Gorno, as if it were a giant flying saucer. She whispered to Joshua, "It can't *fly*, can it?"

"No." With a frown, he pulled specialty folding lenses from his pocket and surveyed the snowy lake scene.

"Well?" she whispered.

"It's deserted."

"Where is everyone?"

"I don't know." Joshua looked up. "I see people moving through the windows."

"But no one's guarding the foundation?"

Joshua pulled off the lenses. "My computer is picking up cameras, infrared triggered lasers, and a low-grade shield."

"Like Michael's shield?"

A smile ghosted Joshua's lips. "Not even close."

Anya craned her neck back. Marli, Elise, and David were prisoners up there. Somewhere. "How do we get inside? If we cross that snow pack, we'll be spotted."

"We'll circle around to the other side. Those pine trees are closer to the support beams than we are here. Then we'll slip by the security system and climb inside."

Her eyebrows raised. "So simple," she said in a deadpan tone. "And what do you mean, 'climb inside'?"

Riding the elevator, of course, would be out of the question. Even if they hacked through security, internal cameras would broadcast their arrival.

"Gorno's got step handles riveted to its support beams. They're for maintenance. Astana had them, too."

An interesting fact that Anya had forgotten. Of course, her father had lectured her and Elise all about Astana's safety systems—especially how to call for help, if stranded at the base of Astana. He had never actually suggested climbing the ladders, however, if the elevator was out of service. A daunting endeavor. Gorno must rise at least a kilometer in the air. Normally, heights didn't scare her—at least, not if she had a parachute. Unfortunately, she hadn't packed one today.

She swallowed. "Right. Let's go."

"First, check your laser charge. I've got a few techy treats Michael wants us to share, too." Joshua pulled off his backpack and hunkered down in the black shade of a pine. The sun had already slipped behind the western mountain, and arctic cold bit into Anya's skin.

Her laser charge was fine.

"Motion sensor. Key code hacker." Joshua handed her the items, and she clipped them to her belt. "Flexible hand-cuffs." He gave her two sets.

These looked like loose, plastic shoelaces. She had never seen anything like them before. "How do they work?"

"Stretch them once, and they'll instantly snap back into place. The stretch releases a solidifying enzyme, so when they shrink around the wrists, they harden to the consistency of an airbird's skin."

"Cool. Another one of ZCA's marvels?"

"An old one." Joshua handed her a pack of energy rations and a water flask. Munching, they headed north, to skirt the lake. While few sparse pine trees populated the northern lakeshore, bare branched, thick bushes were plentiful. It wasn't hard to find a sheltered path to the other side of the lake.

Joshua had not removed everything from his pack. It still looked bulky. "What else did Michael give you?"

"Bombs."

Now she wished she hadn't asked. Pete came to mind, and the way his mission had literally blown up in his face. "You won't set those off—not until you're safe, will you?"

He didn't answer.

A sick feeling arose. "*What* exactly is your mission, Joshua?"

"To disable security and rescue your family."

"And?"

"Permanently incapacitate Gorno."

"What does that mean? Will you blow up the whole city? You'd kill all of those people?" Horror mushroomed. Most of the citizens of Gorno, like Astana, were innocents. Women, children, the elderly. "You can't!"

❊**❊**❊**❊**❊

Joshua wasn't surprised that Anya would immediately jump to the conclusion that he was a cold-blooded monster. He had killed the half-unconscious Altai man by the boulder, after Anya had been shot in the Altai attack. She knew he'd been the clean up man for the military. He had killed hundreds of people in his life, and he wasn't proud of it. His soul was blackened, perhaps permanently. But he had never killed an innocent.

Quietly, he reassured her, "I won't. Not if I can help it. I'll plant the charges in their power generation room, and in their computer and communication centers."

Her look of horror faded. He wanted to touch her pale skin and tell her that he didn't want to hurt anyone, ever again. But he was a soldier. War meant death. He would feed her no false promises.

"Good." Anya offered a tremulous smile. Devotion shone in her eyes—and still, hero worship. One day, she would learn that he was only a man, and not worthy of her. Not in the least. But he couldn't disabuse her fantasy now. Strong confidence in him meant belief in herself, and in their mission. That confidence might provide them the razor thin chance to succeed.

This time, he did allow himself to gently stroke her soft cheek. "We'll succeed, Anya."

Her eyes glowed. Softly, she said, "I know."

Even though he was a realist, for a moment Joshua almost believed it himself.

CHAPTER TWENTY-SIX

ANYA AND JOSHUA crouched in the bushes. The maintenance shacks were ten meters distant. According to Joshua's computer, a low intensity shield encircled Gorno's foundation, including the Tek-Lite diamonite maintenance structures, which were made of a special blend of silicon and steel. Rodent and rabbit corpses lay scattered on the ground, clearly marking the energy field's invisible, electrical line.

It was so quiet. No one seemed to be about, which seemed strange to Anya. And yet, if everything in Gorno was running smoothly, why would crews sit in the cold maintenance shacks?

"Maybe it's a holiday," she whispered.

He grunted. "They know something's going to happen, so they've hunkered into their city to wait."

"Where are their military hangars?"

"To the north. Richert's men will attack there first."

"Maybe we should wait until dusk to break in. It's only another hour. The air battle would camouflage our entry."

"We'll wait thirty more minutes. That'll give us half an hour to get up the ladder. I'd like to time our break-in to Gorno with the first attack."

With a nod, Anya fell silent.

"Stay here. I'll find the source of that energy shield." Computer in hand, Joshua crouch-walked south.

Anya stared up at Gorno's giant, curving steel stalks. What would it be like to climb so high? What obstacles would they meet at the top? How could they possibly break into Gorno?

Her thoughts returned to more imminent problems. How would they breach the deadly energy shield? A stiff, dead rabbit lay nearby, its spine unnaturally arched; a testament that it had died in terrible pain. Even if they did manage to breach the shield, how could they climb up the steel beams without being detected? Surely cameras swept every centimeter of this foundation. Not to mention the hidden lasers primed to fire when infrared sensors were triggered.

Joshua returned. His faint smile lifted her spirits. "I accessed their wireless network."

"What do you mean?" Anya peered over his shoulder. A multitude of pictures edged his computer's main screen.

"Each of these," he tapped the pictures, "are cameras. I can copy the feed, then send a subroutine to each camera, looping the new feed. The cameras will only 'see' what I send them. They won't see us at all."

"Great. But what about the infrared sensors and the shield?"

"I've mapped out a path around and under the sensors. It's logged into my computer's grid, and locked in by GPS. The computer will help us each step of the way. The shield is more tricky. I'll need to disable it for a few seconds. That will probably trigger an alarm."

Any alarm sent to Gorno would likely send down droves of soldiers. Especially if they were on tenterhooks already, waiting for an attack. There had to be another way.

Her gaze returned to the poor, dead rabbit. She said, "Instead of turning off the shield, could we break through it somehow? Or would it kill us?"

"Full strength would kill us. Why?"

"I know breaking through would probably trigger an alarm, too. But the Altai may not find that alarm suspicious. Rabbits hit the shield all the time. Maybe we could trick the cameras when they check. We could send a feed of two new dead rabbits. Security might believe they tried to break through, instead of humans."

"Good idea." His fingers flew over the screen. "I could reduce the shield's power. We'd get a shock, but survive. The fluctuation might be noticed, but I'd program it to occur at the same time we dive through. I'll program the new feed for the rabbits to start the same instant. If Onred's men rewind the footage, we might be in trouble. Those rabbits will appear out of nowhere. But it's a chance worth taking."

Anya was pleased that her idea would help the mission.

"I've set up all the new feeds," Joshua muttered. "Now I'll start them. Then we'll need to move the rabbits."

Anya didn't want to touch one of the cold stiffened corpses, but she gamely picked up a grotesquely twisted rabbit by one of its frozen paws while Joshua retrieved another. Consulting his computer, he headed north again, toward the base of Gorno.

"We'll need to toss them in," he said, "because I don't want our footprints to show up on the new camera feed. And we'll need to be careful. The rabbits can't hit the shield, or security will wonder why they don't immediately see the cause on their monitors. I'm already feeding an old loop so they don't spot us. The new feed will take a minute to make."

"You can have the honors." Anya surrendered her rabbit to Joshua, who tossed it with gentle grace toward the invisible shield. A faint sparkle shimmered, but that was it. His next toss was better. The two rabbits lay side by side.

"Now I'll make the new feed..." Long moments passed. "Done. ...Wait a minute." Joshua swiftly pulled his phone from his pocket. "A text from Michael," he reported. "Onred's transmitting on Alpha."

Anya crowded closer to see.

Onred's hated face filled the screen. "Your double-cross has born fruit, Anya. Your sisters and brother have been tortured. They will be executed in two hours. It will be broadcast on Alpha." The scene switched to reveal her three siblings sitting hunched close together, clothes soaking wet, and shoulders shaking with cold. The camera zoomed in on Marli's bruised, tear slick face. Anya gasped aloud. Marli was shorn bald. All of her beautiful blond curls were gone. Elise's white head looked as smooth as an egg, too. Multiple bruises darkened their faces. David still possessed his hair, but his eyes were swollen shut, and his face was a bloody mess.

Anya gasped aloud. "Marli," she choked out. "Elise! David. *Joshua.*"

He pulled her hard into his arms and she buried her face in his shoulder, trying to muffle her sobs, for fear Gorno's sensors would hear her. All the same, she trembled uncontrollably, and soft, mewling sounds tore into Joshua's shoulder. Wordlessly, he held her tighter, his jaw pressed into the side of her head.

Long minutes passed before Anya could control her grief. She pulled back, sniffing softly. Joshua pressed a soft napkin from lunch into her hand, and she blotted her face. Chin trembling, she looked at him.

The hot, savage fire in Joshua's eyes comforted her. Onred would pay for his crimes. Joshua would see to it. They both would see to it.

"Ready?" His voice was level, but the underlying steel and determination strengthened and steadied her like nothing else could. "We'll need to go through together."

Anya's hand curled around his strong one. "Yes." She was ready to rescue her sisters and brother. At last, cold fury trembled through her. She would rescue her family. And if she saw Onred, she would kill him herself.

She glanced skyward. *God help us.*

❋**❋**❋**❋**❋

At a dead run, Joshua and Anya punched through the shield, arms and shoulders first. White hot current licked through Anya's pores. Pain sizzled. A high-pitched buzz filled her brain, and then she was down, cheek squishing into soft snow.

"Come on." Joshua urged her up, and she staggered after him, zigzagging and then ducking and sliding under invisible infrared sensors, plowing toward the steel pillars. The shock didn't seem to have affected Joshua at all. Anya's head vaguely ached. Worse, her thoughts swam like floating, disconnected electrical fragments.

Joshua directed her hand onto a u-shaped rod, which was riveted onto one of Gorno's steel pillars. His fingers curled over hers, securing them in place. "Are you all right?"

When her disoriented gaze met his, Joshua's eyes narrowed. "Take a breath."

She obeyed. Slowly, her disjointed thoughts fused. "I feel funny. Like my hair is standing on end."

He smiled faintly. "It's not. Are you all right?"

"I'll be fine." She hoped.

"You go first. I'll follow, in case you need help."

He didn't believe that she was fine. Maybe that was for the best.

Rung by rung, Anya slowly climbed the pillar. The Alpha video of her beaten, abused family ran over and over through her head, torturing her. What exactly had Onred done to them? Was he torturing them again, even now? Tears blurred her eyes, but she blinked them back. She couldn't think about it. Not now. Marli, Elise, and David would live for two more hours. She and Joshua needed to quickly get inside Gorno and rescue them.

She focused on the long, endless climb. Half a meter separated each metal step. As they climbed higher, the steps curved with the steel beam so they climbed on top of the supporting pillar, rather than hanging below it. After the first ten steps, she refused to look down. Looking up wasn't much better. Gorno looked as distant as the moon.

"You okay?" Joshua asked, when she paused for the third time.

"Fine." Her thoughts had settled, but the jumpy, shaky feeling in her muscles had not improved. Worry and nerves might explain them better than the lingering aftereffects from the shield's shock, however.

"No one's investigated the rabbits. That's a good sign."

"So far, so good," she agreed, and with determination continued her upward climb.

It occurred to her that their progress seemed too easy. Were they being watched? What if Onred's men waited for them at the top, ready to shoot them, or push them a kilometer to their deaths?

With difficulty, Anya pushed those morbid thoughts from her mind.

It grew darker in slow increments. Gorno seemed much larger now. Anya estimated they had climbed halfway. Her hands and arms ached from clenching the steel steps so tightly. Just the thought of looking down made her hands sweat inside her gloves. It dawned on her that Joshua's fake camera feeds would transmit daylight pictures, even though night drew in about them. She mentioned this to him now, as a way to divert her mind from worrying about her family or falling half a kilometer to her death.

"You're right. But security lights just came on at the base." Anya didn't dare look to see. She trusted Joshua on this point. "Even so, the lighting will be wrong. I'm hoping the air fight will distract them."

They had better get up to Gorno fast, then, before the security personnel noticed something amiss, she reasoned. However, it was difficult to increase her speed, for they were climbing over one of the steeper arcs right now. A slip to the right or left, and she'd plunge to her death.

It was hard to avoid looking down while crawling on top of the curving beam. Anya focused on the half meter wide, silver pillar, and refused to look elsewhere. Closing her mind to all distractions, she focused only upon climbing.

Dusk was deepening into night when Joshua said, "We're almost there."

She looked up. The gigantic base of Gorno, perhaps four hundred meters wide, loomed over them. They had been climbing in its black shadow for the past few minutes. Her wrists and fingers ached with fatigue. She hoped they wouldn't have to escape down this ladder with her family.

"The attack should start soon."

Anya glanced up through the deepening blackness, lit only by Gorno's dark red underbelly lights, trying to see where the ladder ended. A pale, spider thin catwalk appeared to branch from the pillar and lead to a landing platform. Were guards awaiting their arrival? Unfortunately, the way the pillar curved, their backs would be to the platform as they approached the top.

She paused, balanced precariously on the step, and fumbled for her laser, clipped to her belt.

Joshua said, "I've got us covered. Keep climbing."

Trembling more than she liked, Anya gladly abandoned the balancing act and gripped the smooth steel step again.

Thirty meters remained... Now ten. Anya craned a glance over her shoulder. The landing platform looked deserted. She caught a glimpse of an elevator door.

The catwalk appeared at eye level. Thank goodness, it had a railing.

It took a good dose of courage to release the safe ladder and reach for the catwalk's railing. Gripping the rail with all of her strength, she took that first, scary step over the ribbon of open space. Heart pounding and arms shaking, she stepped onto the solid, corrugated latticework of the catwalk. Within moments, she reached the deserted platform. Success. One step closer to rescuing her family from Onred's murderous hands.

Tarp covered equipment loomed in the far corners of the landing. Joshua flipped up the corners, assessing the contents beneath.

"Anything useful?" she whispered. Her gaze darted about, searching for cameras. She spotted two above the elevator door. "Joshua!"

"I already looped the feed," he said absently, squatting by a hydraulic lift machine.

"Can that machine help us?"

"Look overhead.

"A trapdoor." It was at least four meters overhead; unreachable from their standpoint.

"It might open up into a maintenance room." He whipped off the tarp. "We'll ride up together, back to back. Be ready to fire when I spring the door."

With a great grunt, Joshua shoved the machine. It slid a few centimeters. Anya joined him. She wasn't sure how much she helped, but within a minute the heavy machine was positioned under the trapdoor. Joshua offered her a hand onto the small platform. "Ready?"

When she nodded, he kicked the machine into gear. With a quiet whine, they rose toward the steel and Tek-Lite crisscrossed underbelly of Gorno. Joshua's toe tap stopped their ascent. He pulled the key code hacker from his belt and inserted it into the trapdoor's key slot. In a moment, it flashed green and he plucked it back out. As the trapdoor slowly tilted open, the hydraulic lift grunted into gear. Light streamed down. A bad sign.

"Hey!" A man's head appeared.

Joshua fired.

The enemy soldier crumpled out of sight. Enemy laser fire shot down, narrowly missing Anya's arm. Behind her, Joshua fired again.

Their heads swiftly cleared the trapdoor. Laser ready, Anya surveyed the room. It appeared to be the security room. In the far corner, a man at the console reached for his weapon. She fired. A burn mark scorched his uniform, but his weapon snapped up, steady in his hands. Laser fire spit over her shoulder, and the man crumpled.

Tersely, Joshua said, "Out. We're clear."

Anya scrambled out. Three dead bodies littered the small room.

"We've got to be fast," Joshua muttered. "They probably tripped the alarm." He stripped off a dead man's uniform shirt and yanked it over his own. Anya did the same, and when Joshua clipped his transmitter to his underlying snow wear, she followed suit.

She reflected that it was a good thing they had worn black pants. Combined with the stolen shirts, they would be able to blend into Altai's military personnel.

"Hide our coats in the closet," Joshua ordered. "If we make it back here, we'll need them." He flipped through the security guard's keycards. "Good," he grunted, and stuffed them in his pocket.

While Joshua swiftly ripped a board from the computer console and inserted a bomb inside, Anya elected to swipe a key set from a dead man, too. It gave her the creeps to touch his still warm body.

Seconds later, Joshua popped the panel back in place. He'd stuffed the remaining bombs inside his shirt, giving him a paunchy look. Anya didn't like the idea of the bombs being so close to his skin. For all intents and purposes, he was a walking suicide bomber, and she didn't like the thought. Especially since she knew Joshua would sacrifice his life if he believed it would save thousands of Donetski lives.

Surely, it would never come to that.

"When will the bomb go off?" she whispered.

"I'll detonate it with the first attack. It's a small electrical bomb, hooked only into the computer system. It should leave the room intact for our escape, if Michael can't get to us."

So, Joshua intended to retreat down the ladder as a last resort. Maybe if they made it back here safely with Marli and the others, Anya would be more grateful than frightened by that prospect.

Boots pounded in the hallway, and Joshua pressed his back to the wall, laser steady in his hand. Onred's men knew they had broken into Gorno. The war had begun.

CHAPTER TWENTY-SEVEN

LIGHTS FLICKERED in the security room, and Anya's gaze found Joshua's. "Were those the first attacks?"

He nodded. Laser at the ready, he held very still, muscular shoulders bunched, prepared to fire.

The door banged open. Joshua shot the first two men who barged through, then he turned into the doorway and shot two more. Anya winged another. Joshua's grunt signaled he'd been hit, but then he was out, moving down the hall before she could ask if he was all right. He shot the man she had winged, and ran down the hall.

Voices sounded behind them, and Joshua turned and fired. Anya did the same, but wasn't as sure of her success. Another man crumpled. An elevator opened, and Joshua shot the military woman who stepped out. Anya gasped, but followed him in. The door silently slid shut.

"Schematics show communications and main security are on the fourth floor. We'll go there next. Command Central is on the sixth." Joshua fingered his small computer, and an explosion rocked the elevator. "First bomb a success," he said grimly. "Disabling Command Central is key, if all else fails. We've got to get our troops in."

"Give me a bomb. I'll help you."

His gaze held hers for a long moment.

"Don't you trust me?" she asked in exasperation. "I can plant a bomb just as well as you can."

"I trust you." He swiftly unbuttoned his shirt. "I'll give you one, just in case we're separated."

"You mean in case something happens to you." Joshua would never voluntarily leave her.

He did not answer, but unstrapped a thin metal box, perhaps three centimeters by four, from his chest. Wires with clips dangled like spider's legs from two ends. He lifted her shirt and unclipped a loop on her utility belt. The belt tugged forward on her hips as he snapped the box securely in place. Odd flutters tickled her belly as his businesslike fingers tucked black plastic gloves in beside the bomb. "Use the gloves," he instructed. "Strip the wires to the main computer. Then attach the clips. See, the top of the box is a timer. It's set for five minutes."

Anya looked down. His strong, tanned fingers still gripped her belt, as if he had every right to touch her and adjust any article of clothing he wished. Her heart beat harder. She struggled to focus on the digital display.

"The white button increases the time," he said. "Black decreases. Red starts the timer. Understand?"

"Yes." She looked up at him, feeling vulnerable. His brown eyes were hard, as if readying for battle, and yet when they met hers, an odd look softened them. A silent heartbeat passed. Slowly, he tugged her forward and he kissed her. The scorching, possessive intensity made her tremble. "Follow my lead," he murmured.

Unable to speak, she nodded, and the elevator doors slid open.

Lights flickered in the hall they entered. People swiftly walked by, ignoring them. Their stolen uniforms were doing the trick.

Anya followed Joshua's swift footsteps down the corridor and then left, down a narrower one. Double doors inscribed with "Communications Center" ended the hallway. A swipe of the key code access card, and the light flashed green.

Joshua shouldered inside as if he belonged there. He shot the security man at the desk. Still moving fast, he strode into a room covered with floor-to-ceiling computer screens. Half a dozen people manned work stations. Three stood up. Surprise registered when they spotted Anya and Joshua.

"Hey," exclaimed a bespectacled man, fumbling with the laser at his belt.

A burly guard in the corner whipped out his laser, but it was too late. Joshua shot him, and then the first man.

Lasers fired toward them, and Joshua ducked behind the wall. Anya knelt behind the dead guard's desk and shot around it.

Two men rushed the desk. Her laser caught one in the chest. Fire sizzled by her hair and burned into her scalp. Anya aimed for the next man's head, and he cried out and sprawled on the floor. Fear didn't even register in Anya, nor did squeamishness at killing another human being. Just survival.

"Security! Code red. Get up here! Two..." A gurgle ended another man's frantic call for help.

Joshua said, "Cover me," and edged into the room, weapon steady. Everyone lay dead.

Anya followed him, feeling sick, keeping an eye on the door they had come in, and searching for another avenue of escape. How many people had they just killed? An exit across the room caught her eye, and she sprinted to it while Joshua ripped off a computer console and clipped in a bomb.

It was a stairwell. Clanging boots pounded upstairs, growing louder by the second. Thinking quickly, Anya ran up one short flight, and then crouched down, just around the corner. A pair of men appeared, backs to her, heading for the door to the communications room. At close range, even with her mediocre laser skills, it was easy to pick off the first man. The second man whirled on her. He got a piece of her sleeve, and pain burned into her arm. Ignoring it, she blasted laser fire into his chest. He tumbled down the stairs. Silence descended in the stairwell. Anya peered around the corner. No more men. She had been lucky; the element of surprise had given her the advantage. A quick glance at her arm assured her it was only a shallow wound. In fact, it barely hurt. Maybe because of the adrenaline charging through her.

She slipped back into the communications room. "The stairs are clear. Hurry."

Joshua didn't answer. All she could see were his shoulders, hunched over the computer. "There." He snapped the console back in place.

Feet sounded in the hallway, and men barreled through the front door.

Anya fired, bursting laser flashes for stronger impact. The first man went down, but the second man ducked and swiveled to shoot Joshua. Joshua disappeared behind the consoles.

Yellow fire spit at Anya and she gasped, realizing she was the only one in plain view.

More feet pounded up the stairs behind her, so she whirled back upstairs and crouched out of sight, like she'd done before. With a cold-blooded efficiency, that on some unspeakable level frightened her, she shot in quick succession all three men barreling up the stairs.

Her hands shook when she lowered the weapon. How many men had she just killed? And where was Joshua?

She peered into the room again and aimed for a flash of black hair and a moving piece of uniform. A muffled curse told her she'd made a hit.

And then more men poured into the room, ten, fifteen... Anya lost count. She winged several, but they flooded the room like a tidal wave. Joshua!

Where was he? And then a black clad soldier jerked Joshua upright, laser pressed into his temple.

Anya gasped. Joshua's dark eyes locked with hers. His message was clear. *Run. Take Command Central.* Gorno's shield must be deactivated, and their computers destroyed, or the rescue mission would fail.

She gazed at him for a long, agonizing moment. She couldn't leave him.

And yet his black expression seared the word, "*Go.*"

"Get her!"

Anya whirled and sprinted up the stairs.

Men pounded after her. She burst out into the fifth floor hallway and wildly looked left and right. Where to go?

A short distance left, a hall branched to the right. She ran for it. It led to an inner corridor, faced by dozens of doors. Frantically, she tried each one as she passed.

Finally, one opened and she burst inside.

A tall, white-haired girl unfolded herself from a round cushion in the middle of the floor and turned to face her.

Emelie! Onred's daughter.

CHAPTER TWENTY-EIGHT

A SWIFT, TERRIBLE IDEA entered Anya's mind. Laser held steadily between her two hands, she advanced into the room. "Hands up where I can see them."

The willowy girl raised them above her head. No expression marked the smooth, oval face.

Anya searched in her belt for the flexible handcuffs. While pulling them free, she darted behind Emelie, yanked the girl's hands down, and secured them behind her back. "To the chair," she ordered. For good measure, she pulled the straight-backed chair to the center of the room, fastened Emelie's legs to it, and tied her hands to the ladder back.

Emelie said nothing, which seemed odd. Anya's breaths came fast, as she tried to get a grip on her emotions, which threatened to explode. *Joshua.* And her family. How would she ever free them now? This girl had to be the key. But how could she use Emelie to her best advantage?

The television screen beeped across the room. What did it mean? Emelie continued to watch Anya, her face a blank mask. It disturbed her.

On a hunch, Anya pulled the phone she'd been given for the mission from her belt and opened Alpha channel. She didn't dare turn on Emelie's television screen, for fear it had a camera imbedded for a return broadcast.

Onred's face filled the small screen. Glee glittered in his slitted eyes. "A choice morsel has fallen into my lap, citizens of Donetsk." The shot cut away to reveal Joshua, being dragged into a room. His shirt had been stripped off to reveal the bombs attached to his chest. Purple bruised his bad eye, and a red line split his charred cheek. Anya swallowed back a cry of horror and instinctively moved behind Emelie, so the girl couldn't see her distress. Men strapped Joshua to a chair. One pulled forward a machine, and still another attached electrodes to Joshua's neck and his chest, too, by snaking them inside of his black snow wear.

Anya put a hand to her mouth to stop a scream. They meant to electrocute him. Torture him. And in the process his bombs might explode.

Onred's face appeared on screen. His smile curdled Anya's soul. "It is simple, Donetsk. Your destruction has begun. I will extract *all* of your secrets from your leader, and then I will kill him. And when I find the lovely Anya Dubrovnyk, who hides within my city, I will kill her, too. Then the war will end." He cackled. "Donetsk Territory is mine."

More lights flickered. The allied attack was well under-way. However, no explosion had sounded from the communications center downstairs. Had the men found Joshua's bomb? It appeared so.

Then how would the extraction team break inside Gorno? Joshua had only disabled a small slice of their inter-nal security. With Gorno's main security still working, and both the communications center and Command Central still going strong, what were their chances of defeating the city?

Next to none. Anya had to find a way to turn off the shields, and to stop all communications between Onred and his fighters. She had to weaken the city's internal defenses so Richert's men and Donetsk's could overtake Gorno. But how?

Joshua had planned to plant a bomb inside Command Central.

Realistically, Anya didn't see how she could possibly take over Command Central alone and plant a bomb. On the other hand, if she could gain access by computer...

Maybe she could figure out a way to disrupt Gorno's communications network.

Her gaze darted about Emelie's small apartment. A door led to a bedroom. The main living area included a dining table and a kitchen. A faint glow, around the corner in the dining nook, caught her eye. Anya hurried to investigate, and her breath caught. Emelie had turned her dining room into a computer station rivaling a small scale ZCA Command Central. She remembered Marli mentioning that only Astana's technological marvels had intrigued Emelie. Now she understood why. The girl must be a computer genius. A full screen wrapped around three walls, and three separate keypads indicated the multipurpose use of the system.

Images flickered on the screens. A quick inspection revealed the system was logged into Gorno's internal networks, too.

Anya smiled. Returning to the living area, she tilted Emelie's chair back and dragged her backwards into the dining nook, so she could keep an eye on her. Then she double-bolted Emelie's front door and settled down at Emelie's central work station.

"Now," she murmured, "let's see what we can find."

✹✺✹✺✹✺✹✺✹

Pain sizzled into Joshua's neck. His muscles convulsed, and he bit back a moan. The sadistic thugs had already jolted him seven times. His skin burned. "Warming you up," said one fiend.

Gray colors swam in his bad eye and his head felt like it was about to explode. In his dim field of vision, Onred appeared, smiling. Joshua wanted to kick in the demon's teeth.

"So," Onred said pleasantly. "I hope you feel warmly welcomed to Gorno."

Joshua didn't bother to answer.

Silence elapsed. "Fine. This might loosen your tongue." Onred passed a small computer screen before Joshua's eyes. His good eye made out Anya's frightened face. "We've captured your girlfriend. She's eagerly awaiting my return."

The words hit Joshua like a punch to the heart. He closed his eyes. And then the picture swam again through his mind's eye. It was Anya, all right. But behind her had been a darkened doorway...and stairs. The picture was shot before she had fled from the communications room. He gritted his teeth. The lying, two-faced cockroach. Onred would take half-truths and feed on Joshua's fears—if Joshua let him.

He needed to retreat inside of his skull, as he had done so long ago...

"You will do as I say," said Onred's hated voice. To Joshua, the words sounded hollow, as if coming from a great distance. Onred's voice merged with his father's. The liar. The manipulating bastard, goading him, forcing him to hurt the ones he loved most. Never again. *Never.*

Pain flicked into Joshua's cheek, and he opened his eyes. Onred glared back. "Enough of the games. I want information. Give it to me, and I'll set your precious Anya free."

Joshua did not respond.

Onred shoved another picture into his face. A blue ball of fire filled the screen. Michael's shield. The picture must have been shot during the air battle in the canyon. Onred said, "The bird is standard issue. The shield, clearly, is not. Who invented it?"

Joshua said nothing.

The territory baron's voice rose. "Who invented it?"

Joshua remained silent. So, he had been right. Onred didn't want greenhouses or land. He wanted Donetsk's technological inventions.

Onred abruptly motioned. Pain, long and intense, burned into Joshua's chest. He couldn't stop his moan, nor, eventually, the saliva that dripped from his bottom lip.

Onred passed the plastic handcuffs before Joshua's bleary eyes. Following these, he held up other technical marvels, all stolen from Joshua's belt. "Who invented these?"

He remained silent.

"*Who invented them?*" Onred screamed.

"Yankee doodle." Joshua chuckled, because suddenly, it was very funny.

Hot pain sizzled into the back of his head. Mercifully, everything went black.

❋❋❋❋❋

Anya pressed her hand to her mouth, choking back cries of horror. She had pulled up Alpha channel shortly after sitting down at Emelie's computer. She had seen every second of Joshua's torture. And now...was he dead? He lay so still. But his chest moved.

Abruptly, the feed went black.

Anya wiped at the tears slipping down her face. She had to do something. Anything, to free him. But what, and how? Hatred for Onred rose like a black virus in her soul. She wanted to rip out his demonic heart with her bare hands. She wanted to hurt him as horribly as he had just hurt Joshua.

Her watery gaze went to Emelie, and a terrible, awful idea entered her mind. She couldn't.

And yet she could.

First, though, while Joshua was safely unconscious, she needed to figure out how to disrupt Gorno's communications systems. Onred would surely wait until Joshua woke up before torturing him again. Her mind replayed Onred's screaming demands. Richert's oblique, sly hints had proven right. Onred wasn't interested in Donetsk's greenhouses at all. He wanted ZCA's inventions; specifically, the name of the inventor responsible for Michael's new shield. It boggled her mind what Onred could do if he gained control of ZCA's brilliant head scientists. She knew Joshua well enough, however, to know that he would die before divulging that information.

Anya spent the next precious minutes delicately probing into Gorno's computer infrastructure. Emelie appeared to have complete access to every detail of Gorno's system, including security cameras in every corner of the city. Amazing. Anya wondered if Onred knew. And she wondered why the girl wanted such wide ranging access. Did she like spying on all of Gorno's operations? Darker ideas entered Anya's head. Did Emelie spy on *people*? Maybe blackmail them? Or did she merely like the power of knowing that she could single-handedly run Gorno? Perhaps even more disturbing, Emelie clearly could undermine all systems from her own workstation.

Might be interesting to investigate Emelie's personal files.

Anya glanced at her watch, and allowed herself one minute. Swiftly, she scanned folders. Nothing. Then she had the bright idea to enable hidden files. One folder popped up, outlined in purple. It was simply named, "Astana."

Heart rate accelerating, Anya clicked on the folder and another single folder appeared, named "Virus." She gasped, mind racing. Michael was right. He had said a computer virus had attacked Astana's satellite and computer systems. It must have infiltrated and disabled Astana's system before her family was abducted. That meant the virus had been planted prior to the kidnapping. It could have lain dormant for days, or weeks...or since Onred and Emelie had visited Astana for the peace talks.

More facts clicked together. Marli had given Emelie tours all over Astana. Emelie had expressed interest in Astana's technological breakthroughs. Just as Onred had now, she realized. Emelie must have seized one of those opportunities to introduce the virus into the computer system. Probably the children's network, which would explain the puzzling fact of why that system had been corrupted.

The virus had been planted while her marriage—and peace—to the Altai baron were being negotiated.

Anya drew an unsteady breath.

From the beginning, Onred had never intended peace. All along, he had meant to destroy Astana. Relief, mixed with a terrible grief gripped Anya's heart. It wasn't her fault. Fleeing her marriage had not caused Astana's destruction. But somehow that knowledge only made the truth seem all the more terrible, because she could have done nothing to stop it. The two-faced Altai leader had planned Astana's destruction from the beginning. The death of her people was written into this computer code.

With a trembling hand, Anya clicked the folder named "Virus." An executable file and a "readme" file appeared. She read the text file, and then closed her eyes in disbelief. The solution to defeating Gorno lay right here, in Emelie's computer.

CHAPTER TWENTY-NINE

"YOU CAN'T DO THAT, you know." Emelie's thin, quiet voice spoke for the first time.

Anya shot her a narrowed glance. "Just watch me."

"He'll kill Joshua. And Marli. And the others."

For the first time, Anya understood what Joshua had faced when he had ordered the hit on Yegor and his warships when they had rescued Damon. Did the good of the many outweigh the needs of the few? In this case, was Gorno's destruction more important than the possible survival of her loved ones?

Anya smiled. It must not have looked like a nice one, for Emelie paled still further. Her dark, heavily outlined eyes looked like coals in her white face. Anya pulled the bomb from her belt. Using her extra set of plastic, stretchable handcuffs, she snapped it onto Emelie's throat. She made sure it wasn't too tight, so the girl could breathe. Horror widened Emelie's eyes.

Anya dragged the girl back into the other room. Conversationally, she said, "Does your father love you, Emelie?"

"I don't know."

The chair stopped with a squeak before a plain white wall. It could be a wall anywhere. Onred would have no clue where his daughter might be.

"When I broadcast, I'll have to gag you," Anya told her.

"I'm not frightened of you." The girl's pale lips pressed tightly together.

"Maybe you should be," she suggested. "Your father is about to kill everyone I love. I would do anything—*anything*—to stop him." And it was true. Anya felt like she stood at the edge of a precipice. What did she have to lose, besides her soul? She would gladly give that in order to save Joshua and her family. She looked steadily into the girl's eyes. "I've already killed six people today. What's one more?" Of course, those were all in self-defense. Not premeditated murder, like this would be.

Emelie's eyes widened. Tears glimmered. "Don't. Please."

"Please?" Anya retreated to the kitchen to find a rag that would serve as a gag. She also found tape, and returned to Onred's daughter. "'Please' goes nowhere with me. You're a murderess. You've killed *thousands* of people. Don't you think you deserve to die?"

"I didn't!" Emelie gulped out. "I didn't mean to."

"You didn't *mean* to?" Anya said in disbelief. "You created the virus. You installed the virus in Astana's computer systems. And somehow you think it's an *accident* that thousands of people died?"

"I knew he'd disable Astana, but not..." Emelie sealed her lips. Her features hardened, as if retreating inside herself.

"You did it all because your daddy asked you to," Anya said in a patronizing tone.

Hatred gleamed in Emelie's eyes, and her lips sealed more firmly.

Anya was suddenly weary and sickened by the hateful cat and mouse game she played with Onred's daughter. Could Emelie possibly be an innocent pawn in Onred's game? Having younger siblings, she could easily see how Onred could plant the idea of making a virus in Emelie's mind. He'd make it sound like a challenging, fun game to a computer genius. He had probably spent extra time with her, encouraging her. The girl may well have lapped up his approving attention.

Or, perhaps Emelie was just as viperous and lying and manipulative as her father. Whatever the case, Anya truly did not want to hurt the girl. Unfortunately, in order for her plan to work, Emelie would need to *think* she would. Therefore, Onred would believe it, too.

"Open up. Time for the gag," she ordered.

When Emelie refused, Anya pulled out her sharpest, most wicked looking knife from her belt.

Tears in her eyes, Emelie obediently bit down on the wash rag.

Anya taped it securely in place. "Good. Now we'll see just how much your father loves you."

✖＊✖＊✖＊✖＊✖

Joshua woke up. He wished he hadn't. His head pounded, and it felt like a thousand needles poked into his skin.

"Call the boss. He's awake."

Joshua slumped, feigning unconsciousness again. He needed time to think, and to plan an escape.

Something sharp poked into his skull, but beyond a faint twitch of his fingers, Joshua did not respond.

"He's out. That last blast would have fried an elephant."

"What, Boss? ...Okay." A telephone beeped. "Tie him up. Take him to the others. He'll execute them all at the same time."

"When?"

"Now. Or as soon as he can set up a camera in the room." A rough chuckle grated.

Electrodes popped from Joshua's body and hard hands shoved him sideways, so he toppled onto the floor. It was hard to stifle his reflex to break the fall, but he managed to land on his good shoulder. Ropes trussed his hands and feet, and men carried him quite a distance. A door opened, and the men heaved Joshua inside. He landed hard on his back, the breath knocked out of him. The door slammed again.

Tentative hands touched his face. "Joshua? Are you alive?"

His eyes slitted against the bright light. "Marli." The little girl's bald head swam into view, then Elise's joined her. "Untie me."

Marli vigorously shook her head. "I can't. They'll kill you. She cast a fearful look over her shoulder. "They're watching," she hissed. "Pretend you're dead."

❊*❊**❊**❊**❊

Anya set her small phone to "video record" and set it on a table facing Emelie. Her stomach churned with distaste for what she was about to do. Murderess or not, Emelie was only a child. Unfortunately, Anya must terrify her.

The camera recorded Emelie's unblinking, wide gaze for a full minute, and then Anya advanced toward her with the frightening knife gripped in her fist. Emelie's eyes grew wider the closer she came, and when Anya grabbed the teenager's hair and pulled her head back, exposing her neck, a muffled cry tore from Emelie's throat. Anya pressed the blade against the tender skin. She felt sickened by her actions, but managed to level a hard glare into the camera.

"I've got your daughter, Onred. If you kill Joshua or any member of my family, I will kill her, just as she, with her computer virus, killed Astana. Listen closely. Bring everyone to the main shuttle bay. I will exchange Emelie for them there. You have fifteen minutes."

She turned off the camera and replayed the video. Good. She would broadcast it on Alpha after she had taken care of a few more details.

Hatred glared from Emelie's black eyes.

Anya smiled grimly. "You were perfect. Now, I've got another present to prepare for your doting father."

Anya retreated to Emelie's computer command center. Following the girl's blessedly explicit installation instructions, she shot a copy of the virus deep into the heart of Gorno's communications system. She shot another into the security network, which would hopefully disable Gorno's shield so the military air strikes could hit their marks, and another into the environmental controls. She would set the detonation timers after she had accomplished a few more tasks.

It helped that all of the systems were wide open to receiving the fake packets of information, thanks to Emelie's full access to the system. She wondered how Emelie had broken Astana's codes and accessed the computer system—although, to a computer genius, hacking them had probably been simple.

It seemed poetic justice to serve the same destruction on Gorno as Emelie and Onred had unleashed upon Astana. And yet the hardest part lay ahead. Rescuing Joshua and her family from execution might well prove impossible. Onred certainly would not release them in the shuttle bay. Of this, she felt certain. However, if she could divert Onred from guessing her true plan, maybe she'd have a chance to rescue them.

She checked the security channels, and accessed every camera feed in Gorno. It took long, nail biting minutes, but finally a picture flickered into place that lifted her spirits. Marli, Elise, David, and Joshua were held captive together in one room. David lay in a fetal position in one corner. Marli and Elise hovered over Joshua, who lay on the floor, too, struggling against his bonds. Why weren't her sisters helping him?

Joshua unexpectedly freed his hands, and then sat up and untied his feet.

Suddenly, Marli whipped a glance over her shoulder. She cried out. Burly men charged into the room. Joshua leaped to his feet, but a blow to his jaw sent him reeling backward before he could straighten. Joshua spun and punched a foot into the man's throat. The guard went down, clutching his neck.

Three more guards rushed into the room. Before Anya's horrified eyes, two men pinned Joshua to the wall and the other punched his defenseless body until his face was battered and bloody. Eyes swollen shut, he slid sideways.

"Stop it!" she screamed. "*Stop it.* Oh, God help him," she whispered.

The guard delivered one final blow to his stomach, and Joshua toppled over, torso twisting at an odd angle against the wall. In the corner, Elise held a weeping Marli. The guards glared at them and stomped out.

Anya pressed her hands to her face, trying to control her sobs. Joshua looked dead. *Oh God.* He couldn't be. He just couldn't be!

She pushed the tears from her eyes, trying to rally concentration and strength of purpose. It was time to move. If ever she could help them, it would be now. Jaw clenched hard, she layered Gorno schematics on top of the holding cell's location. They were on the sixth floor. Air duct schematics offered direct access. She loaded it all into her phone's GPS, and set the timer for the viruses to detonate in one minute.

Last, and finally, she broadcasted her video with Emelie on Alpha.

Before leaving the dining nook, Anya paused, looking back at Emelie's command center. Images already blurred on the screen. The virus, doing it's work?

She would have to leave Emelie here, alone. If Onred's daughter managed to free herself, she might be able to shut down the virus before it had a chance to finish its destructive work. Anya couldn't allow that. But she couldn't stomach shooting the girl, either, even on blue laser.

Holding her weapon steady in both hands, Anya shot yellow fire into each of the three computer consoles. Their screens went black. The virus was already safely embedded deep in Gorno's computer networks. Emelie's computers were no longer needed.

Anya ran from the dining room. Fury and hatred blackened Emelie's gaze. Anya had cut to the girl's heart. Good. She left without a backward glance.

CHAPTER THIRTY

OUT IN THE HALL, Anya swiftly strode for the fire escape stairs. She passed a woman and a man, deep in conversation. Neither paid attention to her, thanks to her fake uniform shirt. Inside the stairwell, she sprinted for the sixth floor. Halfway up, all of the lights blacked out.

The computer virus. Had it already attacked the environmental systems?

Using only the metal rail as a guide, she hurried to the sixth floor landing. Gaining access to a room—any room—was her next goal. From there, she could climb into the air ducts and crawl to the room where Onred held Joshua and her siblings hostage.

She peeked into the hall. Floor lights edged the dim passage. People hurried from one destination to another, talking to one another in agitated murmurs. Anya slipped into the hall and followed a slim, dark-haired woman who held a clipboard. The woman hurried right, down an adjacent corridor. A quick glance at GPS schematics told Anya it led to Command Central.

She smiled grimly to herself. Hopefully, Emelie's virus would wreak more havoc there than a bomb ever could. Anya continued down the passage, matching the hurried pace of the others. Surreptitiously, she tried door handles as she passed. None moved. Finally, she stopped before one that read "Conference Room." She swiped her key card. When it flashed green, she took a page from Joshua's book and strode inside as if she belonged there.

It was dark inside, except for the faint glow of a computer screen imbedded in a conference table at the far end of the room. Unfortunately, three bulky men hunkered over it. Bluish gray computer light illuminated their faces. One man looked up and frowned. He reached for his collar. "Secur..." Anya shot him. He spun left, clutching his shoulder, and sagged in his chair. Impossible to tell if he was dead. Passed out would do well enough for now.

The other men ducked behind the table, and Anya dove behind a chair. Unfortunately, the chair legs provided little protection from the lasers. Fire shot toward her, and she shoved the chair over. The narrow chair back blocked the laser beam. That time. But it provided scant protection for most of her body. She shot at the men's bulky frames. One cried out and clutched his arm. The other fired at Anya again. The laser caught her boot, and for a second it felt like her foot was on fire. She turned her laser on "stream" and swept it under the table, hitting everything in its path. The other man gasped and collapsed sideways. The winged man still moved, but slowly. Anya fired again, and he stopped.

No more time to waste. She leaped onto the conference table. Her computer phone indicated that access to the air ducts should be about...here. She poked the ceiling, and a square of diamonite moved. Swiftly, she rose on her tiptoes and pushed it aside, then grabbed the ledge and swung herself up by her fingertips. Elbows on the steel frame, she hoisted herself up. No air blew in the pitch black vent. The heating systems might already be compromised. She could only hope. Anya switched on the phone's flashlight, replaced the diamonite square, and crawled fast for the holding cell.

A tremendous blast shook the floor beneath her knees, and she crouched lower, trying to keep her balance. Gorno's shield had fallen. Had Richert's warships struck the vulnerable city? Or Donetski airbirds? At this point, she supposed it didn't really matter. All the same, she wished she could see what was going on outside.

Her phone beeped when she was fifty meters from Joshua's holding room. Alpha channel. She kept crawling, but watched the feed.

The shadowy scene made her gasp. A burly man pressed a gleaming knife tip into Marli's neck.

"Surrender now, Anya Dubrovnyk. In the shuttle bay. One minute. Or your sister dies."

The video feed went to static.

Anya crawled faster. The holding cell should be about...here. A narrow grating appeared and she peered through. Her breath caught in horror. Dim emergency lights lit the room. A guard held Marli by the hair, with the knife still poking into her neck. Another man gripped Elise. Both David and Joshua lay sprawled on the floor, unmoving. A third man guarded the closed door, and a camera on a tripod stood beside him, filming the unspeakably ghoulish proceedings.

"Almost time for night-night," crooned the bald bruiser who gripped Marli. Rolls of fat bulged up from the base of his skull. "I'll make it nice and easy on you. Hold still, like a good girl."

Tears streamed down Marli's cheeks. Her eyes looked wild, terrified.

Anya shoved her laser muzzle flush with the grating, hands shaking. Marli's body blocked the man. His face was too near her sister's. How could she get a good shot at him? She wasn't a skilled markswoman. The side profile of Elise's guard, however, was partially exposed. A bigger target to aim for.

"Boss says now."

Marli elbowed the man. He spit a curse.

Anya shot Elise's guard through the grating. He roared in pain. A black, smoking line charred his shirt.

The guard at the door whipped out his laser and Anya squeezed off another round at him. Out of the corner of her eye, Joshua launched himself onto Marli's captor's back.

The guard at the door thunked to the ground, taking the camera with him. Elise fought her guard. When her captor's back turned briefly to Anya, she shot him again. Fire hit his neck. He collapsed on top of Elise.

Marli was now free, and the knife swirled halfway across the floor. The big, bald man shook Joshua, who was on his back, like an angry bear. Joshua hung on, his elbow tight around the man's neck. The bruiser backed up and slammed Joshua against the wall, again and again. Joshua's head hit hard the sixth time. He released the guard, but landed on his feet. The guard spun and his meaty fist connected with Joshua's jaw. It made a horrible, sickening sound. Joshua slid to his knees, but evaded the next punch.

Marli darted into Anya's line of sight. Now Anya couldn't get a good line on the bruiser, who was sure to kill Joshua. She had to get into the room.

Fury mottled the guard's jowled face, and he lunged for Joshua. Joshua rolled sideways, then lunged up and staggered forward, ramming his shoulder into the man's stomach.

Anya scuttled forward, searching for the entry panel into the room. Here. She shoved it aside and dropped almost three meters down, straight into the fray.

Roaring obscenities, the bruiser beat Joshua, who had collapsed to his knees again. Marli had the knife. With wide eyes and shaking hands, she advanced toward the Altai man.

"No, Marli!" Anya shoved her aside. She shot the man point blank in the base of his skull.

"Watch out!" Elise screamed.

Anya spun. A fourth guard, whom she hadn't spotted, smashed a fist into her face, and pain exploded, so hot and black and fierce she couldn't think.

She fell. Then the guard's face twisted like an overwrought cartoon character, and he crumpled to the ground, too. Elise gripped a laser. She must have retrieved it from the dead door guard.

Groggily, Anya sat up. Pain pulsed in her head, making her feel sick. Marli sobbed wildly, struggling to pull the massive man off of Joshua. Elise ran to help, and Anya crawled to do the same.

They rolled the heavy man backward. He was dead. And Joshua...blood covered his face, and he lay unnaturally still.

"Is he dead?" Marli cried out.

Anya pressed shaking fingers into Joshua's warm neck. A faint pulse twitched beneath her fingertips. "He's alive."

"We've got to get out of here," Elise said, her voice high with fright. "More guards will come."

Anya put a hand to her throbbing jaw and looked up at the opening through which she had dropped. Then she glanced about the empty room. "Stack the guards. We'll climb on them, and then crawl out."

"What about David. And Joshua?" Marli whispered. "They're unconscious."

Anya crawled to her brother. Although his face was terribly bruised, his pulse felt stronger than Joshua's. "David." Urgently, she shook his shoulder. "David! We need you."

After an excruciatingly long moment, her brother's eyes opened. They were black, bleary, and unfocused.

"Can you sit up?" Anya said urgently. Under normal circumstances, she would urge him to lie still until a doctor could determine the extent of his injuries. But if he remained here, Onred would kill him. "Come on," she said, pulling his arm. "We're going to escape. We need your help."

David partially sat up, propped up on one arm. His eyes closed, as if dizzy. "How? I...don't think I can walk."

"Can you crawl?"

"Yes. I think...maybe."

"Elise, you go up first," Anya directed. She climbed to her feet and stood still for a moment, feeling disconcertingly woozy. After a few seconds, the worst of it settled. "Marli and I will push David up to you. You'll pull him through."

Elise was a stronger girl than she looked, for all of her slight figure.

Anya boosted Elise up through the opening, and then she and Marli struggled to get their brother up onto the guards' backs.

Anya held him steady while David slowly rose to his feet. "Hold your arms overhead," she instructed. "Elise will help you through. Come on, Marli. One, two, three..." Anya gripped David by the waist and heaved him upward with all of her strength. Marli did the same. Her little face looked grim, teeth gritted, with the strain of trying to lift her big brother.

"I've got him," Elise said.

"I can help," David muttered. He went up on his elbows at the air duct's ledge, and with a combination of Elise pulling under his armpits and Anya and Marli pushing him up by his knees, he went through the opening.

"Now you, Marli." Anya gripped her sister about the thighs and lifted her. She wavered on the guards' backs, trying to keep her balance. Marli swayed.

"You can do it," Elise encouraged, face pinched. Anya teetered. "Got her." Anya steadied when Elise pulled Marli upward. The last she saw were her sister's feet wriggling through the opening.

Now for Joshua. Anya stumbled off of the dead guards and collapsed onto her knees beside him. Gently, fearfully, she touched his battered face. Was he still alive?

His eyelids twitched before she could take his pulse. Relief made her feel weak. "Come on. Time to escape." She tugged at his arm.

His bruised mouth moved. Blood dripped from his split bottom lip. "No."

"We've got to leave *now*," Anya whipped a glance at the door. "Before more guards come."

"No." His voice was weak, but his swollen eyes slitted.

"Joshua *please*," she implored. "We've got to leave now. Can you stand? I'll help you."

"No." His voice was stronger. "I'll...slow you down."

"Don't be a hero." Tears filled her eyes. "We need you, Joshua. Please."

His hand lifted, and then settled like a heavy weight around the back of her neck. A tiny flexion of strength urged her down, closer to him. His breath touched hers. Behind the swollen, bloodshot eyes, she glimpsed tawny fire. Joshua. Her Joshua was alive and well inside of his mangled body.

"I love you, Anya." Gently, he kissed her. "Go. Now."

Her fingers clutched into the solid muscle of his body. She whispered, "I love you, too." Tears welled. "I won't leave without you. Please. Try to come with me."

"No. Go. While...still time."

He clearly could not move, and she didn't have the strength to lift him. She wanted to rage at him to fight...to try. Not to give up. "No. I won't..."

"Go." That low, forceful command silenced her.

Lips quivering, she stared at him.

"Trust me. One...last time. Go."

Biting her lip, she sat back on her heels. He was a stubborn man. He had chosen his fate, and Anya reluctantly understood that she would not be able to change his mind. The least she could do was obey his last wishes.

"I'll take them to safety," she told him. "And then I'll come back for you."

He closed his eyes, but did not answer. Clearly, he believed he would die a battered, broken man in Onred's prison.

"Anya." Marli's small whimper drew her attention. Her sister was afraid. As she should be. More guards would soon discover their escape.

Anya kissed Joshua's temple—the only spot not battered by bruises or blood. "I love you," she repeated. "And I'll be back. I won't leave you here to die."

Joshua did not respond. Was he now unconscious? Anya wished that she and her sisters possessed the strength to lift him into the air vent. But they had barely managed to boost David through the opening. Joshua was much bigger and heavier. She needed help. She would get it, and then she would come back.

Chewing on the inside of her lip to keep back the tears, she grabbed two of the guards' lasers and piled them into Joshua's lap. When Onred's men came, at least he would be able to defend himself. Then she hoisted herself into the air duct.

Before setting the diamonite square back into place, she looked one last time at Joshua, sprawled awkwardly against the wall. She loved him so much. *Oh God, please keep him safe.*

Gently, she replaced the square. Unchecked tears streamed down her cheeks as she led her siblings away from the man she loved. Using her phone as a flashlight, she headed toward the conference room...and ultimately, for access to Gorno's roof.

CHAPTER THIRTY-ONE

TRAVEL IN THE AIR DUCT was slow. Elise whispered that they hadn't eaten in days. David's slow crawl appeared to be fueled by determination alone. Shivers intermittently racked Marli's small body, for her clothes were still damp from Onred's first torture session.

"Just a little further," Anya encouraged, checking her GPS. Her face still hurt from the teeth-rattling punch from the guard. But she did her best to ignore it, and the slightly dizzy feeling that lingered. Soon, they'd need to drop into a room, find an elevator—if they were still working—and take it to the top floor of Gorno. No easy task. She might need to leave her family in the air duct until she could find help.

Had the extraction team landed yet? And what about Michael? If she made it to the roof, he had said she could activate her transponder and he'd arrive within minutes. Of course, an air battle waged outside right now. But Michael possessed his remarkable shield. He'd make it through. Maybe he could help rescue Joshua, too.

A shudder rippled beneath their knees as they crawled.

"What was that?" Marli whispered.

"Our forces and Richert's are attacking Gorno."

"Richert is *helping* us?" David's voice cracked.

"He's on our side. For now." Anya checked her GPS and slowed down. Here was the conference room where she had first accessed the air ducts. Dared she check inside?

Might as well. She lifted a finger to her lips. "Shh. I'm going down. You three stay here. I'm going for help."

Marli clutched her arm. "Don't leave us!" Her whisper verged on hysteria. "Don't, Anya, please!"

Elise's wide eyes looked frightened, too. She clutched Anya's hand. "If something happens to you, we won't know where to go. Don't leave us. I'd rather die with you than stay here."

David asserted, "I can walk."

"And I've still got the guard's laser," Elise said. "Thanks to our father, I'm a good shot."

The idea of taking her frail family through Gorno's dangerous hallways did not seem like a good idea at all. However, with their frightened, pleading eyes staring at her, how could she say 'no'?

"First, I'll make sure the conference room is safe," she compromised. "If it is, we'll all jump inside. From there, we'll take it one step at a time."

Elise nodded, and the others looked relieved.

Anya pried up the diamonite slab and peered into the conference room. All three men lay where she had shot them. Were they dead, or unconscious? Sickness stabbed at her. How many people had she killed today? She swallowed back bile. No time to think about that now. She had to get her family to safety.

Silently, she swung down into the room. "Come on," she whispered, and helped the others down.

Next, she slipped to the door and peered out. Hordes of people swarmed down the hallways. While the uniform shirt Anya wore would help her blend in, she feared her brother and sisters would stand out like sore thumbs. In addition, every Altai citizen must have seen their faces broadcasted on Alpha.

"They'll recognize you," she whispered. "This isn't a good idea."

Three pale, frightened faces looked back at her.

David slowly staggered to the far end of the room, where the men lay. When Anya realized his intent, she ran to help him. The jackets they pulled off the bulky men were too large, but their black color would help her siblings blend in with the Altai people better than the pale clothes they wore now. Marli drowned in her jacket, but Anya directed her to walk tight in between Elise and herself so others wouldn't notice her.

"When we leave, walk straight, and with purpose, like you know where we're going," Anya instructed.

"Where *are* we going?" Marli asked, hugging the jacket tighter around her for warmth.

"The elevator. I'm hoping generators are still powering them. If not, then the stairs." Although she didn't say it, Anya didn't know how her weak family could possibly climb three flights of stairs. She sent up a silent prayer for help. "We need to get to the roof."

David offered a feeble grin. "Think our guys have landed yet?"

"Maybe." Unexpected goose bumps rippled across Anya's skin. The temperature was dropping. It remained to be seen how much destruction Emelie's virus had already wrought in Gorno. "Let's go." Another blast shook the floor beneath their feet.

Making it to the elevator proved to be easy. People ran in the corridors now, as if panicked. And thank goodness, the elevator door opened.

Inside the elevator their lone companion, a woman, stared at them in suspicion. "Hey. Aren't you..."

Elise shot blue fire into her spine. The woman crumpled.

"*Yeah,* sis." David shot a look of respect at Elise.

Slowly, the elevator slid up.

With a sideways glance at Anya, Elise said, "Did Joshua actually kiss you?"

Anya drew a quick breath of surprise. Her sister had seen. The change in her relationship with Joshua must have come as a shock to Elise. Quietly, she admitted, "Yes."

No surprise registered on her sister's face; just a calm, steady knowing. "You'll go back for him."

"Yes."

Marli squeezed her hand. Approval gleamed in her eyes, and David smiled.

Anya smiled back, feeling relieved that her family, at least, supported her heart's choice.

The elevator slid up two floors, and then one more. She sent up another silent prayer of thanks. Things were going so well. Much better than she had anticipated.

With a soft ding, the doors slid open. A tiny gasp escaped Anya's lips.

A solid, impenetrable wall of uniforms blocked their path. Five men trained lasers upon them.

"On the *floor*," shouted the largest one. "Now!"

CHAPTER THIRTY-TWO

AS SOON as the diamonite slab slid back into place overhead, Joshua forced one swollen eye open. His hands curled around the lasers Anya had left in his lap. Slowly, painfully, he pushed himself into a sitting position. Every muscle in his body ached. Images blurred in his left eye, his head pounded, and he felt nauseous.

Making one determined effort, he rolled to his feet.

"Sorry for tricking you, Anya," he muttered, taking stock of his balance and mental acuity. "But I've got one last mission to finish."

Fingers clumsy, he pulled knives and key cards from the guards' belts, and pocketed one of their phones. When he straightened, dizziness and nausea again overwhelmed him. He gritted his teeth and remained stationary until the pounding in his head became tolerable, and then moved forward.

Joshua swiped the key card in the slot, and checked to make sure the lasers were set to kill. Gathering his mental focus, and tensing his body for combat, he jerked open the door.

✖⁎✖⁎✖⁎✖⁎✖

"On the floor!" shouted the red-uniformed man again. "*Now.*"

Richert's men. Tarim soldiers had already infiltrated Gorno. Relief hit Anya, followed swiftly by caution. Just because they were her uncle's men did not mean she could trust them. Richert probably played a game of his own right now. She didn't know what his ultimate goal was, or what he had ordered his men to do to achieve it.

Anya touched Elise's arm, and the two went down flat on the floor, hands on their heads. Marli and David quickly followed their lead.

Hard hands ripped weapons from her belt, and her phone, too.

"I'm Anya Dubrovnyk," she said. "These are the hostages."

"Yeah? We'll see about that." When the man seemed satisfied that she'd hidden no more weapons on her body, he said, "Sit up. Slowly. Hands over your head."

Anya and her siblings obeyed. Sitting on their knees, they looked up at their captors.

The apparent leader, a burly man with a blond buzz cut, stared back, his thick lips set in a straight line. "So. You *are* Dubrovnyk. On your feet. Slowly."

"We have to get to the roof," she told him. "And I need to go back for Joshua. He's still a prisoner."

"Van Heisman's a prisoner."

Surely he knew that from the Alpha feeds. "I need to go back for him," she repeated. "As soon as my family is safe."

The man eyed her, as if reluctant to agree to her demands. Anya wondered what training Richert had drilled into his soldiers, should any of them have the fortune to run across her, or any of their other top enemies. Kill her on sight? Certainly, he wouldn't allow her to slip through his fingers.

"Exactly where is Van Heisman?"

Anya didn't know if she could trust him. But she did need help. Maybe Michael could help her, if he came quickly. On the other hand, these men were here now...

"He's on the sixth floor," she compromised. "I'll take you to him." And, if necessary, she'd lose them along the way.

"Ty." He nodded to one of his men; a tall, thin young man with a pockmarked face. "Take the kids to the roof. Dubrovnyk stays with me."

Elise's eyes widened. "No!"

Thinking fast, Anya said, "I need to make a call."

"Why?"

"To schedule transport for my family."

The burly man scowled. Clearly, he wanted to deny her request. Something held him back. She wondered what it was. Abruptly, he nodded, and relinquished her phone. "Hurry up." Perhaps he viewed Anya as the main prize. Her powerless family might be expendable.

While lifting the phone to her ear, Anya covertly hit the transponder button on her collar, so Michael could get a fix on her general location. Unfortunately, in order to call Michael, she had to transmit on Donetsk's secure housekeeping network. Alpha was out of the question. Hopefully, the blond giant wouldn't rip the phone from her hand before she could log off.

"Michael. It's Anya. My family's heading to the roof. I'm going back for Joshua. Take them home. Please. Out."

"Give that to me." Richert's man extended a meaty hand.

Anya swiftly disconnected from all broadcast channels. "No."

"No?" Thick blond brows slammed together.

When his considerable muscles bunched, she said, "I need it to find Joshua. And I need my weapons back, too, in case we run across Onred's men."

"We'll protect you."

"Will you?" Her level gaze met his. "What orders did Richert give you?"

"Give me the phone." Menace registered in the low voice.

Anya gave it to him. But she didn't trust him now. She would lose him and his henchmen at the first opportunity.

"Ty, take the kids to the roof."

Ty swallowed. "Release them, Major Barnes?"

"Yes."

Ty directed her family down the hall. They cast terrified looks back at Anya, and she struggled to dispel the notion that they were prisoners being herded away to death camps.

Get a grip, Anya. He ordered them to be released, didn't he? More importantly, she trusted that Michael would soon arrive on the roof. She had full confidence that he'd protect her family with the same ferocity that his brother possessed.

Joshua. She had to focus upon him. He was the one in danger.

Anya pushed the elevator button. "Let's go."

"We'll take the stairs." Barnes' hard fingers gripped her arm. "You'll stay with me."

❋**❋**❋**❋**❋

Two men looked up from a computer monitor when Joshua barreled through the holding cell door. Joshua shot one, and the other got a piece of his jacket before Joshua neutralized him, too. Good thing the men hadn't hit the bombs still strapped to his body.

The room swiveled, and Joshua grabbed the closest object to steady his balance. It was the computer console. When his equilibrium returned, he blinked to focus on the screen. This computer would help him find his prey. He shuffled closer to the keyboard, shoving aside a man on the floor with his foot.

However, his swift keystrokes net nothing but the same blue input screen. The computer appeared to be frozen. Was this why both men had been staring at the screen when he had run in? The computer glitch may well have saved his life.

Joshua rebooted the computer. The screen turned black, and then wavy blue lines bisected it. "Error," murmured the computer. "System is offline. Corrupt files. Fatal error."

Joshua tried to wrap his head around this new development. Gorno's computers were down?

And then he smiled. Pain pulled at his split lip. Anya had done it. Gorno's systems were imploding, just like Astana's had. He chuckled and softly said, "Good girl."

No need for the bombs now. Joshua stripped them from his body, and then pulled out the phone he'd swiped from the guard. Even if Gorno's main computer was down, the phone's memory still held the messages and video transmitted on Alpha. Maybe those would give a clue to Onred's location.

He played the last feed, showing the guard with the knife to Marli's neck. Onred's voiceover, however, was far more interesting. "Surrender now, Anya Dubrovnyk. In the shuttle bay. One minute. Or your sister dies."

Joshua played the previous message, and another painful smile cracked his lips. Anya had captured Emelie, and had threatened to kill Onred's daughter. The woman he loved was brilliant, and remarkably resourceful, too.

Both messages indicated that Onred would be somewhere near the shuttle bay right now. The shuttle bay was located on the third floor.

Joshua cracked open the door and checked the dimly lit passage. People hurried by. A few ran. Although Onred had confiscated his stolen shirt, Joshua's snow wear was black. It would blend in well enough in the dim hallways, and the thin fabric would allow greater ease of movement than a uniform. He felt the visceral need to plant bare knuckles into Onred's face. That enticing thought cleared more of the fog from his head.

Joshua slipped into the hall and headed for the stairs, forcibly shutting out the stabbing pain each movement brought. He strode with calm, deliberate purpose, and no one paid him any attention.

After gaining the stairwell, he joined others trotting downstairs and flipped open the guard's phone. Swiftly, he scrolled through the phone's call list. Sure enough. Onred. Time to trap a serpent.

CHAPTER THIRTY-THREE

ON THE SIXTH FLOOR, Major Barnes demanded, "Which way?"

He still hadn't released his tight grip on Anya's arm, and she was beginning to wonder how she would escape him. On the other hand, maybe a posse of armed men converging upon the well-guarded holding cell would be best.

"Left."

Barnes' men led the way, pitilessly shooting every Gorno citizen in their path. Women screamed. Footsteps pounded down the corridor. More of Barnes' men brought up the rear.

"Here's Command Central, Major."

"How much further?" Barnes demanded of Anya.

"Twenty meters."

"Four men come with me. The rest of you, take Command Central."

Booted men eagerly darted down the hall toward Gorno's central command.

Anya wasn't sure exactly which door led to the holding cell, since she had accessed it through the ductwork. "May I see my phone, please?" Tersely, she explained her previous method of access.

With ill grace, Barnes shoved it into her hand. She drew up the schematics while the major looked over her shoulder.

She pointed. "It's up... *There!*" An Altai man barreled out of the door in question.

Barnes swiftly shot, and Anya just as rapidly shoved the phone into her pocket. When she made an attempt to dart through the doorway, Barnes elbowed her aside. He and his men stormed in first, lasers at the ready. Sizzles spit.

"All clear."

Anya dashed for the cell's open door, and gasped. The gray, dismal room was empty. "He's gone!"

❊∗❊∗❊∗❊∗❊

"What?" Onred snarled into the phone.

Gruffly, Joshua said, "Captured Dubrovnyk. On way to shuttle bay."

"Meet me in conference room nine. Out."

With a grim smile, Joshua pocketed the phone. Onred was about to answer for his hellish deeds.

He exited on the third floor into a crush of humanity. The river of people streamed right, toward the shuttle bay doors. Panic charged the air. Women called for their children, and babies wailed.

Wall markers indicated that the conference rooms were to the left. Joshua shouldered across the torrent of people, heading for the far wall, and then battled east. Twenty yards later, he cut right, down a deserted corridor.

The physical exertion had further cleared Joshua's mind, although his body ached like a son-of-a-gun. He ignored it.

An arrow indicated that CR-9 was located to the left, and down the next corridor. Joshua stopped just short of the corner and pressed his back to the wall, laser at the ready. He shot a quick glance down the passage and then ducked back. From memory alone, he fired upon the two men guarding the door.

Fire flashed at his toes. Joshua chanced another look. He'd missed both. One man ran toward him. The other raised his hand to knock on the conference room door. Joshua shot him first, and ducked back into his refuge spot. He sprayed the hall with laser fire.

All fell silent.

Joshua's gut told him not to trust the signal received by his brain. The remaining guard still lurked around the corner. He waited for Joshua to show his face.

Joshua listened closely for breaths or for stealthy boot steps. Nothing.

He refused to waste time playing hide and seek with the guard. Swiftly, he sprayed the hall again. Hot pain licked into his fingers, and he hurled the laser across the hall just before it exploded with bright, popping "boom." Bits of diamonite sprayed into his face. He bit off a curse. His red fingers burned, but they still worked well enough to rip the spare laser from his belt and spray the hall again.

A man grunted into his transmitter, "Van Heisman... out."

Joshua shot another glance into the hall. The last moving guard, on his knees, swayed backwards. Joshua shot the laser from his hand. The man collapsed, his face slack and white. Dead. Or close enough.

Sprinting now in his urgency to try to catch Onred off guard, Joshua finished the distance and shouldered hard into the conference room. With swift, deadly accuracy, he shot the two men flanking Gorno's leader, and growled, "Hands in the air."

Onred did not comply. Instead, he smiled. "Van Heisman. At last. But the situation appears uneven. Are you scared of a fair fight?"

Joshua carefully checked the conference room for additional guards, and then kicked the door shut. He smiled, showing his teeth. "Not at all. In fact, I welcome it."

Onred grinned. "Good. First, however, I would like to show you something. May I take out my phone?" The obsequious question grated on Joshua's nerves. It was a lie, just like every word that left Onred's mouth. However, much as Joshua longed to shoot the Altai leader right now, killing him with his bare knuckles would prove much more satisfying. Therefore, he would allow Onred this last game.

"Do it." Joshua's laser remained trained on the Altai leader. Onred withdrew his phone and lifted it high. His thumb hovered conspicuously over the "play" button.

Slowly, deliberately, Joshua tucked the laser into his belt. If Onred tried to double-cross him, he could easily kill him before the Altai leader drew his weapon.

Onred's lips curled in disgust. "Fool. Now your fate is sealed. One button push will end life as you know it."

❊ ❊ ❊ ❊ ❊

Heart in her throat, Anya whirled to stare at Barnes. "Joshua's gone. Where could he be?"

Had he escaped? What if Joshua had stolen one of the guard's shirts? What if he was the man who had fled the holding cell area—the man Barnes' men had shot? But a quick glance told her that Joshua was not among the men lying on the floor or in the hall. Another, far worse scenario entered her head. "Onred has him," she gasped. "Come on! We've got to find him."

She darted past a startled Barnes before he had the presence of mind to grab her. Out in the deserted hall, she sprinted for the stairs and whipped out her phone. Where could Joshua be? Had Onred broadcasted again on Alpha? Maybe that would give her a clue...

"Dubrovnyk!" Barnes bellowed. "Stop!"

Anya slammed through the stairwell door, and on impulse, went down. The shuttle bay was on the third level. Maybe that's where Onred lurked. She had told him to meet her there. Maybe Joshua was held captive there, too.

As she clattered down the stairs, she accessed Alpha. No recent feeds to replay. A swift tune into housekeeping net no return message from Michael. Was her family all right?

Footsteps thundered on the metal stairs behind her, and Anya burst onto the third floor. She joined the flood of women, children, and old people surging to the right. Schematics said the shuttle bay was this way, too. Were all of these people planning to escape?

Where were Joshua and Onred? Gorno was huge. What if she was wrong, and they weren't in the shuttle bay? How would she ever find them?

An idea occurred to her. She slowed and ducked down a narrow hallway. Joshua still wore his transponder. A tracking device was imbedded inside—and who knew how to track it? Michael.

Swiftly, she typed into the text channel, "Michael. Need AV's coordinates. Text me!" She sent it. Her digital signature would verify that it was sent from her phone.

She bit her lip, waiting. What if Michael was out of range? What if he was fighting Richert's men? What if her family…

Orange text rolled across the screen. "Kids ok. AV these coord." Three sets of numbers flashed, and she swiftly input them into her computer's GPS. Exact latitude, longitude, and meters above the earth.

"Thanks," she typed back.

"Waiting for you and AV," was the response.

Anya bit her lip in gratitude. "Will text when safe. Out." *If* they escaped.

Her small phone computer indicated that Joshua was indeed on Gorno's third level, and he was eighty-five meters east. Schematics showed the shortest route to get to him.

Anya took off at a sprint and barreled through the crush of people converging on the shuttle bay. No sign of Barnes or his men. Good.

A right turn, and the hall became narrower and emptier as she closed in on Joshua's location. Was he truly Onred's prisoner? More practical matters entered her head. If he was, how could she fight Onred's men and free Joshua? Barnes had taken all of her weapons.

She slowed and tried the few door handles she passed. All locked. According to her computer, the next turn in the hall would bring her to Joshua. Ten meters remained. She pressed her back to the wall just before the final corner. Without a laser, how could she possibly save him? Maybe if she caused a distraction…

She peeked around the corner and took in the closed doors and the two dead men. Joshua must have killed them.

Hope, for the first time, surged. Maybe he wasn't a prisoner. All the same, he could be fighting for his life right now, inside one of those rooms. She had to find a weapon. Anything to help him.

She checked her belt again. Barnes had left nothing. Even though the hall felt colder by the minute, perspiration sprang out beneath her armpits. This wasn't a good idea. But what if Onred was about to kill Joshua? Joshua might need her. Now might be her only chance to save him.

The guards! They must have lasers...

Footsteps whispered behind her. She twisted to look. A black clad man with grizzled hair lunged for her. Terror flashed and she bolted sideways, but not quick enough. A thick arm clamped around her neck. "Gotcha."

Anya tried to lunge forward and bend at the waist, intending to throw him over her shoulder. Unfortunately, his other arm came around her chest with the force of a steel bar and lifted her from the ground. The older man was strong.

In her mind's eye, his face flashed again, and in horror, Anya closed her eyes. It had taken a second, but now she placed him from ancient news clips. Onred's father. Jacan, the jackal. The bestial man who had raised Onred and his brother, Cadmus.

A thick, rusty chuckle rumbled from Jacan's chest. "Onred will be glad to see you."

✖✱✖✱✖✱✖✱✖

"Your phone is not a laser," Joshua told Onred. "How will you kill me?"

Onred cackled and twitched the phone back and forth in his fingers. The screen faced Joshua. "I don't have to kill you. Look." He pressed the button.

Camera footage of an empty elevator rolled. Joshua and Anya entered. After a few murmured words, Joshua tucked the bomb into Anya's belt, and then tugged her close to him. He kissed her with scorching, clearly possessive intensity.

Onred's eyes narrowed when Joshua didn't lunge for the phone, as he had obviously expected. "You'd give up your power for that *girl?*"

Joshua felt no need to respond.

A complacent smirk curled Onred's lips. "If you don't care, then I'll publish it on Alpha." He pushed the "send" button before Joshua could blink.

It didn't matter.

Joshua remained stationary, calculating his game plan. Should he beat Onred bloody, and then kill him? Or shoot him now? Even with reflexes slowed by injury, his military training was so deeply ingrained that he could easily draw and shoot faster than Onred could gain his weapon.

He remained still, watching Onred like a lion his prey. He decided to allow Onred to make the first move. The Altai leader would choose his own death.

Blackness hardened Onred's eyes, and fury tensed his muscles. "Idiot. You should *cower* to me," he screamed.

When he lunged, Joshua was ready. He sidestepped, gripped Onred's wrist and jerked him forward, using Onred's momentum against him.

Onred ducked into a roll and landed on his feet. His lips curled back. "You are going to *die*," he snarled.

Joshua smiled faintly. "After you."

The Altai leader charged again for Joshua. Onred's shoulder hit him, spinning him sideways. Onred turned faster than Joshua had expected. His shoulder hit Joshua squarely in the stomach, and they both went down. The barrel-chested Altai leader was heavy, and he managed to land one smashing fist into Joshua's face before Joshua wrestled on top and landed three blows in quick succession to Onred's nose, jaw and throat. The last made the Altai leader choke.

Onred punched hard into Joshua's sore belly. They grappled, punching and rolling...and Onred attempted to claw and strangle. Pain roared in Joshua's head. Although Onred was strong and uninjured, and a formidable enemy, Joshua would accept no thoughts of defeat.

Onred's fists pounded Joshua's body. The leader seemed to know just the spots where Joshua had already been beaten and burned by the electrodes. Joshua shut out the pain and willed his body to obey him. With one violent effort, he went up on one knee and drove his fist with brutal force into Onred's nose. The Altai leader fell backward. Blood flowed like a thick, red river to his chin.

Taking savage advantage, Joshua's fists drove harder and faster, landing with sickening, cracking thuds. He grunted, "This is for Anya...and Marli, Elise...Damon, David, Astana..." The innocents lost in Astana ravaged his mind, and then strangely, superimposed upon those faces was the image of his father with his lips curled back in the mad snarl he'd always worn when he'd beaten Joshua and threatened his siblings; and forced him to hurt the ones he loved most. "*...and the people you murdered!*" This last fist punch landed on Onred's jaw with every scrap of power he possessed. Onred's eyes rolled up into his head.

A door slammed open.

"Stop! Or I shoot the girl."

A bit dazed, Joshua looked over his shoulder. Jacan held Anya up on her tiptoes, his arm a vice about her throat. A laser pressed into her temple.

Breathing heavily, Joshua muttered in a ragged voice, "Release her."

CHAPTER THIRTY-FOUR

RELEASE HER?

What was Joshua thinking? The man held a laser to her head!

But Joshua remained unmoving, back partially to them, shoulders heaving. On the floor, Onred stirred. "I *said*," Joshua said with slow menace, "release her."

The Altai leader went up on one elbow. Joshua's gaze seemed fixed upon him.

A twisted grin split Onred's lips. "You'd do anything to save your precious Anya, wouldn't you?" With a terrible smile, he looked over Joshua's head, straight into the eyes of his father. At the same time, his hand whipped up, and a blade glinted. "Kill h…"

With unhesitating brutality, Joshua plunged a knife deep into Onred's throat. Almost faster than thought, her protector withdrew it, pivoted on one heel, and the bloody blade shot straight toward her.

Anya gasped and instinctively ducked.

The man behind her screamed. His thick arms loosened, and she sprang free to whirl on him. He lay motionless on the floor, the knife imbedded to the hilt in his eye. She swallowed a violent surge of nausea and turned to Joshua. After taking Onred's phone from his dead body, he slowly rose to his feet. Battered, bloody, and bruised, he stood remarkably steady upon his feet.

Tears blurred her vision and she ran into his arms. "Joshua," she whispered. He felt solid and strong...and smelled of blood.

His arms closed tightly around her. Joshua held her close for so long that she wondered if he ever intended to let her go. She held him tighter. The death and destruction around them sank like a chill into her soul. Joshua had killed tens of people, and she had killed at least nine. So much death and horror. Would they ever be the same again?

Gently, she pulled back. "Let's go. Richert's men are on the roof. Michael's waiting for us, too, with my family."

"Good." His beautiful, tawny eyes closed for a second. Beneath the bruises and blood, exhaustion tinged his skin gray. He didn't move.

"Come on." Tenderly, she took his hand. "You need a doctor."

"No." The word sounded bleak. "I have one more job to finish."

"What?"

He strode from the room, scrolling through Onred's phone directory. "Emelie."

Anya gasped. All of Joshua's stories about being the clean up man for the military flooded her mind. *The only safe enemy is a dead enemy.* She dashed after him. "You *wouldn't.*"

"Emelie planted the virus in Astana. She is responsible for thousands of deaths." He shouldered into a nearby stair-well and headed up them, fast.

"But she's just a child!"

"Fifteen is not a child. And she is Onred's heir."

"Joshua!" She grabbed his arm. "I won't let you."

He stopped. Slowly and carefully, he gripped her arms and said, "She is a risk that must be neutralized. Permanently." He finished the last stairs and strode into the fifth floor hall.

"No!" She grabbed his arm, but he shook her free.

"You would have killed her thirty minutes ago."

"To free *you.* And my family. But now..."

"Now they're free. But this war will continue until we cut off the head."

Was Joshua a monster? Was this man she loved a cold-hearted child killer? "Don't murder her," she cried out. "I'll never be able to look at you again."

He rammed the key card into Emelie's locked door and sent a grim look over his shoulder. "Who said anything about murder?"

Joshua slammed open Emelie's door.

To Anya's consternated relief, the room was empty. Joshua strode from one end to the other, upending the bed, wrenching open closets. She was gone.

Anya watched in silence. "If you don't plan to kill her, then what do you plan to do with her?"

He swore. "Shuttle bay. Now."

She followed in his fast footsteps. Emergency lights flickered. Cold crept through the halls in a thickening, frigid current. Scores of Richert's red-suited soldiers ran through the corridor, mixing with a few blue Donetski men. Black clad Gorno men lay dead. Children's cries reached her ears. Innocents were suffering. They would continue to suffer...for days, weeks, perhaps even months—if they survived that long.

Anya could not grasp the unending horror and misery just beginning all around her. She burst into the shuttle bay shortly after Joshua. Although flooded with people, all of the aircraft were gone.

Outside the windows, a swarm red birds, vastly outnumbering the Donetski blue ones, made short work of the fleeing black ships. For a second, the threatening sight of Richert's dominant forces made her steps falter. If she didn't know Richert was on their side, the sight would frighten her. As it was, she could only feel thankful.

The war was almost over. Just like that.

"Now what?"

Joshua gazed outside, his lips straight and hard. "We can hope justice has been served. If we're lucky, Onred's line has ended forever."

"You would wish for the death of a little girl?"

He turned to her. "No. But I can wish for the deaths of all who would advise her to carry on her father's quest. I can pray for that. And I will."

"Do you really think she's evil?" Anya asked in a hushed voice. "She cried when I held her hostage, just like Marli would. She might have only been a pawn. A little girl trapped by her father's expectations." She looked at Joshua. "But you would understand that, wouldn't you?"

His shoulders relaxed a little. "Yes," he said at last. "I would."

More quietly, she said, "What did you plan to do, then, if you'd found her?"

"Banish her to our northern city."

"To the prison?"

"Yes. If she proved trustworthy...and sane, I would transfer her to the supervised level."

"She would never be free."

"It would be natural for her to want to avenge her father's death. We could never trust her. So no, she'd never be allowed to go free."

"I see."

He turned to her. "Do you?" The weight of the world seemed to deaden those brown eyes.

"I do." She slipped her arms around him and pressed her cheek into his shoulder. And she did understand. He didn't want to ruin a child's life. But Emelie had planted the fatal virus. She was a smart child, and could possibly be a dangerous one, if enough of her father's tainted blood ran through her veins. The safety of Donetsk had to come first.

Joshua's arms closed tightly around her, and remained so for a long time. At last, he touched the transmitter at his collar. "Alpha Victor. Ready for transport."

✖∗✖∗✖∗✖∗✖

Michael instructed Joshua and Anya to meet him at the far end of the shuttle bay. They managed to board before any desperate Gorno people could crowd in close enough to beg passage from their dying city.

Marli greeted them with hugs. The little craft was crowded. It was only meant to hold four, at the most, but including the doctor, eight weighed down the ship.

"We'll make it," Michael assured them. "Doc, take a look at my brother. He's in bad shape." Joshua allowed the doctor to attend to his visible wounds. Dr. Spalding clucked that Joshua would need to spend twenty-four hours in Zyra's hospital.

Anya would be surprised if Joshua stayed until dawn.

They flew into the black night, leaving behind the pale, flickering lights of Gorno. Damon was awake now, to Anya's relief. According to Dr. Spalding, he was recovering, but needed to be admitted to the hospital immediately.

Marli snuggled up against Anya. "The war's over, right?"

"Yes. Onred is dead." And so was his evil father, Jacan. However, Cadmus, the other son, was still alive. He was a wanderer, also nicknamed "The Ghost," and was rumored to live in western Mongolia. Would he take it upon himself to avenge his father and brother's deaths? If so, Richert might be right. Maybe they'd have to fight all of western Mongolia next. But now wasn't the time to think about the unknown future.

"Your face is burned," Elise told Anya. "Hold still. I'll fix it." Elise borrowed the healing wand from the doctor and cool light touched Anya's left temple, and also her bruised jaw. Her temple did burn, now that Elise mentioned it. So did her arm. Anya had forgotten about being shot in the communications center. Her foot burned, too. Why?

And then she remembered being shot in the boot in the conference room. Upon closer inspection, a hole perforated the boot. Her foot was burned, but not too badly. She took the wand from Elise and patched it up.

An hour later, back in Zyra, Joshua, Anya, and her entire family were ordered to report to the hospital. Damon, David, and Joshua were admitted, amid protests. After being re-leased, Anya and her sisters were ushered to a suite of rooms which they were instructed to consider their own, for as long as they wished them.

Anya tucked Marli into bed, said goodnight to Elise, and collapsed onto her own soft, warm bed with the blankets pulled to her chin. Was it possible the war could be over so quickly? All worries of Cadmus aside, they had escaped Gorno. Onred was dead. Joshua and her siblings would live. What more could she possibly want?

All of her prayers had been answered. For the first time, Anya realized the enormity of this simple fact. Tears in her eyes, she breathed a heartfelt prayer of thanks.

She fell deeply into dreams of death, blood, and horror. The souls of the men she had killed tormented her. Guilt plagued her. And worse, Joshua went missing. Where could he be? She searched everywhere, but he could not be found.

He did not want to be found.

At dawn, Anya woke up in a cold sweat. One fact pierced her heart like a knife. Joshua meant to leave her.

She had to stop him.

CHAPTER THIRTY-FIVE

ANYA SLIPPED into the shower, feeling dead tired after the short night of tossing and turning. The warm water revived her a bit. Hopefully enough to survive the coming confrontation with Joshua. Maybe her dream had been a premonition, or maybe only a result of the fear and horror lingering from the attack on Gorno. Soon, she'd find out the truth.

A brush through her hair, clean clothes and wounds tended, she left the room, heading for the main conference room. She had to find Joshua.

The halls were quiet. Too quiet. She hurried faster, but found the conference room empty. She stopped a uniformed man. "Where's Birn and Ray?"

The corporal's eyes narrowed. Puzzling contempt curled his lips. "Command Center's main viewing room. Straight ahead and to the right."

"Thanks." Disconcerted by his attitude, she sent him a frown and hurried to her destination.

A swipe of the Zyran security keycard she'd been given, and she entered the huge room. Floor-to-ceiling windows overlooked the western plain and the eastern, snowcapped mountains. To the south, a gigantic television screen broadcasted footage of a smoking Gorno. Birn, Ray, Joshua, and a few others stood in the middle of the room, talking. If Joshua's set expression and straight, stiffly held shoulders were any indication, the conversation was serious.

Birn caught sight of Anya. "Get out. You have no place here."

"Speak to her with respect," Joshua said in a low, harsh snarl.

"I am baron now," Birn bit back. "I'll listen to your advice, but that woman means nothing to Donetsk. Escort her out, or I'll order my men to throw her out."

Stunned and confused, Anya's gaze went from Birn to Joshua. Birn claimed *he* was baron now? What had happened? How could he strip away Joshua's power, and dismiss her as if she were a piece of trash?

Joshua strode for Anya. His features were like expressionless stone. Firm fingers took her elbow. "Come with me."

Without a word, she obeyed and followed him into an empty conference room. The door slid shut behind them. There, he released her. The burned patch on his cheek had faded to a light pink, and his cuts and gashes were half healed. The skin around his eyes, though, was a pale purple color. His eyes looked black.

"What's wrong?"

"It's my fault," he gritted. "I should have stopped him. I'm sorry."

Now she was even more confused. "You should have stopped *who* from doing what?"

A grimace flickered. "Remember the elevator in Gorno? When I kissed you."

"Yes. Of course." How could she forget? She had wondered if that would be the last blissful moment she'd ever spend in Joshua's arms.

"Onred got it on digital feed. He taunted me with it. I should have shot him before he sent it."

"He sent it...over Alpha?"

"Yes."

Anya felt as if she'd been punched in the stomach. She needed to sit down.

Of course. That explained the corporal's contempt, and Birn's greedy grab for power.

"I can fix this," Joshua said, his voice even.

Anya instinctively stiffened. Her fears from the dream returned with full force. "No."

"Listen," he said curtly. "I can make this all go away. You'll keep power in Donetsk."

But Joshua would not. This was abundantly clear from his set expression. "I don't want power. Not without you."

"You owe it to your family. Renounce me."

"What?"

"Tell Birn and Ray that I forced myself on you. Demote me to an enlisted man. Banish me to Tash."

"No! I won't."

"The Dubrovnyks will retain power. That's as it should be."

"I won't lie. Not for you. Not for my family. For no one." The injustice of the situation caught her by the throat. "This is wrong. *We* saved Donetsk from Onred. Birn has no right…"

"He has every right," Joshua returned quietly. "Renounce me. That is an order, Dubrovnyk."

A laugh battled with her despair. She went to him and gripped the lapels of his uniform jacket. It was her favorite one—the baron's cream jacket with gold trim. She had always thought he looked so handsome in it. "I will never renounce you," she told him. "Never."

"Any…" His gaze flicked over her shoulder.

The automatic door hissed. Someone had come in.

Perfect. Now was her opportunity to end this argument once and for all. Anya's hands slid up and curved around the back of Joshua's neck. His eyes narrowed, anticipating her plan, and he refused to allow her to tug down his head.

No matter. She went up on her toes and kissed him, full on the mouth. His lips felt hard and unyielding, but she pressed closer to him and stroked his hair.

He broke the kiss by turning his face aside. "Anya." Although the guttural word was clearly meant to be reproving, it sounded tortured, instead.

Encouraged, and ignoring their silent, condemning audience, Anya nuzzled his neck and pressed kisses into the strong line of his throat. Now, no one could ever doubt that she was a more than willing participant in the broadcasted elevator kiss.

Joshua convulsively swallowed. "Stop. That is enough."

A throat cleared behind her. "We have news," Ray said. "You're wanted in the Command Center. Anya, too."

✳*✳*✳*✳*✳

Richert's weathered face filled the main viewing screen when they returned to the Command Center. The territory baron's obsidian eyes seemed to bore into the room, as if he could read the thoughts of everyone present. The thick, silvered black brows bristled in their usual, unfriendly manner, but an uncharacteristic smile curled his lips. Unease struck Anya when she saw it.

"Joshua," her uncle growled. "Lost power, eh? Sorry to deliver more bad news. But I have someone you know." When he scowled, the camera zoomed back to reveal a torso shot of Richert sitting at a conference table. Next to him, with a laser to his temple, sat Michael.

Anya gasped. Michael's features appeared stoic, and he very much reminded her of his brother right then.

"What do you want?" Joshua bit out.

Richert cackled. "You haven't seen everything. Yet." He waved an impatient hand, and another video feed superimposed over the bottom corner of the screen. A slow pan revealed a wall shot of the parked birds in ZCA.

Joshua went pale.

Birn scowled. "What's that?"

Anya remembered that for security reasons, Joshua had told his commanders very little about ZCA or its location. Now it seemed to be a moot point. Richert's men had discovered ZCA. The secret was out.

Another screen shot popped into the other corner of the screen. Slovic and many other men knelt in ZCA's Command Central, hands on their heads. Both small screens revealed few actual details of ZCA, Anya realized, but enough so that Joshua would understand that Richert now owned control of their last military stronghold.

"Understand what this means, Joshua?" Richert queried. When Joshua's jaw clenched, the old baron pressed, "What about your men? Do they understand?"

Tersely, Joshua told Birn and Ray, "They have ZCA."

Disbelief registered, and then Ray's face went blank.

Furious color darkened Birn's skin. He cursed the old man.

Richert ignored this. His gaze remained focused upon Joshua. "I've got you. I suggest you surrender Donetsk Territory now. No more bloodshed is necessary."

Anya felt sick. Her head had warned her that this would happen. Her illogical heart had wanted to trust the crotchety, hurting—*megalomaniac*—old man who was her uncle. She wanted to curse the two-faced man and call him every foul name under the sun, but she did not. Trembling with emotion, she turned her back on the screen.

Every man in Command Central mutely turned to Joshua, unconsciously seeking his opinion and his leadership. All except for Birn, who blustered, "We'll fight you to the death, Richert!"

"No," Joshua said. "It's over. After last night, our air fleet is down by more than two-thirds. Without ZCA, we have nothing. Richert knows it."

Birn bellowed, "It's over when I say it's over!"

"Birn," Ray said quietly.

Birn strode to the video console and slammed down his fist. The TV screen froze. "I am baron now. The men will follow *my* orders."

"Logically, victory is impossible," Ray returned. "ZCA houses most of our remaining aircraft. We may have fifty birds scattered throughout the territory. We can't win against Richert with fifty birds."

"Our army is strong," Birn argued. "We can take Richert." Gaze hot and nostrils flaring, he turned to Joshua. "Give me ZCA's coordinates. Our divisions can be there in a day. We'll blow Richert sky high."

"You'd destroy ZCA?" Joshua said with disbelief.

"Better than letting that bastard control it. Give me the coordinates!"

"No."

"I'll throw you in prison!" Birn shouted.

"Birn," Ray interjected coolly. "It's over."

One by one, the other high level commanders in the room agreed with Ray and Joshua's assessment of the situation. Surrender was inevitable. The deaths of more men would be a waste.

Fury pulsed Birn's cheeks. He said nothing for long minutes. Then he slammed a fist onto the viewer button again. Birn's moment of power had come and gone in the blink of an eye.

Richert leaned forward, hands clasped. His glittering eyes looked like black, expectant beetles, eager to devour their territory in one gulp. "Well?" he said with ill-hidden glee. "Have you come to a decision?"

Birn's fists clenched. It appeared he'd sooner vomit than say the words required of him.

Long moments passed.

"Well?" Richert snapped.

With ill grace, Birn spat, "We surrender, you two-faced old coot."

Richert leaned back, his lips curved in a satisfied smile. "Good. Open up a shuttle bay. I'll arrive within the hour to finalize the terms of surrender. And," he finished testily, "I want both Joshua and Anya present."

The screen went black.

Anya crossed her arms and hugged them to her middle. She felt sick to her very soul and trembled with fury. Richert had behaved exactly true to form. Why was she so surprised, then? She wasn't sure what she had expected from him, but this complete stabbing in the back was intolerable. After everything Joshua had done by killing Onred and defeating the Altai regime, they had still lost Donetsk. Not to Onred, but to her equally bloodthirsty uncle.

Without a word, she turned and bolted from the room. She had to warn her siblings. What did Richert intend to do with them all? He had said no more bloodshed was necessary, but why should she trust him now? He had wanted to kill her father. Would Richert want to exact his final revenge upon herself and her siblings—Jason's offspring? She had to prepare her family for the worst.

CHAPTER THIRTY-SIX

WITH A START, Anya discovered Joshua silently matching her stride when she turned into the corridor leading to her family's new suite of rooms.

She dashed tears away. "I'll gather everyone together. We need to warn them."

Joshua took her hand. "Look at me." He stopped, and so she did, too. That direct brown gaze steadied her, and his warm hands enveloped hers. "It will do no good to frighten them," he said quietly. "Let them rest. When we know the terms of surrender, we'll tell them together."

More tears formed. "You don't think Richert will...will *kill* them? Do you think he'll kill us all?"

Joshua drew her closer. "No. I don't."

Her lips trembled. "But how do you know? We're a threat to his power. He's hated our family for twenty-four years!"

"He hated your father and your mother. Richert's ruthless, but he's fair. I don't think he'll condemn the children for the sins of their parents."

Joshua seemed so certain. Could he be right? But after Richert's backstabbing power grab, how could she trust that any decency lived in her uncle?

"I feel betrayed," she admitted, taking a deep breath. "I was foolish. I'd started to trust him...a little. I was so stupid." She bit her lip. "But now... I was so *wrong* about him. I feel like I can't trust my judgment anymore. I'm scared."

"I'll protect you. And I will protect Marli, Elise, Damon, and David, too. Richert will not hurt you. I have a plan. If we need to escape, we'll go together."

Her hands tightened around his. "Yes." She wanted to be with Joshua, always and forever. If that meant they had to live in a freezing cave, or travel halfway around the world in order to be safe, she would be happy, as long as she was with him.

His warm palms gently framed her face and he kissed her. Anya's heart bloomed with joy, and overflowed with love. Fiercely, her arms went around his neck, and she buried her cheek in his shoulder. "I love you so much, Joshua. Please don't ever leave me."

His arms closed around her, but he didn't answer. Fear arose again. She pulled back and searched his eyes. "What aren't you telling me?"

"I'll bargain for your safety. But I'm not sure what Richert will do with me."

More fear welled. Slowly, she said, "You mean you're the real threat to him. Donetsk would follow you to the grave, and Richert knows it."

His features remained impassive. "You will be safe," he repeated. "I will make sure of it. I'm expendable. I've told you that from the beginning."

"You are not!"

Gently, he disentangled her arms. "I need to make preparations before Richert arrives. I'll see you in the Command Center."

He turned on his heel and strode down the hall. It reminded Anya of when he had ordered her to marry Onred, and afterward he had walked away, leaving her alone. Now, at last, she understood what a sacrifice that had been for him. Just as walking away from her now would be a sacrifice, too. She also knew, if necessary, that he would offer his life in exchange for hers. The knowledge made her feel sick and horrified.

One thing remained for sure. She wouldn't let that happen. She would never lose Joshua to Richert's sly, bloody machinations. Never.

❋❋❋❋❋

Anya stood in the shadows of the shuttle bay and watched Birn, Ray, and Joshua greet Richert as he rolled off the shuttle in his wheelchair. It again struck her how frail her uncle looked. His large frame hunched forward, and the black uniform, piped with maroon edging, hung from his gaunt, bony shoulders. The baron's skin and knobby fingers looked as papery as ever, but he held his head erect, with fierce pride. An unknown emotion glittered in those black eyes. Richert saw her, but made no sign of acknowledgement. Neither did she to him.

Four burly guards accompanied the territory baron, along with a young man she guessed to be his sixteen-year-old son. The boy had black hair, like his father, was whipcord lean, and possessed eyes as dark as midnight.

Birn led the way to the Command Center. Richert rolled along next with his men, and they were followed by Ray, Joshua, and herself. Additional commanders awaited their arrival in the conference room. They would be witnesses to the exchange of power.

Richert wheeled up to the long edge of the conference table. Two of his men flanked him, and two stood behind him, hands on their lasers. Anya sat across from him, with Ray to her right, then Joshua, and then Birn at the head of the table. The other commanders sat to Anya's left.

Richert pointed to the far end of the table, where the young man had taken a seat. "Dominic. My son," was all he said by way of introduction. His obsidian eyes gleamed at Anya.

Expression deliberately cool, she broke eye contact and offered a small smile to her cousin. Dominic's lips flickered up in return.

What would it be like to be raised by a bitter man like Richert? Anya felt pity for the boy.

"Tablet," Richert said curtly, and one of the beefy men extracted a tablet from a black briefcase. When the guard plugged it into the conference table, the computer screens imbedded in the table glowed to life. The screen before Anya revealed the document in Richert's tablet. It was simply labeled, "Surrender Document."

"Read it," Richert ordered. "And sign it. Every one of you."

Anya read the brief document. Basically, Donetsk Territory would surrender all territory, cities, greenhouses, intelligence...everything...to Richert, effective immediately. Signatures appeared on the screen as the commanders signed in real time. At the very bottom of the page, Richert signed with flourish. Slowly, Anya picked up her stylus. When Joshua's bold signature appeared, she signed below it. Birn's was a dark, angry scrawl.

Richert smiled and handed the tablet back to the guard. "History is made. From now on, I call the shots for Donetsk."

"Until you're dead, old man," muttered Birn.

Richert scowled. "You are dismissed. Leave your bars with my men. Your new assignment will be janitor in Omsk's prison."

Birn's mouth opened and closed like a fish gulping for air.

"Get out." Bony fingers snapped, but Richert didn't look at Birn again. His opaque black eyes glared at the other occupants of the table. "Any more insubordination?"

Anya itched to tell the old man off, but kept her mouth shut.

Richert's gaze lingered on her. Did a faint smile twitch his lips? The sadistic dictator.

Birn's fist slammed into the wall as he exited.

"Good," Richert said. "Now we can have a civilized conversation."

Unable to stay silent a second longer, Anya demanded, "What do you intend to do with us?"

"If you shut up, I'll tell you."

Anya glared. Richert scowled back.

Anya sealed her lips, and crossed her arms for good measure. Now she was certain that amusement twitched her uncle's lips.

"Good," Richert growled. "You'll have plenty of time to talk later. For now, everyone will listen to me. I've got two orders of business to complete. Then I'll allow discussion."

Anya thought of a particularly pertinent comment she'd like to make, but swallowed it with great difficulty.

"First," Richert said, "Donetsk now operates under the same laws as Tarim. Same goes for Altai Territory, but that's a mess. Onred's daughter remains a threat—she probably escaped, and we can't find Cadmus. We'll sort that out later."

Ray dared to speak. "How are your laws different than ours?"

"Good question." Richert's gaze bored into Joshua. "That foolish protector law is dead. All penalties are erased."

Anya's mouth dropped open. Joshua's lifted brow revealed his surprise as well.

"Other laws will change, too," Richert finished testily. "Lisa will upload the documents to Zyra this afternoon."

Anya's heart pounded unnaturally fast. Why would Richert deliberately state that that one, specific law had changed? She glanced at Joshua. It was almost as if...

"Second," Richert growled, "since all power now cedes to me and my heirs, the current baron of Donetsk must surrender to me all objects of his office. Later, that will include keys, codes, etc. For now—for symbolism's sake—he will surrender the baron's jacket."

Stricken, Anya gazed at Joshua. This moment had been inevitable, of course. But it pained her to see Joshua peel off the baron's jacket that he had worn for so long and so well. Although he'd come into power by a fluke of fate, he had earned that jacket, many, many times over.

Although Joshua's face appeared emotionless when he delivered it to Richert, she knew how deeply it must hurt him to give it up. He had poured his whole life, heart, and soul into Donetsk. And now every bit of the power and respect he had earned would be stripped from him forever. In that moment, she hated Richert perfectly.

"Now what?" Her voice trembled. "Shall we all get down and..."

"Watch your mouth," Richert snapped.

"You double-crossed us, and you want me to stay quiet?"

"Anya."

She fell silent at Joshua's quiet tone, but her cheeks felt hot. He was right, of course. Starting a fight would only deteriorate matters. Richert had won. But it was hard to accept gracefully.

Richert's eyes gleamed, as if pleased by this interchange. His black gaze bored into her. "I've said this before. You look like your mother, but your mouth...and your fiery spirit...come only from your father."

Anya wasn't sure how to respond. It actually sounded like a compliment. Coming from a crotchety, bitter old man who had hated her father, she must be mistaken. "Thank you." Whether she said it to be polite or sarcastic, she wasn't certain.

Richert nodded. "Now, to my final order of business. I am an old man. I've decided to transfer the leadership of Donetsk Territory to someone I trust. It will not be my first-in-command, since I've recently learned that he's been poisoning me."

Anya gasped.

Richert's eyes gleamed. "Ironic, isn't it? That's how my brother died. Now my first-in-command will suffer the same death he designed for me." He coughed suddenly and harshly, and then wheezed for air. One of the guards swiftly put an oxygen mask to his mouth.

Long, gasping breaths later, Richert shoved it aside. "I may die soon. I need someone to take the reins for me. Since I've decided I can trust only family, I'll transfer leadership of Donetsk to my oldest heir."

Anya's gaze swiveled to Dominic. That's why Richert's son had come. Surprise registered on his young face. As well it might. He was still too young to take leadership. Or perhaps that was another of the laws Richert had changed. Did it matter, in any case? Richert was the dictator here. Whatever he said would be. Anya certainly had no say in the matter. Richert only wanted Joshua, herself, and the other commanders present to witness Donetsk's power transfer to his son.

Richert settled Joshua's jacket into neat lines on his lap and rolled back from the table. He slowly steamed for his son.

Anya closed her eyes. This drama was too much. She just wanted it over. She wanted to ask Richert what he meant to do with her family and Joshua. And then they could make plans for the future.

"Open your eyes, Anya," Ray murmured.

When she did, she was surprised to discover that Richert had rolled past Dominic and now rounded the table, heading toward the commanders on her side of the table. He bypassed both of them, too, and halted beside her.

Bewildered, she stared at him. Why had he stopped?

Richert's papery lips cracked into a smile. He cackled. "I've still got some surprises up my sleeve." He lifted the cream jacket and carefully placed it on her lap. "Choose the only man who will fill this jacket properly."

Her fingers cautiously touched the fine fabric, still warm from Joshua's body. "I don't understand."

Richert cleared his throat. "This coat belongs to my oldest heir. Since she is a woman, the jacket will belong to her husband. I'm still a chauvinist at heart."

Richert's meaning finally registered. Shocked, she retorted, "I am not *your* daughter." Her high voice cracked. "I'm *Jason* Dubrovnyk's daughter."

"I thought so, too. For twenty-three years." The old man's eyes glistened. It couldn't be from moisture, surely. "But when I met you...there was just something about you. Your fire and gumption were nothing like my brother." He cleared his throat again. "He was a mean, sadistic brute. That morning, back in Aksu, I took your juice glass and gave it to my lab. They triple checked, to be sure. You are my daughter, Anya Dubrovnyk. Mine and my Rachel's." His hand shook as it smeared a tear beneath his eye. "Like it or not," he added gruffly. "That's the fact."

Unable to speak, Anya could only stare at the testy, unpredictable old baron. He couldn't be right. Her whole world...everything she had ever believed would turn upside down. But she could also see that Richert believed he spoke the truth. He would never give power to Jason's daughter. He would never cry over a girl who wasn't his own flesh and blood.

Her throat felt suddenly full and choked. Her trembling hand smoothed Joshua's fine coat. "They lied to you about the DNA tests?"

"Jason did. I don't know if your mother knew the truth."

Anya swiftly shook her head. "She didn't. I would have sensed...something."

Richert nodded abruptly. "The jacket is yours. Choose wisely." He wheeled around, so his back faced her. "The meeting is over." Over his shoulder, he added, "But we'll share ZCA. I'm no fool."

Dominic, looking as stunned as the other men at the table, rose and followed his father out of the room. He was her *brother*. Her half brother. And Marli and the others were her half siblings, too. But forever in her heart they would be her whole family.

Anya couldn't move. She could barely think.

Ray put a brief, cool hand on her shoulder. "Congratulations," he said quietly, and left with the other commanders.

Only Joshua remained. He took Ray's chair and faced her, his knees touching her own. "How are you holding up?"

"I don't know. I can't...can't get my head around it."

"It will take a while."

Anya ran a palm over the smooth jacket. "The Old Barons' protector law is dead." She couldn't believe it. The weight of it...the relief...she could barely touch the wonder of it.

Joshua smiled. "I heard."

"I almost think he did that...for us."

"I think he did. In Aksu, Richert figured out what I felt for you. I tried to deny it, but he wouldn't bite."

Anya looked down at the jacket. Richert had deliberately abolished the law for them. In her heart, she believed that that had been his complex, inexplicable way of telling her that he loved her. "He wants me to choose the only man who will fit this jacket."

"You have plenty of time to look around. I'm sure you'll have lots of applicants."

She looked deep into his tawny eyes. "Don't joke about this. *You* are the only man who can fill this jacket. I know it, and Richert knows it. You've earned it a thousand times over. No one else could take your place. *You* are the Baron of Donetsk."

"Thank you." Her words had touched his heart. Anya saw it in his eyes. And for the first time, she sensed that he truly believed them, too—that he truly believed in his own worth. The broken boy from Tash was gone. Only her Joshua, the true Baron of Donetsk, remained.

A small smile edged his lips. "Will you marry me, then?"

She laughed. "I guess I'll have to."

That velvet brown gaze became very serious. "Are you sure?"

"Stand up." Anya stood with him, and tugged the jacket sleeve over his tanned hand and up his arm, across his broad back, and helped the other arm through. Then she faced him, her palms on his chest. "If you can handle an unpredictable wife, and elements of chaos in your life..."

"I can think of nothing I want more."

She smiled. "Then I absolutely want to be your wife."

Joshua smiled, too, and his hands ran down her back and drew her possessively nearer. He murmured, "Donetsk Territory needs a baron today."

She grinned playfully. "Do the orders begin now?"

"How about persuasion?" His lips met hers. Warm passion simmered in his kiss, and heat licked through her blood. "Will you marry me tonight?"

At that moment, Anya wasn't sure if she could wait that long. Giddy happiness surged through her. "Yes. Yes, please."

"I love you, my sweet Anya." His low voice sounded like rough velvet. "You have always been the only woman for me." His kiss deepened, until all thoughts left her mind. His hand slid into her hair and gently cupped the back of her head. He kissed her with a warm possessiveness which threatened to steal her heart and soul from her body. With a tiny, joyful sigh, she utterly surrendered her whole heart, soul, and life to this man. No more fears of rejection, nor of Joshua losing his baronship. Just the warm bliss of holding the man she had loved for so long.

She whispered, "I love you, too, my protector."

❀✲❀

ICE MASTER

Ice Chronicles Book Two

If you enjoyed *Ice Baron*, read on for a sneak peek from the
next book in the series!

PROLOGUE

BLOOD PAINTED HER NIGHTMARES; the color of the city that exploded with the fury of a supernova. Thermonuclear clouds boiled in her mind, and red streamed from the dark heavens, spattering death upon the pristine white snow of Kazakhstan.

Upon the land of her enemies.

Much as she wanted to, she could not deny it—as a child, she had helped her father kill the innocents in Kazakhstan. Her computer virus, like the serpent of old, had slithered through their enemy's computers and laid them open to thermonuclear attack.

She was responsible for the murders of thousands of people.

Their tormented, skeletal faces twisted through her nightmares, reminding her of what she had done. Making her wish that she had never been born; making her wish that she had died with them.

For living was her torture.

And every morning, Emelie Stoystiya woke up screaming.

CHAPTER ONE

ZCA, Tarim, Territory, year 3151 A.D.
(Millennial Ice Age, caused by Nuclear holocaust)
Monday

"Your interview is next, Ms. Smirnov." The secretary for ZCA's Commander closed the door behind the second-to-last job applicant, a studious looking young man who held his paper-thin microcomputer in a death grip.

Lee managed a smile. "Thank you." She'd waited all day to interview for this job. It was a job she'd sacrificed everything to gain. Still, she couldn't quite believe she'd made it this far, and actually into the heart of the top security outpost, Zebra Charlie Alpha.

Warm perspiration trickled down the back of her neck and dampened her armpits, too. Abruptly, Lee stood. She managed another small, composed smile for the perfectly coiffed secretary, who wore a ruthlessly pressed black uniform. "I'll return in a moment."

If the previous interviews were any indication, she only had fifteen minutes before it was her turn.

Lee headed into the hall, looking for the restroom she'd seen earlier. She desperately needed a cool splash of water on her face. Emotions rarely got the better of her. She'd trained for many years to hide her feelings.

A Tarim soldier approached. On instinct, her expression cooled into one of polite reserve.

The handsome Tarim soldier—a sergeant, identified by the insignia and medals on his black uniform—smiled as he passed by her in the hall. He tried to maintain eye contact, but she turned aside, into the restroom, which was thankfully unoccupied. She slid home the bolt.

Men noticed her. Although Lee accepted that fact, it meant little. They did not notice *her*. They admired her shell. The lie that science had created.

If the soldier knew her true identity, he'd want to kill her. So would everyone else in ZCA. Especially Michael Van Heisman, the man she would soon meet.

Cool water sluiced over her fingers, and Lee pressed cold, dripping palms to her cheeks. She must land this job. Failure was unacceptable, because it would mean certain death for thousands of people. Her vision dimmed, seeing into the past. The water dripping down her face darkened, too, seeming to congeal into dark copper. The color of blood.

With a shudder, she swiped it off, hard, with the cuff of her sleeve.

She could not tell these facts to Michael Van Heisman.

ZCA's policy on spies and terrorists was well-known; instant imprisonment, followed by a twenty-four hour military investigation and trial. Then, if found guilty, immediate execution. And she'd be found guilty. Guilt already stained her hands and her heart.

In the mirror, worried dark brown eyes regarded her, framed in the face of a stranger. Even though seven years had passed since her five plastic surgeries, Lee still found it difficult to accept that the tall, perfectly proportioned woman was herself.

The jet black hair was her own. Her eye color, a battle fought for and won, remained her own. Microsurgery, however, had changed the interior structure of her eyes so she could not be identified. It had resulted in a year of poor vision. Her fingerprints were surgically altered. Her skin color, a light honey color, was not her own, nor were her slightly tip-tilted eyes, giving her an exotic look. They hinted at an Asian ancestry which did not exist. Her cheekbones were now higher and a bit wider than her natural ones, and her ears had been reshaped. The purpose of the surgeries had been to completely disguise her original features so her true identity could never be discovered.

The sadistic doctors had eagerly sharpened their blades again when she'd turned sixteen, but she had refused further surgery, unable to stand the pain, or the bloody, healing scars.

The mess had all finally healed. It had pleased her uncle that it had only taken one year.

After the surgeries, the new, darker lie of her life began. Lee entered the prestigious Omsk Tech University's Aerospace and Nanotechnical program. She was inserted among her enemies like a black widow among brilliant, beautiful butterflies. She was supposed to learn all she could. To excel. And she had.

Her uncle was pleased. She'd graduated one year early, at twenty-three, and during her time at school had become best friends with Dominic Dubrovnyk, the son of Richert Dubrovnyk, Tarim Territory's baron. And, most important of all, today she would interview with Michael Van Heisman, Commander of Tarim's military and technological powerhouse, Zebra Charlie Alpha. ZCA.

Today, if her interview went well, and if she succeeded in gaining the job of Van Heisman's assistant, all of the plots and plans of her murderous family would ripen to fruition. Her orders were clear. Her debt clear. And finally, she was ready to pay.

It is time.

She looked at herself for one last time in the mirror; into her eyes, the last piece of herself that remained her own. They reflected back the resolve and pain in her heart. Perhaps even a bit of her soul; if she still had one, which was doubtful.

Without expression, Emelie Stoystiya headed for her interview with Michael Van Heisman; the only man who possessed the key to her redemption. And her death.

Uliastai, Mongolia
One day earlier

"Are you ready to die?" Pockmarks covered Cadmus' narrow jaw. His sparse black goatee and mustache failed to hide these physical defects or the cruel set to his lips. "You will be caught. It is inevitable. And Michael Van Heisman will order your execution. Are you ready to succeed with your mission?"

"Yes, Uncle." Emelie welcomed death. And perishing at the hand of her enemy would be poetic; the ultimate stroke of justice against her black soul.

Her uncle's onyx stare bored into her, testing the truth of her declaration. Usually she concealed her thoughts from him, but now Emelie allowed him to witness her resolute, determined passion for the mission. *Her* mission. If Cadmus guessed it differed from his own, he would slit her throat right now.

Unease, like a cold sliver of ice, slid down her skin.

His eyes narrowed. Emelie's expression did not change.

For a slightly built man of medium height, Cadmus, known as "The Ghost," conveyed menace like no other. Personal experience proved he was far more deadly than her blood-thirsty father, Onred, or her grandfather, Jacan, "The Jackal," had been. Once upon a time, eight years ago, when Cadmus had rescued her from certain death in Gorno, she had been grateful.

How quickly she had learned that he worshipped only the two-faced gods of cruelty and selfishness. Malice fed the poison in his soul.

For a moment, her mind drifted to the past...to the inexorable unfolding of events that would soon lead to her death.

After their enemies had invaded Gorno and Joshua Van Heisman had killed her father, Emelie and her uncle had fled to the safety of Mongolia.

Cadmus had immediately scheduled Emelie's life changing appointments with that country's top plastic surgeons. When she'd dared to ask why, he'd snarled, "Your appearance must change. Do you want our enemies to find you? To slit your throat?"

Frightened, Emelie had believed him. She'd suffered through the mutilation of her birth body, and was reborn in a more perfect, foreign one.

That was only the beginning of her uncle's plan.

"You will go to school," he'd told her. "You will become the best student of nanotechnology that ever lived. You will graduate early, and then you will obtain a position at ZCA. Thereafter, you will infiltrate their computer systems, send data on all of their secret technologies to me, and then help me to destroy Tarim and Donetsk Territories."

His cold black eyes silenced the horrified questions on her tongue.

"Good." Sharp teeth punctuated his thin smile. "Your father would be proud."

Emelie didn't want to make her father proud. She didn't want to obey her uncle, either. But since he was her only living relative, and she had nowhere else to turn, she had agreed. However, rebellious plans took shape and fermented in her mind when she entered Omsk Tech.

At sixteen, her uncle's demands had seemed unattainable, but Emelie had achieved them. Cadmus had never praised her. Her performance was expected.

"Good." Her uncle's voice drew Emelie's attention back to the present. "Take note of your final orders."

Emelie nodded, but made no move to withdraw her phone.

For the briefest second, approval glimmered in his opaque gaze. "You will win the job of Michael Van Heisman's research assistant. You will relay their weaknesses to me, and then infiltrate and compromise ZCA's defense systems. Finally, you will make copies of Van Heisman's work, along with all of ZCA's top secret research, and send it to me."

"And then what?" Emilie dared to ask. She cooled her expression to careful disinterest. Her hatred for this man, and the manner in which he'd chosen to manipulate her, just like her blood-thirsty father had done when he'd turned her into a mass murderer, was pushed into a dark, icy corner of her heart. If Cadmus could cold-bloodedly plot to obtain his goals, then she could do it far better.

Cadmus' black gaze sharpened into flint. "Don't question me, *girl*," he spat.

Emelie's clasped fingers tightened behind her back. "What is your ultimate goal, Uncle? To destroy ZCA? And Tarim and Donetsk Territories, too? If so, when? I will need to prepare."

"You will do exactly what I tell you to do." His lips trembled, as if barely suppressing rage.

With dispassionate, clinical observation, she noted the pride that stiffened her uncle's shoulders; a reflection of the virulent arrogance that twisted through his soul. A weakness she would one day exploit. For now, he clearly did not trust her. Did he trust anyone?

Hatred and murderous blood lust ran through Cadmus's veins as thickly and corruptly as it had through her father's. While the city of Altay was still under Cadmus' direct control, reclaiming the rest of Altai Territory from Tarim Territory was his most fervent goal and addiction. Wiping all of Tarim and Donetsk Territories' cities from the Earth came in a very close second.

Cadmus' close friend, the Mongolian leader Naranbaatar, shared similar goals. Mongolia wanted more land. Cadmus had promised to help that country obtain its dearest wish by helping to orchestrate the destruction of Tarim and Donetsk Territories. As a reward, Naranbaatar would give Cadmus Altai Territory, and perhaps a choice bit of Tarim's oil fields, too.

Emelie knew that she was the key to her uncle's plan. Cadmus wanted her to use her vast wealth of computer and nanotechnology knowledge to weaken their enemies' defense shields and allow thermonuclear bombs to annihilate key enemy cities. He wanted to finish the destruction that his brother had begun.

The horror that her uncle contemplated, and that he expected her to achieve, made her normally steady stomach heave. A hellish sense of déjà vu swept through her again.

Was Cadmus insane? Did he think she'd actually do it?

Of course he did.

And so she continued to pretend to be his devoted, obedient niece. That charade meant her own diabolical plan just might succeed. And it guaranteed that she would be the only Mongolian operative he'd depend upon to destroy their enemies. The only one who could save them.

"Yes, Uncle," she said. "I will win the position of Michael Van Heisman's research assistant. I will do everything you ask. As I have always done."

But she wondered about her uncle's ultimate plans for ZCA, which served as the Command Central of their enemies' two territories. Did Cadmus plan to destroy ZCA, too? Or just take it over?

Clearly, he did not intend to tell her now.

Cadmus continued to stare at her. Malice flickered in his opaque eyes. She did not flinch, but returned his stare with a cool, implacable one of her own.

To her surprise, he blinked first. "Good. Time is of the essence. Helene will provide your specialized equipment. You will report to me each day with the phone I provide you. Understand?"

"Yes." She uneasily wondered what his cryptic "time is of the essence" meant.

He stepped toward her, and for an insane second, Emelie thought he wanted to shake her hand. Instead, he grabbed her long hair and painfully jerked her face close to his. "Do not fail me, Emelie," he hissed. "Or the horrific fate you've unleashed upon others will devour you, too. *And* everyone you love. Including your friends in Omsk."

Although she hadn't made many friends in Omsk, Cadmus probably knew every student she had spoken to. The names of her roommates. Every professor she'd liked. The children she'd visited in the hospital, when she'd mistakenly thought good deeds could help heal the black hole of guilt in her soul. And Dominic. Her best friend.

Cadmus would kill the Tarim Baron's son with the relish of squashing a fly.

For the first time, real fear crept into her heart. Her own death did not matter. Cadmus probably knew that. But the murder of the people she cared about...

He was a monster. In that second, Emelie saw this as clearly as if his human facade had peeled away and the demonic being inside screamed at her.

She would need to be very, very careful.

His grip on her hair hurt. To her humiliation, her eyes watered. "I will do as you ask," she promised evenly. "Threats are unnecessary."

He smiled. "Threats are *always* necessary." With a shove, he released her. "Now that we understand one another, go with Helene. After you've received your equipment, rest until it's time for your shuttle to leave."

Apparently, her brief stay in Uliastai was over.

Emelie followed Helene from the room. However, rest was not an option. Instead, she would go to the computer library and download Mongolia's top military secrets onto the microchip in her shoe.

CHAPTER TWO

ZCA, Tarim Territory
Present day

MICHAEL VAN HEISMAN STOOD UP when Adele opened his office door to usher in his last applicant. His long legs felt cramped from sitting behind the desk all day.

The ZCA Commander didn't like to take time away from his real work, but unfortunately he needed help, and he'd waited far too long to find it. Last month, his former assistant had decided to accept a rare teaching opportunity that had opened up in Omsk's premier technical university. As was typical, only the most severe of circumstances made the old professor lose his job. Death, to be exact, and it wasn't a surprise. He'd been ailing for months. Michael didn't blame Devlon for jumping at his dream job. But right now, in the midst of the most delicate, promising research project of his career, Michael needed a new assistant. Now. And only the best would do.

Silently, and with lithe grace, Lee Smirnov entered his office. His secretary softly closed the door behind her.

Although Lee Smirnov's last name was the most common one in Russia, her beauty was anything but ordinary. The digital image on her application did not do her justice. Not in any regard.

His swift, involuntary glance took in her flawless skin, ebony hair and faintly exotic eyes.

Smirnov was at least four centimeters taller than an average woman, with a supple, athletic build. She looked like a runner. Her features were almost disturbingly perfect. Delicately arched brows, aquiline nose, and perfectly formed lips, with just a hint of fullness to them.

Her dark brown eyes met his, and before he could decipher his own response, something flashed in her gaze. Something he could not quite read. Cool, composed detachment followed.

"Ms. Smirnov." He reached across the desk and his large hand enveloped her smaller, slender one. She returned the shake firmly. Michael felt large as he loomed over her. He must have at least sixteen centimeters on her. "Please have a seat."

"Thank you." Gracefully, she did so, and he resumed his, as well.

Michael fanned Lee Smirnov's application documents open on the razor thin computer monitor imbedded in his desktop. He glanced at them again, although he'd already memorized the pertinent facts. He'd scheduled her interview last today for a reason. He'd wanted to compare all others to her before conducting her interview.

"Your resume is impressive."

She inclined her head, but remained silent. That she allowed the facts to speak for themselves impressed him. Although her outward demeanor appeared calm, his highly sharpened perception—only a combination of sharp observation coupled with logical facts, was how he explained it to himself—sensed tension in the erect line of her shoulders and her clasped hands. One of her finger joints was white.

She wanted the job. Badly. And yet he could get no emotional read on her at all. Odd. He decided to start off easy.

"Why should I hire you?"

"I graduated at the top of my class." Her low voice spoke with the faint accent of northern Russia, which was in line with her verified birth records from that harsh, northern area. However, the cultured tone of Omsk softened the accent of her birth. Briefly, he wondered if she'd ever attended diction classes or visited a speech-language pathologist.

Seemingly unaware that he analyzed her every word, she continued, "I've spent the last seven years interning with the top scientists in Omsk and Zyra, in the fields of computer science and nanotechnology." She went into more depth. It mirrored the facts in the documents before him.

"Good." He smiled, but her return smile lagged by several seconds, as if she hadn't expected humor or smiles to take place in the interview. "Do you mind if I call you Lee?"

"Please do, Commander Van Heisman." Another small smile accompanied this statement, but it appeared to be offered for social purposes only. No warmth softened her eyes.

The first two questions had been designed to warm up the conversation, but they hadn't thawed the woman's reserve at all.

Interesting. Michael leaned back in his chair. "On paper, you're qualified for the job. So are two dozen others." He needed to find the absolute best scientific mind, and he wouldn't make this easy on her, although her resume, combined with the letters of recommendation from prestigious scientists he personally knew, seemed to indicate that she was the absolute best.

He said, "This interview will get difficult. Answer as best you can."

She offered an imperceptible nod. Only the slight stiffening of her spine indicated her resolve to master the questions.

Over the following ten minutes, Michael shot rapid-fire questions at Lee. They ranged from the practical to the latest studies in energy creation and computer nanotechnology.

She answered instantly and flawlessly, her voice cool, and her mind easily moving faster than the computers she programmed. He switched tactics midway through and offered new, esoteric theories authored by renowned scientists, as well as theories of his own that no one had ever heard about or studied before.

Again, as before, she answered instantly, with easy brilliance, and she even added insights of her own. The only questions that made her hesitate, for the barest fraction of a second, were a few of his own computer models and theories.

She paused after one particularly challenging question—the answer to which he was still researching and testing answers—and offered another small smile. A genuine one, this time, but it flashed as brilliant as a comet and then vanished, leaving the familiar cool, dark reserve. "Interesting theory."

"Thank you." He smiled. "It's one of my own. One last question. What do you know about ice eleven?"

Without hesitation, she replied, "It's usually made artificially, because the natural formation takes thousands of years to produce."

He waited.

"It has ferroelectric properties, as well as possible piezoelectric properties. The first allows the polarity to be changed with the application of an external source. Piezoelectric elements have applications in biological science, geoscience, as well as electrical and..." Now she did give a noticeable pause. "Nanotechnology."

"Good." No one, except for a select few, including his brother, Joshua Van Heisman, the Baron of Donetsk Territory, knew both the subject and purpose of his latest, top secret military project. But now, clearly Ms. Smirnov—Lee—had figured it out.

The barest smile curved her lips. "Fascinating possibilities, Commander Van Heisman."

He nodded, but didn't elaborate. The woman was brilliant; far more so than her resume conveyed, and that was impressive. His mind told him she was the best candidate for the job. But his gut still couldn't get a read on her, and that disturbed him.

With a finger flick, he closed the folder, signaling the interview was drawing to a close. Her stiff spine relaxed the barest fraction, as he had hoped it would.

Casually, he said, "Tell me the real reason why you want this job, Lee."

Her face blanched, and for a second her eyes widened. They darted in tiny, barely detectable twitches over his face. An interesting reaction, and it didn't settle the questions in his gut. Softly, he said, "The truth, Ms. Smirnov."

She swallowed, and her cheeks faintly flushed, allowing him to see a glimpse of the true woman inside. "I want to make the world a safer place. A better place, Commander."

"Why?"

"I..." For the first time, her gaze briefly left his. "I had friends and family who lived in Kazakhstan. I want to do everything I can to prevent that kind of destruction from happening again."

"You may not be working in defense systems."

She now met his gaze with quiet intensity. "I'll do whatever you need me to do, Commander. If you hire me, I will give every scrap of dedication I possess to my job. I will do everything you ask. And if I come up with theories of my own, I only ask that you might listen to a few."

His lips curved. "I'm always open to hearing new theories."

She nodded and placed her hands on the arms of the chair. "If that will be all...?"

"Not quite, Ms. Smirnov. One last question."

"Of course." Her gaze met his, and quietly waited. She was not a woman who played games, and he liked that.

Michael still didn't have a read on her, but that could be remedied in the near future. He wanted to hire her. Her mind matched his, and she possessed a great deal of potential. She was the most promising scientist he had met in over a decade.

"How do I know another company—or country—won't steal you away from ZCA?"

❈*❈*❈*❈*❈

"How do I know another country won't steal you away from ZCA?"

Lee wondered, for the tenth time during the interview, why Michael Van Heisman's jade green eyes seemed able to read into her soul.

Right now her phone, which was imbedded with an illegal chip that would enable her to speak to her uncle, even within ZCA's protective shield, felt hot in her pants pocket.

The Commander's eyes narrowed beneath his straight, sable brown brows. Silently, he waited for her delayed response.

She should have spoken by now, but her mind, for the first time during the interview, felt sluggish. Slowed by guilt. Guilt that she illogically feared he could sense. And if he did...if he developed any suspicions about her true identity, or that Cadmus had sent her here to obliterate everyone Van Heisman loved, and to steal and destroy everything he'd worked for in ZCA, her life would prematurely end.

For one wild, irrational moment, she wondered if he would execute her himself. His brother, Joshua, had killed her father. Michael Van Heisman could easily end her life, too.

The ZCA Commander certainly looked capable. Not only was he formidable in intellect and perception, but in size, as well. He towered ten centimeters taller than the average man, and muscle broadened his frame, making his shoulders look massive. His short, dark blond hair gleamed an unusual, burnt gold color. Although it looked neatly styled, it also appeared as if he'd run his hand through it recently.

It disconcerted her to notice that this man, her enemy since birth, was handsome, too. She already knew he was young, at thirty-three; he was the youngest man to ever gain Commander status, and he'd done so years ago. He had a square cut jaw, straight nose and firm mouth. Only the jagged scar running from his left ear to his jaw marred his masculine beauty. At some point in his life he had suffered. Or he'd fought someone. If it was the latter, then she had no doubt that he'd won the altercation.

Half of the male scientists she knew were stereotypically thin, and definitely not muscular. The Commander of ZCA was very different. For that matter, so was Dominic Dubrovnyk, her best friend, who even now waited in Tash to see if she'd won the job.

"Well?" Van Heisman's low voice bottomed out in a bass register. It shivered down her spine, and warned that she must speak now, or else risk losing all hope of obtaining the job.

"If you hire me, Commander Van Heisman, I guarantee that I will never seek nor take employment with another company. Or country."

One brow raised. "You're young. Maybe that's a rash..."

"I *guarantee* I will never take another position."

Because working for ZCA would kill her. A just fate. Although nothing could pay the debt demanded by her unforgivable sins, she hoped her true purpose here might save thousands of lives.

Her unwavering gaze held his with fierce promise. "You have my word, Commander."

"I believe you."

Lee couldn't relax yet. "Do you have additional questions?"

"How soon can you start?"

Lee smiled. An unexpected, light feeling of relief instantly tangled with a host of other, darker emotions. "Tomorrow."

Van Heisman pushed back from his desk and with easy masculine grace rose to his feet. "Meet me here at 0900 hours. And ask Adele to give you the keycard to your new apartment in Tash."

He offered his big hand in another shake. His grip was warm and strong, and his fingers finely chiseled; the hands of an artist, or a scientist who worked at the microscopic level.

If Van Heisman wasn't her enemy and she could tell him her true purpose for being here, his handshake might have provided her with a sense of security and stability. Instead, the strength in his grip inspired caution. In order to achieve her goals, she would need to circumvent his security systems and pursue her own agenda without being detected by this brilliant man.

An impossible task? For the first time, she truly wondered. Michael Van Heisman possessed a far more intuitive and effortlessly sharp mind than any other man she'd met before. His potential threat to her mission was far greater than she had previously assumed.

"Thank you, Commander." She returned the firm handshake. "I very much appreciate the opportunity you've given me."

His level green gaze held hers for a moment longer than felt comfortable. But instead of male interest, as she'd received from the man in the hall, Van Heisman's held a bit of warning. She would need to be careful. He didn't trust her yet. She would need to carefully choose her path in the coming days.

"I look forward to working with you during the next three weeks, Ms. Smirnov. The trial period ends then."

Meaning that if she didn't gain his trust, he'd boot her out. She would need to work quickly then, in the event that happened or if someone prematurely discovered her unauthorized activities.

Either of those concerns, however, would become a moot point if her uncle's deadly plan exploded early. She didn't trust Cadmus, and although she'd do her best to trickle as little information to him as possible, he was as nastily unpredictable as a snake. She suspected far less than three weeks remained in which to achieve her goals.

The proverbial tight rope walk to come promised to be difficult.

"I look forward to the challenges ahead, Commander."

Ice Master is now available at Amazon
and Barnes & Noble online!

AUTHOR'S NOTE

I HOPE YOU ENJOYED *Ice Baron*. The story came from a mixture of several ideas coming together at once. Joshua's character came first, and then Anya's predicament as a bride with little choice. I lived every minute with her as she jumped out of the shuttle, trying to forge a better life for herself and peace for her territory. I hope you did, too.

Astana, Donetsk Territory, and the other places in this book are a mixture of fact and fiction. I did extensive research on Kazakhstan and the Tien Shan mountains to make sure that the details of the story, although set in an Ice Age, were accurate.

I had always thought that an ice age would reduce temperatures on Earth by 20 or 30 degrees. Imagine my surprise to learn that during the Younger Dryas ice age, 10,000 years ago, temperatures only dropped by 7 to 15 degrees Celsius. However, that is enough to significantly change the landscape of the earth. As well, to my sometimes crazy imagination, it also seemed plausible that a world-wide nuclear war could disrupt the Earth's atmosphere, and usher in a cataclysmic ice age. Shiver...

One final note. As a small press author, getting books before readers is a real challenge. You can help! If you liked this book, please write a review on Amazon, B & N, or the retailer's website where you purchased the book. Each review encourages Amazon and other online retailers to promote the book to more readers. *Each* and every review counts, and helps so much! Thank you. ☺

I love to hear from my readers. Please drop me a note at jennettegreen@jennettegreen.com. Or, connect on Facebook at: www.facebook.com/JennetteGreenRomanceAuthor.

Best wishes,
Jennette

www.ingramcontent.com/pod-product-compliance
Lightning Source LLC
Chambersburg PA
CBHW061558100726
47898CB00002B/430